Sara Orwig, from Oklahoma, loves family, friends, dogs, books, long walks, sunny beaches and palm trees. She is married to and in love with the guy she met in college. They have three children and six grandchildren. Sara's one hundredth published novel was a July 2016 release. With a master's degree in English, she has written historical romance, mainstream fiction and contemporary romance. Sara welcomes readers on Facebook or at www.saraorwig.com.

Sarah M. Anderson may live east of the Mississippi River, but her heart lies out west on the Great Plains. Sarah's book *A Man of Privilege* won an RT Book Reviews Reviewers' Choice Best Book Award in 2012. *The Nanny Plan* was a 2016 RITA® Award winner for Contemporary Romance: Short.

Sarah spends her days having conversations with imaginary cowboys and billionaires. Find out more about Sarah's heroes at www.sarahmanderson.com and sign up for the new-release newsletter at www.eepurl.com/nv39b.

THE RANCHER'S HEIR

SARA ORWIG

HIS ENEMY'S DAUGHTER

SARAH M. ANDERSON

MILLS & BOON

First Published in Great Britain 2018
by Mills & Boon, an imprint of HarperCollinsPublishers,
1 London Bridge Street, London, SE1 9GF

The Rancher's Heir © 2018 Sara Orwig
His Enemy's Daughter © 2018 Sarah M. Anderson

ISBN: 978-0-263-93610-0

51-0718

MIX
Paper from
responsible sources
FSC® C007454

This book is produced from independently certified FSC™
paper to ensure responsible forest management.

For more information visit: www.harpercollins.co.uk/green

Printed and bound in Spain
by CPI, Barcelona

THE RANCHER'S
HEIR

SARA ORWIG

Prologue

During the night under a starless sky, they had driven their Humvee into an ambush, and now they were barely holding on, pinned down in a firefight with nothing but a crumbling rock wall between them and the enemy. Noah Grant had only cuts and bruises. His two close friends, Mike Moretti and Jake Ralston, also had non-life-threatening injuries. The other member on this US Army Rangers mission, Captain Thane Warner, was hurt badly with wounds to his chest and head, an injured leg and deep gashes all over his body from flying shrapnel.

Mike had applied pressure to two serious wounds, trying to save their captain and friend until help arrived. Their last communication had been cut off, but before it was, Noah heard a chopper was on the way.

An explosion rocked the ground not twenty feet away, sending up a plume of light. Mike turned to punch

Noah's shoulder. As Noah Grant lowered his weapon, Mike told him, "Trade places. Keep pressure on his wounds. He wants to talk to you."

Without hesitation, Noah took Mike Moretti's place, holding Thane's own jacket and Mike's jacket over Thane's wounds, trying to apply pressure to the two most serious ones, hoping his captain and friend could hang on until help arrived.

Thane gripped his arm and Noah leaned closer to hear him over the explosives. With shallow breathing and a hoarse whisper, Thane spoke through obvious pain. "Noah, promise me you'll take two gifts home for me." Coughs racked his body and he grimaced. "Promise me."

"I promise," Noah said without thinking as he concentrated on trying to keep pressure on the wounds.

"Two keys in pocket," Thane said in a raspy, weakened voice, placing his hand on a pocket. "Keys alike. Other one for Jake. Mike has one."

"Don't talk. Save your strength." Trying to keep pressure on the wounds, Noah slipped his hand into the pocket, leaning down closer to Thane. "I have the keys."

Thane's eyelids fluttered and he looked at Noah. "…in box…two packages go to Camilla and Ethan." He closed his eyes and stopped talking. Noah leaned closer.

"Thane. Thane. Hang in there. Chopper's coming. Thane!"

Thane's eyes fluttered and he grasped Noah's wrist with surprising strength. "Promise…you'll give Camilla…gift yourself."

"I promise I'll put her gift in her hands," he said, not wanting to think about actually doing the deed.

"Other present—promise me…you…give to my

nephew…have to…give to him, no one else…want him to see a soldier. Don't give to Camilla… Promise me even though—"

"I promise to put the present in your nephew's hands myself."

Thane's eyes fluttered open and for an instant Noah felt a shock as Thane looked intently at him.

"I promise to place it in the baby's hands," Noah repeated emphatically, startled by the piercing look from Thane.

The last statement seemed to pacify him as he nodded and closed his eyes. "Get Jake."

Noah looked around, spotted Jake and shouted at him. He didn't dare let go of the blood-soaked jackets he held against Thane's wounds.

"Jake," he shouted again and jerked his head when Jake looked around.

Noah turned back to tell Thane that Jake was coming. Anxiety filled him as he saw Thane's eyes were closed, his head turned away. Noah felt for a pulse and was surprised to find one. "Thane," he shouted, trying to keep the man awake until medics arrived. "Thane, stay with me."

Jake slipped down beside Noah just as another explosion ripped the ground in front of them. "Thane wants you to have this key," Noah said, handing a small key to his friend. "He'll tell you what he wants you to do. Hold these against his wounds. Where the hell is the chopper?"

"I don't know, but last I heard it's coming."

"It better get here soon. He's lost too much blood." He leaned close to Thane's ear.

"Thane, here's Jake," Noah shouted and moved away as Jake took over keeping pressure on Thane's wounds.

"Hang on, Thane. Help is coming," Jake shouted, leaning close to Thane as the man stared blankly at him.

Noah moved away, pausing when he heard another sound besides the bursts of gunfire and the explosion of a grenade. Were they going to get some help? He opened his hand that was smeared with Thane's dried blood. A brass key lay in his palm and Noah drew a deep breath. He didn't want to go home and give Camilla a gift from Thane. When they broke up, he didn't expect to ever be with her again and it still hurt to think about her.

He didn't want to see her, talk to her or do anything to stir up old feelings. It had hurt to walk away but he had and now he had to go back to her. He wondered whether he would ever reach a point where he would stop thinking about her.

One

Noah

Six months later, in July, Noah was no longer a Ranger in the US Army. He'd been honorably discharged, armed now with a list of things he needed to do before he settled back into civilian life and took over his ranch again. He'd systematically run through the list until, after tonight, there was only one thing left to do—take Thane's packages to Camilla and her baby. He didn't want to see either of them, but he would keep his promise to Thane. He stood holding two packages. He guessed the one for her baby was a book—that was what it felt like. Both packages were wrapped in what looked like the brown paper of grocery sacks at home. Used paper with wrinkles smoothed out. The other package for Camilla was a box. It wasn't deep, but it was bigger than the book. Each one was tied with brown twine. Neither box felt heavy. A simple delivery. Just hand them to her and get the hell out of her life again. Just the thought of seeing her was stirring up too many unwanted memories.

The first weekend back he'd gone home to see his parents in Dallas. He'd hugged his mother while Betsy Grant had wiped away tears as she smiled at him.

"Mom, don't cry," he'd said.

"I'm just so happy you're home."

"I'm happy to be home and I'll never understand crying for happiness."

Smiling, she'd wiped her eyes and patted his cheek. "Someday you will. Someday you'll have tears of joy and relief in your eyes."

"Don't wish that on me," he'd said, laughing. As he'd hugged her, he'd realized she felt a lot more frail than she had when he had hugged her goodbye before he'd left for Afghanistan.

His dad's handshake had been firm, his smile as warm as ever, but Cal Grant's skin had looked pale.

Tonight he returned to the family Tudor mansion in Dallas and walked in to see his siblings. Noah stepped to Hallie to hug her lightly. His sister-in-law was still a beautiful woman, tall, blonde and brown-eyed.

"We're glad you're home," she said, smiling at him.

He turned to his middle brother and gazed into blue eyes slightly lighter than his own. The two looked alike, except Ben had wavy black hair, not thick black curls like Noah. Noah wrapped his arms around Ben, Hallie's husband, and hugged him. "I'm glad to see you," he said, meaning it.

"I'm glad you're here, bro. Eli was sorry he couldn't get here tonight. He couldn't get out of a dinner where he's a speaker."

"I'll see him soon."

"Come sit and let everyone talk to you," his mother said as they all walked into the big familiar living room with comfortable sofas and chairs. "You can't imagine how glad we all are that you're home."

He sat and talked to his family and once again he was struck by how much his parents had aged in the years he'd been in the military. He heard the front door open, and then his sister, Stefanie, appeared, screeching when she saw Noah. She ran across the room, her black hair flying, to throw her arms around his neck. Laughing, he hugged her and she stepped back, smiling at him.

"I'm so glad you're home."

He looked into her deep blue eyes, so like his own, and smiled. "I'm glad to be home."

She turned to greet the rest of the family, crossing the room to kiss their dad's cheek, going to brush her mother's cheek with a kiss. "This is a celebration," she said.

Noah laughed. Some things never changed, and his little sister stirring up the whole family with her grand entrance was one of those things.

And some things did change, he thought. Like his parents.

As they all sat and talked, he realized how good it was to be home. Nothing was more important than family. This was what he'd wanted at some point in his life. The moment that thought came, so did memories of Camilla and, with them, an unwanted pang that shocked him. After all this time, how could he still miss her? They had broken up three years ago and he didn't want to still miss her. He didn't want to picture her when he thought of having his own family. But he did. She was his wife and the mother of his children in all such fantasies.

But it had to stop. Now.

Banishing those tormenting images, he turned to his father and tried to pay attention to what the man was saying. It wasn't until ten that night, when his folks said good-night and retired for the evening, that he was alone with Ben and Hallie and Stefanie.

"C'mon, Stefanie. Come with me. I'm going to find a book to take home," Hallie said, dragging his sister to the library down the hall.

Noah looked at Ben. "I know the folks usually tell us good-night and leave, but Hallie has left for a reason besides getting a book to read."

"Yeah. Let's go into the study," Ben said, and Noah realized it was something serious. He followed his brother.

Ben switched on the lights and Noah glanced around the familiar room that served as his dad's home office. Then his attention shifted to Ben.

"What's up? I have the feeling there's something you've been waiting to tell me."

"There is. I told Mom I would tell you and you can talk to them about it tomorrow, but she can't talk without crying."

"Oh, damn," Noah said, sinking into a leather chair. Instantly he remembered his dad's pallor and quiet manner. "It's Dad, isn't it?"

"You noticed. I figured you would. He—he has heart problems. Since you've been gone, he's had a heart attack and he's had bypass surgery."

Noah felt as if he had been punched in the chest. He hurt and he looked down, remembering his dad in earlier years. "Dammit."

Ben took a seat beside him. "Dad isn't strong any

longer, but he walks on a treadmill several times nearly every day."

Noah looked away, remembering moments as a kid when he'd had fun with his dad, playing ball, swimming.

"That's a hell of a thing to come home to," he told Ben. "How's Stefanie handling it?"

"She's hovering over him, which seems to make them both happy. Mom, too. Between work and her social life, Stefanie keeps busy, so she's okay. She's running the north Dallas Grant Realty office and she's very good at it." He shook his head as if amazed at how well she handled the family's real-estate business. "I thought she was too much a social butterfly to be a sharp businesswoman, but I was wrong. Last spring, she spent a month in our south Texas home and had it all done over. And I think she has plans for the Colorado home this fall. I don't know where she gets the energy. Even with all that on her plate, she moves in social circles and supports several charities. I've got about three I devote time, effort and money to, while Eli has about five. You know how Dad taught us all we need to give back to the community, so here we are, doing what he expected."

"I'm sure he's proud of you all."

Ben looked at him squarely. "We're all proud of you serving in the Army in the Rangers."

Noah shrugged. "Our dad served. Our grandfather. Our great-grandfather. It's a family tradition. But one from this generation is enough. Don't you go sign up."

Ben held up his hands, palms out. "No danger of that. I have my hands full here." He ran a hand through his hair. "When Dad had to step down, I took over the main real-estate office. You know, it might be a good thing if you come in about once or twice a month just so you know what's going on and you're able to take over if I'm away."

"Okay, but I'm sure you have some vice presidents who can step in."

"Oh, yes. I just want you to know about the business since Dad is out."

"And in turn you'll come out to the ranch and spend a couple of days per month."

"Noah, ranching is your deal and maybe Eli's occasionally. I would be lousy—"

Noah laughed and waved his hand. "Don't worry. I'm kidding. You barely know a horse's head from its rear, so I don't think you'd be of much help anyway."

Ben sat back, looking relieved. "Don't scare me like that." Then he sobered. "Back to Dad. I told him I'd tell you about his heart. He said he has a doctor's appointment tomorrow and they're running some tests. He said to give him a couple of days and then come by. I think those doctor appointments wear him out. So much that he doesn't even venture into the office any longer." Ben leaned forward. "Don't panic, Noah, but I'd really like you on the board."

"The ranch is my life. I'll be on the board, but I won't take an office job." He got up and paced the den. "You know, when you leave home, you think you're coming back to the same life, but you never do," he said. "Well, hell, this one hurts and it's just going to hurt more as the days go by." He stared into space a moment, lost again in memories of his dad. He turned to Ben. "Thanks for telling me."

"Yeah. I hated to have to tell you."

"I'm glad I didn't know it over there. Losing Thane was hell enough. We've been friends since we were schoolkids. His wounds were too bad and they couldn't save him. How're things with you?"

Ben shrugged. "Business is good. On the home front there have been some tense moments—" He paused to look at Noah. "Hallie and I have tried since we first married to have a baby. Especially since Dad's heart problems. We wanted him to know his first grandchild." Ben shook his head and glanced at the closed door. "The docs say we're both okay, to just relax, that pregnancy will happen. It would give Mom and Dad so much pleasure." He paused a moment as Noah resumed his seat, then met his brother's eyes. "I hate to ask, but…have you seen Camilla?"

At the mere mention of her name, his insides knotted. "No, but I will. Thane asked me to take gifts to her and to her baby."

"She was only married two, three months at most. Then the guy was gone. He was there long enough that she has a baby. He left town before their divorce and I've heard he doesn't have any interest in the kid."

"Doesn't matter. It's over between us," Noah said, his stomach tightening even more. "I'm too much the alpha male for her, which is the pot calling the kettle black, to quote the old saying. And she loves Dallas and won't even visit my ranch."

"Sorry. You two seemed close."

They had been once. They'd dated for a year before he joined the Army. "Not any longer." Noah stood. "I better go and let you get home."

They walked back to rejoin the others. He glanced at Stefanie. "If I know you, you're just getting ready to start your evening. You're probably meeting friends."

Smiling, she wrinkled her nose at him. "You might be right. You can even join us."

"Thanks, but not tonight." He turned to his brother. "I'll call and see Dad when it's convenient for him."

Ben nodded, then reached out to hug his brother.

"Damn, I'm glad you're home," he said.

"Let me know if you need me. I have something I need to do in Dallas before I go to the ranch and I'll spend a bit longer in Dallas to be with Dad more."

"That will be good. I'm sorry about you and Camilla."

It still hurt too much to talk about her. "Thanks. So am I, but I'm not giving up ranching. I sure as hell can't change my personality."

He said good-night to Stefanie and Hallie. "See you both soon," Noah said as he made his way to the door.

Stefanie asked him to wait, walking outside with him.

"How is it with Camilla?" she asked as they headed toward her car. "Have you seen her baby?"

"It's finished with Camilla, and no, I haven't seen her baby," he said.

"Sorry, Noah, if you're unhappy about it. Come out with me Friday night and have some fun."

He laughed and squeezed her shoulder. "You'd take the old man out with you? Thanks, but I'll pass this time."

"You're not that much older than my crowd and you're not as old as some of them." She smiled at him and touched his arm. "Think about it. Also, I'm a co-chairman for the Heart Ball—"

He stopped her with a grin. "I'll take a table and however many tickets that means."

"Ahhh, thank you! It's still three months away but it's never too soon to sell tickets." She opened her red sports car and turned back to him. This time he noticed her expression had sobered. "Ben told you about Dad, didn't he?"

"Yeah, he did. I'll go by and talk to Dad soon. He has a doctor's appointment tomorrow."

"It breaks my heart, but I don't want to be sad around them. He seems to be doing okay, but I'm sure you see a difference."

"Of course I do." He reached out to her. "If you want a shoulder to cry on, I've got one."

She gazed up at him. "There will be times I'll need it. You're a wonderful big brother."

He smiled and pulled her to him in a hug. When he released her, he held open her car door, then closed it when she was in. "See you soon," he said as he turned for his car. As he opened his car door, he glanced back to see her backing out of her parking place. He left, driving to the condo he maintained in Dallas while he thought about his dad, and then his thoughts shifted to Camilla. He would see her—after all this time. His pulse beat faster when he thought about her while at the same time memories of the past clutched at his heart. He had put this meeting off long enough. Even though it might very well open old wounds, the time had come to see her and fulfill his promise.

Stefanie

Stefanie drove to her condo in downtown Dallas. She ran a family office in a suburban area, but she liked the town condo. When she was inside, she walked to the window to look out at the city without really seeing it. Her thoughts were lost on her oldest brother. She was thankful he was home. Noah had a steadying influence on everyone in the family.

She could hear the gruffness in his voice when she had asked about Camilla, and her anger flashed. She'd liked Camilla—until she'd hurt Noah. She'd hurt him before he ever left for overseas and that had worried Stefanie. She'd feared he wouldn't have his mind on his job as much if he was worried about Camilla—something that could be fatal in hostile territory.

She thought about Camilla, who was pursuing an art career. Stefanie had always wondered if she had married to spite Noah because her husband was gone in a couple of months. Camilla probably hadn't planned on a pregnancy. The guy hadn't even wanted his baby.

Stefanie thought about Noah, looking preoccupied tonight, learning about their dad and coming home to unhappiness with Camilla. Noah needed to meet someone, someone who was fun to be with, someone who would get him over his breakup.

Stefanie knew some really gorgeous women who would be perfect for Noah. She knew two women in particular who came to mind right away. Better still, one of them was going to be in Vivian Warner's wedding party when Thane's widow remarried next week. She could call Vivian. Noah needed someone who would make him happy.

And Stefanie needed to think of a way to get Camilla away from Dallas and out of her brother's life.

If Camilla was away from Dallas, maybe Noah would be more interested in going out and meeting new friends.

Camilla

In her large art studio at her Dallas home, Camilla stepped back to look at the canvas on an easel. She

had a commissioned family portrait of two children
she was painting from a picture she had taken with
her iPad. She usually got up early to paint while Ethan
slept. She would hear him on the monitor when he
stirred.

It was quiet, peaceful in her studio, and on breaks
from painting, she could watch the sunrise over her
backyard.

Light spilled into the room and over easels holding
watercolor paintings, charcoal drawings and portraits.
One wall held a massive landscape painting. There
were shelves filled with art bottles of acrylic paints
and tubes of oils. Two sinks were near a worktable.
Sunshine splashed through the floor-to-ceiling glass
wall that gave a broad view of her gardens. Stacks of
drawings and prints were in bins along a wall. She had
a patio door open to let fresh air in and a slight paint
smell out. She had a studio in her condo, another studio in an office in downtown Dallas, but this was her
favorite place to paint. She also had an art gallery in
Dallas.

As she cleaned her brushes, she glanced over at a
black-and-white pencil sketch propped on top of a cabinet holding her paints. The sketch was Noah, one she
had done from a picture after they started dating. She
still liked it. All in shades of black and gray on a white
background, she had made his eyes a vivid blue, trying
to reproduce the color of them. He had a faint smile and
his black hair was its usual unruly tangle. That mass
of tangled curls was gone when she last saw him with
his military cut.

She stared at his picture a moment, dreading seeing
him again while at the same time missing him, wondering what the future held. Guilt plagued her and memo-

ries taunted her, memories of his kisses, moments in his arms.

With a shake of her head, she continued to put away brushes and pencils. In the cabinet were scrapbooks with printouts of pictures and artwork she had done.

She had attended a musical at the Music Hall last night, and during the performance, her mind had wandered to Noah. He was out of the military now.

On the wall behind a massive wooden desk was a wall calendar with the art jobs she had pending and due dates. She had appointments written in, important events she would attend, including her widowed sister-in-law's upcoming wedding. Noah would be there and their paths would cross.

She thought over what she'd heard: Noah Grant was home. She couldn't get him out of her thoughts. She couldn't understand her reaction to hearing the news. She hadn't seen him for two years, not since he'd been home on furlough. Even back then he was exactly what she disliked in a man—a take-charge male—yet when she heard he was back, her heart had raced and longing shook her. For just an instant, she forgot their fights and arguments and remembered only the good moments. Noah making her laugh, Noah holding her, kissing her. Noah taking her to bed, where she'd run her hands over his smooth back. Noah—

Stop it.

She had to listen to that sane inner voice telling her to rein in those errant memories. Yes, they'd had moments of ecstasy, of bliss, but those times were over.

So why did the mere anticipation of seeing him make her heart flutter? Why did she have such an intense reaction to him?

Their last time together had ended in a bitter breakup

and she had been the one who'd enacted it. She told him they had no future. She had a father who made all the decisions and ran their house with an iron fist. All her life her mother had given in to her dad. Too far back to remember exactly when, Camilla had vowed she would never live a life where she had to constantly give in to someone else about everything. She had to make some of her own decisions beyond what she would wear and whom she'd invite to the next party.

Her brother, as much as she had loved Thane, had been another take-charge man. But she wouldn't allow herself to choose a man like that for a husband.

At least her dad led a quiet life. Noah, on the other hand, liked challenges.

Noah and she were such opposites that she couldn't understand the attraction she felt. She was going to Shakespeare in the Park tonight. Noah would never go with her to Shakespeare, the opera or the ballet. He seldom went to art galleries with her. She loved city life, operas, chamber music, her art. Noah was a billionaire rancher, but a cowboy at heart. He loved his ranch, boot-scootin' honky-tonks, country music, competing in rodeos, flying his planes. He was exuberant, filled with life, and he'd take charge wherever he was. She didn't want to tie her life to a cowboy who was 100 percent determined to do things his way.

So why did she almost melt when she looked into his vivid blue eyes? Why did his kisses set her on fire? He could make her forget the world, forget what she liked and didn't like. So easily he could make her want to be in his arms. And that was what he had done the last time she had seen him when he had come home to Texas on a furlough.

They had started out fighting and arguing and ended

up in bed in each other's arms. He had charmed her as he usually did.

For all their differences and her wanting to avoid getting entangled with a wild, take-charge rancher who liked challenges, she had been charmed, dazzled and unable to resist the mutual attraction, and she had spent the weekend in his bed. Now she was going to face the consequences.

When Noah had been home on furlough, he had been more appealing than ever. He had filled out with broad, muscled shoulders, a hard body in prime shape with a narrow waist, endurance that made him fabulous in bed. Just thinking about seeing him again made her pulse race and her insides get tingly.

She didn't know how she would deal with him. No matter how much she planned to stand firm, to resist him, she feared that all he had to do was wrap his arm around her and kiss her and her resistance would disappear into thin air.

On the other hand, he could be stubborn, determined and unyielding. Which made her wonder how forgiving he could be. She couldn't answer that, because there hadn't ever been an occasion between them for her to gauge his ability to forgive.

Thinking of seeing Noah made her shiver.

She heard the monitor and left to get her fifteen-month-old son.

He had gone back to sleep and she stood beside his crib, love filling her for her baby. Ethan lay curled on his side. His long black lashes cast dark shadows on his rosy cheeks.

Camilla ran her fingers lightly over her precious sleeping baby. His mop of curly black hair reminded her of his dad. He held a frazzled-looking teddy bear in his arms—the toy he held like a security blanket whenever he'd get sleepy. The bear's stitched black nose was smashed from Ethan rubbing noses with it.

She touched Ethan's curls again. Guilt was a heavy shroud that had fallen over her. This was Noah's baby and he had no idea that Ethan was his son.

Two

Camilla

All during her pregnancy, everyone assumed she was carrying her ex-husband Aiden's child. When she realized they did, she let everyone go right on believing that. By the second month after they married, Aiden and she were divorced. When the baby was born, it was easy to keep up the deception. She had been divorced and Aiden had left town six months before Ethan was born, so no one questioned her naming her baby Warner, her family name. Aiden had been a rebound marriage, a fling, a mistake, and she never wanted to keep his name and he had no interest in her baby.

Little Ethan, like Aiden and Noah, had black hair, so no one suspected anything.

Though she'd already broken up with Noah when she started dating Aiden, she'd been pregnant. Noah had been back in Afghanistan, his furlough over. As well as their relationship.

She'd known Aiden since college and she married him on the rebound. She had thought he would be a dad for her baby, but she knew the second week of the marriage she had made a mistake and she felt he wasn't happy, either.

They really weren't compatible. By the second month he'd wanted a divorce and so had she.

People still didn't realize this was Noah's baby. While guilt plagued her because Noah had a right to know the truth, she knew he would want to take charge of the situation. He would want control over her baby. Maybe her own life in some ways would be out of her hands.

At some point she had to let him know about Ethan, but she dreaded it more than anything in her life. She was not going to let him know yet. Ethan was the joy of her life now. She didn't want to lose him. Nor was she ready to share him. Noah was a rancher, but she loved city life and wanted her son in Dallas.

Though she'd spent time on her grandfather's ranch, she wasn't fond of them. Being on a ranch made her think of Winston, her little brother who had fallen through the ice at their grandfather's ranch when Winston was four. Thane had pulled him out of the icy pond. Later Winston had developed pneumonia and died. It always saddened her to think of that time.

The entire year they'd dated, Noah had never declared his love, but he'd made it clear that if he ever wanted to marry, his wife would have to live on his ranch.

Yes, suffice it to say, she and Noah had hugely different lifestyles. Noah wasn't going to change and she didn't want to change, either.

She brushed her fingers so lightly over Ethan's soft curls, feeling them tickle the palm of her hand. Wanting to lean down and kiss him, she resisted because she was afraid she would wake him. The minute Noah knew about their son, she was certain he would want to take charge of Ethan's life and maybe hers, too. She would see Noah when Mike Moretti and Thane's widow, Vivian, married. Their wedding was coming up this next weekend, and both she and Noah would be in it. Ethan was too little to go to this wedding, so she didn't have to worry about having Noah and Ethan in the same place.

Aside from Mike and Vivian, she moved in a circle of friends now who did not know Noah, so she hoped she'd be able to drag out the deception a little longer.

Over the last almost two years there'd been times she'd considered telling Noah about his son, but she'd always backed off. Now, as she looked at her baby and fought the urge to hold him in her arms, she knew despite her guilty conscience, she had to continue to keep Noah away from him. It was too terrifying to tell him the truth.

Noah

Tuesday afternoon, Noah sat across from Mike as they ate burgers together on the patio of a popular lunch place in Dallas. "I'm glad about you and Thane's widow," Noah told his friend. "I guess it was good you told Thane you'd go to work for him when you got out of the military. I think it gave him peace of mind to hire you and know if something happened to him, you'd go home to run the ranch. He may have hoped all along that you would marry Vivian."

"I'm sure he was taking care of Vivian and taking care of his beloved ranch. He had everything all lined up if anything happened to him." Mike put down his burger and wiped his mouth on a napkin. "Now you have an errand for him."

"Right," Noah said, looking into his friend's alert brown eyes. Mike's black hair had a slight wave and was longer than when he was in the service, but still cut short. "I had to promise Thane I would put his package into Camilla's hands myself. The baby, too. Her baby isn't going to know or care what's going on and probably won't even know he has a present."

Mike laughed. "Thane probably hoped you'd get back with his sister."

"That won't happen. She told me a definite goodbye and she married after I left. She divorced him a few months into the marriage and now has his baby. Camilla and I are history. I'm too much the alpha male for her."

"We're all alpha males, and her brother definitely was, too."

"She has said the same thing about her brother." Noah shrugged. "I can't change something as basic as that. It's who I am. I don't know how we got together in the first place. We're opposites. She likes opera, art galleries and big cities. I like my country-western music, rodeos and the ranch. In short, we were never meant to be. It's over."

"Sorry. Life can get complicated. Thane probably wanted you to get back together so that her child would have a good dad around."

"She's from a very wealthy family. In addition, she

does well with her art, some pieces bringing big bucks before I left for the service. She does watercolor landscapes, murals, also portraits and has done some portraits for celebs for impressive amounts of money, so she doesn't need one bit of financial help. Also, she has two more brothers, Mason and Logan. As far as I know, they'll be around some for her baby. When I left for the service Mason had a financial consulting firm in Austin and Logan is head of his Dallas oil company. Maybe being in a war made Thane sentimental. I don't know. All I have to do is take the present to her and give the baby his present and say goodbye."

Mike paused as he went to take another bite of his burger, and his eyes met Noah's. "Sorry, buddy. She'll be in our wedding because she's family and a friend of Vivian's."

"It won't matter. While it's over between us, we can be civil to each other. I'll see her at your wedding and then it's goodbye and we probably won't cross paths again."

"She's a good artist and highly successful, which made her instant friends with Vivian. Vivian shows Camilla's art in her galleries. Camilla is good at what she does. Her art is bringing in higher returns and it's selling better than ever."

Noah was glad for her. She'd always been talented. But enough talk about Camilla. He changed the subject quickly, before Mike could go on about the woman. "Speaking of a wedding, too bad Jake won't be out of the military and back for your wedding."

"We waited for you. I'm not waiting another month for Jake to get back, even though I count him as a close friend," Mike said.

"I'm sure he'll understand."

"He won't care if he isn't in a wedding except that he'll miss a party. Jake loves a party."

After reminiscing a bit about their good friend and Ranger buddy Jake Ralston, Mike asked after Noah's plans now that he was home.

"I'll stay in Dallas for the next month to get business taken care of, see my family some, and I have Thane's gift to Camilla to deliver. Eventually, I'll go back to my West Texas Bar G Ranch."

"That's the best possible plan," Mike said, smiling. "If you want to buy a really fine horse, come by our place."

"I'll do that. When is a good time?"

Mike shrugged. "With our wedding coming up this weekend, either come out today or tomorrow or wait a couple of weeks until we return from our honeymoon."

"Thanks, Mike. I'll give you a call or text when I'm ready."

"Great. You know where the ranch is. Stay for dinner and get to know Vivian if you can."

"Thanks," he said and Mike nodded.

As the hour passed, they finished lunch and finally said goodbye. Noah left, thinking again about delivering the gifts from Thane. When he sat in his car, he called a phone number he still could remember easily and drew a deep breath as he waited to hear Thane's sister, Camilla Warren, answer.

Camilla

Camilla's heart skipped a beat when she looked at the name on the caller ID. Noah. She hadn't talked to him since the two weeks he'd been home on a furlough. Since they'd made a baby together. Sex with Noah had always been fabulous. In bed, they were compatible, in sync. Not so much out of the bedroom. A relationship between them never would have lasted. And now he would never forgive her deception.

She stared at the caller ID while the music on her phone continued to play, indicating an incoming call. She didn't want to answer. She and Noah had nothing to talk about and he should know that she would not go out with him. She couldn't imagine he would want to ask her out after the harsh words they'd had when they last parted. She didn't want to see him and she didn't want to talk to him.

His call kicked over to voice mail and minutes later her heart skipped another beat when she listened to Noah's familiar voice.

"Camilla, your brother has a gift for you. It's important because he went through hell—" Noah paused and tears stung her eyes because she loved her older brother and she knew Noah and Thane had been close friends since they had been in middle school.

She could hear Noah take a deep breath. "Thane went through hell to make sure I knew what he wanted. I promised him I would give a package to you. He was insistent I put it in your hand myself. Sorry Mike could have given it to you, but that wasn't what your brother wanted. This was a final request of a dying buddy, a man whose memory I will always honor, and I'm going to keep my promise to him and put his gift into your hand as he asked. Also, he gave me a present for your baby, his first nephew. I'm to give that present to him. I'll call again for a time." There was a brief pause, and then he added, "It's Noah, by the way."

She heard the click and dropped her phone to cover her face with her hands and sob for the big brother who had been killed, a brother who had been a friend and a second dad. He wasn't coming home. And she knew she was also crying over Noah, the man she had once loved with all her heart. The man she had to keep out of her life at all costs. Yet now there was a reason she had to see him, because she could not refuse her brother's dying request, either.

Thane had known she couldn't refuse to see Noah. Too easily, she could imagine her brother's motive in getting Noah to deliver the present to her. Even from the grave, he was taking charge of someone else's life. This time, hers. Thane was determined that Noah learn about Ethan. After the baby was born, Thane had written her and asked if Ethan was Noah's. He was the only person who had come up with the truth. She couldn't write back and admit it, though. Just the fact that she'd stalled had given him an answer. And then he'd gotten a call through to her and they had argued about it.

Thane tried almost as much as her dad to take charge of everything in his life. But he couldn't convince Camilla to tell Noah the truth.

She sighed as she wiped her eyes and tried to regain her composure. She would have to see Noah and accept her brother's present. To do so, they should make arrangements to meet as soon as possible and get it over and done. But she was not going to let him see Ethan. Noah could give her Ethan's present. Her son wouldn't know what was going on, anyway.

She picked up the phone to send a text to invite Noah to come by. She had no intention of telling Noah ahead of time that Ethan would not be home. Noah would simply come another time. In minutes she received an answer and a time, which she accepted. She sighed as she wondered how she would get through seeing Noah tomorrow. Not only then, but at Vivian's wedding.

Vivian would marry Mike Moretti, another Ranger buddy and rancher who had been in Thane's outfit. Thane had hired Mike to replace their retiring foreman. Vivian knew about Camilla's breakup with Noah, so she had been sympathetic when she'd asked Camilla to be in her wedding, telling Camilla if she was uncomfortable accepting, she would understand. Camilla wanted to say no and stay far away, but she couldn't. For Thane's sake—and she truly liked Vivian—she would be in the wedding, which Vivian had originally said would be small with just family members and very close friends. That had changed because there were so many family members. Mike and Vivian both had brothers and close friends. One of Vivian's brothers would be best man. Noah would be a groomsman. Noah's sister, Stefanie, would be a bridesmaid.

Camilla hoped she could get through seeing Noah, talking to him, being in the wedding with him, without any tears. She was the one who had broken up the relationship and she thought by now she was over him, but hearing his voice not only made her cry, it made her weak in the knees and swamped her with longing to have his arms around her and to kiss him again— something she didn't want to feel. She had no future with Noah. Her feelings hadn't changed one tiny degree regarding his alpha-male ways. She just had to get through tomorrow's meeting and get through the wedding, and then Noah would be out of her life.

After the wedding, she didn't ever have to see Noah again. She would cling to that thought like a lifeline.

But first she had to make it through tomorrow.

* * *

The next day at noon her heart fluttered as she changed clothes for the third time. She shouldn't care how she looked or what she wore. She and Noah were finished forever and she would take the package and baby present her brother had sent and say goodbye and Noah would be gone. She lived in Dallas, and Noah lived two hundred and thirty miles away in West Texas on his Bar G Ranch. Now, if only her heart could get the message that seeing Noah wasn't important. Her heart was pounding, her hands were icy, her breathing was fast—why couldn't she get over him? She didn't want a future out on a ranch with a strong alpha male whose life choices were mostly the opposite of hers.

Annoyed by her reactions to seeing him, she took a deep breath.

Her door chimes made her jump and she realized how tense she was. She took another deep breath, glanced at herself in the mirror and shook her long, straight brown hair away from her face. Her gaze skimmed over her pale blue cotton blouse, matching slacks and high-heeled sandals. Then she hurried to the door, swinging it open and feeling her heart beat faster as she looked up into Noah's vivid blue eyes. In that instant, two years' worth of time vanished. In some ways it could have been yesterday when she'd last seen him. In other ways, change was evident. He looked older, taller, more broad-shouldered and even more incredibly handsome. His thick black hair was a mass of unruly curls above the most vivid blue eyes she had ever seen.

Looking like the rancher he was, Noah was in civilian clothes: fresh, dark jeans, a navy long-sleeved shirt and black boots. A short black beard was a new addition. He looked like a strong, handsome Texas cowboy, not a billionaire rancher and former officer of an elite military outfit. She couldn't speak and she wanted to walk into his arms and kiss him. She had thought she was getting over him, but the instant she looked into his eyes, such intense longing filled her that it hurt. For a moment they stared at each other and she realized he was as silent as she.

"Come in, Noah," she said quietly, her voice a whisper. Her pulse raced and she couldn't tear her gaze away from his. She couldn't move. Her heart pounded and she made an effort to step back so he could enter. When he did, she caught the scent of his aftershave. As he stepped in front of her, he paused to look down at her. She couldn't breathe while she wondered if he could hear her heart pound. He turned and walked on. Taking a deep breath, she closed the door and walked ahead of him into the living room.

"Where's your baby?" he asked, following her. "I expected you to be holding him."

"Actually, Noah, my mom came by and took Ethan with her. One of her friends is here from out of town and she wanted to show him off."

She entered her living room and turned to face him. He had a slight scowl and his gaze had grown cold.

"Camilla, I told you that I have Thane's gift to you and one to your son. What's his name—Ethan?"

"Yes—he's named for my uncle. I'm sorry," she answered, raising her chin, trying to get some force into her voice so she didn't sound guilty or intimidated. "I know you told me that you wanted to see Ethan, but this was special to Mom, and her friend will only be in town today. Besides, he's a baby," Camilla stated firmly and had a sinking feeling when his expression did not soften. "Ethan is fifteen months old. He won't know or care if you put that present in his little hands or not. That's ridiculous. He doesn't even know how to open a present. He'll probably chew on it. I'll get it to him and put it into his hands." Changing her tone, she waved her hand. "Have a seat, Noah, and relax," she said, motioning toward an armchair.

Noah shook his head. "Thanks, Camilla, but I have other places to go."

Why did his words hurt? He was stiff, cold and angry. She didn't want to react to him, to ache to be in his arms and to remember far too vividly his kisses.

"Do I get my present?" she asked.

He crossed the room and she couldn't resist letting her gaze flick over him. Her pulse raced as she noted differences. He stopped a couple of feet in front of her. Her gaze lowered to his mouth and she couldn't get her breath. She realized how she stared and her gaze flew up to meet his, and for a few seconds, she saw scalding desire, a hungry look that made her weak in the knees. She was the one who broke up with him, so why was she about to go up in flames just facing him now?

She fought to regain her composure, or at least feign it. Searching for something to say, she came up with a lame comment. "I think you're taller, Noah."

"I am," he answered. "I got measured enough in the Army to know I'm taller than when I went in. Taller, heavier, stronger and hopefully tougher. We'll see the next time I participate in a rodeo." He reached out, holding a package. "Here's your present from Thane, Camilla. He had very specific instructions for me."

Momentarily lost in thoughts about her brother, she accepted the small package and ran her hand over the ripped and wrinkled brown paper, tied tightly with twine. She thought about Thane, dying in Afghanistan, so far from home and family, having a present for her and one for Ethan. "Thank you. I'm glad you and Mike and Jake were with him. He died doing what he wanted," she said and stopped talking for a moment because tears threatened. "When I kissed him goodbye, I wondered if I would ever see him again," she whispered and turned her back to wipe her eyes. She tried to get her emotions under control and shifted her thoughts to Noah and the present, turning back to face him.

"Sorry, Noah. Thane was really special."

"Yes, he was. He was special to all of us under his command."

She took a deep breath. "You did what he wanted. I'll tell Ethan, when he's old enough to understand that Thane very specifically wanted you to bring his present home and he wanted you to place it in Ethan's hands yourself."

"And that's what I intend to do. I'll have to come back," he said, and she could hear the reluctance in his voice.

A chill slithered down her spine because she knew Noah would do whatever he said he would. She knew far too well how tough and unyielding he could be when he thought he was right.

"Noah, you're busy. I'm busy. Ethan is a baby and Thane wasn't thinking about how little Ethan is."

"Camilla," Noah said in such a cold voice that she stopped talking instantly. "Thane knew exactly what he was doing and saying. Those were the words of a dying man giving his last wishes. I promise you, your brother's thoughts were clear, and with great effort and some of his last breaths, he made me promise to put that gift into your baby's hands. He specifically said to not give it to you."

She felt heat rise in her face. She loved her brother, but he had always meddled in her life. This was why she wouldn't tie her life to a man who was an alpha male through and through. Her controlling brother had even managed to wring promises from his men that would bring about the results Thane wanted. He was just as bad as her father.

Her father had never been deeply interested in his kids. Early on, Thane took over being a second dad to her and sometimes he'd interfered in her life if he'd thought it was best.

She smiled sweetly. "All right, Noah. You can give the present to Ethan personally. I'll call you. It won't be this week because we have commitments, but next week should work."

Noah nodded. "If possible, as soon as you can. I want to get this done. I gave your brother my word that I would."

"Sure. You want to get back to your ranch, don't you?"

"You can't imagine how much I want to. It's been two years since I even saw it, back when I was on that furlough. You should have come out there with me at least once, Camilla. It's beautiful."

She shivered. "Noah, I've told you—we used to go see my grandparents on their ranch and it was never beautiful. It was scary and had snakes. I was bitten once, but it wasn't a poisonous one. My grandfather spent his time and money gambling and that ranch was insignificant to him. So were his grandkids. I hated it, and after my grandmother died, my grandfather let everything go. The house was dark and depressing. I told you—that's where my little brother, Winston, drowned. Our grandfather let us play on a frozen pond and the ice cracked. We all went in and that icy water was terrifying and I had nightmares about it for a couple of years. Thane pulled Winston out. He was only four. He got pneumonia and died. I've told you before."

"Yeah, I've heard Thane talk about it. That doesn't mean all ranches are dark, dangerous, gloomy and sad. That was your grandfather's doing."

"I'll agree with you on that one."

A faint smile raised one corner of his mouth. "Something we finally agree on."

"I've lost two brothers and an uncle because of accidents or violence. At least you can take care of yourself. When we were dating, maybe I should have gone to your ranch with you and you should have gone to an opera with me."

"I can't recall being invited to an opera."

"You would have turned me down."

Again, she saw a faint, crooked smile. "You should have tried me, Camilla. You'll never know whether I would have or wouldn't have."

They looked at each other and she felt that same pull, the attraction that was as intense as it had been when they dated. He had the most vivid blue eyes she had ever seen and they held her captive right now while her heart pounded. She couldn't breathe, couldn't look away and couldn't move.

"I'll see you next week," he said gruffly. But as his gaze lingered on her for a minute after he spoke, longing swamped her. She could just reach out and pull him back into her life. That thought came and immediately she stepped away from him. He might not ever want to be in her life again and she didn't want him back. He hadn't changed; he'd still try to run everything. Just like Thane. She knew Thane had been trying to get them together again or he would never have sent a present for Ethan and asked Noah to place it in Ethan's hands.

"I'll call you before I come out," Noah added, still standing in the same spot and looking at her.

Just as she'd expected, he turned the tables on her, taking charge of their next meeting. "Please do call. My schedule varies from week to week. I have a painting I'm working on."

"I'll call. You look great, Camilla," he said and his voice suddenly had a rasp that made her pulse jump. His gaze ran briefly over her from head to toe and back to look into her eyes. He might as well have run his fingers over her. She tingled from his glance—a mere glance—and she reacted to him.

"Thank you. So do you," she said in a voice that was almost a whisper.

"I don't know why in hell you fell in love with me when you knew from day one the things I like and do, the kind of man I am," he said. His eyes blazed with anger and a muscle worked in his jaw.

Her temper flared over his comment and she leaned closer to him, as she breathed deeply and looked at his mouth. "Oh, I think you know full well why I fell in love with you," she said, reacting with anger and longing. Her emotions were raw and she hurt and was angry with him, while at the same time, she couldn't stop wanting him, his kisses and his arms around her.

Annoyed with Noah and herself, she slipped her arm around his neck, standing on tiptoe to kiss him, running her tongue slowly over his lips for seconds before his mouth opened on hers. His arm banded her waist tightly, yanking her against him, and he leaned over her, kissing her, thrusting his tongue over hers. It was a hot, demanding kiss that made her heart pound while she moaned with pleasure and forgot momentarily all their differences.

Abruptly he swung her up and released her. Both of them gasped for breath as they stared at each other. "Well, I knew there had to be some reason you liked me. That one hasn't changed. It's a package deal—it's all of me, the bossy male, the rancher, the cowboy and rodeo rider, the pilot." He glared at her and her heart still pounded. "I should go," he said.

He turned and left, walking toward his black sports car. She watched as he walked away with purpose, standing straight, looking like a soldier, someone who was accustomed to walking with shoulders back and chin up.

"The truth is, you don't want to change," she said softly, knowing he was out of earshot and couldn't possibly hear her. "You're not going to see Ethan," she whispered. "Not next week or next month or next year. Thane was meddling in my life, doing what he thought was best because he loved both of us, but it wasn't best for any of us—not for me, not for you and not for Ethan."

Her conscience hurt when she remembered Thane's call to her, the heated arguments between them—something she'd never had before in her life—and now her brother was gone and she wanted to say she was sorry she had argued with him. She wasn't sorry for what she had done and was still doing, but she was sorry she had fought with the brother she loved so much.

She had told him that she had rights and he was butting into something that was none of his business and could hurt three people.

He had told her what she was doing was wrong and

Noah had legal rights that she was violating. Thane had said she should rethink what she was doing before she hurt three people badly.

She thought about Noah and whispered to him even though he had driven away. "You can keep Thane's present to Ethan. It won't be half as important as keeping you from giving it to him. If the day ever comes when you see Ethan, the moment you do, you'll know you're looking at your son. And if that happens, all hell will break loose between us, Noah Grant."

Three

Noah

As Noah drove away, he took deep breaths and relaxed his grip on the steering wheel. It had hurt far more than he had expected to see Camilla again. He thought he was getting over her, but the minute she opened the door, he knew damn well he hadn't gotten over her at all. He had just been busy trying to stay alive and do his job.

While he hurt, he wished he didn't care. He and Camilla had no future together and he didn't want to see her again because today had torn him up. She hadn't looked happy, either.

She had been prettier than ever, looking gorgeous, and his knee-jerk reaction had been to want to wrap her in his arms and kiss her for the next hour and carry her to bed.

He couldn't ever do that again.

He struck the steering wheel with his hand. He needed to get to the ranch and outside where he had hard, physical work. The Army was over. His life with Camilla was over. He had to move on and get a new life and try to forget her.

He hadn't helped himself by asking her why she fell in love with him when he knew what she liked and they both were tense and angry. Her kisses made him want to promise to change, to do whatever she wanted, but he hung on to his wits enough to know that he couldn't stop being decisive, controlling, demanding. He loved the Bar G Ranch and didn't want to give up that life. He'd lived in Dallas and worked in the family business and he'd had more of that than he wanted. That wasn't the life for him.

He drove carefully because he was upset and his mind was elsewhere. It was not until he was in his own condo that he could let go, let the memories that tugged at him come, the regrets, the anger, the longing he couldn't control.

He brewed coffee, poured a mug and went out on his balcony to look over the city of Dallas. He was high enough up that the horns and clatter of trucks were muffled.

He sat and sipped his coffee and thought about what else he had to do before he went back to the ranch, yet every few minutes, his thoughts would return to Camilla. He had to let go because they would not get back together. The differences were too big, too basic. She felt he was too strong an alpha male, making decisions and taking charge, because she had grown up with two take-charge males—Thane and her dad. She said her mother had given in to her dad always. Noah felt certain that wouldn't happen with Camilla. She was about as strong-willed as he was if she stopped to think about it. Would she really have liked him better if he couldn't take charge, couldn't make decisions and act on them? He didn't think so.

She hated her grandfather's ranch, thus she disliked all ranches. He knew her memories were terrible at her grandfather's place because her little brother had caught pneumonia from his fall into an icy pond and had later died. That would be a bad memory, but Noah didn't think his ranch would trigger any such memories. He should have tried more to coax her out to his ranch.

She loved life in the city. He loved it out on his ranch, which she had never even visited. They weren't going to work through their differences because neither of them would change. In bed was the one place where they had absolutely no disagreements. She was fantastic, instantly and intensely responsive. He sipped his coffee and made an effort to get his thoughts off sex with Camilla. The big deal was to give Camilla's baby his little present. Why the hell Thane had been so insistent on placing that present in his little nephew's hands, Noah couldn't imagine, unless it had been that the little kid had no dad and Thane hoped Noah would be enough interested in the child to try to work things out with Camilla.

Noah had always wondered if she'd married on the rebound because it had been so fast, coming up right after he had been home on furlough and they had gone another—and final—round in their battle over his alpha-male, take-charge way, their city versus country life.

A part of him suspected that Thane wanted them back together and thought her fatherless child might draw them closer. That wasn't going to happen. Noah knew Camilla hadn't changed. She didn't want any part of him in her life.

He sipped his hot coffee, closing his eyes, lost in memories of holding and kissing her that he couldn't push out of mind. She was still the sexiest woman he had ever known. She dazzled him, and until he'd left for the Army, they'd had fun together. He had been staying in Dallas some of the time, or coming in from the ranch often to take her out, and for a time, they seemed to be getting closer. Until he started inviting her to his ranch.

Give the baby his present and tell her goodbye. After that and Mike's wedding, there won't be any other reason to try to see her.

His logical mind gave him clear commands, but he couldn't stop the memories that clutched at his heart. Memories of one of the last times they were together, when he invited her to his ranch and she turned him down, leading to an argument as he tried to talk her into coming for a weekend. Finally he had stepped closer to slip his arms around her.

"Here's where all our arguments vanish," he'd said quietly. His mouth had covered hers and his tongue had gone deep while he kissed her. He'd held her close against him with one arm, his other hand slipping lightly over her curves, sliding down over her trim bottom, and then he'd shifted, his hand drifting beneath her dress to caress her breast. She'd been soft, wonderful, sweet-smelling, absolute temptation. He'd been lost. Her softness had made him shake.

For a moment she'd stood still in his arms, but with a moan, her arms had circled his neck and she'd thrust her hips against him, clinging tightly to him as she kissed him passionately in return, and he hadn't wanted to ever stop.

He'd leaned over her, pouring himself into the kiss as if he could kiss away her reluctance and make her want a life together. Make being with him more important to her than her dislike of country life and her views on alpha males. Their moments of intimacy were the best possible, but it always came back to the truth: he couldn't change the kind of man he was and make false promises that he never could keep and he didn't want to give up his ranch. City life wasn't for him.

Shifting, he'd slipped his hand beneath her dress, caressing her silken thighs so lightly, hearing her moan as she moved against him. Then he'd forgotten all their harsh words and impossible goals as he leaned down again to kiss her.

"I want you, Camilla," he'd whispered minutes later, running his hand lightly over her nape and then holding her close.

She'd inhaled, closing her eyes to kiss him in return. She'd moaned softly and run both hands down his sides. "Noah, this isn't going to solve anything."

"Shh. For a few minutes shut out the world. We'll talk about it later."

"That just means you're going to do what you wa—"

He'd kissed her so she would stop talking and there were no arguments. The sex had been hot, irresistible, and he'd picked her up to carry her to bed, where they forgot their differences.

Hours later, he'd slipped out of bed, gathering his clothes to shower and dress. When he'd come out, she'd been waiting. She had showered, pulled on jeans and a blue T-shirt.

They'd faced each other in silence. "We didn't solve one thing. You just took charge and swept us into making love."

"It looks as if we're caught up in irreconcilable dif-ferences because I can't stop being an alpha male. And frankly, I don't want to give up living on my ranch. That's my life."

"And I don't want to leave the city life. Noah, why are we even arguing? You haven't proposed. We're not that deeply involved."

"One of us was," he'd said. "All right, Camilla. I guess we say goodbye. I'm going to the military, any-way. I won't be around for a few years."

She'd flinched and drawn a deep breath. "We're just opposites and neither one of us wants to change."

"I guess you're right. One goodbye kiss," he'd said, kissing her again, knowing he had lost her. Hurting, getting aroused again, he'd held her tightly and they'd kissed.

He'd released her abruptly and stepped back, clench-ing his fists so he wouldn't pick her up and carry her to bed. "This is goodbye. It's what you want. Not what I want. You're very special, Camilla. I am who I am and I guess you can say the same about yourself. You fuss about your brother being an alpha male, as well as your dad, but that didn't stop you from loving Thane and turning to him when you had a problem. Aw, hell. There's too much about me you don't like—too much you love that I don't want any part of, like living in the city and working here. I'm here now more than I want to be so I can take you out. Well, that's over. I'm going into the Army and I'll be gone. We just said goodbye."

Tears had spilled over and run down her cheeks, but her frown had kept him from closing the space between them to take her into his arms.

"You're right, Noah. I don't want to live on a ranch

or in the country. You're a strong man and you'll always want life your way."

When he'd started to reply, she'd held up her hand as if to stop him. "I know what you're about to say—that I have a strong, take-charge tendency myself. Maybe so. We're opposites in too many ways. All we have that goes smoothly is sex. That's breathtaking. But there's more to life than that. We have to get out of bed, and from the moment we do, we're opposites. So I guess it is goodbye," she'd said, wiping her eyes.

"You know how I feel about you, but I have to be honest and I have to be me."

He'd turned and walked out of her condo, knowing it was the end of their relationship and wondering how long it would take him to end his feelings for her.

The memory faded, but instead of feeling like three years ago, the pain of that breakup and goodbye was fresh. His feelings for her hadn't ended as he had thought they would when he was on active duty. He'd thought he was getting over her and then one glimpse of her set him back. There was one ray of hope for getting past the hurt from their breakup—he had done far better when he was away from her.

As soon as he delivered her baby's present and was in Mike Moretti's wedding, he would rarely ever see her. Thane was gone now, so his friendship with her brother could no longer throw them together. He planned to stay in Dallas for several weeks to be close to his dad. He would have to come and go from the ranch and spend more time in the city than he had originally expected.

There hadn't been a beautiful, fun, sexy woman in his life since he went into the Army. If he found one, maybe he could move on completely and the hurt over Camilla would lessen and disappear.

Convincing himself that life would improve, he tried to focus on the things he needed to get done while he was in Dallas. He needed to go see his dad. After that, he wanted to go by the family's commercial real-estate business. The company headquarters of Grant Realty was in downtown Dallas, which was run by Ben, and they had two suburban offices covering the metropolitan area of Dallas and Fort Worth, Eli running one of those and Stefanie managing the other.

And he also needed to deal with Thane's final wishes. Camilla ought to have her baby home and available for him to visit early next week. Before that, Noah would see her in Mike's wedding because he would be a groomsman and he knew she would be one of the bridesmaids, and then Camilla would be out of his life. They would be finished and he could say goodbye and, hopefully, forget her.

The next morning when Noah stopped at the back of the house, his parents were sitting in big rocking chairs on the veranda. He joined them and sat talking, taking his time and enjoying the morning, seeing his folks and gazing at their yard filled with flowers, a lily pond with a waterfall and fountains. He knew that around the corner on the east side of the house, there was another large veranda with an outdoor living room and kitchen. Beyond it was a sparkling swimming pool with more waterfalls and fountains.

"Let's go to my office," his dad said, and Noah nodded, strolling slowly beside his dad through the hall to the large home office. Cal Grant entered and crossed the room to sit in the big leather recliner he'd had for years. Noah turned to close the door and then sat in a hard, wooden rocking chair.

"I remember when your feet didn't touch the floor when you'd sit in that chair," his dad said, smiling at him.

"Yeah. I remember sitting here getting lectures about my behavior," Noah replied, and his dad chuckled.

"They must have done some good. You turned out to be a good man."

Noah looked into his dad's eyes. "Ben told me about your heart attacks and your bypass surgery, Dad. I wish I could do something."

"This came sooner than I thought something would, but I'm doing okay. I walk on a treadmill some, try to eat right. I feel okay."

"That's good news. I'm just sorry about what you've been through and that I wasn't here."

"You were doing a service for me and for all of us. Your mother is in a dither over this, so the less said around her the better. I feel better now that you're home. That's good."

"It's good to be home."

"You'll be going to your ranch soon."

He nodded. "I have Mike Moretti's wedding to Vivian Warner coming up and I'll be around here for a while after that. We'll get to see each other."

"Noah, you faced that you might not return when you enlisted. With old age, it's a given. We have trusts set up, the business is taken care of and I'm out of it. I've had a really good life. Financially, there shouldn't be any problem or even responsibility for your mom. Harvey's been our accountant for years and he'll handle things. If something happens to me, just give her your love and attention the way you always have. Take care of Mom and try to not grieve. I've had a good life."

"There's no way in hell anyone can avoid grief. Not when you love someone," Noah replied, not wanting to even contemplate losing his father. Surprisingly, another thought entered his mind. Camilla. He wondered if he was going to miss her for the rest of his life, too.

He leaned toward his dad. "If there is anything I can do to make life easier, you tell me. Would you mind if I go to one of your doctor's appointments with you? I'd like to meet and talk to your doctor."

"I knew you would," his dad said. "Look on my desk. I wrote the names and numbers of all the docs I've seen. Feel free to call and talk to them. I told them you probably would when you came home. Also, you can look at my calendar on the desk and see my appointments. I'd be happy for you to go along."

"Thanks," Noah said, getting up to walk to his dad's desk.

"Are you seeing Camilla now?"

"No, sir, that's over. It was over before I enlisted."

"Sorry, son. She seemed nice and we've missed seeing her, but some things just don't work out. We were saddened over Thane and we're both glad you're home. You've served and Mother needs you. We're both going to need you this year."

"Yes, sir, I'll be here, and you call anytime you need me no matter what hour it is. I've got a pilot's license and my own plane. I can get here from the ranch easily in no time."

"Thanks. I'll do that."

"I better run, Dad. You'll see me a lot now that I'm home and especially when I'm in Dallas," Noah said and realized he might have to rethink the time he intended to spend on his ranch. "For now I've got some time, so I'm staying in the city."

"Good. We're always glad to see you, but don't stay

on my account. I'm getting along fine." His dad stood and they faced each other.

Noah stepped up to wrap his arms around his dad and hug him lightly, realizing how frail his father had become. "Life is tough, Dad," he whispered.

"Yeah," his dad answered. "So are you." They stepped away and his father placed his hand on Noah's shoulder. "You'll do what you have to do and do it well. You always have."

"Thank you," Noah answered. "I had a good teacher." They smiled at each other and turned for the door that Noah stepped forward to open.

Noah's mother had been sitting where she could see them and she stood to walk into the hall. "Can you stay?"

"I have to go now, Mom. I'll be in touch and you call me whenever you want. I'm close and I can get here easily."

"Thanks, Noah. You come home when you can. We're so glad you're back and we want to see you."

"Thanks," he said, opening the door to go out the back steps. They followed and stood on the veranda as he crossed the shady drive to his car.

He climbed in, waved and drove away, wondering how well his dad really was. He glanced at the time. He had a few errands to run, but his mind wasn't really on those tasks. Instead, he thought of Camilla. The mere mention of her name conjured up memories of kisses, stirring desire and lusty thoughts that were unwanted. How long would it take him to forget her once he walked away this time?

And why did that prospect hurt so much?

Four

Camilla

Friday afternoon before Camilla had to dress for the rehearsal dinner and party Mike and Vivian were having, she picked up Thane's letter and stood looking at the envelope.

She had put off reading it because she knew it would hurt and she would miss Thane more than ever. Also, she suspected he would try to explain why he had asked Noah to personally deliver her present and Ethan's. She didn't want to read a letter from her beloved brother urging her to marry Noah. It had been a few days now since she had seen Noah and she hadn't called him about Ethan. She was certain when she saw him tonight at the rehearsal dinner he would ask her about Ethan and she could say she forgot.

She propped Thane's letter on a vanity, running her hand over it again because it was a tie to her brother, something he had sent to her, written, handled, wrapped for her, and it seemed a tiny part of him. "You should have stayed home the way Vivian and I wanted you to," she whispered, closing her eyes.

She opened her eyes and turned her back on Thane's letter. She might read it after the wedding when she wouldn't see any more of Noah. At least that was what she hoped. Noah could be mule-stubborn. At the thought that he wouldn't give up seeing Ethan, a chill slithered over her and she shivered. She had to keep Noah away from Ethan. She was doing something she shouldn't, but she still wasn't ready to share her son and she didn't want to marry Noah solely because of Ethan. They had too much between them to make a relationship work out of obligation alone.

She turned and looked at the dress hanging in her closet, eager to get out of the funk that thoughts of her late brother and Noah had put her in. Festive and lively, the sleeveless dress was a scarlet red with a scoop neckline and a straight skirt ending above her knees.

Mike and Vivian would have the rehearsal at the church and then the wedding party would go to a downtown club for dinner. As Camilla dressed, her thoughts of Noah returned. She had mixed feelings. She dreaded seeing him because she hadn't called him to come give Thane's gift to Ethan. The last time with Noah had been painful and she didn't want another confrontation. Also, when they were together, there had been fireworks with hot kisses. She had dreamed about him every night.

Within days he would vanish out of her life. She would not tie her life to a strong alpha male, especially one who liked the opposite of most things that she liked. On one of life's most basic needs—where to live—they were poles apart. Noah would have all sorts of ideas about raising Ethan and she suspected they would battle each other at every turn. She didn't want his interference with her baby.

Their baby.

At the thought, a twinge of guilt disturbed her, but she tried to focus on the wedding and think about her friends that she would see tonight. At the same time, excitement skittered over her nerves and she could not get Noah out of her thoughts. Underneath all her dread was a thrill at seeing him again that she couldn't shake and didn't want to feel. When—and how—would she get over Noah?

She was still asking herself that question when she got to the church.

The wedding party met there to run through what everyone would do at the upcoming ceremony. When Camilla stepped out of her car, she glanced at a black sports car pulling in at the end of the row. In seconds Noah stepped out and in a few more seconds she would catch up with him.

In a navy suit and white shirt, with a black Western hat and black boots, he looked incredibly handsome. Her heart thudded as he faced her, and she was glad he couldn't know how her pulse raced.

Noah

When he saw Camilla, he drew a sharp breath. In high heels, and a sexy red dress that showed a lot of her gorgeous long legs, she looked incredible. With each step she took, her silky hair swung across her shoulders. While his pulse raced, he couldn't stop looking at her. As he stared and walked toward her, she smiled faintly, her full rosebud lips curving as if in an invitation. He wanted to walk up to her, put his arms around her and kiss her. His heart pounded while he clenched his fists and reminded himself that she was off-limits and out of his life. She would not be seated by him, nor would she do anything with him tonight. If he didn't want to hurt more than ever, he would stay away from her.

Mike had called to ask if he wanted to be seated with Camilla, and Noah told him no, that it was definitely over between them.

As she neared, he smiled. "You look stunning," he said and meant it. His voice had a raspy sound because he was aroused. He wanted to whisk her off somewhere they could be alone, where he could hold and kiss her and just look at her. She took his breath away and he knew the luscious curves beneath that dress.

She smiled slightly in return, but her hazel eyes were cold. "Thank you, Noah. You look very handsome."

"Thanks, Camilla," he said, falling into step beside her. "I'll ask now before we get involved in the wedding. You were going to call me about bringing Thane's present to your son."

She shook her head. "Noah, sorry. I'm busy right now. It's been a hectic summer. I'm sorry I didn't get to call you, but when I'm home and see my calendar, I'll call this week. You said you'd be in Dallas awhile," she said.

"I'll expect to hear from you this week. I want to get this done."

"I understand and I'll call you."

He reached out to get the door, but he didn't open it for her. With wide eyes she looked up and his heart pounded.

"You really do look gorgeous," he repeated softly, aching to touch her.

"Thank you again," she whispered.

His heartbeat raced as he gazed down at her and remembered her kisses the last time they had been together. His heart pounded. How was he going to get over her?

"We better go inside," she said, smiling at him.

"You're right," he replied and opened the door for her. After she entered, he followed her in and then went the opposite direction so he could let his heartbeat slow and his temperature cool.

Camilla

Camilla glanced over the people standing in clusters in the foyer. She spotted Vivian and headed toward her. She couldn't resist glancing over her shoulder and saw Noah with his back to her, talking to Stefanie Grant, his younger sister. Camilla's heart was still racing from just walking past him through the open door as he held it for her. When she had, she'd caught the faint scent of his aftershave that triggered memories of when they'd kissed. She remembered the feel of his slightly rough stubble against her face and his strong arms around her. After this wedding it might be life without Noah in it. Just the thought hurt, yet she couldn't change her mind. No matter how much she missed him, wanted him, dreamed about him, she couldn't deal with his strong alpha ways and his cowboy lifestyle out on a ranch.

Smiling, Vivian looked radiant, and Camilla remembered Vivian had that same radiance when she had married Thane. Thane had looked as if he was the happiest man on the planet and Vivian had looked as if she adored her new husband. Camilla hurt for losing her brother, as well as losing Vivian in the family.

Wearing a pink suit with a sparkling diamond necklace, Vivian hugged Camilla. "You look great tonight. I love your dress."

"Thanks. You look beautiful and I'm happy for you. Everyone says Mike is a great guy."

"I think so," Vivian said, her eyes twinkling.

Camilla's smile vanished and she touched Vivian's wrist lightly. "I know you're supremely happy, but I also know this has to have moments that are hard for you."

"A little," Vivian admitted, "but I'm marrying a man who is as understanding as your brother was. I can't believe I've found two of them. Well, Thane found Mike for me. He is understanding and it takes away a ton of sadness. I'm so happy and we're happy," she said as she glanced across the room at Mike again and back to Camilla.

Camilla felt her insides clutch. Would she ever find that kind of happiness with someone? A dull ache enveloped her as she looked around.

In that moment, Camilla realized Vivian might have been a closer friend if she had tried to get to know her more. She regretted she hadn't because Thane had loved her, and the little Camilla had been around Vivian, she had liked her, too. She and Vivian both shared a common bond of being artists.

"I'm happy for both of you and I'm certain this is what my oldest brother wanted to have happen. He was always trying to take care of everybody, sometimes to the point of meddling in lives," she said, and Vivian's smile broadened.

"Yes, he did, and he had an uncanny way of being right about what he thought everyone should do," Vivian replied. "He chose well. Mike is a great guy. Camilla, when things settle after the wedding and honeymoon,

I expect us to still get together over our art and I want to keep showing your paintings in my galleries."

"Thanks, Vivian. That's good to know."

"I'm glad your other brothers could get here for the wedding. They're already here. I've talked to them," she said and looked around as Camilla did.

"Ahh, excuse me. Mike is motioning and he's with the minister, so we're probably getting ready for the rehearsal. The sooner we do that, the sooner we can go to dinner."

"Of course," Camilla answered and watched Vivian walk away. She was certain Thane had sent Mike home not only to run the Tumbling T ranch, but also to meet and marry Vivian. She was equally certain her brother had wanted Noah to get back with her. She sighed. That would not happen.

"Hello, little sis." She turned to face her two older brothers, Mason and Logan. She hugged Logan, gazing into hazel eyes like her own. He was thirty, single, and they saw each other often in Dallas events. He liked the same things she did and both had season tickets to the symphony and to the Dallas operas. They both knew Noah was the father of her child, but unlike their oldest brother, Logan and Mason were willing to let her live her life her way, and they respected her choices, for which she was grateful to both of them.

In spite of that, it was Thane she had always felt the closest to and had confided in as a child.

Mason gave her a quick hug and smiled. Mason looked more like their dad with brown eyes and blond hair.

"I want to come see my little nephew while I'm home. I don't want him to forget me."

She smiled. "He won't forget you and we'll be glad to see you."

"That includes me, too," Logan said.

"You both are welcome anytime. Just let me know to make sure we're there."

She knew her brothers—they came alone to the rehearsal dinner, but each one would probably leave with a pretty woman.

Shortly, they went through the rehearsal. She was paired with one of Mike's brothers, Tony Moretti, and Noah was with one of Vivian's unmarried friends, a tall, striking redhead named Mia Mason.

As she chatted with various members of the wedding party, she turned to face Stefanie, Noah's sister. Stefanie smiled at her.

"Hi. I want to talk to you, Camilla. Maybe we have a minute now."

"Sure, Stefanie. What's up?" she asked, looking into another pair of thickly lashed vivid blue eyes. Stefanie's black hair was long and wavy, a tangle of silky strands. Noah's sister was beautiful with rosy cheeks, full red lips and a gorgeous figure. She seemed to have boundless energy and an optimistic outlook on life that Camilla envied. A fun person, Stefanie was more outgoing than her older brother and Camilla enjoyed knowing her. Although she didn't know her well, they moved in the same social circles.

"I have a deal for you," Stefanie said, wasting no time. "We have some property in Chicago I've been working on and we just sold one of the smaller suburban buildings to a prestigious art gallery. We sold it to them before it ever went on the market and they got a good deal. They're extremely happy about it."

"Congratulations! That's quite a coup for you." Camilla smiled, surprised at Stefanie telling her all this.

"Thanks. They're thrilled and so grateful for letting them have an early shot at the space. The thing is, I showed them some of your landscapes and they loved them. I think they may contact you for a showing in their new gallery."

"Stefanie, that's fabulous," Camilla said, meaning it. "I'll let you know if I hear from them. Thank you. I'd love to have a showing in Chicago."

"I thought you would," Stefanie said. Something in her smile gave Camilla a thought. She wondered if Stefanie wanted her to spend time in Chicago in order to get her away from her brother and out of his life. She was doing that anyway, but she still was happy about the chance to showcase her art in Chicago.

"I'm excited over this. Is the name of this gallery secret for now? I know some of them."

When she looked down at the card in her hand, she gasped. "Stefanie," she said, smiling at Noah's sister, "I've been to this gallery—just to look—and I've seen their ads and a few lists of artists who have some showings there. This is fabulous. I can't thank you enough. This is wonderful."

"Don't get too excited until they actually call, or you can call them and see what happens," Stefanie said, smiling and sounding pleased. "Part of their interest in you is doing it as a thank-you to us for giving them an early chance to purchase the building, because it's a fabulous building in a great location. Part of it is your art. They liked your work, so good luck with it. Contact them and see what happens. You have nothing to lose."

"No, I don't. This is just marvelous. Does Noah know about this?"

"No. I thought the two of you—" She waved her hand.

"You're right. We're not seeing each other, but I

wanted to make sure. I'm thrilled about this opportunity. Thank you for showing them my art."

"Glad to. I hear you're a mommy now. Congratulations. I'm sorry about the divorce, but I know you're happy with the little baby."

"I love him with all my heart," she said and gazed into Stefanie's blue eyes. A twinge of guilt filled her because she was keeping Stefanie from knowing her little nephew. "I'll let you know what happens. Thank you again."

"Good luck with it. I hope it goes really well," she said.

Camilla watched Stefanie walk away. Whatever Stefanie's motives, Camilla was thrilled over the prospect of getting a showing with that gallery. She slipped the card into a pocket in her dress.

To her relief, at dinner she was seated at the opposite end of the table from Noah, near Logan and Mason and between more of Mike's family. She did have a good time at moments, but she couldn't shake her awareness of Noah, and occasionally, she couldn't resist glancing his way. Three times he was looking right back at her, which startled her each time, and she could feel a flush crawl up her cheeks even after she had turned away. Once when she looked, his dark head was bent close to Mia Mason, who was laughing, and it hurt to see them having fun together.

Still, the prospect of getting more deeply involved with Noah wasn't appealing, either.

By ten o'clock, the party began to break up. She watched Noah leave with Mia and wondered if they were going out somewhere for a drink, going home together or if he was just walking her to her car. It hurt to think about him moving on, having a life with someone else in his arms, going out with another woman, marrying her. She gave herself a mental shake. She had to stop thinking about Noah.

It was easy to tell that to herself, impossible to do.

She glanced at Mike and Vivian, who were holding hands, smiling at each other, and she felt another pang. She was happy for them. Her brother had been on target on that one. Mike really was a great guy.

As she expected, Logan told her goodbye and left with one of the pretty bridesmaids.

Mason waved as he left and one of Vivian's pretty relatives was with him.

As she drove home, she wondered if Noah could be put off indefinitely about the gift for Ethan. He hadn't seemed too concerned tonight. But it wasn't like Noah to let something go, so she better start figuring out exactly what she was going to do. Guilt still nagged at her, but without a doubt Noah would want in his son's life.

When she arrived home, she talked to her nanny briefly before telling her goodbye and going to Ethan's room. She stood beside his crib, gazing down at him and brushing soft curls back from his forehead.

"I love you, my sweet baby. You look like your daddy," she said wistfully.

She thought of Noah and from out of nowhere came an errant thought. A wish that Noah was standing beside her and they could enjoy their son together.

She had no idea where that wish came from…but she knew it could only ever be that. A wish.

Five

Camilla

With a sigh and determined steps, she tiptoed out of the nursery and walked into her bedroom to pick up the box from her brother. She carried it to her rocker, kicking off her shoes and turning the box in her hands.

She tried to untie the twine. It took a long time and she rocked as she bent over it, determined to avoid cutting the twine he had used. She knew it was foolish, but she wanted to keep the box just the way it had been in Thane's hands. It was her last tie to her big brother. She missed him and it hurt unbearably. She looked at Ethan's picture, his smiling baby face, and love filled her, along with the knowledge that she would risk her life to save him if she had to. And she always felt gratitude for the men and women who served in the military to keep peace and America safe, even though she was thankful her other two brothers had not joined the military. Thane had been special, a brother and sometimes another dad to her. The thought of him dying from injuries in a foreign country hurt badly.

It took a long time, but she finally unwrapped the twine and then the paper around a box, constantly aware that it was last handled by her brother. The box contained something wrapped in more brown paper and beneath it a white envelope with her name scrawled across it. When she opened the brown paper wrapping, a bracelet of gold links fell out into her lap. She picked it up and slipped it on. It looked old in the soft light. She rubbed it against her cheek and wiped away tears as she picked up the envelope to find a letter.

Camilla,
If Noah brings this to you, then it's because I won't be coming home to you. Your worst fears for me came true. Even though I've made the ultimate sacrifice, if I had to make the choice again, I would still go into the service.

I hope your feelings change about Noah being a rancher. I've been to his ranch, and I promise you, it is not like our grandfather's ranch at all. Go and see for yourself. Noah is not a compulsive gambler as was Granddad, who paid no more attention to his ranch than he did to his grandkids, namely us. As for worrying about alpha males— you're a strong woman and can hold your own. You are closing yourself off from happiness. Don't shut your baby away from it. He should know his daddy.

I want you to know I will always love you, my baby sister. I wish I could see your little boy grow up and I wish I could be part of his life. I hope I have done some small part in keeping America safe for him to grow up in freedom the way we did.

My deepest brotherly love to you. Hug my little nephew for me. Please let him know the fine man and soldier who is his daddy. He needs his dad in his life. He needs both of you—a family like we had.

Here's a bracelet I bought. It's old, but pretty, and I thought of you.

Thane Warner, Captain, US Army Ranger

She put her head in her hands and cried. "I miss you," she whispered. Finally, she wiped away tears and folded the letter to put it back into the envelope. She stared into space as she contemplated her brother's words. She didn't know if she could ever tell Noah about his baby. If she did, it would turn both her life and Noah's upside down again and be another upheaval even bigger than when he enlisted. Guilt plagued her and she stared down at Thane's letter. She knew what he wanted her to do, but the minute she did, Noah would take charge and want to do things his way. And she couldn't allow that.

"I'm sorry, Thane. I can't do it," she whispered, tears falling again. She shook her head. "I just can't tell him. Ethan is a happy baby now even if he doesn't have a daddy," she whispered. "I can't deal with Noah taking over my life and Ethan's."

She stood to get ready for bed, her thoughts on Ethan. It was for the best that she avoid the man altogether. Then she realized what awaited her tomorrow. It was Vivian and Mike's wedding, which meant she would see Noah again.

* * *

The sunny day was perfect for a wedding. All the bridesmaids wore short, straight black dresses with white chiffon scarves at the vee necklines. As Camilla walked down the aisle, she glanced ahead. Mike and his grooms-men stood waiting and her gaze went to Noah, who was watching her from under his dark lashes. Her breath caught and pain squeezed her heart. Noah was more handsome than ever in a black tux. She once thought she'd walk down the aisle toward him as her groom.

At that lost dream she felt longing for Noah tug at her heart and looked away. But as she reached the point to turn to join the bridesmaids, she made a mistake and glanced at him again and her heart thudded. Nearly stumbling, she took her place and turned to watch the next bridesmaid come down the aisle. Mia's gaze was on Noah, too, as she walked.

In minutes Vivian came down the aisle. She looked radiant in a crepe sleeveless dress with a round neck and short, straight skirt. Camilla was happy for her and for Mike. Once again, Camilla was certain this was what Thane had wanted when he couldn't come home. If only Camilla could be so certain that her brother was right when it came to her.

For the first time, she gave some thought to what she was doing in keeping Ethan from knowing his dad. Was she cheating her baby out of a close, important re-lationship that would help him grow into the wonder-ful man his daddy was?

She barely heard the service for thinking about Noah and then it was time to process back up the aisle. All through the pictures she was conscious of Noah. He spent his time talking to Mia and Stefanie and then at the reception he was with Mia. Camilla stood watching him and thinking about Thane's letter. It was later in the evening when Mia finally moved away from Noah and Camilla crossed the room to talk to him.

"Noah, wait." He turned and her heart raced. Was she making the wrong decision for the wrong reasons? Was it Thane's letter or was it that she had lost Noah and she didn't want to let go? She couldn't answer her own questions.

She stood in front of him. "I can meet with you this week if you want to give Ethan his present. I need to talk to you anyway."

"Good. How's Wednesday?"

"Wednesday's fine. I'd like to talk to you first, so can you come at about two because Ethan will be taking a nap then—at least, I hope he'll be."

"Sure," Noah answered. "I'll be there at two."

"Good. We need to do this before you leave for your ranch."

"Yes, we do, even though I'm not going as soon as I had originally planned."

"Well, I may not be here too long," she replied. "I don't know whether Stefanie told you or not, but she gave my name to an art gallery in Chicago. They contacted me today and offered me a showing, so I'll be going to Chicago soon. I've told Stefanie thanks because it's a wonderful opportunity."

"She didn't mention any of this to me, but that's good news for you."

"Also, that package you brought had a letter from Thane urging me to let you meet Ethan."

The corner of Noah's mouth lifted in a faint smile. "Thane was always arranging everything in his life and I'm sure he couldn't resist arranging his baby sister's, too."

Shaking her head, she smiled. "No, he could not." For a moment they were both silent. "Well, I'll see you Wednesday afternoon."

"Thanks, Camilla. I want to get this done and keep my promise."

"My meddling brother," she said, shaking her head as she walked away.

In her heart she wanted nothing more than to be here with Noah and to leave with him. But her head told her differently. The man had a love of everything country, wanted to be a rancher 24/7, had a need to take charge always. They were simply not compatible. Monday night she had tickets with a friend to the symphony. Tuesday, she had agreed to an appearance at an art gallery showing her work. That evening she was attending a charity dinner. Noah wouldn't want to be involved in any of those activities.

She hadn't slept much last night after she had read Thane's letter. His words had made her think. Was she cheating her baby out of knowing his dad? She hadn't really looked at it from her baby's standpoint until she read Thane's letter. Noah would be a wonderful dad; she had no doubt of that.

Her eyes sought him, and she saw him leaving with Mia. Pain stabbed her heart. Out of the corner of her eye she saw Stefanie, who was also watching Noah, and she saw the smile on her face as he left with Mia.

Maybe her earlier suspicion had been right. Stefanie had arranged for the Chicago contact to get Camilla out of town. Away from Noah. Still, it was a wonderful opportunity, one she intended to take full advantage of to further her career. Besides, she knew Noah and Stefanie were close and Stefanie probably was concerned about her brother and his happiness. She couldn't fault Stefanie for that.

Noah had a nice family. She had met all of them, been with them for parties and family gatherings. For the first time she realized she was keeping Ethan not only from his dad, but also his grandparents and aunts and uncles. And he was the first grandchild. Ben and Hallie did not have any children. Eli wasn't married and neither was Stefanie.

The thought stuck with her all the way home. When she got in, she dismissed the nanny and went to check on Ethan. Tenderly she touched his forehead as he slept. He looked so much like Noah. It was his blue eyes and black curly hair.

Tears ran down her cheeks. "I love you, Ethan," she whispered. And in that moment she knew that her son should know his daddy. She was cheating him out of a tie that was one of the most important in life.

She shut the nursery door and went into her bedroom, where she picked up Thane's letter, running her hand on the paper. "Thane, you sent Mike and Noah home with promises to you to do things here that you knew would change lives. But, as usual, you're right. Ethan should know his dad because Noah is a fine man and has a wonderful family. But I don't want to lose my baby doing this. Noah can be stubborn and hard." Tears stung her eyes and she covered her face to cry, shaking because she was so scared she would lose Ethan.

Noah would instantly step in and she would have to share Ethan almost immediately, so she'd better pull herself together and start thinking about what to do when she told him he had a son.

Was she going to be strong enough to do that?

Noah

Wednesday morning Noah felt he was beginning to fit back into his life as it was before he went into the Army. He knew his sister was matchmaking, but so far she was doing a good job of it. He liked Mia, he had fun when he was with her, but his mind still continued to drift to Camilla. It had hurt to watch her walk down the aisle and know that someday she would marry someone else. How long would it take him to get over her?

Sometimes he would see a tall woman with straight brown hair and he'd go out of his way until he could see whether or not it was Camilla.

He was glad she had set a time for him to deliver Thane's gift to his little nephew. He had expected to do that and then he would say a permanent goodbye to Camilla. Eventually, he would go to the ranch, where physical work would keep him busy, and he'd do better about getting over her. Now, because of his dad, he wanted to stay in Dallas longer, and seeing Mia a few times had helped a little.

For the twentieth time that morning, he checked his watch. It was hours yet before he'd go see Camilla. He had to bank his eagerness to see her and to stop checking the time, but he was so curious as to why she wanted to talk to him. He'd just have to wait to find out.

About midmorning he pulled into his parents' drive.

He went by to see them nearly every morning and often in the evening.

As long as he was in Dallas, he wanted to spend what time he could with them. He enjoyed his dad's company and Noah was glad that he had the chance to thank his dad for being the best father ever.

After visiting his parents, he stopped at Ben's office.

Then, finally, at twenty minutes before two, he drove to Camilla's house. It was in a gated area with winding drives past elegant mansions with tall oaks casting cool shadows. Behind a high wrought-iron fence stood a large two-story colonial. Well-tended flower beds bordered the front porch. A splashing fountain was in the center of the circle drive. Her home was beautiful, which didn't surprise him. Her family was wealthy and he knew she had investments in family businesses. Plus, from what he'd heard, her art was bringing in more.

When Camilla swung open the door, his pulse jumped. In a blue T-shirt and tight jeans, she looked gorgeous. His reaction to seeing her was just as strong as it had been that first time after coming home from the Army.

"Come in, Noah," she said, stepping back.

Carrying the small parcel from Thane, Noah entered, following her into her living room, his gaze on her tight jeans and trim butt as she walked ahead of him. Once again, he realized he hadn't lost any of his desire for her.

"Can I get you something to drink?" she asked, turning to face him.

All he wanted to do was step closer, wrap his arms around her and kiss her. Instead, he shook his head. "Thanks. I'm fine."

"Have a seat. I want to talk to you."

His curiosity grew because whatever she had to tell him, she was worried about it.

She sat on the edge of a sofa and he sat facing her in a wingback chair. Her hands were locked together in her lap and her knuckles were white. Startled, he reached over and placed his hand on hers. Her hands felt like ice and he looked up to meet an even more worried gaze.

"What the hell, Camilla? What's wrong?" He thought about his dad's heart trouble and a cold fear gripped him.

"Noah, I've just had so much difficulty with our breakup. I can't deal with your male ways sometimes. You know you take charge. I don't want to spend weekends on your ranch. I don't even really like country music. We're not compatible."

"I've got all that, Camilla. We've been over it," he said, watching her wring her hands, which he'd never seen her do before. He leaned close and covered her hands with his. "Camilla, are you ill?" he asked gently.

"Oh, no. No, it's not that," she said, sounding startled. He waited while silence stretched between them. He couldn't imagine what was wrong.

"Camilla, just tell me," he coaxed softly.

"This morning I started to call you a dozen times and cancel seeing you today. I don't want to do this."

"You're not sick, but you have to tell me something unpleasant that you don't want to tell me. Is that what's going on?" She bit her lip and stared at him. "Something is worrying you and in some manner it involves me or you wouldn't be telling me all this. What the hell is wrong? Just say it and let's go from there."

She took a deep breath. "I've done something I should not have done and Thane knew it."

Noah frowned because he had no clue what she was talking about, but at least she didn't have a dreaded disease and he was relieved for that. He removed his hands from hers and thought about the letter from Thane. "What on earth has your brother asked you to do? And it involves me. He was trying to get us back together just like he got Mike and Vivian together, wasn't he? You don't need to get so totally undone over that. I can't imagine anything you've done that you shouldn't have unless he's given you a guilty conscience over breaking it off with me. Is that it?"

"Absolutely not," she said, shocking him.

"Then what the hell could possibly be this bad that Thane knew and that affects me?"

"I haven't told you something I should have told you, so just get ready for a shock." She reached over beside her on a table and picked up a framed picture that had been facedown. He'd noticed it but had given it little thought. "Here's Ethan's picture. Noah, please forgive me and try to understand."

He took the picture, and as he looked down at it, he felt his heart clutch.

Six

Noah

As he stared at the face of the boy in the photo, he remembered how Thane, when he had been wounded and barely conscious, suddenly had looked at Noah with clarity and determination and told him in a strong voice to put his nephew's present in the baby's hand. Thane had been determined that Noah see Thane's nephew. Just as determined as Camilla had been to keep him from seeing the child. Speechless, he looked at the picture again and knew he was looking at his own child.

His eyes met Camilla's. Tears spilled over and ran down her cheeks.

"I got you pregnant when I was home on furlough before you married?" he asked, knowing that was the only time it could have been.

Nodding, she closed her eyes. "Yes."

Still stunned, he could feel his heart pound. "Why didn't you tell me?" he couldn't keep from asking. "Oh, dammit, Camilla." He looked at the picture, at the baby with black curls and blue eyes, and he felt as if he held his own baby picture.

"He has to be over a year old now."

"He's fifteen months," she said without looking at him. She had a handkerchief over her eyes as she cried. "Noah, I'm sorry. When I had him, you were overseas."

"Have you heard of a father's rights?" he asked, and he couldn't keep the anger out of his voice.

"I know I did something wrong, but we weren't getting along."

"This never once occurred to me."

"It hasn't to most people."

"But Thane… When did he see Ethan? Thane wasn't home after Ethan was born."

She shook her head. "Thane hounded me to send a picture. I didn't send it until I got him to promise he would keep what I wrote to himself. Thane always kept his word. I wrote Thane the truth and that I hadn't told you and I sent him a little picture. Of course, he urged me to let you know."

"I can't believe you kept this from me and my family." Noah stood and walked away from her, taking the picture with him to look at it while fury rocked him. "Anyone who sees this baby would know he's my child. I can dredge up baby pictures that look just like this."

"I know." Tears still ran down her cheeks and she wiped her eyes.

Noah thought about all the time she had known that he was a dad.

"We need to work out what we're going to do," she said.

"Oh, yeah. Camilla, I want my son."

She lowered the handkerchief to look at him, standing and facing him. "Noah, I'm sorry you didn't know sooner. It wouldn't have brought you home any quicker. Please forgive me."

"It wouldn't have brought me home sooner, but my family would have known they had a grandchild."

"You can tell them today and I can take him to see them this week."

"Dammit," he said, fury making him hot as he stared at her. "I'll take him to see them. But that's not the point, Camilla. It's time. Time matters. For fifteen months—for almost twenty-four months, counting your pregnancy—my parents could have looked forward to and enjoyed knowing their grandson before I came home."

"They can now, Noah."

He walked closer to her. "Camilla, while I was gone, my dad had two heart attacks and heart surgery. Time does matter and you cost them months of happiness," he said, his words cold and bitter.

All color drained from her face. "Oh, Noah, I'm so sorry," she said, putting her hand up as if to reach to touch him, while tears poured down her cheeks. But she put her hand down and looked away. "I didn't know and I never thought of something like that. Did Thane know about your dad?"

"No. Ben just told me when I got home."

"That's dreadful and what I did is dreadful. I didn't know about your dad. I'm so sorry. I've made some big mistakes. Is your dad's health why you haven't gone to the ranch?"

"Yes. I'm staying in Dallas for a while so I can be with my parents."

As he thought about what he wanted to do, he faced

Camilla. "I want my parents to know Ethan. I want Ethan with me half the time." Color drained from her face. Even so, she raised her chin.

"I've been thinking about it. We'll have to work out how we'll share him, but for right now, since you don't know him or how to take care of him, move in with me. I've got a big home and it's already arranged for a baby. I know moving to my house will put a temporary crimp in your social life, but for a little while, move in and let Ethan get used to you and get to know him. That way, I'll be here for him, because he needs me, Noah."

As he thought it over, anger still burned in him, but she made sense and his son needed his mother. "You're probably right. I can do that."

"I'll give you a tour when we can. I have a big studio here and I paint early in the mornings, but we can adjust that. There's plenty of room.

"I need to fly to Chicago next week to arrange my art show. It'll leave you two here together. My mom will keep him in a pinch, so take him to her when you need to go out. I have two nannies I use and I'll leave their names. Once you introduce him to your family, I imagine your parents will want him sometimes, too."

"Yes, they will. Right now the only symptom Dad seems to have is he's more tired, so my mom can take care of Ethan and I'm sure she'll want to. Ben and Hallie will probably want some time with him. They've tried to get pregnant and haven't been able to. This will take some pressure off them and that may help because the doctor said they were physically able to have a baby."

He ran a hand through his hair. "Dammit, Camilla, family is the most important thing in life. My family means the world to me and I want a family of my own, but I also never wanted to rush into a relationship and marry until I knew damn well the woman was the right person for me. Right now, marriage isn't a solution for us at all and I'm sure you agree."

"Yes, I do, Noah. We have big problems between us."

"This hurts," he said. Camilla stepped close to him to put her hands on his shoulders. His heart drummed, and in spite of his shock and anger, he still wanted to put his arms around her.

"Noah, I made the wrong choices. I've hurt you and your family and I'm truly sorry. I hope it isn't too late to make up for that."

He was torn between desire and anger. Right now, he was aware of her hands on his shoulders, of her enticing perfume, of her big hazel eyes with long brown lashes. His gaze lowered to her full lips and his pulse pounded. She always smelled sweet and her softness was irresistible. He fought the urge to wrap his arms around her and kiss her, and he simply nodded. "All right, Camilla. We'll go from here."

She dropped her hands and stepped away, but turned back. "If you want a DNA test, we can do that. I promise you, this is your baby, but if you would like a DNA test, I'll get one for you."

He shook his head and held up the picture she had handed to him. "This is like looking at my own baby picture. I don't need a DNA test."

"That's what Thane wrote after I sent him Ethan's picture. He didn't know you when you were a baby, but he must have seen pictures of you. Ethan has your black curly hair and your blue eyes. You'll see."

He heard a baby cry on a monitor.

"There he is, right on cue," she said. "I'll go get him."

She left and Noah looked at the picture again. He was a dad—no nine months to get ready for that news.

His anger was fading and he was beginning to think about the immediate future. He would move in with Camilla. That made the most sense. He couldn't imagine how they could live under the same roof without giving in to sex, which would only lead to an even bigger emotional risk. But she was right. He needed to learn how to take care of his baby, and he couldn't take his child away from his mother and put him with strangers.

He was going to have his son in his life and he just hoped he didn't have to fight Camilla in court about it. He wanted equal time, joint custody, whatever it took. He thought about Mia. He'd liked going out with her the couple of times they'd dated, when he'd thought Camilla was out of his life, but that had all changed this past hour. Seeing Mia would have to be put on hold. Right now he needed to get to know his son and he needed to be able to deal with Camilla on some level because they would have to both be involved in their child's life.

He heard her talking before she entered the room and then she came through the doorway with a baby in her arms. He felt as if a giant hand squeezed his heart and all his anger evaporated. He couldn't take his gaze off the baby, who was wearing little jeans, socks and a red T-shirt. He had black curly hair as tangled as Noah's had been as far back as he could remember. The baby had rosy cheeks and big blue eyes. He held a little brown stuffed bear in one arm and kept his gaze on Noah, seeming to be as curious about Noah as Noah was about him.

Noah's heart pounded and he felt overwhelmed. She walked close, stopping in front of him, and Noah could smell baby powder. "Here's your son, Noah," she said softly. "This is Ethan. It's officially Ethan Warner. By the time Ethan was born, Aiden and I had officially been divorced for months and there was no reason to take his name. Aiden knew the truth, that this was not his child, and he left Texas and said he wasn't coming back. Everyone who knew me didn't question that I named him Ethan Warner because Aiden was long out of my life." She smiled at her baby and then looked at Noah. "Do you want to hold him?"

Emotions ran through Noah: joy, gratitude, curiosity, amazement and uncertainty. "I don't know one little thing about babies even though all my siblings are younger than I am." He looked at Camilla. "Will he be scared?"

"I don't think so," she said and placed the baby in Noah's arms. Ethan was warm, smelled of baby powder and was astonishing to Noah.

"My son," he said in amazement. He looked at Camilla. "You should have let me know. I might have been able to get home for the birth. How long were you in labor?"

"Not long. He weighed eight pounds and one ounce."

"I think he's a fine-looking baby."

She smiled. "I think so, too."

"Our baby. That just isn't real yet. You went all through that pregnancy without me. Did you have morning sickness?"

"No. Everything about my pregnancy was easy except the daddy part, and that was my own doing."

Noah looked at Ethan. "Hi, Ethan," he said, and Ethan smiled, reaching tiny fingers to touch Noah's beard.

Camilla placed her hand on Noah's shoulder. "Daddy," she said clearly. Then she looked at Noah. "Ethan's a man of few words, so don't expect much in the way of conversation."

Noah laughed. "I think he's fascinating." His smile faded and he looked intently at her. "This baby is going to bless my whole family. In a minute I'll call them. I know they'll be home tonight. Can I take Ethan to meet them?"

"Noah, he's your baby, too. Of course you can," she said.

"Can he stay overnight with them soon?"

"Of course. You don't need my permission for those things because you're his dad."

"I'm on a roll. Maybe I should ask if I can take him to the ranch."

She drew a deep breath and he smiled.

"I'm teasing you right now. The day will come when I will want to take him to the ranch, but not now." He looked at Ethan again. "He's marvelous. Ethan, you're a first-class baby," he said. "Does he sleep through the night?"

"Nearly always. He's been an easy baby. And a happy baby."

"That is really good news," he said, turning to look at her again. She gazed back with a worried frown and he turned to his baby. "I'm a dad. That is the most wonderful news."

"I didn't know you'd be this happy about it."

"I'm in awe. I'm thrilled. I need some dad lessons. I don't know how to take care of him."

"That's why I suggested you move in here. I can show you how."

Noah couldn't seem to take his eyes off the child. "Ethan, I'm your daddy."

"Daddy, Ethan," she repeated and placed her hand on Noah's shoulder again. Ethan held one arm out to reach for Camilla, so Noah handed her their son.

"I think he's had enough of me."

Camilla took him. "You did well for the first time and he liked you."

"I'm glad you know his signals. All he did was stare and smile. I'm going to call my folks and tell them I want to come by and talk to them, that I have a surprise. Then I'll come back and get you and Ethan and take you over. We're not going to just walk in the door with him and announce that I have a son."

"Just go and talk to them, and when you're ready, call and I can drive to your folks' house. You don't have to come back to get us."

"I'll come get you because it will give them a chance to get used to this idea of being grandparents. Stefanie is going to love this." He turned to look at Camilla, who stood only inches away, and she gazed up at him. Once again she had tears in her eyes.

"Why the tears now?"

"I've made a muddle of things and I'm so sorry, especially about your dad. That possibility never occurred to me. We still have big problems separating us. This baby needs both of us."

"Yeah, I know. I'll worry about that one tomorrow. Just take tonight and let's celebrate. He's still under your roof and he's with you and he's with me. My family will be thrilled beyond anything you can imagine. Frankly, I'm thrilled, Camilla. I didn't know I would feel this way about a baby, but I do."

He looked intently at her and slipped his hand behind her head.

"It wasn't my fault, but I'm sorry I wasn't there with you when he was born."

Her expression changed as her eyes widened and she looked surprised. "I'll admit, Noah, I had some rough moments because you weren't here. My brothers tried to make up for it, but Mason and Logan have busy lives and they're single. They were nice to try to be there for me. Logan lives in Dallas, so he was around often at first. Thanks to you for saying that now. And I'm sorry about your dad. If I had known…" Her voice trailed away.

Noah looked at Ethan. "This will make up for it in a lot of ways. You can't imagine how happy Ethan is going to make my family. It'll help us get through what's happening and what's to come." She looked up at him and Noah wanted to wrap his arms around her and Ethan, and he wanted to kiss away all the problems between them and take her to bed with him. Taking a deep breath, he turned away, because that wasn't going to happen and their problems would not go away.

"Oh, here's the package from your brother that I'm to put in Ethan's hands. I don't think I have to do that now. I get what he was after. He wanted me to know you and I have a son."

"Yes, he did. Thane was a wonderful big brother, but sometimes he meddled."

"Thank God he did this time," Noah said, giving her the package.

She turned it over in her hands. "I have this instead of my brother," she said. "I miss him."

"I know. He was a great guy." Noah pulled out his phone. "I'll head home now. I hate to leave. Let me get some quick pictures. Can I take this one now?" He held up the photo she'd shown him. "I'll give it back."

"Keep it, Noah," she said, smiling at him as he took the small framed picture of Ethan. He took some more pictures on his phone and she smiled. "Noah, stop.

You'll have fifty pictures in another minute. We have loads and you'll take a bunch at your house."

He smiled and stepped to her. "I'll stop and I'll go see my folks. I know things aren't great between us, but for tonight, let's forget the differences and celebrate my discovery that I'm a dad."

"It won't solve a thing, but I'm willing to have a celebration tonight. Sort of a temporary truce, if there is such a thing."

"Goodbye, sweet baby," Noah said, leaning down to look Ethan straight in the eye. Noah laughed and straightened. "He is a man of few words. When do they start talking?"

"He should by now. It varies, but he's going to be one that's on the late side. He says some words. *Bye-bye*, *bear*, *mine*—he has a tiny vocabulary. It'll come, Noah."

"Well, I think he's marvelous. Maybe babies should wait and come when they are about twelve months old. They're more interesting."

"I don't think pregnant mothers would vote for that one," she said, smiling and shaking her head. "You've really surprised me once we got past the shock and anger, which I understood and expected. I didn't expect this enthusiasm and joy, but I'm so glad and so relieved."

"I've never really given a thought to being a dad. Well, I'll run," he said as he opened the front door. She followed him outside and stood on the top step of the wide front porch.

"Goodbye, Ethan, you adorable child. Ahh, Camilla, this is wonderful news. It'll complicate the hell out of your life and my life, but it'll be worth it. I'll call you after I talk to my parents," he said and went to his car in long strides, soon leaving down the long, sweeping drive and heading for his parents' home, happy that he was going to have great news for his whole family.

Stefanie, though, might have a moment or two because she was friends with Mia and hoped Mia would replace Camilla in his life. He'd had fun with Mia. She was gorgeous, sexy, appealing, and she accepted him totally as he was without wanting him to transform his life and turn into a different kind of man. For right now, though, he wanted to get to know his son. That came first.

And if the time came when Camilla was part of the bargain, he'd deal with it the best he could.

Camilla

Camilla went inside and closed the door, looking down at Ethan. "Now you've met your daddy and surprise, surprise—he loves you a whole, whole lot. Surprised me because I never expected that reaction." She thought about Noah's dad and hurt for Noah. She was sorry about his dad's heart trouble, but medical science could do wonders. "Tonight is great, but tomorrow, your daddy and I will have to start making decisions and it's going to be, oh, so tough," she told Ethan, who chewed on his bear.

"In the meantime, let's get out your best outfit so you look your cutest to meet your grandparents. You'll meet your paternal grandparents tonight and maybe aunts and uncles. They won't be able to resist you and your charming ways, especially since you had the good sense to look like your dad," Camilla said as she took Ethan to her room to bathe him in her bathroom. She'd picked up Thane's package before she'd left the living room and now she placed it on her dresser before taking Ethan to bathe him. She would open Thane's little package afterward.

Later, after bathing Ethan, she put him on the floor, where he could play with his toys while she got ready. First, she picked up the package from Thane and sat on the floor with Ethan to carefully open it, once again feeling a tie to her brother. When she unwrapped the brown paper, she held a child's book of nursery rhymes. She opened it. Thane had written:

> To Ethan:
> I hope your parents read these verses to you and you like them as much as I did. I wish I could watch you grow up. Hug your mommy and your daddy for me. I love all of you.
> Much love to my nephew from Uncle Thane

Camilla hurt and missed her brother. What a sacrifice soldiers made to give up their lives. Wiping away tears, she couldn't be annoyed with him for making sure that Noah learned that he had a son. She should have let him know when she was pregnant or shortly after she gave birth to Ethan. She never expected him to be so thrilled and happy over becoming a dad.

She put the wrappings and the book back on her dresser and her thoughts shifted to Noah again and how happy he had been over Ethan. Never once had she expected Noah to be so delighted to discover he was a father. She knew a tough time lay ahead. He'd made that clear tonight. For the rest of her life she would remember tonight when he said, *I want my son*. That was the downside. He would fight to have Ethan equally. Her family was wealthy, but Noah was wealthier, even without his family's fortune. He could certainly afford the fight.

He said to take things a day at a time and that was what she would do tonight. Tonight should be filled with joy for Noah and his family.

And what about later tonight?

She suspected he would stay tonight in a guest bedroom in her house. If they started sleeping together, she would just have a far bigger hurt when he moved out. She had to guard her heart because when he was happy, Noah could be incredibly charming.

But could she keep her distance, not only resist him, but keep her hands off him?

Noah

As he drove, Noah smiled. He called Ben's secretary and asked her to do a big favor and call Ben's best florist to order a huge bouquet of flowers sent ASAP and to put it on Noah's bill. He gave her Camilla's name and address. He asked them to put a small stuffed toy in it, if possible. Ben's secretary knew Noah and she laughed and said she would.

He was a dad and he had an adorable baby who looked just like him. This would be such good news for his parents. He wasn't going to think about what could have been or what should have been. They would learn about Ethan now and go from there, and from tonight on, it would be fun and exciting to have a baby in the family.

Once again he thought about Mia. Tomorrow he would call her and tell her about his son. She might not be thrilled to learn he was a dad.

Problems lay ahead with Camilla, too. They hadn't

solved anything. They had probably complicated their lives and they might be headed for a huge court battle over rights.

Within minutes he turned into the familiar big circle drive and parked in front of his parents' two-story Tudor mansion that had an east wing and a six-car garage with an apartment over it. Ben's car was in the wide drive with Stefanie's red sports car parked behind it. Eli's car wasn't there, but he worked later and lived farther away. Noah had told Ben to round everyone up, that he wanted to talk to all of them and that he had a surprise. Noah had ordered a big rib dinner to be delivered to the house and he caught the enticing scent when he stepped onto the porch.

Excitement gripped him and he knew he would remember this day for the rest of his life. He wanted to laugh and shout for joy. In the coming days he intended to focus on his baby. He and Camilla hadn't settled one little thing and now the stakes would be infinitely higher with their baby in the middle.

Their baby... How good that sounded. He refused to consider any if-onlys. He crossed the porch and entered, hearing voices and laughter in the big living room.

"Hey, I'm here," he called, entering the living room and greeting them individually as he moved around the room.

Ben turned and smiled. "Okay, he's here and he's got a surprise for us and a big grin, so it's a good surprise. Let's hear it and then I'll go get you something to drink. Get us out of this suspense. You look as if you just found a gold mine in your yard."

His dad was still seated, not coming to his feet as he had always done when someone entered, and Noah hoped he was feeling reasonably well. His mother entered with a tray of crackers and healthy fruit and veggie snacks that she put on a table.

"Well, what is this big surprise you have?" she asked him. "And don't tell me you got us all together to hear about a new bull or new horse."

"Oh, it's better than a new horse," he said. They all gazed at him, waiting, Ben with his arm casually across Hallie's shoulders, Stefanie's eyes sparkling.

"I'm not sure where to start," he said as he looked around the room. "Camilla and I— Well, you know we had stopped seeing each other when I left for the service. But when I came back for a furlough about two years ago…" He noticed the minute he said Camilla's name, Stefanie's sparkle vanished and was replaced by a frown.

He started again. "Camilla had some news for me—a big surprise. I'll bring her over this evening, but I wanted to tell you first." He crossed the room to his mother to put his arm around her. "Mom and Dad, all my family, I'm so happy and I hope you are, too. I'm the father of a fifteen-month-old boy, Ethan."

His mother hugged him while Hallie shrieked with joy and rushed to hug him next. His dad stood to shake his hand and then Ben clapped him on the back. He glanced across the room and saw Stefanie with a deep frown as she stared at him. He smiled at her and turned to his mother.

"You're bringing them over for us to see your baby tonight?"

"Yes, I am. I think he's adorable."

"Noah, Camilla has let everyone think her baby was fathered by the man she married and divorced," Stefanie said.

"Yes, she didn't correct anyone about it. I'm sure some people knew, but none of us. Thane knew the truth and wrote her, urging her to tell me and all of us, so she has."

Ben shook his hand while he grinned. "I'm so happy for you. You can't imagine. This is a blessing for all of us."

His dad put his arm across Noah's shoulders. "That's the best news I've had in a long time, son. You'll be a fine dad."

"If I am, it's because of you," Noah said, hugging his dad.

"Hey, bro, I just got here. What's this about you being a dad?" Eli, Noah's youngest brother, asked, crossing the room to shake Noah's hand. Noah looked into another pair of eyes as blue as his own. Eli's black hair had a slight wave like Ben's.

"That's right, Eli," Noah said. "Camilla and I have a fifteen-month-old boy, Ethan Warner."

"Congratulations! Fantastic, man! Wedding bells will come next, eh?"

"Don't go so fast. I'm just trying to adjust to my new status as a dad."

"When do we get to meet the little guy?"

"As soon as I go get them. I wanted to come tell you first before I walk into the house with him."

"Noah, go get your baby for us to see," his mother said.

"I'll get the drinks," Ben said. "What do you want, Eli? Your usual vodka?"

"You got it, but stay here and I'll get the drinks." Eli left for the bar with their mother going along talking to him. Noah turned to face Stefanie.

"Noah, don't you want a DNA test before you announce you're the dad? Camilla might be saying this to get you back."

He laughed. "Stef, I don't need a DNA test. This is my baby."

"You don't know that for certain," she said.

"She might be right," Ben replied.

"I'm the oldest, so none of you remember me as a baby, but you've seen plenty of my baby pictures. How's this?" He went to the entryway to a table where he had placed the framed picture facedown when he had arrived. Carrying it, he returned to the family room to his sister and Ben, who had moved closer. "Here's my baby, little Ethan."

"Noah—" Stefanie started to say as she took the picture and looked at it. Frowning, she raised her head. "You have a baby picture just like this. Have you seen this baby?"

"Yes, I have. That's his picture, but it looks like one of mine."

"Sure as hell does," Ben added, peering over at the photo. "I've seen your baby pictures and they're interchangeable with this one." He walked away to get his drink.

Stefanie let out a long breath and shook her head. "He's your baby," she said, sounding shocked. "I didn't think this would really be your baby, but it is. There is no denying it—he looks like every one of us in this room."

"Stef, don't sound as if the world just ended. This is great news for our folks, and it's good news for Ben and Hallie because it takes the pressure off them," he said, speaking softly and talking fast. "Stop matchmaking for me. And tonight, enjoy your new nephew. You're Aunt Stefanie now."

"Oh, my, I'm an aunt." She looked up at Noah and smiled. "I'm sorry about you and Camilla, but this is wonderful. This is good for Mom and Dad. I'm sorry, Noah. I want you to be happy and you seemed happier with Mia than you've been with Camilla, but this is your baby. Mercy, he looks just like you."

"He certainly does look like me. He's got my wonderful disposition, too," he said and smiled. Laughing, Stefanie still stared at the picture. Noah patted her shoulder. "Lighten up, Stef. This is good news. You're going to like being an aunt and he is one happy baby."

She looked up, sighed and then nodded. "Sorry, Noah. I just worry about you and I think Camilla is going to hurt you."

"Let me worry about that. Enjoy my son."

"My, oh, my. Your son. I can't believe it."

"C'mon—we'll show Mom and Dad his picture. I have some pictures I took with my phone, too. In just a few minutes, I'll go get Camilla and Ethan."

"Have you told Mia?"

"Not yet. I just found out and I wanted the family to be the first to know. I'll call her tomorrow. Stefanie, Mia and I have a good time, but there's nothing serious between us. Stop matchmaking. And speaking of—who are you going out with?"

"Don't start in on me. As far as Mia is concerned, I just want you to be happy and you haven't been."

"I've been overseas fighting and going through losing Thane and some other buddies. Things will straighten out with time," he said, wondering if and how they really would. His life had just gotten a lot more complicated.

"Okay. Go get this little baby of yours. I can't believe I'm an aunt. Aunt Stefanie." She laughed. "I want to meet my nephew. I hope I like him."

"I think you will. Pretend he's me."

Smiling, she shook her head. "Go get this baby for us to see before Dad gets too tired to enjoy the moment."

"You're right. I'm gone. You can show the picture around."

"You realize you just tied your life to Camilla's for a long time."

"Yeah, I know." He turned and left to get his baby. His baby—he was still in shock. On the way he made a stop to buy champagne.

When Camilla opened the door, he drew a deep breath. She had changed into tan linen slacks and a matching linen blouse and she looked gorgeous. He looked into her wide hazel eyes and his heart beat faster as desire filled the look he received in return.

"Come in," she said, and her voice was breathless. When her gaze went to his mouth, he fought an inner battle because he wanted to take her into his arms and kiss her. Trying to control his desire, he stepped inside and walked past her. As a faint whiff of her perfume teased him, he fought the urge to look around at her. How was he going to live in the same house with her and keep from carrying her off to bed?

Seven

Camilla

Camilla's heartbeat jumped to a faster pace. Noah stood facing her and he was so good-looking, he took her breath away. Her heart pounded, and desire, the longing to take two steps and put her arms around him, was intense. In spite of all the problems, she wanted to walk into his arms and kiss him. But she knew that was impossible, would only create bigger problems. Trying to bank her longing, she smiled at him. "We're ready to go. I have Ethan's things. But first I have to ask—was your family happy?"

"They are overjoyed and can't wait to see him. You look gorgeous," he said, making her heart beat faster when she looked into his eyes and saw the desire that filled his expression.

"Thanks." She looked at Ethan in her arms in a navy jumper and white shirt. "How does he look to you?"

"Perfect. Hi, Ethan," Noah said, leaning a little closer. She could detect Noah's aftershave and that made her think of kissing him. She looked at her baby in her arms and tried to stop thinking about Noah.

Ethan smiled and held out his arm.

"Hey, he wants me to take him. You think?" Noah's dark brows arched in surprise.

"Don't sound so shocked. Maybe he senses something. Let me get his things. He never travels lightly. We'll go in my car because of the baby seat."

"Okay. I'll take Ethan and you put this in your fridge." He handed her a bottle of champagne. She'd been so intent on looking at Noah that she hadn't noticed it till now. "We'll celebrate when we come home. When you're ready, we'll go," he said, taking Ethan from her.

Noah's warm hands brushing hers and just that slight contact sizzled. She was grateful for the champagne that she had to refrigerate.

When she returned to the living room moments later, Noah turned to her. "I'll drive if you want."

"Sure," she said, giving him the keys with another brush of hands. They looked at each other at the same time and she realized he had felt something too from the casual brush of hands.

"Why do we do that to each other?" she asked.

"Who can explain attraction? We're as different as fire and ice."

"Well, I'm rather happy for some of those differences," she said, knowing she shouldn't flirt with him or encourage the attraction.

Noah must have known it too, because he held his ground. "We're complicating our lives from the first moment. But somehow—"

"Let's go," she said, not wanting to play with the fire that was burning between them.

She turned on the house alarm and followed him out to the car.

When they arrived at the front door to his parents' house, she handed Ethan to Noah. "You take him in and show him around."

The minute they entered the living room, everyone huddled around Ethan. Noah handed him to his mother, who turned to take him to his dad. Noah stepped back beside Camilla. One glance at him and she guessed that he was thinking about losing his dad. Impulsively, she took Noah's warm hand.

When he turned and focused on her, she dropped his hand. "Sorry. I just thought you were worrying."

"I was. It's a bittersweet moment."

Noah glanced down at Camilla and laced his fingers through hers, holding her hand and stepping a fraction closer, making her think about going home with him and making love, something she wanted more each time she was with him even though she knew she needed to keep her distance. Working out how they would share Ethan could pose monumental problems on top of the ones they already had.

"Go join them, Noah. I'll take some pictures." Noah crossed the room and stood close to his parents while they held Ethan. She looked at all the black-haired, blue-eyed Grants. Ethan fit right in and looked like one of the family. Only Noah's mom had blue-green eyes and red hair with white strands now. His dad still had some black in his hair, but it was mostly gray, making her think that was the way Noah would look someday. She realized this would probably be the only time she would be included in a Grant family gathering. She and Noah were no longer a couple and he would be taking Ethan alone to see his family. That realization hurt, yet every time she questioned her feelings about Noah being a rancher and another alpha male, she came back to the same decision—that wasn't what she wanted in her life. But moments like this still hurt.

Stefanie glanced her way and then crossed the room to her. "We didn't mean to leave you out. Everyone is so excited over Ethan. I can't believe I'm an aunt. He is precious."

"Thanks, Stefanie. Go back and join the family. Ethan is new to all of you. I've had a lot of time to look at him. I don't mind."

"Why don't you join us?" she replied. But before she turned to go back, she said, "I'm surprised how happy he is, and he's not scared of all these new people passing him around and looking at him."

Camilla smiled. "Maybe because all of you look just like he does, he feels comfortable."

Stefanie laughed. "If you're okay, I'm going back. I don't know beans about a baby, but this is fun and wonderful for my folks."

"I'm glad," Camilla said, keeping her smile, but she hurt because she wasn't part of the family and she wouldn't ever be.

Noah

While Noah talked to his siblings, he watched Camilla, who sat with his parents, helping them with Ethan if they needed it. His gaze slid over her and his heart beat faster. She looked radiant tonight, laughing and smiling with his family, happy with her little boy. Even though he knew he couldn't, he wanted to take her home to bed, to hold her and make love to her, to shower her with gratitude for this baby. As she talked to his folks, she shook her head and her hair swung away from her face and Noah could remember how it spread over his bare shoulder when they were in bed together, an image he needed to get out of his thoughts now.

The family and Ethan seemed to have a fun time and finally Ethan slept in Noah's dad's arms while his mother was beside them, looking at Ethan every few minutes. When Camilla glanced at Noah, he suspected she was ready to go home because the hour was getting late.

"It's a weeknight and we should go now," Noah said as he stood.

As he expected, it was another thirty minutes before they were in her car with Noah driving and Ethan asleep in his car seat. They spoke about how happy his family was, how eager to hold Ethan. But all Noah could concentrate on was Camilla. She was three feet away in her seat, yet he could feel her.

At her house he helped her put Ethan to bed and finally stood beside her over Ethan's crib. Noah draped his arm casually across her shoulders as he stood looking down at Ethan.

"He's a marvel to me. I wish I'd been here when he was born."

"We can't undo that now."

They walked out of the room together and he still had his arm across her shoulders. "My room adjoins his," she said. "I can put you in an adjoining room on the other side, or there's a big suite across the hall."

"Give me the suite and I can spread out, unless that's an inconvenience. You have a big house for one person and now a baby."

"I have a big art studio downstairs and I wanted lots

of room for Ethan. My family is here sometimes, too."
She shrugged. "It is big, but I like it. I have someone
who comes to clean it. Someone to take care of the yard.
And I have a nanny who's here when I need her. And a
backup nanny. But Ethan is easy, so I take care of him
most of the time myself. My folks really aren't into bab-
ysitting, but they keep him occasionally."

"Sounds like you have things worked out. Let's go
open the champagne and celebrate my fatherhood."

She stiffened and for a moment he thought she would
decline. Perhaps because she too thought that champagne and celebration could lead to kisses and bed?
Just the thought made his heart beat faster.

"By all means," she finally said. "I didn't know how
you'd take the news, but you've been great and I think
you're going to be a wonderful dad."

"I hope so. I had a good model."

Camilla

The lights were low in her big family room, giving
a cozy atmosphere that couldn't quiet Camilla's nerves
as she watched Noah open the champagne and pour the
bubbling liquid, half filling two flutes. He had rolled up
his sleeves and unfastened the top buttons of his blue
shirt. His thick curls were a tangle and some fell on
his forehead. In the low light he looked strong, handsome and sexy, and she felt she was headed for disaster
if she didn't walk away in the next few minutes. She
couldn't leave, though. She had spent too many nights
missing him, wanting him with her. Knowing better,
she still couldn't resist this small celebration with him.
He was home safe from fighting and he had been great
with Ethan. Ethan was happy with Noah and with his

whole family and that was definitely a cause for celebration. She knew problems were ahead because she and Noah had different outlooks on life and they both were strong-willed people.

He picked up one flute to hand to her and then took the other for himself. He turned to her and held up his glass. "Here's to you, Camilla, for giving me our son. He is already a joy for me and my family."

Noah's voice was husky, his blue eyes dark with desire, and she felt headed for catastrophe as she clinked her flute lightly against his and sipped her champagne. She remembered how she had wanted Noah at her side when Ethan was born. She wanted Noah's strong arms around her now. She wanted his kisses, his loving, even though a night of kisses and hot sex would just make life more difficult.

"I'm still shocked how happy you are about Ethan."

"Of course I'm happy about him. Family is everything, and you saw what a joy he was to my family." He gazed at her and set his drink on a table, turning to take hers from her hand and put it beside his. Her heart drummed and she knew she should stop him, but she couldn't say anything. She ached to kiss and hold him and find the paradise they once knew when they were together.

"Noah, this is just going to complicate our lives all over again," she whispered while her heart pounded. She gazed up at his thickly lashed eyes that made her pulse race.

"Darlin', we complicated the hell out of our lives when I got you pregnant. There's no going back on that one. I know we've got bad times ahead of us, but tonight let's really celebrate. We're Ethan's mom and dad, and tonight let's rejoice in that and in each other.

We can go back to the fight tomorrow or next week or whenever. I know we will go back to it because it goes deep and isn't something that has an easy fix. Just one night's celebration."

His seductive request was too tempting, but she knew she would have monumental regrets because she wasn't getting over him. And he was right—the problems weren't going away. Noah would always be an alpha male, always be a rancher. No matter how big a folly tonight might be, she couldn't resist. He was looking at her now as if she were the only woman on earth and as necessary to him as breathing.

"Noah, we're going to have giant regrets, but I can't say no to you when you're so overjoyed about our parenthood. Ethan is a constant joy. You'll love him so much and your family will, too. I guess we'll just sink into more difficulties and go ahead and celebrate tonight. Just tonight. It was a lonely childbirth in spite of my family. You weren't here and didn't know and neither was Thane. Frankly, Logan and my mom finally came to the hospital just before he was born, but I didn't know they there until quite a while after he was born. Mason sent a huge bouquet and came the next week. I'd like to celebrate tonight because I couldn't when he was born."

Noah slid his arm around her waist and she felt the solid muscle. He pulled her up tight against him and her heart pounded.

"Tonight, I want to forget everything except becoming a dad. I want you, Camilla."

"Ah, Noah, we shouldn't—" She couldn't keep from saying the words, even though she had already decided she would celebrate with him tonight and she had known that that meant making love.

"Oh, yeah, we should, and you want to. Oh, baby, do you ever want to. It shows in your eyes." He tilted her chin up and looked at her intently. "Tell me you don't want me to kiss you."

"Noah—" She hurt and she should tell him, but she wanted to kiss him with all her being.

"That's what I thought. You want to kiss as badly as I do." He bent his head and his lips covered hers and she opened her mouth to kiss him in return, wanting his kiss with all her heart. His arm tightened around her and he leaned over her. She wrapped her arms around his neck to cling to him as she kissed him, her tongue sliding over his, his tongue stroking hers and her mouth.

She moaned with pleasure while her heart pounded and she thrust her hips against him. He was hard, wonderful, holding her easily with one arm while his other hand ran lightly over her curves, caressing her.

She slipped her hand between them to unbutton his shirt completely and then slide her hand over his bare chest, tangling her fingers in the curly black hair.

"Ah, darlin', how many long, empty nights I've dreamed of holding you, touching you and kissing you."

His words were seductive, his hands magic on her, his mouth setting her ablaze with longing. "Noah, you'll never know how much I've missed you and wanted you," she whispered, turning her head and then running her tongue over the curve of his ear while she ran her hand along his thigh.

"I want to touch and kiss you all night long. You were my dream, my wish, my longing while I was gone," Noah said between kisses as he unbuttoned her blouse and pushed it away. When he slipped his hand beneath her bra and cupped her breast, she gasped as he caressed her.

"You're so soft. There were too many lonely nights, too much violence, too much fighting and too much dying. This is life and love and hope. I can't tell you how many nights I've dreamed of you and wanted you in my arms. You've given me the greatest gift possible. I want you, Camilla," he whispered, peeling away her bra and slacks. He held her, his gaze roaming over her.

"Beautiful," he said in a hoarse voice.

"Noah, we're just going to make things worse," she whispered, but she didn't really care. She had already made her decision to make love to him, to stay in his arms all night long.

"Tonight that is absolutely impossible," he whispered and kissed away her protest. She was lost to the moment, wanting him. It had been two years since she had been in his arms and they had made love. She suddenly wriggled free and pushed against him, unfastening his belt, her hands shaking with haste as she continued to peel away his clothes. She paused while he yanked off his boots.

"I have to kiss you, Noah," she whispered. "You just take my breath away and I want to kiss you. I have to touch you," she repeated, trailing her hands on his thighs, following her fingers with her mouth and tongue, taking his thick rod in her hand and kissing him, stroking him, running her other hand so lightly between his legs and over his thighs.

He inhaled deeply, winding his fingers in her hair, tangling it. He picked her up to place her on the bed, moving on top of her. His eyes blazed with passion as he gazed down at her, but his hand was incredibly gentle when he brushed long strands of hair from her face.

"You're beautiful. You're sexy and I want you. I want to kiss and touch every inch of you and make you want me and want to make love all night long. I need you and we're just getting started." He bent his head to kiss her belly while his hands were all over her, caressing her breasts, her nipples, her inner thighs as she writhed and moaned with pleasure as much as need.

He trailed his tongue over her belly, up over first one soft breast and then the other, stroking lightly, slowly circling her nipples while his hands played over her.

"Noah…" She gasped. "Come love me," she said, tugging on his arms. He rolled her over on her stomach.

"Shh, let me kiss you. I've dreamed of you, your gorgeous body, your softness, your fiery sexiness." He trailed kisses along the backs of her thighs. Her hands knotted the sheet as she wriggled and let him kiss and touch her.

"Oh, Noah," she gasped, lost in sensation, wanting to kiss him, wanting him inside her, wanting his hardness, his hands all over her, her mouth on him.

He sat up once, pulling her up to face him. He wrapped his arm around her waist, leaning forward to kiss her. He raised his head to look at her again and she gazed into blue eyes that had darkened with passion.

Noah rolled on his side, taking her with him and gazing at her before pulling her close and kissing her, a kiss that made her want him desperately.

"You had my baby. Ah, darlin', we have a beautiful, wonderful son and my family already loves him and for that I will always be grateful to you. I want to make love to you, feel and caress and kiss you all night long. I want to find what really excites you."

"You have, Noah. Just holding me and kissing me." She turned his face to her and gazed into his eyes before leaning close to kiss him, running her tongue so slowly over his lips first.

He made a growling sound deep in his throat while his hand went to the back of her head to pull her forward and his tongue went deep into her mouth as he kissed her hard in return. Featherlight, his fingers caressed her breasts, and then he shifted to his side. His leg slid between hers, keeping hers apart while his hands moved over her intimately, rubbing and caressing her.

"Noah, I want to kiss you," she whispered, shifting to push him down. She moved over him, leaning close to run her tongue over his belly and his manhood, taking him in her hand to stroke and excite him as he had her.

"I want your mouth and hands all over me," she whispered. "I want mine all over you. I've dreamed of making love to you, dreamed of you being here with me."

Sitting up, he pulled her into his arms to kiss her passionately again, a kiss that made her heart pound and made her feel that, for the moment, he loved her with all his being. A kiss that made her feel as if they were the only two people in the world and they would always have each other. His mouth, hands and body, his thick manhood, mesmerized her.

While he held her tightly, she couldn't think beyond the moment or look at reality. Right now they kissed each other and that was enough.

He stepped off the bed to get a packet from his wallet.

"I'm on birth control," she said. He came back to bed to place the condom beside the bed and stretch out beside her, drawing her into his embrace again.

"I think you told me that some twenty-four months ago."

"That was a fluke. It'll work this time."

"At the moment, I don't care. I can't change my plans at this point unless you absolutely want me to."

"I want you to kiss me."

"Anything to make the lady happy," he whispered, pulling her into his arms and kissing her.

She wrapped her arms around him, kissing him in return until he moved between her legs and paused to put on the condom. She watched him. He was hard, ready to love her, and the sight of him made her heart race. Noah was incredibly handsome, virile, so sexy. Tonight she couldn't, wouldn't, resist him. She would relish every moment of lovemaking and not think about tomorrow.

He lowered his weight and kissed her, entering her slowly as she wrapped her long legs around him and clung to him with her arms around his broad back that tapered to his narrow waist. She ran her hand over his hard bottom. He was all muscle, so incredibly appealing. She tightened her arms around him as he moved slowly, and she raised her hips to meet him, holding him close.

"Ah, Noah, I want you." She gasped, pleasure washing over her as he withdrew and plunged in again. She shifted higher, wanting him, moving beneath him until he began to thrust faster, and she moaned softly, holding him tightly, feeling the pressure coil inside as it built, until her climax burst and she cried out in pleasure.

"Noah." She sighed and thrust with him as he reached his climax and then sagged against her, turning to kiss her.

"Camilla, this was better than I dreamed of. I want you in my bed, in my arms all night."

"This time is okay, Noah. Tonight is a celebration of Ethan's birth and of you learning you're a dad. Tonight is special."

"Damn right it's special. In every way it's fantastic,

being a dad, making love to you, holding your naked body against mine. This night is paradise on earth for me."

"It is for me, too," she whispered. "You can't imagine how sexy you are, how I want you and how marvelous this is."

"Yeah, for several hours," he said, and she heard a bitter note in his voice. She placed her finger over his lips.

"Celebrate and be happy this night. Right now, we have a baby. We have good news, raging sex and each other to hold and kiss. That's a blast."

Stroking her breast lightly, he ran his tongue over the curve of her ear and then turned his head to look into her eyes before he kissed her lightly, a sweet kiss. His arm slipped beneath her, drawing her against him and holding her close.

She felt his warm, hard muscles against her, his arms around her. She was wrapped in his embrace and she kissed his jaw lightly, taking her own advice and not thinking beyond tonight. She reflected on being with his family and how happy they had all looked.

"Ethan must have sensed how happy everyone was with him. He was happy as could be even though I'm the only one there he really knew. I told you—he's a good baby."

"That's because he takes after his dad," Noah said and she laughed.

"That's where he gets his good looks. He gets his good disposition from me."

"I'm still in shock. Maybe this is the best way to find out. No worries and what-ifs about his birth. I love him."

"Noah, I've been thinking since we were with your

family. I named Ethan for my uncle Ethan, as you know. My dad was okay with that because he's never liked his name, Mervyn Osbert Warner. He actually asked me not to use his name. I loved Uncle Ethan and spent more time with him and my aunt than I did with my mom and dad. Anyway, I've been thinking. How would you like to change Ethan's middle name to your dad's name? Your dad has a very nice name."

Noah shifted, sitting up slightly to look at her. "You're willing to change?"

"I think I owe you and this is one thing I can do. Hopefully, it will mean something to your dad. And maybe to you. It would be Ethan Caleb Warner."

Noah slid one arm under her and picked her up to kiss her. After one startled moment, she wrapped her arms around his neck and kissed him in return, and forgot about baby names even when he released her.

Feeling dazed, wanting to pull him back and kiss him again, she looked up at him.

"Thank you, Camilla. I think my dad would feel really great to know he has a little grandson named after him. If you're sure, I can take care of getting it done."

"I'm sure."

He drew her into his arms again, trailing his fingers over her, caressing her with light touches that made her feel cherished and important. She was fascinated by his marvelous body and ran her hands over him, feeling his erection come to life again, which excited her. He shifted, putting his hands on her waist.

"I want to look at you this time," he whispered, pausing to get a condom and put it on. He placed her astride him, entering her, filling her. His hands toyed with her breasts, stroking and caressing her and running his hands over her bottom. She closed her eyes and tossed her head back while he thrust into her and in seconds they pumped wildly together.

"You're beautiful," he said hoarsely, his thrusts making her cry out with pleasure. Caressing him, she rocked with him while tension built. She cried out with need, moving faster, reaching a climax when he did, and together they went over the edge.

When ecstasy enveloped her, she collapsed over him, her hair spreading over his shoulder. He held her tightly with one arm while he slowed and finally was still. His hand stroked her, brushing her long hair from her face, running over her back and down over her bottom.

"You have a fantastic body," he whispered. "Beautiful, so beautiful. So soft. You're a temptation that I dreamed about when I was gone and couldn't be with you." He ran his hands all over her and she clung to him, wishing they could hold the night and everything would be like this with them all the time.

She would do like Noah. Take this moment and not think about tomorrow or what decisions they would have to make. His body was strong, fit, perfect. They had hours for lovemaking and she wanted every minute. She hadn't faced fighting or death or the other things he had overseas, but she'd been alone, and had lost a brother she loved and had a baby without Ethan's father being here or knowing about him.

She wanted a night of passion, hot, thrilling sex and excitement with a man in peak form, muscled, able to love her into oblivion, a man she cared more for than was good for her.

As dawn spilled through the cracks around the closed shutters, Camilla slipped out of bed to open them and then came back to find Noah propped up with his hands behind his head, watching her.

Laughing, she slid beneath the sheet. "I thought you were asleep and wouldn't see me. I'm letting the sunlight in."

"I guarantee you, I'm happy to watch you because you're luscious. See what you do to me with just one glance at you?" he said, taking her hand and placing it on his thick erection.

Her smile vanished as she drew a deep breath and turned to kiss him, and in minutes they made love with her astride him, her eyes closed as she rode him while he pumped hard and fast. When they climaxed at almost the same moment, she cried out with pleasure and fell across him, her long hair spilling over his shoulder. When she slid off to stretch beside him, he pulled her close against him.

"That is the way to wake in the morning," he said.

His voice was a deep rumble. She ran her fingers in the hair on his chest. "I'm going to shower. Ethan will be awake before you know it and he doesn't wait happily for his breakfast. When he wants to eat, he wants to eat."

"Ahh, our adorable son. Thank you again," he said, kissing her lightly.

"You're very welcome," she said, smiling at him.

"I remember you saying you paint early in the morning. Am I ruining your schedule?"

She smiled. "Completely, but there are no complaints. I'm not on a tight deadline here, so it's fine if I miss some mornings."

"That is very good news. I need to get up, too. Although I'd rather spend the day in bed with you, I want to get started on his name change. The sooner the better."

Noah stepped out of bed and her gaze ran over his body that was hard, fit and strong, aroused right now.

"When it comes to sex, you're insatiable," she remarked, looking up to find him watching her.

"That's because you're absolute temptation and keep me constantly aroused. All I have to do is look at you or think about you."

She caught up the sheet and tugged it off the bed to wrap up in it. "Now I'm modestly and properly dressed," she said as she started for the bathroom. "You can shower down the hall. You have your own suite here, remember."

"I remember, but I definitely prefer this one." He blocked her way, smiling at her and wrapping his arms around her. "Want to see how long it takes me to get you immodestly and improperly undressed?"

Laughing, she wriggled, and he let her go. "No way. You go shower—a cold shower to cool you down—and I'll see you at breakfast and you can learn how to feed your son. He can do fairly well with parts of breakfast all by himself. It's better to feed him the messy stuff before he puts it in his hair."

"Oh, gross." Noah grimaced. "I'll get dressed in something washable," he said, gathering his clothes. "This is the part of baby care that mamas do so well and dads need to let them do it."

"Don't you wish. You need this experience. It is definitely part of being a dad."

She hurried past him to head to her bathroom and get ready for the day. Excitement coursed through her and she felt happiness she hadn't known in a long time. Their night of celebration was over and reality would crowd back in and fill their lives, and the sexy, fun relationship they'd had last night would be a memory. All she had to do to keep nights like last night happening was accept Noah the way he was now—a strong alpha male, a rancher, a billionaire who worked at ranching because he loved it. A cowboy country boy through and through, while she was a city girl. If she could accept all that completely, the problems would vanish. She didn't want to live on a ranch, give up her art galleries, opera, stage shows and city life.

As she stepped into the shower, turning on the water, she thought about Noah being such a domineering male. She had grown up promising herself she would never marry an alpha male because of the way her mother had given up a lot of things she wanted to do or did things she didn't want to do because her dad had made all the decisions. She had asked Vivian once how she dealt with being married to the strong-willed man that Thane was. Vivian had her art and she wasn't interested in ranching, yet there she was, living on a ranch because that was what he'd wanted them to do. Vivian had just smiled and said that Thane had made up for doing things his way by doing things for her and she just went ahead and did what she wanted some of the time.

Camilla suspected it was a very small "some of the time." Just the thought of living on a ranch held no appeal. She might try to adjust to that one, but the alpha-male thing—that was his personality. That wasn't going to change one bit.

Camilla showered, washed her hair, dressed in jeans and a short-sleeve blue T-shirt and went to Ethan's bedroom, which adjoined hers. He was standing in his crib and held out his arms when she came inside.

"Mama, up," he said, waving his arms.

"Good morning, my sweet baby," she said, smiling as she lifted him out of the crib. She kissed his rosy cheek. "I love you, Ethan. Today we're going to show your daddy how to feed you breakfast and what you like to eat. You have a smart dad, so he'll get it."

The art showing in Chicago was coming up and it would be wonderful exposure for her art, but it would take her away from Ethan and Noah. She needed to let Noah start taking care of Ethan so he could when she was gone, even though he would have all the help he wanted from her nanny and his family. She knew Stefanie had wanted to get her away from Noah, but that had been before any of them had known about Ethan. Stefanie could not have been nicer last night. Right now, Noah and his family were all enchanted by Ethan. She knew, though, that she and Noah had tough times ahead working out how they would care for Ethan. It scared her to think about it because Noah could be tough and forceful. He wouldn't back down from what he wanted. She couldn't bear to think about sending her little baby off to stay with Noah for any length of time.

Each time Camilla started to rethink her feelings for Noah and his lifestyle, she came right back to the same conclusion. She needed someone in her life who wasn't a rancher, who wasn't such a strong alpha male.

She was going to lose Noah at some point. She was certain he would marry one day. For the next eighteen years at least, they would have to be in touch with each other, sometimes a lot, because of sharing their son. Was she ready for that? Each time she went over that question, the answer was no.

Their problems loomed as big as ever. She hoped that these happy moments they'd spent together would move them toward working out an agreeable arrangement for Ethan. She hoped, but couldn't imagine it happening. The thought of losing her baby half the time tore at her and made her want to lock her door and never see Noah again. Yet when she was with him, they had moments like old times.

Her phone rang and she saw it was the gatekeeper, who said a floral company had a delivery for her.

She told him to send it in. "We're getting pretty flowers that you'd love to eat, but you can't," she cooed at Ethan as she carried him to the front door. "I don't know who is sending them, but we'll know in a minute." She glanced out the sidelight to see a deliveryman taking out a giant bouquet of mixed flowers from his truck. He pulled out another large bouquet of roses. She opened the door and watched as he continued to set gorgeous bouquets out and then he picked up two and carried them to her front door. "Good heavens," she said, glancing at Ethan, who wiggled to get down. "Look, Ethan, we're getting flowers. Lots of flowers."

"Ms. Camilla Warner?" he asked.

"I'm Ms. Warner. You can bring those in here," she said, holding the door open. "Just set them on the table, please."

He went back to get two more vases. She signed that she received them and he left. She walked around looking at roses, lilies, daisies, stalks of blooming ginger, anthurium, gladiolas and tulips. A white teddy bear was in the center of a large blue bow around one vase. She opened the small envelope and removed a card.

You should have had this when Ethan was born. He's wonderful. Noah.

"Look what your nice daddy did. Your very sexy daddy. If it wasn't for you wanting your breakfast, I could go back and thank him for this right now."

Ethan started taking off down the hallway to the kitchen, and she followed.

"Ethan," she said softly, putting him in his high chair and giving him some little circles of dry cereal to munch while she washed and cut up strawberries for him. She put a little plastic bowl of strawberry slices in front of him. "Now please eat your breakfast so I can go back to bed with your daddy, which is a lot of fun."

"I'll second that suggestion," came a deep voice.

She spun around, feeling her cheeks grow hot as she blushed.

"I should have just wrapped a towel around me and come down and gotten you and Ethan and gone back upstairs. He surely has something that will entertain him," Noah said.

"Unfortunately, he likes people around when he's awake, so no, you can't just send him off to play," she said, feeling tingles as her gaze flicked over him in tight jeans and a fitted black T-shirt that showed his muscles.

She crossed the room to him, put her arms around his neck and looked up at him. "Thank you for the gorgeous flowers. I think they probably had to close the store after filling your order. And I see a teddy bear in it that I assume is for Ethan."

"You assume right. You're welcome."

Noah smiled at her as he put his hands on her waist. "If you can get little one to cooperate and go play with his toys or whatever he does, then we can go back to bed."

"You weren't listening a minute ago. He has no intention of entertaining himself. Quite often, he gets his way."

"That's not fair because I damn sure don't."

"Are we going to start the day with a fight?" she asked sweetly.

"No, we're not. We'll start with me getting to feel

how soft you are, check how great you smell," he said, inhaling, "and see if you can still be as sexy to kiss in the early morning as you were in the night." He kissed away any answer she may have had.

He held her close against him as he kissed her passionately, leaning over her until she clung to him and kissed him in return. By the time he released her, she gulped for air.

"It can be so damn good between us," Noah said.

"Yes, it can," she agreed. "But we have some big decisions to make and some big problems to work around," she said, studying him intently. What they'd shared last night and just now hadn't solved anything, and had pulled them a little closer together—and would make it hurt more if they couldn't work things out.

"I have to get his breakfast," Camilla said, passing Noah. "You can watch and learn," she added.

"After that kiss, right now, there's only one person I can watch. You watch him and I'll focus on your gorgeous body and think about how it felt against mine."

She pulled out a container of rolled oats and poured some into a bowl with water. "He's messy with oatmeal, and when he's not hungry, he uses the spoon to throw food around. I try to anticipate that and take his spoon away from him."

"I don't suppose telling him no does any good."

"It makes him laugh."

"I don't think you know how to be forceful."

She turned to look at Noah. "Uh-huh. I want to see this. You'll melt like hot butter when he starts smiling at you."

"He learned that from you."

"I don't believe I see you giving in to me on a regular basis."

"Maybe you're not using the right enticement. Now, last night, you could have gotten anything you wanted."

"We weren't going to do this," she said, and his smile was gone.

"I had high hopes for this celebration lasting a while."

"Noah, you know we're just setting ourselves up for a bigger hurt."

"We've already hurt each other, so that would be nothing new. In the meantime, relax. Celebrate with me for a few days. We might work better together later." He grinned again and she could feel herself weakening.

"You owe me this, Camilla. I didn't get to celebrate when he was born and you did."

She shook her head as she smiled. "Noah, you're manipulating me, but you know I can't say no to that one."

"Good." He leaned closer and slipped his hand to her nape, caressing her lightly and stirring desire. "I think you like celebrating with me."

"You know I do," she whispered, looking at his mouth, and then he kissed her. His arms wrapped around her and her heart pounded as he kissed her possessively.

"In some ways it's very good between us. We're good together."

Her heart missed a beat as she gazed into his blue eyes. "Yes, we are."

"Look, just come look at my ranch. Let me take Ethan and you and come see the place. It's not going to be one bit like your grandfather's."

She drew a deep breath. "Noah, there's just no point in it."

He frowned slightly. "Camilla, we have moments that are good. We have moments that are fun. The sex couldn't be better. We could be a family now."

"Yes, we can if I would compromise and do everything the way you want. I don't hear you offering to live in Dallas."

"I am what I am, Camilla. I'd be lying if I said I'd change. I don't consciously think 'I'm an alpha male, so I'll take charge.' There are just a lot of times someone needs to take charge and so I do. We're both strong-willed. You can't tell me you're not."

"I know," she said. "I am who I am. I can't change and neither can you."

He placed his hands on her shoulders. "We have a big reason to try to stay together. Come for just a couple of days and see my ranch."

She took a deep breath and thought about last night in his arms.

She looked at Ethan and knew she had to do what she could to work with Noah. "Let me think about it."

Noah smiled. "Thank you. Look at your calendar. You know I'm free. Right now, I'm going to call my attorney and get his middle name change started. We'll have to go to court, I'm sure. Later today I'll get some of my things moved over here." He left the room and she shook her head as she turned to give Ethan more of the slices of strawberries.

"I think your daddy just wiggled out of feeding you breakfast today. I think he's going to change your life and mine a lot. I know you'll be happy with what he does. I can just hope for the best for all of us." As she heated up his oatmeal, she told him, "It looks like we're going to a ranch. You'll probably like it."

But would she?

Honestly, she felt she owed Noah some favors for not telling him about Ethan sooner, but extending this celebration would just make it hurt more than ever when they parted, and they definitely would part. He hadn't declared he was in love or even suggested marriage. She hadn't changed her feelings, either. She didn't want a ranch life and she definitely didn't want a lifetime of dealing with another strong-willed male. Yet this time with Noah made her realize one more thing. One thing that presented an insurmountable problem.

She hadn't gotten over him at all.

Eight

Camilla

During the morning Camilla received another call from the art gallery in Chicago, and when she finished, she booked a flight to Chicago.

She had left Noah in the nursery with Ethan and she wondered how things were going. She went to find them.

Surprisingly he was in the backyard, standing beneath a big oak while Ethan sat in the grass. "What are you doing?"

"I thought he needed to be outside. Does he have a swing?"

"No, he doesn't. I never thought about a swing."

"They have baby swings and we can fasten him in and he'll love it. This tree is perfect. I'll get one today and put it up. You'll see. He'll like to swing and you'll like having a swing for him."

"Okay." She leaned down and handed Ethan the ball

that had gotten away from him. Then she looked back at Noah. "I made my flight arrangements for Chicago to see the art-gallery people. They're really eager to show my paintings and I need to go talk to them. I owe your sister thanks, even though I know she did it to get me away from you."

He shook his head. "I think she'll stop. Frankly, I think she wants us together now because of Ethan," he said and gave Camilla a big smile.

"I know she loves you and she seemed truly thrilled over Ethan."

"She is," Noah said, glancing at Ethan, who was now happily pulling out grass. "She wants to keep him sometime and I told her she could."

"That's nice, Noah. He has a wonderful family with your family."

"Good."

"Now, while I'm shopping for baby furniture, do you want me to get my nanny to take care of Ethan, or would you like to take care of him?" They'd already agreed that Camilla would outfit a nursery for his Dallas condo.

"Let me," Noah replied. "I'll get my folks if I have difficulty. I may just stay right here because you're set up for a baby. I'm glad I'm going to start getting my condo that way." He pulled out his wallet. "Here's my credit card."

She took it and slipped it into her pocket.

"I've been thinking," he said. "Whatever you buy, get two, and we'll have the second one shipped to the ranch and set up there."

"You want it all alike?"

"Yes, because Ethan won't care and I don't. And it'll be easier for you. Later when he outgrows the baby stuff, we can do something more original."

She shook her head. When Ethan outgrew the baby furniture, she would probably not be the one buying furniture on Noah's behalf. It might be his wife—a thought that she didn't like to consider.

She looked at Noah standing in the shade, looking up at the tree, his thick black curls in their usual appealing tangle. He was all hard muscles from his head to his feet, handsome, sexy and exciting. She wanted to be in his arms, but that was putting off reality and the problems they needed to solve. Right now those problems seemed monumental and without a happy solution. When they parted this time, after being together with Ethan, she suspected it would hurt more than it had the first time when he left for the Army.

She forced herself to abandon that line of thinking and focus on the task at hand. "Okay. Two sets of furniture it is. Just one question—can you clear enough space for a suite for him in your condo now?"

"I've been thinking about that. Go ahead and buy it, so it's all selected, and tell them I'll call and give them an address to deliver it to. I may get them to hold part of the order and just buy a house here so we'll have a yard. I can get my brothers and Stefanie to find some likely houses for me fast."

"There's one for sale a block south of here. Then we'd be in the same neighborhood and it would make sharing Ethan easier."

"Give me the address and I'll ask about it and look at it. It won't take long for me to make a decision."

"They have a sign in the front yard. I have a listing for this area. I'll leave the name of the current owners, the address and their phone number on the kitchen table for you."

"Good."

"I'm leaving now. You're sure you'll be okay with him?"

Noah nodded. "We'll be fine."

She left him with Ethan and spent the next hours selecting baby furniture for the ranch and for Noah to have in Dallas.

All the time she did, she was aware she was setting up a nursery and a playroom for Ethan, but she wouldn't be with him when he was with his dad.

It was almost five when she returned that afternoon. While she had been shopping, she had been in touch with Noah by phone and text, and he'd assured her they were doing fine. When she got back to her house, she found him putting together a baby swing. But no sign of their son.

"Ethan is at my folks'," he explained. "I'll go get him whenever you want or we have a dinner invitation, thanks to Ethan."

"Whatever you want to do. I'll be happy to see your family again."

He picked up the baby swing he'd finished. "Now I'll put this in the tree. C'mon. You can hand me stuff. Did you get the furniture?"

"I think I did—two of everything and the furniture will be delivered this Thursday to the ranch. They will hold the rest here until we give them an address and instructions where to deliver it."

"Thank you. C'mon," he said, carrying the baby swing and rope outside to the tree.

"You need a ladder."

"No, I don't," he said, jumping up and grabbing a limb. He caught it easily. She watched him swing himself up and climb to the next limb, muscles flexing as he moved with ease, proving how fit he was. He had two lengths of rope looped around his shoulder and in minutes he had one end of each length around a branch with a length of rubber from an old garden hose to protect the tree. He knotted each length and dropped to the ground, landing on his feet. He inserted the ends of each length of rope in the back of the swing and secured them with knots. "Now he has a swing."

Noah turned to look at her and then arched an eyebrow as her gaze ran over his chest and she drew a deep breath. His hand closed on her arm and he stepped close to put his arm around her.

"Noah, we're outside."

"There's no one here except us and this is your house with a high fence, bushes and trees and all the privacy in the world. When you look at me the way you just did, there's no way I can resist kissing you," he said. He kissed away an answer, picking her up while he kissed her.

She wound her arms around his neck, holding him and kissing him in return. She tingled from head to toe. Noah was sexy, incredibly appealing with solid muscles, fit and agile. In spite of all the differences and problems between them, she wanted to be in bed with him, all that strength and energy turned to blazing sex. She moaned softly, her breasts tingling, wanting his hands and mouth on her and his body against hers.

She wasn't aware of her surroundings until he let her stand in his bedroom as he peeled away her clothes and she removed his.

"You have an incredible body," she whispered, running her fingers over him, feeling his rock-hard chest.

"Baby," he whispered, "that's my line. You definitely have the incredible body and I can't ever get enough. In bed is where we're in total and absolute agreement."

He showered kisses across her belly, his one hand caressing her breast as his other hand made feather strokes along the inside of first one thigh and then the other. The light, slow brushes of his warm fingers moved up slowly until they touched her intimately, and she gasped.

He covered her mouth, kissing her deeply, sensations bombarding her, sizzling torment making her want all of him. His hand continued to tease her nipple and stroke between her legs, making her want more.

In minutes, he laid her on the bed and got a condom. As soon as he had it on, he moved over her to enter her. She clung to him, lost to sensation, and nearly immediately reached a climax. She held him tightly, knowing soon he would leave her arms, leave her bed and, all too soon, leave an emptiness in her heart.

The first of the week Noah went with his dad to meet his doctor and Noah sat through the exam. To his relief, the report had been positive. His father wasn't going to get over the heart trouble, but they could keep it stable and his dad comfortable. Noah felt free to ask questions, and then when they left, Noah stepped back briefly to ask some direct questions about his dad's outlook. He joined his dad in the waiting room and relayed what he had learned that was positive. He felt better about his dad. He would be less worried going to the ranch when he finally decided to do so. Now, with Ethan in his life and his family so delighted to have him around, Noah felt he needed to stay in Dallas for a while longer. He had to admit, Camilla held him in Dallas and he didn't want to question too closely how important she was becoming to him because they had such huge differences that had not only never changed, but now became even more important with Ethan in their lives. They had a baby now and the nights with her were magic. Could they ever reconcile their differences?

A few days later Noah and Camilla stood in the empty courtroom and had Ethan's name officially changed to Ethan Caleb Warner.

When they left the courtroom with the offical papers in Noah's hand, he glanced down the empty hall and drew her to him.

Startled, she looked up at him.

"Thank you for doing that. It will mean so much to my dad and my family and it does to me." He kissed her briefly and Camilla smiled at him.

"Wait until we're home and I'll really thank you," he said, slipping his arm across her shoulders as they turned to leave.

That evening they were invited to Noah's parents' house for dinner for a celebration of the name change. It was a warm night and they'd planned a cookout.

They went to their suite to change, and a half hour later Camilla heard him knock on her closed door. She was in the en suite putting her hair in a ponytail while Ethan was sitting on the floor in her bedroom playing with his toys. She called out for Noah to enter.

"Hey, little buddy, come here," she heard him say as he came in. "You look very spiffy in your light blue jumper. I hope you can stay that way for an hour so all the folks will be impressed by how cute you are."

"Dada," she heard Ethan say, followed by Noah calling out, "Hey, Camilla, he called me daddy."

She came out of the en suite laughing and shaking her head as she saw Ethan in his arms. "I heard. I've been trying to teach him to say 'Daddy.'"

"'Dada' is close enough," Noah said. When he looked at her she suddenly wanted the evening to be over and to be back home with him. He looked so handsome in navy slacks and a pale blue shirt open at the throat.

She felt him rake his gaze over her red cotton summer dress. "I have my hands filled with baby or I'd come kiss you. You look fantastic," he said.

She smiled at him. "I was about to say the same. My goodness, you are a handsome man."

"Let's go get this evening over with so I can carry you off to bed," he said, sounding as if he was barely able to get his breath.

Her smile vanished. "Noah, what are we going to do? We've got this intense attraction that neither of us can resist. We have a precious baby between us. At the same time, we're polar opposites in lifestyles and temperament."

His smile disappeared and she regretted putting a damper on the moment. But it was the truth. And it hurt. She knew what she was losing when they really split apart. This was just a brief, temporary truce because of Ethan. None of her basic feelings had changed, but Noah's appeal was intensifying. She was headed for a huge heartbreak.

"I can't give you an answer, Camilla. I am what I am. I know we have a physical relationship that's fantastic. I think about you constantly and I'm instantly filled with desire when I see you. I don't have an answer for how we can work out a relationship where we're both happy. It's that simple. At the same time, the attraction continues to grow. At least for me. I've told you that family is everything and I want one. We're halfway there."

"Noah, other than the fact we have a baby, we're not even close to halfway there."

He frowned. "Family is important to me. It's a high priority. And it involves commitment, deep love, sharing, making adjustments, and right now, we don't have that. Being together, some of that might come. It sure as hell won't come if we're totally separated. And you were right about me moving in with you being the best way to learn how to take care of Ethan. I want us to be his mom and dad and be together, but that won't work unless we have those things I just mentioned— love, commitment, adjustments. There's no point in getting into a relationship that isn't going to work and you know it."

"Yes, I do," she replied, hurting, feeling as if the gulf between them just widened when he stated all those qualities of a strong relationship and announced they didn't have any of them. "You're right. Without love, marriage isn't going to work."

She hurt badly and just wanted to walk into his arms and hold him tightly and have him offer some small changes, but she knew that was a dream. Maybe she should think about what she could change. The minute that thought came, she thought how her mother had spent a lifetime changing what she wanted in order to shift her life to what Camilla's dad wanted.

She slipped on the gold bracelet Thane had sent home to her and held out her arm. "Look, here's what my brother asked you to bring to me."

Noah took her wrist in his warm grasp. "That's beautiful." He looked up at her and slipped his hand lightly on her nape. "And so are you," he said, his voice getting a rasp. "And this is a good moment—here's a gift from me this time," he said, reaching into his pocket and withdrawing a small box.

Surprised, she took the box and looked at him.

"Go ahead—open it. That's for Ethan, for the name change."

She opened the box and removed a small jewelry box and snapped it open. "Noah," she said, picking up a gold chain with a sparkling diamond pendant. "It's beautiful. Thank you," she said, knowing she would treasure his gift just as she did her brother's, but with Noah, she couldn't fathom his true feelings. Was the gift purely gratitude for Ethan—or did Noah feel anything deeper?

"Put it on me. I'm wearing it tonight," she said, putting the necklace in his hand, turning and lifting her hair. She felt his warm fingers brush her nape.

"There," he said.

She turned to look into his blue eyes that were filled with desire. She stood on tiptoe, slipped her arm around his neck and kissed him.

Instantly, his arm circled her waist as they kissed.

She wiggled away. "Thank you. I'll thank you more later. Right now we better go." She started packing all the things she would take for Ethan, although she suspected someone would play with him every second of the evening. Noah's family had seemed enchanted by him the last time they were with them.

Her guess proved correct as every member of Noah's family had to hold him when they arrived.

She had to show everyone her necklace from Noah because of Ethan and her bracelet that Thane sent home to her.

Before dinner she stood on the veranda close to Betsy and Cal, who were seated. Cal held Ethan and they both played with him and talked to him. Camilla was talking with Stefanie and Hallie while Noah and his brothers hung out across the veranda.

Camilla thought about what a wonderful family the Grants had, and now Ethan would be one of them. She felt another pang of longing to be with Noah, to be part of this family and to have that for Ethan. It hurt more today to hear Noah talk about love and commitment when he had never come close to indicating he loved her or that he wanted to make a commitment. She hadn't either, but it was because he hadn't.

She had to admit, she was probably as determined and strong-willed as Noah, and that wasn't a good combination. Neither one could change a basic personality. She looked at Noah, who was laughing at something Ben said. Noah's gaze shifted and met hers and she felt as if he'd touched her.

Looking into his blue eyes always made her pulse beat faster at first glance. Noah was a force to be reckoned with—absolutely the most desirable man she had ever known. Her insides knotted because she was pained with wanting him. Too much of the day she hurt over the thought of Noah leaving her life. She had made one mistake in a relationship—marrying a man to try to get over Noah. She didn't want to make another big mistake here and lose the love of her life. And she did love him. Years ago she had never told him because she didn't think he loved her. They hadn't talked about marriage and now she didn't think he ever would. Had she made a big mistake then by not visiting his ranch and at least trying to see if they could work things out?

His gaze still held hers, which surprised her. What was going through his thoughts? Did he hurt the way she did?

Then Ben must have said something directly to him and he turned back to his brother.

They had dinner and she sat between Stefanie and

Hallie, across from Noah's parents, who flanked Ethan's high chair. They obviously relished every moment they spent with the baby. Noah sat at the other end of the table, with his brothers.

She hadn't spoken a word to him all evening and she couldn't help but feel as if a wall had come back between them. But why?

After dinner, she found him in the den, deep in conversation with Ben. He looked up and walked over to her in the doorway. "Camilla, we need to talk," he said, leading her into an empty adjacent room.

"Is everything okay?" she asked him.

He nodded, but his eyes didn't meet hers when he spoke. "I've been thinking about us. I can think more clearly when we're not just the two of us—then I get sidetracked and want to kiss you." He took a deep breath… "Sooner or later, we're going to have to come to grips with how we'll share Ethan. And it will have to be official. I don't want a handshake deal. I want an agreement in court that is legal and binding. I want joint custody and I want him half the time."

Half the time? Joint custody with Noah? He had told her that before, but he was emphatic about it now. Pain gripped her heart like a vise and she had to fight back tears because they had to face all his family as soon as they walked out of this room.

"I understand," she said, certain that Noah wasn't going to be easy to deal with. She had known this was coming, but it still hurt to hear him state his demands. She knew for certain Noah would fight for what he wanted.

Right now she couldn't face this. She couldn't even look at him.

"I'll join you in a few minutes, Noah," she said, turning to go to a bathroom where she could close the door and have privacy.

She leaned against the door and wiped at the tears that spilled out. They had been getting along and she didn't know what made him think about the future, but the time would come soon when they would go their separate ways, and when it did, they had to make arrangements to share Ethan and she was going to hurt more than she ever had in her life. She loved her son and she loved Noah. She would lose Noah and she wouldn't have Ethan half the time. Half of all the time he was growing up. That sounded unbearable.

Because of his dad's health, she knew she wouldn't have to deal with Noah leaving Dallas for a while, and she tried to focus on that and push worries out of her mind, at least until she was home and away from his family. Taking a deep breath, she left the bathroom and went back to join them in the great room. When Stefanie saw her from across the room she shot Camilla a long look. She wondered if Noah had told his sister he was unhappy. Camilla knew little sister Stefanie was protective of her older brother; it was written all over her face.

Before she could go speak to Stefanie, Noah came over. "I think Ethan will crash soon. Are you ready to leave?"

"Sure," she said, gathering their things.

It was another half hour before they had said their goodbyes and were in the car. The minute Noah started driving down the long circle drive, Ethan was asleep in his car seat.

"My dad is so happy with Ethan and he's over the moon with having him named Ethan Caleb Warner. That was a wonderful gesture," Noah said.

"You have a wonderful family and that makes me happy for Ethan."

"They all love him, that's for sure," Noah said. She watched him drive, looking at his handsome profile, the dark curls falling on his forehead. In spite of the differences between them, in spite of their eventual joint custody of their son, she couldn't deny her attraction to him. Neither could she deny that she wanted to be in his arms.

He was incredibly handsome, more so than he had been before he had gone into the Army. She had already faced the fact that she was in love with him and headed straight for disaster, but tonight, if he wanted to make love, she'd step right into his arms.

Later, when she was in bed in his arms, she shifted so she could look at him. "Noah, I thought of something else. I'd like to have Ethan christened while your dad is able to attend and enjoy the event."

Noah rolled on his side and propped his head on his hand. "That would be great. I hadn't given that a thought, and guessed you had already had him christened."

"No. By the time Ethan was born, I missed you being here—I just put it off. Once I started putting it off, it was easy to continue to do so. Now would be a good time."

"My folks would really like it." Noah placed his palm gently on her cheek. "Naming him after Dad, christening him so Dad can attend—you are doing a lot for me and for my family."

"I think I owe you," she said quietly, her heart beating harder because she wanted everything to work out between them and it never could. "Noah, I'm trying. I want to work things out between us for Ethan's sake," she admitted. She couldn't change the basic issues she had about Noah being such an alpha male and being a cowboy. It didn't matter about the money—rich or poor or anywhere in between, a cowboy at heart was a cowboy and wealth or lack of it didn't matter. In spite of his fortune Noah was a rancher and a cowboy. The more they were together like tonight, the more she was going to be hurt in the future. When he walked out of her life, would she ever stop missing him?

He pulled her close to kiss her tenderly and she wrapped her arms around him, holding him tightly, knowing she would lose him and wondering if she would love him all her life.

"I don't suppose you've thought about working in Dallas and giving up the ranch?" she asked him. "You're living here anyway."

He rolled back to look at her again. "No. I'm a rancher and my dad is doing okay. I've talked to his doctors. I've been gone so much the last three years I needed to see the folks, and now with Ethan, that's all the more reason to extend my stay in Dallas, but eventually, I'm going to my ranch. I want you to come see it, Camilla. If you will, that would be good news."

She gazed into his unfathomable blue eyes. Why was he pushing her to visit his ranch? Hope blossomed in her heart. Did that mean his feelings toward her were changing, becoming more serious?

Noah had never declared love and neither had she. She'd felt she loved him before he joined the military, but it was not enough to overlook what she didn't like. What she felt for him had grown stronger since he had learned about Ethan. Now that Noah had learned he was the father of her baby, he had done all the right things. He had been filled with joy over the news, sorry he hadn't been with her, instantly joyous and loving his baby, taking Ethan and her to introduce their son to his family, and later celebrating just the two of them, a smoking-hot, passionate celebration of the birth of his son. He was irresistible in so many ways, but then there was the other side—the alpha male. She would not follow in her mother's footsteps and fall in love with one then spend a lifetime with a man who made all her decisions for her.

Especially since she was not like her mother. She could be as stubborn as Noah, which meant they'd probably butt heads every step of the way. She would know more about how they could work together when they started working out custody of Ethan. Just the thought of that gave her a chill. She was going to lose her baby part of the time.

And she had no idea about the depth of Noah's feelings for her. He had never given any indication of being in love, much less that he wanted anything permanent. And she still didn't think they could ever work past the problems.

Yet if she was falling more deeply in love with him and if there was a shred of hope to work out custody of Ethan without a battle and heartbreak, she should go see his ranch. A few days in the country wasn't much. She could do that, just visit. After all, she wanted Noah in her life—but on her terms. The realization shocked her. She turned to look at him as he lay beside her on the bed, running her finger along his jawline, feeling tickles from the black stubble on his jaw.

"Noah, I'll visit your ranch," she said, and he shifted, propping his head on his hand to look at her.

"You and Ethan will go home with me?" She heard the surprise in his voice and he was staring intently at her.

"You've asked me several times. You and I are sharing Ethan now and that means we will be in each other's lives to some extent for at least the next sixteen or so years. I should at least have enough of an open mind to accept your invitation to visit."

He gazed solemnly at her and she wondered what he was thinking. He leaned over and wrapped his arms around her, sat up and lifted her to his lap.

"You always surprise me," he said. "There will never be another surprise as big as Ethan, but this is a surprise and I'm glad. Even if you hate the place, at least you'll have been there. That's good, Camilla. That's called an open mind."

"Don't be a smart aleck and don't push your luck."

He studied her and she had no idea what ran through his thoughts until he pulled her to him to kiss her. In minutes they rolled down on the bed and he caressed her, running his hand lightly over her, and she forgot everything. Everything except desire.

Sunday, they stood at the front of the church while the minister and assistant pastor went through the christening ceremony of Ethan Caleb Warner while Noah's family and Camilla's family stood with them. Afterward, they all went to the country club where Noah had a private room reserved and dinner catered.

It was three in the afternoon before Noah, Camilla and Ethan went back to Camilla's house. Ethan was asleep and Noah carried him to his crib, standing and looking down at his son.

Camilla came in and stood in the doorway watching Noah. When she finally joined him, he put his arm around her.

"He's still a marvel to me. I just can't believe I'm a

dad. He's a super son. He was so happy and good today and everyone loved playing with him."

"Were you half that good?" she asked. "And don't say, 'Of course.'"

He smiled. "Let's get out of here before we push our luck too far and wake him." He ushered her out of the nursery. "To answer your question, no, I can't recall great praise about what a happy, good baby I was. Don't ask me questions like that. Ask Mom."

"I'll bet you were born giving orders."

"I'm not that bossy."

She shot him a look that told him she didn't believe that for a second. They started walking down the hall. "You remember that I leave tomorrow for Chicago, right? I'll be back Tuesday. Are you going to stay here or at your mom's?"

"I plan to stay here. I can take care of a little baby until your return."

She smiled. "Well, you know where to get help if you need it. We still have the nanny on call, even if we've never had her out here since you moved in."

He took her hand in his. "Come with me," he said and walked her into his bedroom. "The monitor is on, Ethan is sound asleep and all's quiet on the home front. I've waited way too long and you'll be gone tomorrow night," he said as he wrapped his arms around her and leaned down to kiss her.

She slipped her arms around his neck, kissing him in return, reveling in the moment, knowing that all too soon now, Noah would move on and her life would change again—a forever change—without Ethan half the time. The thought suddenly struck her. Was she cheating their son out of a family because she disliked the country? She might be getting ahead of herself because Noah had never told her he loved her, much less talked about commitment. He loved his ranch so much, he might not want commitment from someone who didn't love it the way he did.

He raised his head to look at her. "Something wrong?"

She looked into curious blue eyes. "You're too perceptive sometimes. I was thinking about us."

"I'll try to keep your mind more on us," he said, leaning forward to kiss her again.

As desire swamped her, she forgot their problems. She wrapped her arms tightly around his waist and kissed him back. Then she stepped back to unbutton her blouse as he watched her.

She unbuttoned it and then reached out to unfasten his belt. He shed his shirt and jeans quickly, and then she walked into his arms and stopped worrying about their future.

Nine

Noah

Noah turned into Camilla's drive and parked, smiling when he saw her car. She was home from Chicago and he was glad. He'd missed her. He was happier when they were together, which made him examine his feelings for her. He had never gotten over her, not even after their big blowup before he went into the Army and not after three years when he'd seen her only once.

The first time he had seen her when he returned, his heart had felt as if it would pound out of his chest and desire had been a flash fire sweeping over him. That reaction hadn't changed.

But he didn't want to lock himself into a marriage that wouldn't work. That would be worse for his son than no marriage between his parents. Noah knew they could be compatible, but they also were two strong-willed people who could dig their heels in and refuse to cooperate with each other.

Family had always been all-important to him. He loved his family and wanted his own to be as harmonious. That took some work and giving. His mother gave big-time, to his way of thinking, but she made that marriage work. And she was happy. He felt certain about that. He didn't know if he could have that with Camilla. He didn't want to live in Dallas and work in the family business and be a suit. He loved the ranch and ranching. That was a divide between them that he couldn't overlook or bridge.

She couldn't accept his being an alpha male and he didn't know any possible way he could change that one if he wanted to in the worst way.

He didn't know the sum of his feelings for Camilla because he always came up against these two problems in their relationship and it stopped him cold. She would never marry him as long as these two things were part of her life or his. They had to be worked out before he could ever truly love her enough for a big commitment. Which might keep them from ever being a family. That hurt, but it would hurt more if they married and then were unhappy and divorced. He didn't want to make a mistake that would hurt his future and his baby's future.

He walked in the door. "Honey, I'm home," he called.

Smiling, she came out of the library and his heartbeat quickened again. She wore a short, straight navy business skirt that made her legs look great, and a matching blouse. Gold bangles were on her wrist and she had her hair looped and fastened on the back of her head.

"You're gorgeous, and did I ever miss you."

She walked into his embrace and put her arms around his neck. "I'm glad, because I missed you," she said without smiling at him.

"Something wrong?"

She shook her head. "No. Just that we're not always going to be together."

"Pretend for tonight. Mom and Dad wanted to keep Ethan again tonight and I told them yes, because I want to be alone with you," he admitted, nuzzling her neck, inhaling her perfume, glad she was in his arms.

"I'd think your mom might be getting a little tired of him."

"Are you kidding? Hallie has been there the whole time and she and Ben slept over there last night to be with him, and they might again tonight. Stefanie loves to play with him and rock him. It's a wonder Eli didn't come over, too, but...well, he thinks he's a cute little kid, but Eli likes his peace and quiet at night, or his girlfriends."

"I'm glad Hallie and Stefanie are there because they have more energy and they can help your mom."

"How was your trip? Is the art show on?"

"Actually, it is. It will be in October, a while away, but they book ahead. Once I show there, they will keep my art on display for six months."

"I'm glad it went well."

"It did except I missed you and Ethan."

He leaned down to kiss her, but she pulled back. "Noah, let's talk about our situation," she said, stepping out of his arms. "Sit, and let's talk."

He wanted to carry her to his bed, but realizing she looked concerned, he nodded.

She sat in a straight-back Queen Anne chair and he

sat facing her, aware she wasn't sitting on the sofa where he could touch and hold her. Even her voice sounded tight when she spoke.

"We were going to celebrate the night you learned about Ethan. One night. We're still together—which I'm happy about, but I feel sort of in limbo. We're not really off and we're not really on. You're here under the same roof to learn how to deal with Ethan, but that didn't include sleeping together, which we're doing."

He leaned toward her and took her hand. "Have you ever heard that old expression 'Go with the flow'? For right now that's what we're doing. I'm learning to be a dad and getting to know my baby."

"Before I drop the matter, I don't think you've disliked being here in Dallas with Ethan and me," she said, and immediately he knew she was going to talk to him about living and working in Dallas, which he did not want to do. And right now, she was inches away, and she had been away since the night before last. They could come back to the problems, but he wanted her now.

"Let it go for tonight, Camilla. I missed you too much to get into a discussion about our future." He kissed away her answer, pulling her up against him. His hand went to the hem of her skirt and slipped her skirt up, sliding up and caressing her legs.

"Damn, I missed you," he whispered. His fingers now worked the buttons of her blouse and soon he pushed it off her shoulders and leaned back slightly to unfasten her lacy bra and toss it away. He cupped her breasts and rubbed her nipples lightly.

She gasped and cried out. "Noah, I want you," she whispered.

She tugged free his belt buckle and unfastened his

jeans, freeing him in minutes, her fingers moving frantically.

She stroked his manhood, caressing him, kneeling to run her tongue over him, almost sending him over the edge. He wanted to take time, to pleasure her until she was as desperate to make love as he was. But he couldn't wait. He needed her now. He yanked away her panties and then lifted her high to stroke her nipple with his tongue, and then he lowered her onto his erection. She locked her legs around him and they moved together. She clung to him with her eyes closed and her head thrown back, her long hair swinging while he pumped fast. Her hands on him tightened and she cried out as she climaxed, but instead of slowing, she kept thrusting her hips, shifting wildly until she reached another climax.

In minutes she clung to his shoulders, lowered her legs and stood. "Hold me," she whispered. "I feel as if I'm going to melt."

"You're fantastic," he whispered, caressing her, showering light kisses on her forehead.

He picked her up to carry her to the shower, where he peeled away his socks and boots and her shoes. He stood her on her feet and turned on the warm water. His hands were all over her, caressing her, sliding over her curves. And in seconds, he was hard.

"Noah, you're insatiable and you're strong enough to do this all night long."

"Let's see if you're right."

At dawn she fell asleep again in his arms and later woke to roll over and run her hand lightly over him.

He was aroused and she kissed his shoulder. "You never stop."

"It's because I'm with you." He turned to look at her, smiling, slipping his arm around her.

"This isn't the real world."

"Shh. Enjoy today. I promise, the real world will come in time. I keep hoping for a miracle. I want you in my bed."

She started to answer and he kissed her, ending their conversation because this situation wouldn't last and they hadn't solved anything between them.

When he awakened, an hour had passed. He held Camilla close against his side. She was warm, soft, her skin smooth and silky. He wondered how deep her feelings for him ran. Neither of them had ever declared love, and love was the game-changer. Love made all the difference.

They needed to talk and get out of this limbo that couldn't last. When he got a chance, when Ethan was asleep so they wouldn't be interrupted, he wanted to talk to her about the future. It was time for him to move on. He dreaded it, but it might as well happen. He didn't want to hurt her, nor did he want to be hurt, but they needed to get on with their lives.

Camilla

It was morning when she stirred and looked around the empty bed and could smell something enticing emanating from the kitchen.

She rolled out of bed, grabbed a robe and went to her bath to shower. Twenty minutes later she walked into the kitchen.

In a T-shirt and tight jeans, Noah stood there stirring something in a skillet. There were two glasses of orange juice on the table.

She crossed the room and slid her arms around his

waist to hug him. "Good morning, very sexy man," she said, unable to resist him even when she knew every caress, each kiss would just make saying goodbye worse when the time came.

"Hey," he said, turning and putting down a spatula. "You look and smell good." He wrapped his arms around her and kissed her.

When he released her, she felt dazed.

"I just need to eat to maintain my strength to keep up with you."

"Breakfast and maybe then bed. Want an omelet? I make the best one ever."

"You're so modest. We need to work on your lack of confidence," she teased. "Of course I want one of your delicious omelets." She poured two cups of coffee and carried them to the table and in minutes he came with a platter that held the golden omelets. Bowls of blueberries and sliced strawberries and kiwi were on the table, as well as toasted wheat bread.

He sat facing her. "I could get very used to this, Camilla." He looked serious and sounded sincere. She couldn't stop the words that hurtled from her mouth.

"Settle in the city, Noah."

She felt as if a barrier appeared between them the moment he turned away. "This might please you," he said. "Eli has found three houses in this neighborhood that I have appointments to look at today. You're welcome to look with me if you want."

Her heart missed a beat. Would he possibly get a house in town and give up the ranch or would it simply be a replacement for his condo? "I'd love to look with you. Whatever happens, I'm thrilled you're looking for a house in this neighborhood."

"Don't get too excited. I'll always have a place to

live in Dallas and I'll always spend some time here. Just not most of the time. I'll pick Ethan up this morning and bring him home. I imagine he's worn my folks down by now. Let's talk about going to the ranch. Neither of us has anything in particular scheduled right away, right?"

"Yes, I'm free."

"Good. I'll call to get the house ready. How about going the day after tomorrow? We can spend the weekend there. Better yet, stay a few days into the week so you can see what it's like."

"That's fine with me, Noah."

He leaned closer and placed his hand on her waist. "I'm glad you'll visit the ranch."

"You expect me to love it, don't you?"

"I hope you do. It's my way of life. That isn't going to change, Camilla."

"Noah, we've never talked about a future together."

His blue eyes darkened and his hand tightened slightly on her waist. "No, we haven't, but we're sharing a child now and we've shared a bed plenty of times and it's been damn fabulous. If we could work out the problems, then we might have a future to talk about. We don't now," he said bluntly, and a pain enveloped her.

"I've told you, family is all-important to me, and there has to be certain things for a family to function well. It won't work for us to marry and you live in Dallas while I live at the ranch. That wouldn't do a bit of good for Ethan. Or for us. There has to be real love, deep and strong. We have a lot of strong feelings for each other, but with the problems, we're not there yet on unconditional love. If we marry for the wrong reasons, it won't last, and I don't want that hurt. We just need to keep trying to work things out until we do or until we know for certain that we never will. Then we say goodbye and figure out how to share Ethan."

His blue eyes were icy. Noah had his moments when he was unyielding. This was one of them.

"I'm willing to try, Noah. That's why I agreed to visit your ranch."

"I'm glad. That's a first step. We'll just see how that goes."

Camilla reached across the table and put her hand over his. "If only it could stay this way, Noah. We can do so well together and Ethan would have a mama and a daddy."

When his surprise changed to a shuttered look, she withdrew her hand.

"Right now I'm in the city 24/7 but I won't be much longer. This is to get to know Ethan, to learn how to care for him, to let him become accustomed to me and being around my family. Staying year-round—that's not going to happen," he said, and she heard that unyielding tone that she had heard before.

"I'll go pick Ethan up and leave him with you if that's convenient."

"Yes, it is."

"Before I go to my folks' house, I have an appointment this morning with my attorney, Camilla."

She gazed into his unyielding blue eyes and a cold chill gripped her because she was afraid they were headed for a court custody fight. "You don't think we can work this out between us?"

"You tell me. You don't like ranch life and I'm too much the alpha male for you."

All their closeness from the past days diminished.

"Noah, I don't want to fight you."

His blue eyes were the color of a stormy sky. "If you don't, we need to work things out in a way that satisfies me."

Which meant she was going to have to share her baby with Noah, and not under one roof. Noah would take Ethan to the ranch and she wouldn't be with him. Was she making a giant mistake by not yielding to everything Noah wanted?

"Excuse me, Noah," she said, leaving the table and taking her dishes and wondering if the last few moments had been a turning point in their relationship and the harmony and compatibility were over.

She was loading her plate into the dishwasher when he came up behind her.

"I'll finish. You go do what you want," he said.

She turned to look at him. "What I want is to avoid fighting with you," she said, and they gazed at each other. After a moment he stepped close to put his arms around her.

"I don't like fighting, either. We have too much that's great between us. I want us together, Camilla, but we have to have certain things for a family to work, and we don't have those things at this point. Let it go for now. Visit my ranch and see if that makes any difference for you."

She looked up at him and fought tears. "That's hard to do when you're talking about a lawyer," she whispered. "I think you expect me to make all the adjustments."

He stared at her. "I'll have to think about that one. I can tell you right now, Camilla, I'm not giving up being a rancher. I've worked in the company business and that life is not for me. I'm not a suit. I'm a cowboy and that's what I'm going to do." With that, he walked out of the kitchen, leaving her feeling as if she was heading straight for another heartbreak.

Could she deal with a male who was so strongwilled? Could she imagine life out on a ranch if Noah and Ethan were there? Was she making a disastrous mistake in not accepting Noah's way of life? She always came back to the same answer.

She didn't know.

Ten

Camilla

Two days later she was in a limo as they drove out to a waiting plane that belonged to Noah. She knew he had a pilot's license, but he wasn't flying today.

The plane was comfortable with plush seats and a big-screen television. Noah had some new toys for Ethan, who was happily playing with a stuffed tiger that roared. But most of her attention was on Noah. He was in tight jeans, a Western-style shirt and a Stetson, looking like the handsome rancher he was.

As her gaze ran over him again, she thought about their lovemaking in the early hours of the morning. The more they had sex, the more she wanted to. She was certain she was setting herself up for a terrible broken heart because she couldn't imagine working things out. He wouldn't change and she couldn't stop wanting her way. This visit to his ranch had pleased him enormously. He had been charming and sent her flowers again. But what she wanted was for Noah to make some concessions.

As she watched Noah play with Ethan, she felt another stab of pain because Noah was a great dad and it was too bad he'd be with his son only half the time. Ethan needed both of them.

She wouldn't let herself think about being married to Noah. She didn't think they would last together more than a few months and she'd already had a brief marriage. She thought about Aiden. She knew the first week she had made a mistake marrying him. She didn't want another marriage that crashed and burned in two short months.

Noah placed his hand on her wrist and she looked at him.

"We're about to fly over my ranch," he said.

She looked out the window, her gaze skimming the miles of mesquite and cacti below with an arroyo cutting through the earth in a jagged gash. And then they flew over another fence and the mesquite and cacti were gone, replaced by pasture, and she saw cattle by a large pond. They flew over more fences, and horses were scattered on more grassland. They flew over a stock tank. She saw a pickup driving on a dirt road, stirring a plume of dust, then more areas of mesquite, more cattle. She knew ranches were big, but Noah's was larger than she had envisioned.

"This is all your ranch?"

"All of it. Even beyond what you can see. We can circle it if you'd like."

She shook her head. "I'd rather get there. We might be pushing our luck with how good Ethan has been buckled into that seat."

Smiling, Noah nodded and turned his attention back to Ethan.

She took the opportunity to study Noah. The sight of his well-shaped hands made her remember how they felt on her skin. She drew a deep breath and looked up to meet his gaze.

His chest expanded as he drew a deep breath. "Save those thoughts and come back to them when we're home," he said in a husky voice.

She could feel her cheeks grow warm. "You're too dang perceptive," she said and turned to the window. Soon the pilot announced the landing, and as they came in, they flew over structures spread out in all directions. She felt as if she was looking at a small town of large impressive houses, of long barns, corrals and outbuildings.

Noah had put a map on her iPad and sent her a virtual tour of the house, so she had an idea what to expect, but seeing it in real life was different because his home, the grounds, the outbuildings, everything was far bigger, more lavish than she'd expected.

Her attention was caught by the views of a sprawling stacked stone mansion with porches, balconies off the second-floor rooms, slate roofs, a large pond in front of and around one side of the mansion with splashing fountains. Three statues of mountain lions were in well-tended flower beds in the front. And then the plane banked and she glimpsed a landing strip on his ranch. As they came in, she saw a waiting limo and a chauffeur in boots, jeans and a Western hat.

After introductions, they were driven around to a back entrance. As they circled the mansion that looked like a castle out on a windswept mesquite-covered flatland, she was surprised by the house. His condo in Dallas was beautiful and covered the entire top floor of a tall building owned by Noah, but this went beyond that, went beyond even his parents' home. Finding it in the middle of nowhere made it even more impressive.

The chauffeur held the door and Noah took Ethan, holding him easily. The chauffeur brought their things and a man came out the back door to greet them.

"Camilla, this is Terrance Holidaye, my house manager."

"Terrance, this is Ms. Warner, and this is my son, Ethan Warner."

"Ah, fine fellow. So happy to meet you, Ms. Warner."

"I'm glad to meet you," she said, smiling. "And thank you. We think Ethan is a fine fellow, too," she said, and they all smiled.

"Let me take that bag for you," Terrance said, taking a bag Camilla carried that held some of Ethan's things.

They crossed a porch that had hanging plants, pots of flowers and palm trees. Terrance held the door for them and they entered a wide entry hall with a splashing fountain, a two-story-high ceiling with an enormous crystal chandelier, paintings on the walls, benches upholstered in leather and a stone floor.

When they entered the kitchen, she was even more surprised because it was a huge room, with doors open to the back. She met Gilda Bascomb, his cook, a smiling, gray-haired woman. Enticing smells filled the kitchen as Gilda stirred something on the gas range.

When they walked back into the hall, Noah smiled at her. "Welcome to Bar G Ranch."

"Thank you. This mansion doesn't really reflect you."

"How so?" he asked, sounding amused.

"You're sort of laid-back and this is showy. It's spectacular, breathtaking, very impressive."

"Well, what do you know—I've impressed you," he said, looking more amused. "Now if I could just get you to like it, it would be worth the cost and the trouble."

"Noah, we don't have any commitment to one another," she reminded him, and again, that wall seemed to rise between them and his smile faded.

"No, we don't. We just have a baby." His voice was cold and she knew she had dampened the moment, which she regretted, but it was the truth.

"You said you have a nursery ready and baby-proofed."

"Yes. It has furniture, but I'd like to leave the decorating to you if you would like to do it."

"Sure. I can do that," she said, wondering to what extent their lives would be interwoven.

"After you selected the furniture and I had it sent here, I contacted my house manager and told him I wanted the nursery and the family room baby-proofed. He has children, so I'm confident those rooms will be safe for Ethan."

"That's great, Noah."

"Mama," Ethan said, dropping his toy, holding out his arms and wiggling to get out of Noah's arms.

Camilla scooped up the toy, took Ethan and gave Noah the stuffed tiger.

"Here's the family room," he said, as they exited the kitchen into the hall and walked through wide double doors. The big room was two stories high with a beamed ceiling and polished dark wood walls, with one wall all glass. Another wall had floor-to-ceiling windows and large double doors with the upper half allowing a view of an outdoor living area with a large fire pit in the center and an outdoor kitchen. Off the patio was a fenced, lit, kidney-shaped swimming pool with palm trees at one end, and boulders and waterfalls and a fountain in the center. Cabanas to one side were partially hidden by flowers and palm trees.

"You have a palace here. How do you keep the palm trees from freezing?"

"There's a framework that isn't visible when it isn't used. It pulls a canopy over them and that's enough protection. Plus they're sheltered from the north wind by the house. I had the fence put in immediately after learning I'd have a baby here. Later, when he's older, I'll have a little kid pool built."

She turned to look at the family room again. "This is beautiful, Noah." She noticed a baby gate secured at the staircase to keep Ethan from climbing to the second floor that had a library circling the room. "It does look baby-proof." The tables were bare and the large fireplace had a bumper pad on the hearth. "Terrance did a good job."

"That's good to hear." Noah stood facing her and she realized he was watching her intently.

"What? I know I don't have food on my face."

"Just wondering if this is like your grandfather's house. You didn't like going there."

"There is nothing here to make me think of his ranch," she said, realizing Noah wanted her to see she had a mistaken view of ranches by thinking they would all be like her grandfather's. "Not even remotely. No, Noah, this will never remind me of my grandfather's ranch, which he didn't keep up. This is entirely different, except it is still far from the city."

"Ahh, the city," he said. "Your opera and shops and traffic and noise. We don't have that here," he said, reminding her of how opposite they were. He walked closer to place his hand lightly on her shoulder and twiddle with long locks of her hair. They were opposites in so many ways, but the physical attraction was mutual. "I'm glad you came to visit," he said, sounding sincere. "That means a lot, Camilla."

He leaned down to kiss her, a light kiss, but one that made her want to forget their differences and step into his arms.

"Dada, up."

She moved back and looked down at Ethan, who was holding Noah's leg.

Noah laughed and picked him up. "I don't think he wants me kissing Mama."

"I think he just wants to join in the hugs and kisses," she said, smiling at Ethan.

Taking Ethan when he reached for her, Camilla kissed his cheek and then looked at the room again. "This is a wonderful home, Noah."

"Inside that big closet, there should be a toy box—no lid—and some new toys, but let's go upstairs now and let me show you your suite, mine and the nursery. We can settle in, and when you want to, and Ethan is ready, I'll show you the rest of the house."

She smiled at him. "That ought to take about how many hours?"

"We can break it up," he said, pausing at the foot of the stairs. "Let me carry him up the stairs," he said, taking Ethan before she could protest.

"Why do you have this big a house on your ranch?" she asked. "You don't have anything like this in Dallas."

"This is home. It's comfortable and exactly what I want. And I have the family out here at least once a month—or I did until I went into the Army. They haven't been out since I got discharged, but Stefanie told me they're coming soon."

She wondered if Mia would be on Noah's ranch, and she didn't like to think of him with someone else, but felt it would be her fault if he was.

"And I assume that all these people who work for you live on the ranch," she said.

"Not all of them. I furnish a house here for any employee who I feel will be here a long time." He led her down the second-floor corridor and stopped outside one of the rooms. "Here are Ethan's digs. Keep in mind his suite isn't finished yet."

"Do you mind if I hang one of my paintings in his room? I have three I've done for him that I haven't put up yet."

"I'd be glad to have your paintings."

They walked into a large playroom, and through an open door beyond it, she could see the crib.

"This suite has a bedroom, a playroom and a bathroom. And there's an adjoining suite where a nanny can stay."

He held Ethan with one arm and took her arm with his other hand. "Your suite is right next door and you have a connecting door to this room." He turned to her. "But I hope you're in my bed. We'll come back to that later when we've put the little one to bed," he said, and desire darkened his blue eyes. "I hired my cook to stay with Ethan when we go out tomorrow night. She has three little grandchildren, so she's been around babies, and she's worked for my family for twenty-two years. I hope that's all right with you."

"Yes, it is," she said, realizing from the moment she told Noah about Ethan, Ethan's life, as well as hers, had begun to change. He would be gone part of the time, influenced by Noah, would get to know and love his new family, who hovered over him more than hers did. She had known when she told Noah about Ethan there would be no going back. She just hoped there wouldn't be anything disastrous ahead.

"Now come see my suite," Noah said, leading her to cross the hall.

When they entered his suite, she saw a huge bedroom with floor-to-ceiling glass on one side that gave a panoramic view of his gardens and pools and lawn. He had a custom-made bed that was longer and wider than a king and covered in a dark blue comforter with a dozen pillows.

The floor was highly polished hardwood. Across from the bed was a huge TV. He had a glass-and-mahogany desk with two computers and four screens.

"Noah, you have a beautiful home."

He walked to her and placed his hands on her shoulders. "I hope you love it here. I'm glad you agreed to visit."

She looked up into blue eyes filled with desire. With one hand, he lightly caressed her nape with feathery touches. She wanted his arms around her, wanted to kiss him. At the same time, she couldn't keep from thinking about her visit to the ranch. She had done what he wanted by agreeing to come. In addition, she'd had Ethan christened, specifically as a favor to Noah because of his father not being well, and she'd changed Noah's middle name. She had made all the moves, all the concessions so far, but not Noah. He was just like Thane and her dad. They were all nice men, but they just managed to believe that their worlds revolved around them and ran them the way they wanted.

She suspected this trip to the ranch—while definitely not what she'd expected—was only going to emphasize that, once again, she was dealing with a strong alpha male.

They spent the next hour getting familiar with the common living area of the house. They had lunch on the terrace with Ethan in his new high chair that she had bought in Dallas and Noah had shipped to the ranch. Later after Ethan's nap, they all got into a pickup, Ethan riding in the baby seat already installed in the back seat, and Noah drove them to one of the barns. He carried Ethan through the empty barn to a corral with horses. When one came to the fence, Ethan's eyes grew big as Noah let him pet the horse.

Camilla watched father and son and felt another clutch to her heart. Noah was so at ease on his ranch, so happy here. She had agreed to stay at least until Wednesday and let Noah follow his regular routine on the weekdays so she could see what life was like. She knew he wanted her to like it the way he did.

Could she?

Noah

That evening they had a steak dinner that Noah cooked on the grill and they ate in the informal dining area off the kitchen that overlooked the patio and pool. Ethan was in his high chair between him and Camilla.

She looked relaxed and at ease in jeans and her hair in a ponytail. Noah wanted her to like the ranch. Until she'd said she was willing to visit, he'd felt they didn't have a future together. When he had come home from the service, he had never planned to get back with her, but the instant he knew about Ethan that had all changed. He wanted Ethan to have a mom and dad and he felt Camilla would be the best possible mom because Ethan was her own baby and it was obvious she loved him deeply.

Noah thought about their nights together. Her attraction for him hadn't diminished one degree since they'd been apart. She was still the sexiest woman he had known, irresistible in too many ways, and he had never really gotten over her. But he wasn't turning his life upside down, giving up being a rancher and moving to Dallas because that was what she liked best. Even if she liked the ranch, he was still too much the alpha male for her. That was something he couldn't change. If she couldn't adjust to it, there wasn't much he could do. So he took charge. So what? Would she prefer a guy who would stand back in a crisis and let the house burn down and him with it if no one else saved him?

Noah shook his head. And as far as he was concerned, Camilla was as strong-willed and decisive and as take-charge as he was. He had talked about this one time to her brother. He remembered Thane laughing and saying, *You two will always butt heads, but she can hold her own with you. She ought to see it in herself, but she doesn't. She couldn't be like our mom if she tried.*

He suspected Thane was absolutely right.

Now, his ranch was another matter. He might figure out something. Maybe spend some time in the city— he was there to see his family anyway—and get her to spend some time on his ranch. After all, she'd finally come to visit the Bar G. That was a big indication that she was trying to work things out because until recently, she wouldn't even consider visiting.

Then it hit him. She was his guest at the ranch. She'd had Ethan's middle name changed to Noah's dad's name. She'd had Ethan christened. Noah had done nothing to work out the problems between them. Maybe he did need to give in a little on the ranch and stay in Dallas. But before he made that move, he wanted to be sure of his feelings for her. From the first time he saw her again, he'd known he wasn't over her. But before he could explore those feelings, he learned about Ethan and the baby changed everything.

Noah glanced at his desk, where he had the picture of Ethan she had given him. Ethan was a marvel and Noah already loved him deeply. How could a baby ensnare his heart so easily? Ethan didn't talk. He babbled and toddled around, but Noah loved him and thought he was adorable.

He knew the depth of his feelings for Ethan—it was boundless, unconditional love. How deep did his feelings run for Camilla? If he loved her, would he be thinking of getting a lawyer and, if necessary, initiating a custody suit? How much was he willing to sacrifice or change in his life to keep her? Could they ever work out their differences?

When she put Ethan to bed and tiptoed out of his room, Noah was waiting. He crossed the hall to wrap his arms around her.

"Noah, I want to sleep close to him."

"I have monitors that pick up every little sound. He'll be fine."

"Still, I would—" Noah kissed her and stopped her argument, and by the time he stopped kissing her, she didn't protest when he picked her up and carried her to his bedroom to make love.

Camilla

Noah took her and Ethan to show them the animals on Friday and he even took the baby for his first horse ride. Holding him, he rode slowly around the corral, going at a walk. Ethan looked delighted.

Finally late Friday afternoon Gilda drove from her ranch house to take charge of Ethan so Camilla would be free to dress. Camilla wondered about the evening ahead. She had gone dancing once before with Noah in Fort Worth and at the time it had been fun. Noah was the one who had taught her the two-step.

She dressed in a tight-fitting red knit shirt with a scoop neck, tight jeans, a wide hand-tooled leather belt and black boots. She wore a black Resistol, and let her hair fall loosely down her shoulders.

When she came downstairs, Noah crossed the hall to place his hands on her hips. "You look smokin' hot, darlin'."

She smiled. "I could say the same to you. I just kissed Ethan goodbye and he's happy with Gilda, so they seem to be doing all right."

"She's good with kids. I've seen her with her own grandkids and ranch kids. Let's go have some fun," he said, slipping his arm around her waist and walking toward the door to the portico where he had parked his pickup.

They drove to a small nearby roadhouse where music blared, neon lights flashed outside and the parking lot was filled with pickups. Inside, the music was loud, compliments of a drummer and two fiddlers. The scrape of boots on the floor was a constant swish as dancers circled.

When they reached a booth and slid into it, Camilla laughed. "You must know everyone in the next six counties. I'd guess it's taken us thirty minutes to get here from the door. I got some 'drop dead' looks from women, so you must be a popular guy out here."

He grinned. "I know what kind of looks you got from the guys. And you met about eight who work for me. They'll come ask you to dance."

A waitress in tight black slacks and a black T-shirt took their order and then Noah asked Camilla to dance.

During the evening as she circled the floor with him, she realized this was the most fun she'd had in a long time. Noah was filled with energy. He was happy, enjoying the night, and she was having fun with him.

It was almost midnight when he caught her around the waist and lifted her in the air as the music stopped. "Let's go home, okay?" Noah suggested, and she nodded.

He took her arm and in minutes they were in his pickup, headed back to his ranch. She threw her hat in the back and leaned against the seat, watching him drive. "Noah, that was fun. How often do you do that?"

"About once every month or two."

"You love this life, don't you?"

"Yes. If you'll visit me again or come to the ranch on a regular basis, I'll have a studio for you. Also, it's not as far from here to Taos and Santa Fe as it is from Dallas. I can open an art gallery in Santa Fe if you'd like. I don't know one thing about an art gallery, but you do. You could hire people to run it."

Startled, she shifted to face him as he drove. "I don't know. I'll have to think about coming here on a regular basis. I'm sure it would be a quiet, peaceful place to paint. I'll think about it," she said, watching him, reminded again that she was the one being asked to yield on some of their differences. So far, Noah still hadn't done one thing in that respect.

After a moment of silence, he spoke. "Camilla, thanks for deciding to come visit my ranch. That's a start on working things out between us. Ethan should have a mom and dad in his life, if we can work things out. That may not be possible, but coming to the ranch to visit is a start."

She gazed up at him and wondered if they were one bit closer now than before she told him she would visit his ranch. Maybe it would finally come down to whether Noah loved her or not, and so far, she didn't know. She wasn't going to declare her love when he never came close to saying he loved her.

Would she ever know the extent of Noah's feelings for her?

Eleven

Camilla

"I'm glad to be home," Noah said, unbuttoning his shirt. She turned to him, looking at the open vee of his shirt and his muscled chest with the thick black curls across it, and her mouth went dry.

"You look sexy tonight," he said, looking at her with desire filling his expression and making her pulse race. "You take my breath away and you have every time I've looked at you."

She caught his wrist. "Let's go to the bedroom now."

He picked her up and carried her easily, setting her on her feet by the big bed. He turned on one small lamp and then faced her, slowly peeling her out of her shirt and jeans. She held his shoulders while he pulled off her boots.

She stepped closer, her breasts just touching his chest while she disposed of her bra and panties. At the same time, he undressed. He was aroused, thick, hard and ready.

She leaned slightly closer and rubbed her bare breasts against his chest. He inhaled deeply and cupped her breasts in his hands. His hands were calloused, but his touch was gentle, light while his thumbs circled her nipples.

She gasped with pleasure and ran her hand over his chest, down over his flat, muscled belly. She knelt to stroke and fondle his hard rod, her other hand slipping between his legs to stroke him lightly. She ran her tongue over him and then took him in her mouth.

He inhaled, his hands tunneling in her hair while he let her caress and kiss him. With a groan, he pulled her to her feet to look into her eyes, a stormy, heated look of burning desire that sent a sizzling thrill over her.

"I want you," he whispered. He ran his hands slowly over her, caressing her breasts, down to her belly, down between her legs, rubbing her lightly. She gasped, closing her legs over his fingers as he stroked her and sensations rocked her, building in her until she grasped his arms and release shook her.

He kissed her hard, a demanding, possessive kiss filled with passion and desire and setting her ablaze again. She clung to him, rubbing against him, while his fingers played with her intimately, and within moments she was lost to sensation.

"I want you," she whispered, running her tongue over his ear.

He picked her up to carry her to bed, yanking away the covers and placing her on the bed while she watched him, wanting him, tingling from head to toe with longing for his hands and mouth on her again.

He rolled her over, getting above her and sliding his

thick erection between her legs while he trailed kisses on her nape and reached beneath her to fondle her breasts.

With a moan, she rolled over, raising her legs to put them on either side of him.

Instead, he caught her ankles and put her legs on his shoulders, giving him access to her, to stroke and tease her. He ran his fingers over her and then his tongue.

"Noah, I want you," she whispered, clutching the bed, unable to reach him.

Sensations tantalized, built desire until suddenly he moved her legs to the bed and reached for a packet to put on a condom.

He entered her, thick and hard, moving slowly. Crying out, she arched and clutched his hard butt, pulling him toward her, wanting him in her to the hilt.

He eased back and she cried out again as he slowly filled her and withdrew. "Make this last. I want to love the night away," he whispered, entering her and withdrawing even more slowly, driving her to arch beneath him, to cry out for him.

He fought to keep control as long as he could, trying to pleasure her, to build the need, to make the moments sexier with each thrust. But he couldn't maintain his control any longer and he thrust into her, moving fast and then faster, pumping while she matched his moves and clung to him.

Rocking with him, she stiffened and arched against him as another blinding climax slammed into her. Dimly she heard him say her name and then she felt his own shuddering release.

He lowered his weight on her and they held each other, bound together in a rapturous union. She ran her hand lightly over his smooth, muscled back that was damp with sweat.

He turned to shower light kisses on her face and both of them were still breathing deeply.

Sometime later—she currently had no idea about time—he shifted and drew her into his arms, holding her. "You're fabulous," he whispered. "Better than I dreamed about."

She looked at his mouth while she slipped her hand behind his head and pulled him closer to kiss him.

"I want you in my arms all night." He held her close and they were quiet. She wondered if he was drifting off, but she didn't want to call his name and end the euphoria that enveloped her.

"Camilla," he said quietly. His voice was deep and she looked at him as he held her close. "This is one thread that holds us together."

She looked in his eyes and had to agree. Being in bed with Noah was great, but not enough in the face of the issues separating them. She had visited the ranch and she would stay this week to see how daily life would be, but Noah was going to have to do some giving, too. She wasn't going to be the only one. Why couldn't he see what he needed to do?

He trailed his hand over the curve of her hip, and when he pulled her against him, she felt his manhood that was already hard again.

"You never stop," she whispered.

"You're the one who started this, just by being in my bed," he answered and kissed her. His fingers slipped between her thighs, and in no time she no longer cared who'd started it. She only knew she wanted to finish.

"I want you in me, loving me," she whispered, running her fingers lightly over him, more aware of his fingers playing between her thighs, another delicious torment that was driving her need to greater heights. He retrieved a condom and then moved over her. For one moment as he looked into her eyes, she felt wanted, but she knew that was an illusion. He wanted her now and she would take that. After they climaxed together, she fell back into his embrace.

She gasped for breath. "You really are insatiable."

"You make me want you. I've dreamed of you, fantasized pleasuring you, wanted to kiss and touch you," he said.

His words made her tingle all over. But there were never words of love from him. Never a declaration. She felt a clutch to her insides, an ache, because if he wasn't in love, they could never work out sharing Ethan.

He tilted her chin up while he looked into her eyes. As she gazed into his face, she couldn't guess what he was thinking or feeling.

"I hope you like the ranch, Camilla. We're going to have to find some common ground to work out keeping Ethan."

His answer hurt and she felt that if she wanted a life with Noah, she would have to always do everything his way. She couldn't constantly be the one to yield. Even then, there were no words of love from him. Not even a hint.

Noah was tough and he would stand firm for what he wanted. Tonight might be a goodbye of sorts. Their lives would be intertwined because of sharing Ethan, but this closeness would vanish. And all because she was the only one in love. And that hurt.

They slept in each other's arms. Waking in the night, she held him tightly and asked herself the same questions again. So much with Noah was wonderful, but if he wasn't in love, she didn't see much hope for them getting together to raise Ethan. She loved Noah, but was her love enough to tie her life to a male who so far hadn't made an effort to agree to anything she wanted?

With a sigh she turned to place her hand on his chest. Instantly his hand closed over hers. Turning, he drew her against him and held her as if he really loved her, but she assumed he didn't and what he did feel might vanish in the next months.

Twelve

Camilla

The plane touched down in Dallas before sunrise on Thursday. She hadn't been able to sleep on the flight, too wrapped up in memories of her time at the ranch. They'd gone to church on Sunday, meeting locals and eating at a café with his friends and neighbors. Then the first two days of the week, Noah had been up and gone doing his ranching work by the time she got up and she'd had the days with Ethan. When Ethan had napped, she'd worked out in Noah's home gym. And each night they'd shared a bed, and some of the best sex Camilla had ever experienced.

They lay down for a quick nap when they got to her house, and when she woke, Noah's side of the bed was empty. She dressed quickly and went to find him. She located him in the kitchen cooking breakfast. Her gaze ran over his tight jeans and blue-and-red plaid shirt.

"We're matching," she said, pointing out her red shirt and jeans.

Smiling, he turned off the burner and glanced at her. "Ethan is still asleep. I want to talk to you and hopefully this will be a good time. Can you wait for breakfast?"

He looked somber and she felt chill bumps rise on her arms. She had a feeling he had made some decisions, and dread filled her because his jovial manner was gone.

"Let's go into the family room," she said. "We'll hear him on the monitor."

Noah brought in two cups of coffee and set one beside her on a table.

He sat facing her in a brown leather wingback chair. He had one foot up on his other knee and watched her closely. "I wanted to talk while Ethan is asleep because we'll have fewer interruptions."

He sipped his coffee, she suspected more as a delay tactic than because he really wanted it. He put the cup down and met her eyes. "Listen, Camilla, we both know what this is about. We both need to think about what we want to do in our future. It's been wonderful to be with both you and Ethan. In a way I want to just keep on like we are now, but we know we have to make some decisions. We could go on this way for a lot longer, but eventually a time will come when we'll need to decide our future, and I think it's time now."

His words sent a shiver through her. She had known this was coming, but it hurt to hear it.

Not waiting for her reply, he continued. "I know how to take care of Ethan now and I have resources and a family who want him every second I'll let them have with him. You and I have talked about the future, but really haven't settled anything. I've told you what I want—a real family, a family that is together. A family where each member feels love and commitment. I don't want a long-distance relationship and I can't quit ranching and work in an office. That may be selfish, but there it is."

"So where do we go from here, Noah?" She had no answer because the answer she wanted to hear wouldn't happen. She wanted them to stay together. She wanted Noah to be in love with her, to love her the way she did him. And she did love him. She would always love him. But Noah couldn't feel that way about her or he wouldn't have said what he just did. He wouldn't want to move out and leave her. If he loved her, he would stay. She fought back tears because she was terrified of what Noah would suggest for Ethan.

"Listen to me," Noah said, leaning forward, gazing into her eyes. "I want to work things out, Camilla. We have some great things going for us. The sex couldn't be better. We both adore Ethan. We both want to be a family for him. We are his parents and I want us together with him," he said, looking directly into her eyes.

Her heart jumped when he said they both adored Ethan and they both wanted to be a family for him. The words gave her hope.

"If we can't work this out, then I want custody half the time."

Like a popped balloon, her optimism fizzled. She felt like she couldn't draw in oxygen. "Noah, we've been doing well together. Surely we can work this out."

"Before we get to a protracted court custody battle and there's no chance of turning back and feelings are hurt, why don't we try something? Let's have a trial run. I'll take Ethan for a week and then you take him for a week. Let's do that for a month and then see how we feel about things before we get lawyers involved," he suggested.

"I knew this was coming, but that doesn't stop it from hurting," she said and covered her eyes. "I'm sorry, Noah. I've never been away from him except for a night or two when he was with your folks. I can't imagine…" She let the unspoken words float between them as she took out a handkerchief and wiped her eyes.

He walked over to her to place his hands on her shoulders. "Camilla, we have never talked about love. I've skirted that the whole time I've been here and so have you. Neither of us has ever said 'I love you' to the other."

Her heart pounded and she wondered what was coming. A declaration of love? Reasons why he couldn't say it?

He gave her neither. "I'm still exploring my feelings," he said. "All the years in the military, I tried to get over what I felt for you. Now, since knowing about Ethan, I haven't really explored my feelings or let go because I felt like I would get hurt. You've never said 'I love you.'"

"You haven't either, Noah. It's hard to say 'I love you' when the other person doesn't say it. That's awkward." She was tempted to tell him now, though, before he walked out of her life.

"To be honest, Camilla, I've tried to keep from falling in love because I felt like it was inevitable that we would part. I still live and work on a ranch and I'm still the kind of man you dislike and we're still opposites in a ton of ways. When I marry, I want it to last. I want forever. I want what my family has. I can't marry and love a woman unless I can have that kind of love with her."

She stood to face him and placed her hands on his

arms. "I don't know if we can ever work things out. You haven't made any effort to change except to move in with me to get to know Ethan and how to take care of him."

She had listened to him, hurting when he said he didn't know what he felt, hurting even more at the thought of giving up Ethan for a week. She'd known this would happen, but they had so many happy moments together she'd begun to hope for more. And they had made love constantly, something merely physical and lusty to Noah, but something emotional and honest for her. Each time they made love, it reinforced the love she had for him and made her hurt more than ever. If he didn't declare his love for her, did she want to tell him she loved him? Noah could view sex as sex. She couldn't. Sex was all tied up with love and intimacy. He hadn't made promises and hadn't declared love, but she'd still lost her heart to him long ago. She'd loved him the night she got pregnant. The only decision now was whether to tell him.

"Are you willing to try a week on and a week off for the next month?" he asked her.

"I don't see that I have much choice here, but that's better than getting lawyers involved. Noah, you told me you don't know the depth of your feelings. I don't know the depth of mine, because there are some things, like moving to your ranch, I don't think I could do, not for the whole year. But I do know that I love you. I've loved you for a long time and I missed you and cried over you while you were away in the Army."

He frowned and stepped closer. "Camilla—"

She held her hand up for him to stop. "You don't need to say anything now. Just tell me—when are you moving out?"

"I hadn't thought that through, but probably today. I'll pick Ethan up this weekend and start my week."

"It'll be a huge change to lose both of you at once. Let me start with Ethan this week and you take him the following week. Will you do that?"

He nodded. "All right. I'll move out today. I'll get my things. Camilla—"

"Let's give this a try. I told you I love you. I don't want you to make any declaration or say anything in response to that until you've given it more thought. I want you to be sure of what you tell me."

He nodded. "I'll do that. I'll skip breakfast and get my things together and we'll get this done. One thing I'm very sure about is how much I'm going to miss both of you. But if we get together, I'd want you on my ranch year-round. I don't want a part-time wife or a part-time family."

She nodded and could feel tears on her cheeks. "I understand. That's why I went ahead and told you what I feel. I didn't think it'd make any difference."

He walked out of the room and she felt sure he was walking out of her life. They would see each other and interact because of Ethan, but a more intimate relationship with him was over forever.

That knowledge, together with the fact that she would have Ethan only half the time, hurt terribly, and she sat in the chair, putting her hands over her face while she cried.

Noah

Noah had his things gathered up and in his car before Ethan woke up. When he heard his son rouse, he went to the nursery. Camilla was already there, picking him up. She turned and saw Noah.

His heart felt as if a fist squeezed it. She had been

crying and for once Ethan looked solemn. He held out his arms to Noah. "Dada," he said. "Up."

"May I have him? I'd like to hold him a few minutes before I leave."

"Of course," she said, handing her baby to Noah. Her hands were like ice and he felt bad about hurting her and he was still surprised by her firm declaration of love. He hadn't thought she was in love, real, serious love, and it had shocked him to hear her say that.

He held Ethan, looking at him, knowing he was going to miss him. Was he making a mistake by not telling her he loved her and proposing so they could all stay together? But he couldn't. He had to be sure of his feelings. He didn't want a marriage that would end in a few years.

"Ethan, I will miss you," he said, hurting and wondering if he was bringing all sorts of heartache on himself. Yet if he stayed months longer and then had to leave, it would be even more difficult.

He handed Ethan back to her and put his arm around her. "I'll miss you, too, Camilla. I'm headed for the ranch, but you can always get me by phone."

"Goodbye," she whispered and turned away. "Let yourself out, Noah."

He knew she was crying and he felt terrible as he walked out of the room and the house. He was flying back to the ranch later and he planned on working hard until late tonight. It was his way of getting over telling her goodbye.

First, though, he would go by his folks' house and break the news to them. He'd already sent a text to his siblings. All of them would miss Ethan, but when it was his week, he would take Ethan to see their parents and they could all go there to be with Ethan.

Camilla

Camilla was sure Ethan picked up on her heartache and that was why he'd lost some of his smiles. She finally sat on the floor to play with him, but after a few minutes, she looked at his black curly hair, thought of Noah and started crying again, causing Ethan to cry.

"We miss him, don't we?" she asked her baby.

"Mama," he said and patted her knee.

She hugged him and cried, missing Noah, hurting because she loved him. Could she possibly stand living on that ranch year-round? She had always said she wouldn't leave the city. Part of the year wouldn't be so bad, but year-round? How much could she live there?

She shook her head. He hadn't asked her to move there and he hadn't proposed or said he loved her. In fact, he had admitted he didn't know what he felt.

"I miss your daddy," she told Ethan, and he gazed solemnly at her. He held out his arms.

"Up," he said, and she pulled him close to hug him.

She spent the day playing with him. She postponed painting, an appointment, shopping for new clothes for Ethan. She could do all that the next week when Noah had him. Right now, she just wanted to be with him, hold him, read to him and play with him. She missed Noah more as the hours of the morning passed. How long was she going to miss him this badly? She didn't think she would ever get over him.

Noah

Friday, a week later, Noah drove his pickup back to the ranch house from the pasture. He was dusty from moving cattle from one pasture to another with a bunch of cowboys. He got a cold beer and sat on the patio, looking at his pool before he went up to shower. He wasn't sleeping nights and it hurt far more than he expected to be away from Camilla and Ethan. It hurt far worse than it had when he had broken up with her and gone into the Army. He missed his son. He missed Camilla, especially at night. She had visited the ranch, stayed longer than originally planned. She had been more cooperative than he had been actually, he realized. He spent all sorts of time in Dallas. Couldn't he live with a wife who visited the city some?

He heard a car and saw a red sports car whip around and park at the back gate.

He smiled. Stef. He'd be glad to see her.

She jumped out and slammed the door, rushing through the gate, and he wondered what was up because she was charging toward the porch. He stood up and waited until she was close and he held up his beer. "Want a cold one?"

She rushed in front of him and stood with her hands on her hips. "No, I don't. You're a miserable louse."

He had to laugh. "Hello to you, too. What bee got into your bonnet?"

"It isn't funny, Noah."

He realized she actually was mad at him, something that had rarely happened since they'd been teenagers. "What the hell, Stef? I've been out here working my tail off. What did I do?"

"You moved out and left Camilla and Ethan."

His smile vanished. "We didn't have anything permanent. We're doing a trial run of alternating weeks with Ethan. We'd planned to do this all along. I just moved in with her to get to know Ethan and to learn how to take care of him. You knew that. Sit down and we'll talk."

Instead, she held her ground. "I went over to see her and she couldn't talk to me without getting tears in her eyes. And I miss Ethan."

"Stef, butt out. I don't want to rush into marriage. And Camilla's already had one divorce."

"Well, yeah, she married on the rebound because she was hurting over you and she was already pregnant."

"Did she tell you all that?"

"We got to be close friends. Actually, we're sort of related now because of Ethan."

"Stef, this isn't any of your business."

"You don't say. It will affect our whole family." She stared at him. "So how are you getting along out here?"

"Don't start in on me. I miss them. I knew I would."

"Do you really? You seemed real happy when you were with them. Are you real happy out here now?"

He sighed deeply. "Do you know this is absolutely none of your business?"

"Are you really happy?" she asked, sounding sincere. "I'm worried about you."

"I'm okay, and no, I'm not so happy. She won't marry me and live out here year-round."

"Sometimes you can be annoyingly stubborn. That's simple to fix. Come to Dallas some of the time. You think you're not coming to see us? You spend plenty of time there. Noah, you're hurting yourself. You're hurting Camilla, and worst of all, you're hurting Ethan."

"You can't tell me he misses me. He's a little baby and they adjust."

"He needs his daddy and you know it. You're unhappy and it's all your own fault. You'll just have him half of the time. He needs both of you all of the time. I love you and I'm worried about all three of you. It's you causing the trouble and hurting yourself. She said you don't love her."

"I don't know what I feel."

"You're smarter than that. I'll tell you what. If you don't know what you feel, I think you're in for some rough times. Unfortunately, you cause others to hurt."

She got ready to leave. "I've had my say. Now I'll drive back to the city, and I'm going to tell Camilla you're not happy either and then I'm going to play with your son. I'll ask her out with my crowd Saturday night and see if that will cheer her up a little. Ben and Hallie will keep Ethan."

"Now you're interfering."

"No, I'm not. You moved out. She's free as a bird. I hate to see you hurt yourself and keep yourself from happiness. You're just being plain stubborn, Noah." She looked around at the ranch. "This is nice, Noah, but it's just a house. It doesn't mean anything by itself. Now, I know you could be happy out here in a shack, but the ranch is just mesquite, cattle and horses. If you want that more..." She threw up her hands. "I miss Ethan and I'm going back to Dallas to play with him. 'Bye, Noah." She left as fast as she came and in seconds the red sports car roared away.

Noah stood looking at his ranch, thinking about Ethan and Camilla. Stefanie had been right about everything. He would spend time in Dallas with his family. He had good people working for him who could manage the ranch just fine in his absence. His wife didn't have to stay year-round on his ranch.

He was definitely unhappy at the moment. He missed them both. The big question was: Did he love Camilla?

Thirteen

Camilla

Camilla stood pushing Ethan in the swing. Noah called and said he wanted to come talk and she couldn't keep from hoping it was something good and that he wasn't coming to tell her about seeing his attorney. She knew it was probably wishful thinking but she couldn't help it.

Stefanie called too and asked if she could come get Ethan. Her folks wanted to see him and she did, too.

Camilla thought about Noah coming. He would want to see his son, but he could go on to his folks' house, which he probably planned to do anyway, so she told Stefanie to come get him.

She heard a car and saw Stefanie drive up, so she got Ethan out of the swing and picked up the bag she was sending with him.

In minutes he was buckled in Stefanie's car and

she was gone with a wave. Camilla was happy for the family to have Ethan, but when Noah took him for his week, it was going to hurt badly. Would she ever get accustomed to kissing him goodbye and being without him?

She walked back to the house and heard the second car and saw it was Noah. He stepped out and her heart thudded. It took an effort not to run and hug him. He looked incredible, tall, handsome, filled with energy that showed in his walk. He had on jeans and boots and a blue cotton Western-style shirt and his black hat.

She had missed him more than when he'd left for the Army. If he started talking about sharing Ethan, she hoped she could hold back the tears this time.

As he came closer, she was aware of her own clothes—cutoffs, a navy knit shirt and sneakers.

"Hi. You just missed Stefanie picking up Ethan. He's at your folks' house if you want to go see him when you—"

Noah didn't stop. He walked up, wrapped his arms around her and kissed away her words.

Her heart thudded and she clung to him tightly with her arms around his narrow waist. Still kissing her, he picked her up and carried her into her house, not putting her down till he reached the family room.

He tossed his hat to a chair. "I've missed you."

Her heart began to pound. He hadn't kissed like he was going to talk about attorneys and taking Ethan half the time.

"We've missed you. Ethan looks for you. I know he's missing you, so I hope you have time to go see him."

"Camilla, I've got something to say and I don't want to waste one more minute to say it. I want to see if we can work out something where I'll be on the ranch part of the time and we'll be in Dallas part of the time." He took her hand. "I love you. I thought about my feelings for you and they run deep. I missed you the whole time I was in the Army. I kept thinking I was getting over you because I didn't see you, but the minute I saw you when I came home, I knew I wasn't over you at all."

"Oh, Noah, I love you. I have for so long—way before you went into the Army." She threw her arms around his neck and kissed him.

When he raised his head to look at her, he still held her tightly in his arms. "I can come to Dallas—I always have. Are you willing to spend a lot of time on the ranch? I'll spend a lot of time in Dallas."

Laughing with joy, she nodded. "Yes. Oh, yes. We'll be a family, Noah. We'll be together."

He reached into his pocket. "Camilla, will you marry me?"

Joy burst in her and she tightened her arms around him, standing on tiptoe to kiss him. He held her tightly while they kissed and then she leaned away. "Yes. Yes, yes, yes, I'll marry you. Today if you want. Oh, Noah, I love you and have loved you for so long. I've been miserable without you."

He released her and took her hand. "I love you and want to marry you." He opened his hand to put a small box in her hand.

She looked at it and then opened it to find another fancy box inside. She opened it and gasped. "Oh, my! That is the most gorgeous ring ever!" she said, looking at a huge diamond with smaller diamonds around it.

He took it from her to slip it on her finger. "If it doesn't fit we can take it to the jeweler."

"It fits. It's magnificent. My, oh, my."

"It is only a symbol of what I feel. I love you," he

said. "Come on. I want to go get Ethan and you can show the family and tell them."

"Should we have a wedding date? They'll ask."

He shook his head. "Let's do that later. I want them to know and I want to see Ethan." He hesitated a moment. "Maybe we should let him stay with them tonight. We have some catching up to do in the bedroom."

She wrapped her arms around his neck again, looking at her ring sparkle before she turned to him. "You've made me the happiest woman in Texas today!"

He laughed and hugged her. "I'm definitely the happiest man," he said as he kissed away her answer.

* * * * *

HIS ENEMY'S DAUGHTER

SARAH M. ANDERSON

To Kristi—I'm so glad you've come into our lives!

One

It took everything Chloe Lawrence had to keep her winning smile locked into place.

"Miss," the stock contractor said, taking off his hat and slicking his thin hair back before replacing the Stetson, "this isn't how we did things back when your father was in charge."

The first time some grizzled old coot had said that to her, she had been genuinely shocked. For all intents and purposes, Milt Lawrence hadn't been in charge of the All-Around All-Stars Pro Rodeo since her brother Oliver had wrestled control of the family empire away from the older man four years ago. The All-Stars was one of the family's many holdings, had been ever since her father had won the rodeo circuit in a poker game thirteen years ago.

Oliver had managed the rodeo from a distance while simultaneously running their main company, Lawrence Energies. Which meant that, on the ground,

Chloe was the Lawrence the stock contractors had been dealing with.

"Mort," she said, keeping her voice warm and friendly instead of angry. "This is just a slight change in who's qualified to compete."

Which was not necessarily the truth.

Allowing women to compete with the men was anything but *slight*. But it wasn't like she was suggesting they cut calf-roping or anything.

Dale Jenkins, an older man with his stomach hanging over his belt buckle, stepped in front of Mort. "What Mort is trying to say," he drawled, "is that of *course* we're still interested in supplying the All-Stars with our stock. But you're *just* the Princess of the Rodeo. You're good at it, of course," he added, as if that somehow made it better. "But…"

He aimed a big smile at her, one that Chloe recognized. But that *just* grated on her every nerve.

When she'd been younger and so excited to open and close every rodeo, Dale had given her that exact same smile and patted her on the head as if she were a puppy and told her that she looked "right pretty up on that horse."

If he patted her on the head now, she might break his hand.

"Gentlemen," she said, putting as much force as she could into the word. "There is no harm in trying something different. If it works, the All-Stars will gain viewers, fans and sales. When those three things combine, you know what that gets us?" She waved her hand to encompass Dale, Mort and the other cowboys paying attention. "More money. A rising tide lifts all boats."

"Women ride barrels," said a crusty old fart named

Dustin Yardley. He stalked right into her personal space. "You're asking us to be part and parcel of something we didn't sign up for. The All-Stars is a men's rodeo." He gave her a look that was so mean she had to fight the urge to take a step back. She wouldn't show fear before these men.

Of course, meanness was Dustin's natural look, so it was hard for Chloe to tell if he was extra condescending today or not. "And we," he went on, "are the *men* who make the rodeo work."

Oh, that absolutely did it. She had heard some version of that speech in Des Moines, Kansas City, Shreveport, Memphis and, worst of all, in Fort Worth. Now she was hearing it in Sikeston, Missouri.

None of the stock contractors or riders or promoters had ever had an issue with her running the All-Stars when her brother Oliver or her father, Milt, were nominally in charge. All she'd had to do then was phrase her orders as coming from her family.

From a man.

But this year was different. At the beginning of the season, Oliver had ceded all control, real or imagined, to Chloe. He was way too busy to handle the All-Stars. He'd gone and fallen in love with Chloe's oldest friend, Renee Preston—who came with a certain amount of scandal, what with her being pregnant with her dead husband's child and the rest of her family under indictment for running a massive pyramid scheme.

And besides, Oliver *hated* the rodeo. Chloe still didn't understand why. She loved it and she'd been pushing for more control over the All-Stars for years. It hadn't been until Oliver had gone behind their father's back to give her the television distribution negotiations that she'd been able to prove her skills.

And prove them, she had. She wasn't *just* the Princess of the Rodeo. Not anymore.

Or so she'd thought.

This season should have been Chloe's victory tour. Finally, the rodeo she'd loved since her father had won it was hers and hers alone. The TV deal was just the first step. She'd also launched her own line of couture cowgirl clothing named—what else?—Princess of the Rodeo and it was selling well. Sure, the workload was insane and yeah, she didn't get much sleep anymore. But her brother had managed the rodeo while running a billion-dollar energy corporation. She could juggle some cowboys and clothing. She *had* to—this was just the beginning.

She had plans. Great plans.

Plans that required people to go along with them.

The one variable she hadn't accounted for. Damned people.

She gritted her teeth. "*Mister* Yardley," she said. She didn't have time to stand around debating. She just needed them to nod and smile and say they'd be happy to try something new. "I'll be sure to pass that sentiment along to your wife and two daughters, who delivered the agreed-upon calves to the Bootheel Rodeo last year—by themselves—while you were recovering from surgery. How's the heart, by the way?" She did her best to look sweet and concerned.

Not that Yardley was buying it. His eyes narrowed as his lip curled. He was not a man who took kindly to having his authority questioned, especially not by someone who was just a *princess*. "Now you look here, missy," he began, his cheeks darkening.

That's when a male voice behind her said, "Problem?"

Inside, her heart sank.

If she had expected anyone to barge into this situation, it would have been her younger brother, Flash Lawrence. He was not only a Lawrence heir but also a cowboy who rode for the All-Stars. He was legendary for three things—his charm with the ladies, the chip on his shoulder and his short-fuse temper.

She'd had plenty of trouble in Omaha when, in the middle of a similar conversation with similar contractors, Flash had decided Chloe's honor needed to be defended. It had taken all of her negotiating skills to get the police to drop the charges.

She would be so lucky if it was Flash who'd spoken. But today was not her lucky day.

Yardley smirked as he made eye contact with the man standing behind Chloe. The very last man she wanted to deal with. She would take a hundred Jenkinses and Yardleys and Gandys rather than deal with this *one* man.

"Pete Wellington," Yardley said and Chloe didn't miss the sudden warmth and good cheer in his voice. "What a surprise to see you here."

He didn't sound surprised. In fact, none of the men she'd been trying to reason with looked shocked that Pete Wellington had ventured from his East Texas ranch to drop by the All-Stars rodeo in Missouri.

Dammit.

"How've you been?" Mort asked, then he cut a glance at Chloe. "We'd love to see you at the rodeo again."

Yeah, that wasn't subtle. But before she could point out that Pete Wellington hadn't had jack crap to do with the All-Stars in years, Dale spoke. "You here to compete?" he asked, beaming widely. "We sure do miss seeing a *real* professional in the arena."

Lord, why didn't they just roll out a red carpet and

lick his boots clean? Chloe had to fight back a scream of frustration. She didn't like it when people took pot shots at Flash, but the fact was he was a damned good rider. He'd earned that seventh-place world ranking on his own, no matter what anyone else thought.

"Now, gentlemen," Pete said from behind her and she had to repress a shiver at the sound of his voice, deep and rich. "You know I retired from riding years ago."

"Doesn't mean you can't make a comeback. It'd be an improvement. A *huge* one." Yardley started to step around her to shake Wellington's hand, but Chloe wasn't having any of it. Pete's father, Davey Wellington, might have founded this rodeo, but he'd also lost it fair and square in a poker game to Chloe's father, Milt.

She wasn't going to let anyone cut her out of *her* rodeo. Especially not Pete Wellington.

Just as Yardley stuck out his hand, Chloe spun to face her nemesis, *accidentally* hip-checking Yardley. "Whoops," she said, working hard to keep her eyes innocent when Dustin stumbled. "Why, Mr. Wellington," she cooed. She'd once heard Flash call him that and Pete had snapped that *Mister* Wellington was his father and she absolutely wasn't above using every single weapon at her disposal. She batted her eyelashes and shifted so her breasts were at their best before finishing, "I didn't see you join us!"

She looked up at him through her lashes—a move that usually gave her total control over the situation. But Pete Wellington wasn't distracted by a pretty face. If that were possible, she would have had him eating out of her hands for the last ten years.

Instead, he said, "Well, well, well. If it isn't the Princess of the Rodeo." His tone was only slightly mocking. "You've got things well in hand, I see. As usual."

Chloe refused to react. She didn't even allow her cheeks to heat as the old farts around her started chuckling. She'd been performing in public as the Princess of the Rodeo since she was sixteen, three years after her dad had taken over the circuit. Every weekend, at the featured All-Around All-Stars Rodeo, Chloe opened and closed the show by riding a horse into the arena and carrying a huge American flag.

The All-Stars was the big leagues for cowboys who wanted to demonstrate their skills at calf-roping, bronco-busting, team roping, steer wrestling *and* bull riding. It didn't bring in as much money as the Total Bull Challenge, which was strictly bull riding. But Chloe had plans to change that.

The first step was to find her breakout star—who was absolutely not her brother Flash. She'd love to find a female rider, a positive role model to bring in younger girls. After all, that strategy had worked wonders for the Total Bull Challenge's bottom line when June Spotted Elk had worked her way up through the ranks. Why shouldn't Chloe replicate that success?

Pete smirked down at her while Dustin chortled behind her. They were the reason that, at this very moment, she wasn't replicating any success.

She *hated* Pete Wellington and his smug attitude and his built body, not to mention his freaking amazing jaw that only looked better with a five-o'clock shadow. And his eyes! They were almost gray when he looked down at her from under the brim of his brown cowboy hat but, depending on the light, changed to either light blue or green. Oh, how she hated Pete's eyes in particular. They were simply the most beautiful color she'd ever seen and some days, all she wanted to do was stare into them endlessly and watch them shift with the changing light.

But more than that, she hated the way he looked at her. Would it kill him to acknowledge that she was a damned good steward to his beloved rodeo? That she ran a tight ship and got things done—like television distribution and increased revenues?

Apparently, it would kill him because she only saw mocking contempt in his eyes. His lips curved into something that could have been a heart-stopping smile on a man with a soul but on him was nothing but a taunting sneer.

He was in Missouri for one reason and one reason alone—to knock her down in front of the very men she most needed to buy into her new plans.

If that's how he wanted to play this, fine. It wasn't her fault his father hadn't been able to hold his liquor. Nor was it her fault that the man had been a lousy poker player who hadn't known when to hold 'em or when to fold 'em. But Pete acted as if she'd stolen his rodeo. As if she'd been there, pouring Davey Wellington another shot of whiskey and whispering in his ear.

Basically, he looked at her like she was the devil incarnate and he treated her accordingly.

She was only too happy to return the favor.

"It's true I have much more to get my hands around than you do," she replied easily, keeping everything light, as if she weren't intentionally insulting his manhood. "But it's so nice to see you getting out and about again." She patted his upper arm, pointedly not noticing the way his hard biceps tensed at her casual touch. "You let me know if you need any help dealing with the crowds. I know it can be overwhelming if you're not used to it."

Any hint of a smirk on his nice, full lips died, which only made her smile broaden. But instead of launching a counterattack, Pete swallowed hard and said, "Big night?"

"Been sold out for weeks." Of course, part of that was because Dwight Yoakam was the closing act. It'd been a huge get, bringing a country star of that magnitude to this tiny corner of Missouri.

But she was going to put on a hell of a rodeo while she had butts in the seats. She had to. If this didn't work... no. There was no *if* here. It would absolutely work. When the rodeo took off, she'd be the one holding the reins.

She braced herself. Now he would come up firing. Now he would try to destroy her with a witty comeback. She could see the cords on his neck straining as he ground his teeth. No matter what he said, she wouldn't let him get to her.

Now. Surely *now*.

"Pete, maybe you can make the little lady see sense," Mort said.

"About what?" Pete replied, but he didn't look away from her.

"About women," Dustin said. He whipped his hat off his head and slapped it against his leg. "She doesn't know what she's talking about."

Pete stepped back and looked Chloe up and down, his gaze traveling the path over her blinged-out cowgirl shirt and customized jeans—both from her Princess of the Rodeo clothing line—way too slowly for her taste. "I don't know, guys. She looks pretty qualified in the woman department, if you ask me."

Chloe blushed. She didn't want to, didn't want Pete to know that his words could affect her at all—but she couldn't help it. Was he...protecting her? Or just ogling her?

What was going on?

"She wants to let women compete!" Dustin all but roared.

"Don't get us wrong," Dale went on in his pleasantly condescending voice, "women can ride the hell out of barrels."

"And they're good-looking," Mort unhelpfully added.

Chloe managed not to lose her ever-loving mind. But she couldn't stop herself from gritting her teeth and closing her eyes. Their words shouldn't hurt. They wouldn't.

"But you put a pretty little thing out there in the arena with a man and he's gonna get distracted," Dustin said, disgust in his voice. "And a distracted cowboy is a hurt cowboy. You know that, Pete."

Pete cleared his throat, making Chloe open her eyes again. He had to be *loving* this open rebellion. Hell, she wouldn't be surprised if he'd orchestrated this whole scene. She glanced around—yep. They'd amassed a crowd of about twenty people. Lovely. There would be plenty of witnesses to her humiliation.

At least Flash wasn't here. There wasn't a single bad situation her brother couldn't make worse.

Then the weirdest thing happened. Pete Wellington—a man who had never bothered to hide his hatred of her—lowered his chin and, from under the brim of his hat where no one else could see it, winked at her. Before she could figure what the hell *that* was supposed to mean, he stepped back.

"You're right," he said to Dustin in particular and the crowd of cowboys in general. "I happen to know firsthand that, because we don't have mixed competitions, no one has ever been injured in the All-Stars rodeo."

Chloe blinked. Was that…sarcasm?

In her *defense*?

What the hell was going on?

There was a three-second pause while Pete's words settled over the crowd before the first chuckle started. Another joined it and soon, all the guys who'd ridden in rodeos, past or present, began to laugh.

"Face it, boys," Pete went on, "we've all been stepped on by a bull or thrown by a bronco." Heads nodded in agreement. It was practically a sea of bobbing cowboy hats. "Women have nothing to do with the bones I've broken or the bruises I've suffered—no offense to my momma, who tried to keep me out of the arena. I say, if women want to compete on our teams and they can help a team win, why wouldn't we want that to happen?"

The bobbing stopped and Dustin pounced. "Are you serious, Wellington?"

"Have you ever seen my sister rope a steer?" Pete shot back. "She could give any man in this arena a run for his money."

Chloe stared almost helplessly up at Pete. He hadn't gone in for the kill. He really was defending her.

When he looked down at her, an electric shock skated over her skin. Then he completely blew her mind by saying, "If Chloe says it's a good idea to open up the team competitions to women, then it's a good idea."

"You can't seriously think *she's* had a good idea." Dustin spat into the dirt.

"Do I look like I'm joking?" Pete shot back.

Chloe gaped at the man.

Who the hell was this Pete damned Wellington?

Two

Pete couldn't remember the last time he'd had this much fun. Chloe Lawrence looked exactly like a fish stunned to find itself in the bottom of a boat instead of the bottom of a lake. By God, it was good to get the upper hand on the woman, for once. Everything was going according to plan.

Pete cut a glance back at Chloe. If he weren't enjoying himself quite so much, he'd be tempted to feel sorry for her. She was normally so high and mighty, the kind of smugly self-assured woman who thought she was better than everyone else, especially him. She never missed the opportunity to rub his face in the fact that the All-Stars wasn't his rodeo anymore.

Now he'd turned the tables and he was going to enjoy rubbing her face in it. These men didn't owe her any particular allegiance and they all knew it.

But that fleeting moment when Dustin took a swipe at her, where pain etched her delicate features, didn't make him feel like he was winning. It made him feel like an ass. He felt like he'd seen that look before, a long time ago. Probably when he'd said something cruel. He couldn't remember what and besides, Chloe always gave as good as she got, so he wouldn't bother to feel bad about past insults.

He pushed back against that wisp of guilt because it was small and easily ignored. Hey, he was not the bad guy here, never had been. All he wanted was what was rightfully his. It had nothing to do with Chloe personally. It had everything to do with her lying, cheating family.

But even as he repeated that familiar truth, his gaze was drawn to her again. The fact that she was the most gorgeous woman he'd ever had the displeasure of butting heads with only made it worse. In another lifetime, the one where his family still owned the All-Stars, he and Chloe wouldn't be on opposite sides of a never-ending war. She would've been just another gorgeous face and Pete would've been free to...

Well, he would've had his rodeo back.

The rodeo was *his*, dammit. The Lawrence Oil All-Around All-Stars Pro Rodeo circuit was comprised of individual rodeos that were hosted from small towns to big cities. Most of the rodeos, like the Bootheel Rodeo in Missouri, predated the All-Stars by decades.

When Pete's father Davey had started the All-Stars back in the eighties with a group of his friends, he'd had big plans. More than just a bunch of individual rodeos—with individual winners—Davey Wellington had seen a way to crown the world's best All-Around Cowboy. It'd been a crazy idea but then, Davey had been just crazy enough to make it work.

Every rodeo that wanted to count toward the world

rankings had to be approved by the All-Around All-Stars. The summers of Pete's childhood had been spent with his dad, driving from rodeo to rodeo to see if that local rodeo was worthy of being counted as an All-Star rodeo.

God, those had been good days, just the two of them in Dad's truck, sending postcards back to Mom. As far as he could recall, those summers had been the only time Pete had ever had his father's undivided attention. Pete might not have been there when Davey decided to settle the matter of who the best cowboy was forever, but by his father's side, Pete had literally worked to build the All-Stars from the ground up.

Rodeo was family. The All-Stars was *his* family, his father's legacy. It was his legacy, by God. Except for that damned poker game. Milt Lawrence had all but stolen the All-Stars from Davey when the man was deep into his whiskey and nothing Pete did could change that. And God knew he'd tried.

When Armstrong Oil—Lawrence Oil's main competitor—had tapped oil on his ranch and Pete had suddenly become quite rich, he'd tried to buy the All-Stars back from Milt Lawrence. Hadn't worked. Neither had any of the lawsuits that had followed.

The Lawrences were like leeches. Once they'd latched on, they weren't letting go until they'd drained the All-Stars of all its history, meaning and money. It was time to try a new line of attack.

One that relied on grumpy old farts. "You can't be serious," Yardley snarled. "We had a deal."

Pete glared at the man. He should've known better than to trust Dustin Yardley with something like this.

"What deal?" Chloe snapped. Any trace of confusion was gone from her face. She jammed her hands on the sweet curve of her hips and glared at Pete. Because of course she suspected the truth.

It was no accident that Pete was in Missouri today and it was no accident that he'd come upon the scene with Chloe being browbeaten by a bunch of old cowboys.

"What deal?" Pete echoed, trying to sound innocent and hoping that Dustin would get the damned hint to shut his trap.

Chloe had been running the rodeo by herself for a few months now and the buck stopped with her. She couldn't hide behind her daddy's boots anymore, and her brother Oliver? He'd been useless from the get-go, relying on Chloe as his liaison. In theory, the decisions had come from Oliver but Chloe had been the show manager.

When Oliver had officially stepped away from managing the rodeo earlier this year, Chloe hadn't hired anyone else to help run the show. She should have, though. She had to be drowning in work. They were a long way from Dallas and Chloe had no backup.

Managing the All-Stars was a full-time job and she'd also started that Princess clothing line. His sister, Marie, had bought a couple of shirts, ostensibly so she and Pete could make fun of the latest tacky venture from the tacky Lawrences. But Marie—the traitor—had actually liked the clothing so much she'd bought a few more pieces.

Chloe could have her little fashion show—Pete didn't care about that at all. But she was going to ruin his rodeo and he wasn't going to stand for that.

The contractors and local rodeo boards—they wanted to work with him, not her. Not Oliver Lawrence. And they'd never trusted New Yorker Milt Lawrence, with his fake Texas accent.

Pete could rally everyone who made the All-Stars work and get them to go on strike unless the Lawrence family either divested themselves of the circuit or paid Pete his fair share of the profits—going back thirteen long years. The rodeo was worth a lot of money—money that by rights belonged to the Wellington family.

But money wasn't why he was in Missouri this weekend. Between oil rights and cattle, his ranch was worth millions. No, this was about his father's legacy—about Pete's legacy. He wanted the All-Stars back.

So he'd proposed a solution to the stock contractors. The locals threatened to mutiny and, when things looked bleak, Pete would ride to the rescue, Chloe's knight in a shining Stetson. Chloe would be so grateful for his support that she would agree to Pete working for the All-Stars in one capacity or another. And once he was in, he'd slowly begin to crowd Chloe out.

It was a hell of a risky plan but he'd tried everything else. This would work. It *had* to. By this time next year, Chloe would be completely out of the picture and the All-Stars would be his.

Provided, of course, that Dustin Yardley didn't blow the plan to bits before it got off the ground.

Chloe swung back to him, her eyes narrowed. Suspicion rolled off her in waves. "Is there something you'd like to tell me, Pete?" She bit off each word as if it had personally offended her.

He had to make this look good. The plan would work fine even if she was a little suspicious of him, but he needed her to hire him on. Pete was walking a fine line and he knew it.

"Steve Mortimer gave me a call. He's under the weather and wasn't able to get his horses here, so he asked me if I could help out. I guess he must've asked

Dustin first, but you know Dustin." That wasn't exactly how it'd happened. It'd cost Pete a pretty penny to get Steve to stay home this weekend. The man did love his rodeo. But then, so did they all.

Chloe gave him a hard look before her entire face changed. It was like watching a cloud scuttle past the sun because suddenly, everything was brighter. Yet, at the same time, that look irritated him. Like she'd flipped a damned switch, Chloe Lawrence looked instantly dumber. If Pete hadn't watched it happen, he might not have noticed the difference.

He'd say this for Chloe Lawrence—she was a hell of an actress.

She swung around to face Dustin. An inane giggle issued forth from her mouth. She was smart, Pete had to give her that. Dustin Yardley would never admit to being outmaneuvered by a girl.

"I'm so glad Mortimer trusted you enough to call you first," she said, her voice rising on the end as if she were asking a question.

Pete frowned at her. He understood what she was doing, but that didn't mean he had to like it.

Then again, when had she ever done anything he'd liked? He didn't like the way she ran the rodeo. He didn't like the changes she wanted to institute. He didn't like the way she used the rodeo to promote her own princess-ness.

The All-Stars wasn't about Chloe Lawrence. It didn't exist to sell clothing or stuffed animals or—God help him—Lawrence Oil, a subsidiary of Lawrence Energies, owned solely by the Lawrence family. The All-Around All-Stars existed for one reason and one reason only—to celebrate the best of the best of ranchers and cowboys. To take pride in ranching. To connect them to the tough men and women who had tamed the Wild West.

None of those things applied to Chloe Lawrence. She'd been born in New York, for God's sake.

Dustin looked confused. The man was mucking this up. Then, at the last possible second, Dustin got a grip on the situation. "Yeah, good old Steve. I, uh, didn't have any room, uh, in my trailer. For his horses. I was glad Pete was able to pick up the slack."

Yeah, *that* was believable.

"But that doesn't change anything else," Dustin went on, talking over Chloe's head to Pete. "It's not right to have women riding in our rodeo. They're distracting and they could get hurt. She's the goddamned Princess of the Rodeo. She shouldn't be making decisions like this, and God save us all from that arrogant ass of a brother of hers."

"Which one?" someone from the crowd asked.

"They're both asses," Dustin announced with grim satisfaction.

Pete watched the tension ripple down Chloe's shoulders and he knew without even looking at her face that she had lost her innocent mask and was about to tear Dustin a well-deserved new one. But before she could launch into her tirade, Pete stepped forward. "How about a compromise?"

"How about you go screw yourself?" Chloe said under her voice.

Pete damn near bit his tongue, trying not to laugh at that quiet jab. Never let it be said the woman didn't give as good as she got.

"Ms. Lawrence isn't wrong," he went on as if she hadn't just insulted him. "A rising tide does lift all boats. Making the All-Stars bigger will mean more money for you, for the riders and, yes, for management. And she's not wrong that having a woman ranked in the top ten in the Total Bull Challenge has brought in a lot more money to that outfit. Are you guys trying to tell me you would rather remain a second-tier rodeo organization rather than open up the All-Stars to new blood?"

Dustin glared at him, but that was to be expected. Pete was more concerned about what Mort and Dale and the riders would think. If other people bought into Dustin's way of thinking, Chloe would dig in her heels and the rift could tear the All-Stars apart. A flash of terror spiked through him. That was definitely *not* part of the plan. He wanted his rodeo back intact, thank you very much.

Chloe turned so she could look at Pete sideways. "Have you been replaced by aliens or something?" she asked in that same quiet voice, and oddly, he was reassured that she didn't sound inane or ditzy.

He wanted to deal with the real Chloe Lawrence. No tricks, no deceptions.

Which was ridiculous because he was actively engaging in deception as they spoke.

"Doesn't sound much like a compromise," Dustin grumbled.

"I'm getting to that." Pete put on a good grin, the kind he used in bars on Friday nights when a pretty girl caught his eye. "We all want to make more money and Chloe has a few interesting ideas that are taking a lot of her time and attention."

She kicked at the dirt. "A *few*?" But again, she was talking only to him.

He ignored her, knowing it would do nothing but piss her off. "Maybe it'd be best if we let her focus on high-level marketing and expansion stuff, the kind that will bring in new viewers and new fans, and leave the nitty-gritty details to someone who doesn't mind getting his hands dirty, someone people know and trust."

"We?" she challenged. Damn. Pete had been hoping that would slip right past her.

"Someone like you?" Dale said on cue. Thank God someone was hitting their marks today.

"I am going to kill you," she whispered even as her eyes lit up and she smiled as if this were a great idea. *"Slowly."*

He ducked his head as he stepped around her. "You can try," he whispered back, and then he turned his attention to the gentlemen gathered around him. "What do you all say? Does that sound like a workable solution? Chloe can keep doing her part to move the rodeo forward and I can handle everything else." He winked at the crowd where Chloe couldn't see it.

Dustin looked like he wanted to challenge someone to a gunfight, but Pete had most everyone else and that was the important part.

"Might not be a bad idea," Dale mused. "After all, we know and respect Pete."

Pete couldn't see Chloe's face, but he heard the sharp intake of breath at what wasn't said. Sure, they all knew and respected Pete—but they didn't respect her. It didn't matter how long she'd been riding at the All-Stars rodeos.

She would never really belong here. It was high time she realized that.

"Well," she managed to say in a voice that sounded relieved, if a little airheaded. "I'm so glad *we* were able to find a solution that works for everyone! And Mr. Wellington, I'm extra glad you are able to bring your horses all the way to the Bootheel." Her grin was so bright it about blinded him. "I'd like to remind everyone that showtime is in three hours and we do have a sold-out crowd tonight and an almost sold-out crowd tomorrow night. Let's give these people a reason to come back that doesn't involve funnel cakes."

She got a little bit of a laugh for this and she kept that big smile going, but Pete could see the light dying in her eyes a little bit.

Good. That's just what he wanted. He didn't feel the least bit sorry that she'd been overthrown in a mutiny. It was past time she found out what it was like to have a usurper sitting on the throne of one's inheritance.

Still... Watching her grit her teeth as she shook hands with cowboys bothered Pete a little bit. These men had been nothing but rude to her today. Some of them had dressed it up with prettier language than others, but still. She had to pretend like this was all hunky-dory because if she punched someone like her brother would've, they'd start in on how it was more proof that women shouldn't be in charge of these things.

That's just the way it went. What was done was done and the end justified the means. He had successfully accomplished the first step in taking back *his* rodeo and he couldn't afford to let things get personal. Nothing he felt for Chloe was personal and that was *final*.

She turned to him. "When you get time," she said, sweetness dripping off every word, "I'd like to go over your new duties with you."

Which meant she was going to try to destroy him. Pete grinned. He'd like to see her try. "Absolutely," he told her, fighting the odd urge to bow. "You're the boss."

Fire danced in her eyes, promising terrible, wonderful things. She tilted her head in acknowledgment of this false platitude and then sashayed off, her head held high and her hips swaying in a seductive rhythm. Pete knew he wasn't the only one watching the Princess of the Rodeo leave him in the dust. The woman was an eyeful.

Just as she got to the gate, she turned and looked back over her shoulder. Sunshine lit her from behind, framing her in a golden glow. Damn, she was picture-perfect, every fantasy he'd ever had come to life. If he didn't know who she was, he'd be beating these other idiots off with a stick to get to her first.

But he did know. She was an illusion, a mirage. She dressed the part, but she was nothing but a city slicker and interloper. A gorgeous, intelligent, driven interloper.

Their gazes collided and his pulse began to pound with something that felt an awful lot like lust. Even at this distance, he could feel the weight of her anger slicing through the air, hitting him midchest.

Oowee, if looks could kill, he'd be bleeding out in the dirt.

With a flip of her hair, she was gone.

"Well, how about that," Dale said, laughter in his voice. "You got your work cut out for you, Pete."

Oh, yeah, he was going to have his hands full, all right.

It was time to show Chloe Lawrence that the All-Stars was his. But she wasn't going to make this easy.

The thought made him smile. He was already starting to like this job.

Three

Chloe's hands were shaking as she sat at her makeshift makeup table in her makeshift dressing room. Which made applying her false eyelashes somewhat of a challenge. She forced herself to take a few deep breaths.

She was going to kill Pete Wellington. It wasn't a question of *if*. It was a question of *how*.

She'd love to run him down with her glossy palomino—but Wonder was at home, enjoying her hay and oats at Sunshine Ridge, Chloe's small ranch retreat northeast of Dallas. With all the things she had to juggle, she couldn't handle taking care of her horse, too. It wasn't fair to Wonder and it wasn't fair to Chloe. So she was borrowing a horse for her big entrance tonight.

Frankly, it didn't feel right running Pete down with a borrowed horse. Too many complications.

That man was up to something. If Steve Mortimer had had a problem getting his horses to the Bootheel, he would've called Chloe. It was obvious Mortimer had no such problems.

What kind of deal had Pete made with the stock contractors?

And how did backing her up when she was under siege figure into it? Because he wasn't doing it solely out of the kindness of his heart. This was Pete Wellington she was talking about—there was no kindness in his heart. Not for her or anyone in her family. She didn't want to offer him a job. She didn't want him anywhere near her. But...

If she didn't hand off some of the responsibilities to Pete, would people break their contractual obligations in protest? She could hire someone else but then she'd have the exact same problem—the people who made the rodeos work would balk at dealing with an outsider. By the time she found a workable solution, the All-Stars might very well die on the vine. And who would take the blame for that?

She would.

Maybe she could arrange a stampede. Watching Pete get pulverized would be immensely satisfying.

There. Her hands were steady. Who knew thinking of ways to off her nemesis would be so calming?

Now she applied the false lashes easily. She wore them for the shows because she was moving around the arena at a controlled canter. If she didn't have over-the-top makeup and hair—not to mention the sequins—people wouldn't be able to see any part of her. She'd be nothing but an indistinct blur.

And if there was one thing the Princess of the Rodeo wasn't, it was *indistinct*.

She was halfway through the second lashes when someone knocked on her dressing room door. If one could call this broom closet a dressing room, that was. Hopefully, that was Ginger, who sat on the local board of this rodeo. If anyone could talk some sense into those stubborn old mules, it'd be Ginger. She took no crap from anyone.

Chloe still had an hour and a half before showtime, but the gates were already open and she needed to be out in the crowd, posing for pictures and hand selling the Princess clothing line. She was behind schedule thanks to Pete Wellington, the jerk. She finished the lashes and said, "Come in."

Of course it wasn't Ginger. *Of course* it was Pete Wellington, poking his head around the door and then recoiling in shock.

"What do you want?" she asked, fighting the urge to drop her head in her hands. She didn't want to mess up her extravagant eye shadow, after all. Then she'd be even further behind schedule.

He was here for a reason. Was it the usual reason—he wanted his rodeo back? Or was there something else?

"I want you to put on some damned clothes," Pete said through the open door. At least he wasn't staring.

Chloe frowned at her reflection. "It's a sports bra, Pete. It's the same one I wear when I go jogging. The same basic style women across the country wear when they're working out."

It was a really good bra, too. Chloe had perfectly average breasts. And she'd come to a place in her life where she was happy with perfectly average breasts. She liked them. They were just right. Anything bigger would make cantering around arenas every weekend downright painful.

That didn't mean she hadn't gone out of her way to buy a high-end sports bra that provided plenty of padding. Everything about the Princess of the Rodeo was bigger, after all. She did a little shimmy, but nothing below her neck moved. She was locked and loaded in this thing and her boobs looked good. And completely covered. "It's not like you can see my nipples or anything."

"Dammit, Chloe, it's a *bra*," he growled back through the door. "I can't... You're... Look, just put on some clothes. *Please*."

Oh, she liked that note of desperation in his voice. Was it possible she'd misread the situation? For almost ten years now, she and Pete had been snarling at each other across arenas and in parking lots. She'd always thought her physical attributes had no impact on him because he'd never reacted to her before in that way.

But he was reacting now. She could hear the strain in his voice when he added, "Are you decent yet, woman?"

She stood, her reflection grinning back at her. "I don't know what you're complaining about," she said, plucking the heavily sequined white shirt off the hanger and sliding her arms through the sleeves. "I'd be willing to bet large sums of money you've seen your sister in a sports bra and never thought twice about it. And yes, I'm decent."

"Let's get one thing straight, Lawrence—you are *not* my..." Pete pushed his way into the dressing room, which was not designed to hold a man his size. The space between them—no more than a foot and half—sparked with heat as his gaze fell to her chest. "Sister," he finished, his voice coming out almost strangled as he stared at the open front of her shirt.

"Thank God for that," Chloe said lightly as she brushed her hands over the sequins—which conveniently lay over the sides of her breasts. "I pity Marie for having to put up with you, I really do."

She'd never had a problem with Marie Wellington, who worked her wife's ranch in western Texas. But then again, Marie had made it clear some years ago that she didn't care if the Wellingtons got control of the All-Stars or not. "It's just a rodeo," Marie had confided over a beer with Chloe one night. "I don't know why Pete can't let it go."

In the years since then, Chloe hadn't gotten any closer to finding out why, either. But if the man was going to torture her, she was going to return the favor—in spades.

Her hands reached the bottom of the shirt and she took her time making sure the hem was lined up.

Pete's mouth flopped open as Chloe closed the shirt, one button at a time. She probably could've asked him for the keys to his truck and he would've handed them over without even blinking. She had him completely stunned and that made him...vulnerable.

To her.

She let her fingers linger over that button right between her breasts as Pete began breathing harder, his eyes darkening. The cords of his neck began to bulge out and she had the wildest urge to lick her way up and down them. The space between them seemed to shrink, even though neither of them moved. Her skin heated as he stared, tension coiling low in her belly.

Crap, she'd miscalculated again. Did she have Pete Wellington at her mercy? Pretty much. But she hadn't accounted for the fact that desire could be a two-way street. He'd always been an intensely handsome man. She wasn't too proud to admit she'd had a crush on him for a couple years when she'd first started riding at the rodeos, until it became clear that he would never view her as anything more than an obstacle to regaining his rodeo.

But the way he was looking at her right now, naked lust in his eyes instead of sneering contempt?

He wanted her. And that?

That took everything handsome about him and made him almost unbearably gorgeous. Her pulse began to pound and, as she skimmed her fingers up her chest to ostensibly reach for the next button, she had to fight back a moan.

"There," she said as she fastened the last button, and dammit, her voice came out breathy. "Is that decent enough for you?"

Pete's gaze lingered on her body for another two seconds before he wrenched his whole head up. His eyes were glazed. She probably couldn't have stunned him any better than if she'd hit him on the head with a two-by-four. Chloe had to bite her lower lip to keep from saying something wildly inappropriate, like *I'll undo all of those buttons while you watch* or maybe just a simple, effective *your turn*.

Talk about wildly inappropriate. Instead, she said, "What do you want?" because that was the question she needed the answer to.

His presence wasn't an accident and he was plotting something. But her words didn't come out as an accusation. At least, it didn't sound like one to her. It almost sounded like…an invitation.

He swallowed hard, his Adam's apple bobbing with the motion. The look in his eyes said one word and one word only—*you*. "We, uh, have to talk. About the job."

Right, right. The job. The rodeo. The feud between their families, going back over thirteen years. The way she knew he was here to undermine her but she wasn't sure how supporting her was going to help with that.

None of that had a damned thing to do with the way his eyes devoured her.

She turned and bent at the waist to check her makeup in the small travel mirror. Pete made a noise behind her that sounded suspiciously like a groan. She glanced back at him in the reflection and saw that he was, predictably, staring at her behind. "Yes, the job. The one you volunteered yourself for?"

"Yeah." He swallowed again. "That job."

She reached over and picked up her chaps. They were show chaps, bright white leather that had never seen a speck of dirt or a spot of cow manure. With supple fringe at the edges, the chaps had "All-Stars" worked in beads running vertically down each of her thighs and then, at the widest part of the chaps at the bottom, "Princess of the Rodeo" had been spelled out in eye-popping gems of pink and silver. Nothing about these chaps were subtle and everything was designed to catch the eye. She always wore the white outfit on the first night of the rodeo. The second night, she had another matching outfit in patriotic red, white and blue. Those chaps were so covered with rhinestones she needed help mounting up in the saddle.

"What I'm trying to figure out," she said, propping one leg up on the chair and strapping the chap around her upper thigh, "is why you want the job, Pete. By all accounts, you don't need the money. I know Marie's ranch does well, too."

Chloe had done her research—he was quite well off. He wasn't at the same level the Lawrence family was, but his net worth meant he didn't *need* this job. Gorgeous, wealthy, rugged—Pete Wellington was a hell of a catch no matter how she looked at him.

And she was looking at him right now. He stared at her with naked desire and she could feel her traitorous body reacting. If it weren't for his hell-bent vendetta, she'd be tempted.

A shudder worked through her body as she went on, "And you haven't exactly shown a willingness to work beneath a woman in general or me in specific."

He had his thumbs hooked into his belt, but he was gripping the leather so hard his knuckles were white. She'd put a lot of money on the fact that he wouldn't be able to tell her what she'd just said.

But this man was just full of surprises, wasn't he? "I never said I have any problem working under you," he said in a low voice that made that tight coil of desire in her stomach painfully tighter. "In fact, I'm beginning to think it's a good idea to have you over me."

Her fingers fumbled with the strap and she had to stop before the heavy leather fell off her leg entirely. Her hands were shaking again, but this time it wasn't with rage.

Damn this man. Even when he pissed the hell out of her, he still had the capacity to make her want him. At least this time, she knew she'd made him want her, too.

It wasn't so much cold comfort as it was outright torture, however.

She took a deep breath, hoping to clear her head—but it didn't work because now his scent was filling this tiny space. Leather and dirt and musk. He smelled exactly like a cowboy should, rough and maybe a little dirty but so, *so* right.

"Good," she managed to get out, but she didn't sound in charge by any stretch of the imagination. "I'm glad you're coming to your senses." There. She managed to get the straps on the first chap done and turned her attention to the second chap. Which required her to switch legs. She leaned into the mild stretch and this time, Pete definitely groaned.

She couldn't think of anything to say that wouldn't come out as "Could you help me with this?" and no matter how hot he was making her, she was absolutely not about to have sex with Pete Wellington in a glorified broom closet.

Or anywhere else, she mentally corrected.

Sex with Pete Wellington was completely off the table. Or any other flat surface. That was final.

So she kept her mouth shut as she worked at the buckle. When she had that one done, she belted the chaps at her waist, which finished the whole look off with the giant belt buckle that had *Princess* worked in Swarovski crystals. Her dad had commissioned it for her when she'd turned eighteen.

She turned back to the mirror, trying not to look at the man behind her, but it wasn't easy. He must've taken a step forward at some point because he loomed over her now. She could feel his breath messing up her carefully curled hair and it was tempting—so damned *tempting*—to lean back into that broad chest, just to see what he'd do. Would he push her hair to the side and press his lips against the little bit of skin right below her ear? Cup her breasts through the sequins? Run his hands down her waist and around to her denim-clad butt?

She physically shook as these thoughts tumbled through her mind. She never hooked up at any of the All-Stars events—which was both company policy and her own personal rule. Cowboys were off-limits. But she lived out of a suitcase seven months of the year, which didn't make it easy to have relationships, either.

It'd been too long since a man had gotten this close to her.

Why, oh why did it have to be Pete *freaking* Wellington? He might be turning her on and she might be driving him crazy, but a little raw sexual attraction didn't change anything. He wasn't here by accident and she couldn't give him any more leverage over her. For all she knew, this attraction was part of whatever con he was running. Get her in a compromising position and blackmail her or something.

She leaned forward and plucked her white Stetson out of its travel case. The hat had a fancy sparkling crown that matched her chaps. She carefully set it on her head, making sure not to disrupt the curls she'd teased into her hair. There. Now she was the Princess of the Rodeo.

"Chloe…" Pete spoke the moment before his hands came to rest around her waist.

Her breath caught in her throat at the feel of his strong hands touching her. Had they ever touched before?

Ten years they'd been dancing around each other, slinging insults and innuendos in a never-ending attempt to come out on top—but had they ever actually *touched*?

She didn't think so because she would've remembered the electric feel of his fingers on her body, the rush of heat that flowed out from this connection.

How would his rough, calloused hands feel against her bare skin?

"Yes?" Her gaze caught his in the mirror. She wanted

to cover his hands with her own, lace their fingers together. She wanted to pull him closer.

She had lost her ever-loving mind.

But even that realization didn't make her move. She couldn't. She had to know what he was going to say. His mouth opened and she held her breath.

Bam bam bam. The crappy door to this closet practically bowed under the force of the pounding as Flash called out, "Chloe! You in there?"

Pete dropped his hands and backed up so fast he tripped over her rolling luggage and all but fell into the far corner of the tiny space. Chloe tried not to groan out loud. There was no situation her brother couldn't make worse. "Yeah, I'm almost ready." To Pete, she hissed, "Here's the deal, Wellington. I know whatever you're doing is a trap, but…"

"But?" he replied, almost—but not quite—pulling off a nonchalant look. He was breathing too hard to look casual about anything.

She didn't miss his lack of a denial. Right. Nothing like a confirmation that he was completely untrustworthy to help squash her rampant desire.

She took a deep breath, inhaling more of his scent, and did something she'd sworn she'd never do. She admitted weakness to Pete Wellington. "But you're not wrong that I need a little help handling the stock contractors and the cowboys. Do you legitimately want to work with the All-Around All-Stars Rodeo?"

He had the nerve to look indignant. "Isn't that all I've ever wanted?"

"No," she whispered furiously. "You've always wanted to put me in my place."

"Did we determine if that was above me or below me?" he asked with a sly grin.

And just like that, they were right back to the same place they'd always been. She ignored his question. "I will tolerate your presence as long as you do what I say, when I say it. If you can convince the locals to get on board with my ideas, then you can stay. But the moment you undermine me, you're gone and I'll see to it you never set foot at an All-Stars event ever again. Understood?"

Flash banged on the door again. "Chloe? Is everything all right? I heard Pete Wellington is here. Do you know what that asshole wants?"

Irritating little brothers would always be irritating, even if they weren't little anymore. She had no idea if she was pissed at Flash or thankful that he'd interrupted the madness she and Pete had been barreling toward at top speed. "One second, for God's sake," she snapped. She jabbed a finger in Pete's direction, but she made sure not to touch him. "Understood?"

It took him a while before he responded. She could practically see the lust fading away, replaced with his usual condescension. "Understood, *boss*."

"Can you handle leaving my dressing room without getting caught?"

He gave her a dull look. "Go before he breaks down the damned door."

She threw the door open—which conveniently slammed into Pete's chest. She gave him one last warning look and then had to dodge Flash's next knock as she quickly walked away from her dressing room. "What?"

Thank God Flash followed her. He already had his chaps belted on, but unlike hers, Flash's weren't all that flashy. Dirt and muck from the arenas he'd been riding in for the last six years had permanently worked into the creases. Chaps that had once been a light brown with a darker brown diamond pattern down the leg were now just…dirty brown. "Who's the act tomorrow night?"

"You had to interrupt me getting ready to ask me a question you could have looked up on the internet?"

She was *so* done with this day, honestly. She needed a stiff drink and maybe a video call with her sister-in-law, Renee Lawrence. She and Renee had been best friends back when Chloe had grown up in New York City, before Milt Lawrence had won the All-Stars in that ill-fated poker game and relocated his entire family to Dallas.

A few months ago, Renee had gotten into a little trouble—which was the nicest way anyone could say her husband had committed suicide rather than face charges for his part in what the newspapers had dubbed the Preston Pyramid, the largest financial con in American history. Renee had come to Dallas looking for Chloe but had found Oliver, the oldest of the Lawrence children and somehow, two people who had driven each other crazy as kids had absolutely clicked as adults. Now one of Chloe's oldest, dearest friends was her sister.

She could use some girl time, frankly, away from the overwhelming masculinity of the rodeo. Renee had no history with Pete Wellington either, so Chloe could work through her suddenly complicated feelings.

But instead she had Flash.

Her brother scratched the back of his neck. "Yeah, yeah, I know. I was just wondering…you know, if the act had changed."

Flash was many things—a cocky pain in the butt, mostly—but hesitant wasn't one of them. To see him hemming and hawing was unsettling, frankly. "What? Were you hoping to see someone else?"

"Never mind. Forget I said anything."

She stared at her brother. Why did she think this was about a woman? When it came to Flash Lawrence, he only cared about two things—women or earning his place at the All-Stars table.

Then it hit her. "Is this about Brooke Bonner?"

"No," he answered quickly, but his cheeks shot red. "Uh-huh."

At the All-Stars rodeo in Fort Worth early in the season, Brooke had been an up-and-coming country star. And it hadn't escaped Chloe's notice that Flash and Brooke had both disappeared about the same time after the rides and before Brooke's show. They'd had to delay the start of the concert for twenty minutes before Brooke had reappeared, claiming she'd gotten lost backstage.

If Chloe had the time or mental energy, she'd go for Flash's jugular over his country-star crush because the man had earned more than a little crap for all the times he'd made Chloe's life that much more complicated. But today, she didn't have it in her. She was late, still flustered from whatever the hell had happened between her and Pete and still furious that none of the stock contractors were willing to agree to her ideas until Pete declared them okay. So instead of ribbing her brother, she only said, "If there's any change in the music line-ups, I'll let you know. Okay?"

"Okay, thanks." Her baby brother smiled at her, the good smile that drew buckle bunnies to him like moths to a flame. But underneath that cocky grin was relief.

"But," she went on, "you owe me." Before Flash could interrupt her, she went on, "Yes, Pete Wellington is here. And I've hired him—on a trial basis," she practically had to shout over Flash's holler of disbelief.

"He's going to run interference with the stock contractors. I'm asking you as a sister and ordering you as your boss not to start anything with him. Okay?"

"Have you lost your ever-loving mind?" Flash demanded, scuffing the toe of his boot into the dirt. "You can't trust that man. He's out to take us all down."

"Who said I trusted him?" No, she didn't trust Pete at all. But aside from Flash, she was alone in that judgment. Everyone else here had made their feelings crystal clear—they'd pick Pete over her every day of the week.

She just needed a little help while she pushed the All-Stars through this transition phase, that was all. She'd make full use of Pete's ability to get cowboys to shut up and go along with the plan and then, when she had the All-Stars positioned properly, she'd cut him loose.

All there was to this…relationship with Pete Wellington was a calculated risk. He was betting he could trick her out of the rodeo, somehow. She was betting he was no match for her. He might be gorgeous, wealthy and awfully good with a rope, but she was a Lawrence.

Flash looked doubtful, so Chloe went on, "Look—trust me. I know what I'm doing and I know what he's trying to do—but I can handle him. Just don't pick a fight with him, okay?"

"If you need someone to run interference, why not just ask me?"

The hell of it was, Flash meant that. He hadn't seen the messes she'd had to clean up after all his other attempts to "help." Flash would always be a big bull in a very tiny china shop.

"Because," she explained, "you want to be a rider, not a Lawrence. You start meddling in the show management and no one will ever believe you've earned your ranking."

Flash was hell-bent on being one of the best all-around riders in the world, which meant riding with the All-Stars. But the problem with riding the rodeo circuit your family owned was that no one believed he hadn't just bought his way into the rankings. Everyone—even the competitors who watched him ride night after night—believed he was here only because he was a Lawrence.

"Fine," he grumbled. "You're right. But why does it have to be Pete?"

Chloe grit her teeth. "Because everyone else already respects him. They listen to him." And not to her.

She pushed that thought aside and went on, "If I bring in someone new, it'll take months—maybe years—before they're willing to try something different and I have plans, Flash. I want them in place before the next season starts." That was the one area where Pete had her up against a wall.

No, no—wrong mental image. Because Pete would never have her up against a wall.

But she needed his connections and goodwill *now*.

Flash scowled. "If Pete gives you any crap at all, I'll beat the hell out of him."

"Agreed," she said and then pasted on her big smile as a family with two little girls spotted them. "Well, now—who are these two beautiful princesses?"

The girls squealed and hugged her and Chloe posed for pictures with the mom and her daughters and then, with surprisingly good humor, Flash posed with the dad.

By then, other people had noticed the Princess of the Rodeo and a crowd formed. As Chloe posed for another picture, she saw Pete Wellington in the distance, talking with a few of the riders. As if he could sense her gaze upon him, he turned. And tipped his hat in her direction.

Another thrill of pleasure went through her at the gentlemanly gesture. No, she didn't trust him. Not a damned bit. But it looked like they were working together from here on out.

This was a bad idea.

After what had almost happened in the dressing room? It was a horrible idea, one that almost guaranteed failure.

But as long as she kept her fantasies to herself and Pete's hands off her body, it'd be fine.

No problem, right?

Four

Pete watched the opening procession from the top of the bull chutes. God, he'd missed being up here.

Chloe was, predictably, first in line. His gut tightened as he looked at the way she sat in the saddle and remembered the way she'd looked in nothing more than a pair of skin-tight jeans and a bra, for God's sake, acting as if that were the most normal thing in the world. To say nothing of the way her nimble fingers had worked at the buckles of those ostentatious chaps as she strapped them on over her long, lean thighs…

He cleared his throat and shifted his legs, trying to take the pressure off his groin as Chloe stood in her stirrups, her ass cupped by those chaps.

When she'd first started this princess crap, Pete had been twenty-three. That he remembered clearly because his dad had stopped by for his birthday and…well, Pete wasn't proud of what he'd done. But he'd been twenty-three and pissed as hell that the Lawrences were making a mockery of his rodeo. He couldn't take out his anger on a cute teenager like Chloe and her dad would've pressed charges if Pete had punched him. Besides, it'd been Davey Wellington's fault that Pete had lost his whole world in one drunken bet.

Even now, the betrayal still burned. The All-Stars had been the one thing he'd shared with his father and yet, Davey Wellington had just drunkenly gambled it away like the circuit hadn't meant anything to him. Like…like all the time he and Pete had spent together at rodeos hadn't meant anything.

When Pete had come into his oil money, Dad had been sick, with just a few months left. Pete had sucked up his pride and made Milt Lawrence an offer to buy back the All-Stars so that Pete and Davey could have a chance to relive those happier times. Pete had been determined to make things right. He'd even offered to let Chloe keep riding as the Princess of the Rodeo, if it would've made her happy.

Only to have the old man laugh in his face and have security escort Pete out of the building. Then he'd promptly kicked Pete off the All-Stars circuit.

After that, it was *war*.

Pete looked at the arena, at the families having a good time. His gaze traveled back behind the chutes, where riders and cowgirls were all humming with energy for the competition and he felt it again—that sense of homecoming. This was where he belonged. All of this should've been Pete's. Now that Dad was gone, this should've been his family because rodeo was family.

Instead, it was Chloe's.

But not for much longer.

Chloe was announced and she kicked her horse into

a gallop, an enormous American flag billowing above her head. Pete followed her with his gaze. He wasn't staring. Everyone was watching her circle around the arena at top speed, expertly guiding her borrowed mount through the curves.

Huh. He didn't remember her riding quite so well. It'd been a while since he'd been able to bring himself to watch this farce. The last time he'd suffered through Chloe riding had been...a few years ago. Four, maybe?

She looked good up there.

She'd looked good in that closet, too, buttoning her shirt over her breasts, her breath coming hard and fast when he'd stepped in behind her and rested his hands on her waist. If Flash hadn't interrupted them...

"Do you have any idea what I'm going to do to you if you screw with my sister?"

Speak of the devil. Pete refused to cede any space as Flash Lawrence squeezed in next to him at the top of the chute, his big black hat pulled low over his head. A nervous energy hummed off Flash, which made him a decent rider in the arena and a loose cannon out of it.

Pete gave it a second before he replied and he made damned sure to sound bored as he said, "I imagine you'll talk a big game, throw a few wild punches, then get drunk and stumble off with the first buckle bunny who catches your eye. As usual." He was speaking from personal experience with Flash. The kid had caught him by surprise one night and given him a hell of a black eye.

Of course, Pete had returned the favor. Anyone who was old enough to get drunk and start a fight was old enough to finish one—on the floor, if need be. Which was where Flash had wound up after Pete had started swinging. It hadn't been a fair fight—Pete had a solid ten years on the kid and at least forty pounds. But Flash had started that one.

Out of the corner of his eye, Pete saw Flash's shoulders rise and fall. Pete couldn't tell if that was a sigh of resignation or a man fighting to keep control. But then Flash tilted his head and looked at Pete from underneath the brim of his hat. "You just can't let the past go, can you?"

Irritation rubbed over Pete's skin. "Sure I can. I don't hold it against you that you jumped me at a honky-tonk, do I?"

Flash snorted. "Yeah, you're clearly over it." He shifted, angling his entire body toward Pete. "We both know you're not here because you've moved on, Wellington." His voice dropped as the music shifted and the local rodeo queen led the rest of the procession out. He was quiet until the music hit a crescendo. "You hurt my sister and you won't have to worry about a barroom brawl."

"That sounds like a threat, Lawrence." But Pete was almost impressed with the bravado the kid was pulling off. Chloe wasn't the only one who'd grown up, it seemed.

Flash cracked a grin but it didn't reach his eyes. Those were hard with something that looked a lot like hatred. Pete recognized that look all too well. "Of course not, Wellie."

Pete gritted his teeth but otherwise didn't react. No way in hell he'd let someone who willingly chose to go by *Flash* get under his skin for a stupid nickname.

Flash slapped him on the shoulder and leaned forward. "It's a promise," he whispered and damn if a chill of dread didn't race down Pete's back because Flash Lawrence was doing a hell of a good job at pulling off *menacing.* He moved to walk past Pete but paused and added, "We'll be watching." Then he was gone.

The national anthem began to play and Pete whipped off his hat as Flash's words echoed around his head. Had the kid caught wind of Pete slipping out of Chloe's dressing room? Or was he simply fulfilling his brotherly duty?

Didn't matter. Either way, Flash hadn't told Pete anything he didn't already know.

The Lawrences didn't trust Pete.

They'd have to be total idiots to do so and, sadly, they weren't that stupid. But Pete knew that'd be the case going in. For his plan to work, he didn't need them to trust him.

He just needed a foot in the door and, for the time being, he had one.

He had to make the most of it because if he screwed this up, he'd never get his rodeo back.

The last of the crowd was filtering out under the starlit sky and the last chords of the last song were fading from the air when Chloe finally dragged her boots back to her dressing room, where Pete had been waiting for her for at least forty minutes. The sound from the concert back here had been distorted something awful, but he hadn't wanted to risk Chloe trying to give him the slip.

She was moving slow, her head down and any trace of the princess long gone. "Chloe."

She pulled up short. "Oh, it's you."

"Yup, still me," he agreed. For some reason, he wanted to grin at her.

"Are you going to follow me into my dressing room again?" Her bright show smile was nowhere to be seen.

She looked worn out. The fancy rodeo queen–style dress she'd changed into for the concert was literally weighing her down. The long, sequined skirt glowed in the dim light. Even in near dark, the woman still managed to shine.

He'd never seen her look so…less than perky. He should enjoy the fact that she looked like a bull had run over her because it was just more proof that she couldn't handle running the All-Stars. Oddly, though, that wasn't the emotion that snuck up on him. Instead, he felt an odd urge to wrap his arm around her shoulder and kiss her.

On the forehead, that was. Nowhere else.

He cleared his throat. "Nope." To hell with it. He did grin. "Not unless you want me to."

She made a noise of disgust. "Don't make me shoot you." But she said it without animosity as she trudged past him.

He caught her by the arm. Despite the summer heat, her dress had long lacy sleeves. "I do need to talk to you."

She opened her mouth as if she wanted to argue with him, but then stared down to where he was touching her. "Do you promise not to barge in on me this time?"

Something in her voice kicked his pulse up a notch. Yeah, he was fully aware she'd been messing with him earlier, using her stunning body to distract him and he wasn't too proud to admit that it had almost worked.

Okay, it *had* worked.

But that teasing sensuality was gone now and she sounded soft and vulnerable and it absolutely shouldn't affect him because he didn't like Chloe Lawrence. He didn't want her and he certainly didn't care one whit for her.

He let his hand trail down her arm until his fingers brushed against hers. Then he leaned in so he could say, "I promise," close to her ear.

She inhaled sharply, but only said, "Wait for me," before she pulled free and disappeared into her private closet.

Pete kicked up a heel on the nearby fence and exchanged a few pleasantries with the remaining riders milling around backstage. The only people still here were either roadies tearing down the stage or riders hoping to get an autograph after the concert. Most everyone else had secured their animals and headed to the bars. The stock contractors were long gone.

Pete scratched the back of his neck and did his level best not to think of Chloe changing clothes. He failed.

When had she changed out of her button-up shirt and jeans into that formal dress for the concert? Was she still wearing that sports bra? Or had she slipped into something slinkier, maybe something lacy that matched the dress? Something that cupped her breasts like a lover's hands and...

Pete slammed the door on any thoughts about Chloe's breasts, clothed or otherwise. He was thinking about... the long night ahead of him. Yeah, that was it. He didn't technically have a place to sleep tonight because his plan had come together way too late to get a room in this small Missouri town. All the hotels were sold out and had been for weeks, if not months, so he'd be in his truck tonight.

He looked up at the night sky. Chloe probably had a room, complete with a nice big bed, all to herself. Would she go right to sleep or would she shower to wash off the dust first?

Dammit. It was fine if she flaunted her hot body in an

attempt to throw him off his game. Her looks were just another weapon at her disposal and this was war. He expected nothing less. It was *not* fine if he let her succeed.

He wanted it in writing that he was the show manager. He'd already laid out a contingency plan if Chloe balked—he would skip the next rodeo in Terre Haute but he'd be back at the one in Little Rock. She might get rid of him once, but he wasn't going away.

He could do this. He could take back his rodeo a bit at a time and then…

And then what?

The door to her dressing room opened and there she was, almost unrecognizable. Gone were the big hair and the sparkly, over-the-top clothing. Her hair had been pulled back into a low tail and she had on flip-flops. Chloe wore a soft pair of black pants that fit her like a second skin and a loose tee that hung off one shoulder, revealing her bra strap. It was not the wide, white strap he'd gotten an eyeful of earlier, but something dark and, God help him, *lacy*.

"You're still here. Plotting, I presume?"

She said it in such an offhand way, as if it were common knowledge that he was out to undermine her and not a point of contention between them. And she said it without the least hint of drama. He was her problem and she was going to meet him head-on.

Was it possible he was starting to do the unthinkable? Was he starting to *respect* Chloe Lawrence?

God help him, he just might be.

"We didn't discuss terms earlier."

She adjusted a small duffel slung over one shoulder and tilted her head to the side. The mass of hair she'd bound back fell over one shoulder and he had to fight the urge to bury his hands in it.

"Earlier?" she asked. "Ah, yes—when you freaked out and then watched me get dressed. You're right, I don't remember much discussion happening then."

He might have underestimated this woman. "I don't think 'freaked out' is an appropriate—"

"Freaked. Out." Then the worst thing in the world happened. She smiled. Warmth bloomed in Pete's chest as the moonlight glinted off her mouth.

"Surprised," he corrected.

"Fine." She looked around and rolled her shoulders as if they were tight with tension. Pete had to clench his fists to keep from stepping behind her and rubbing his thumbs into her exposed skin. "This is probably a terrible idea."

"Which part? The part where I barged in on you? Or the part where you agreed to hire me?" It felt risky asking that, but hey—maybe being casual was the way to go. If she let down her guard...

"The part where I ask if you want to get something to eat."

"Now?" It was out of his mouth before he could stop it.

"Filled up on funnel cakes, did you?" He couldn't see it, but he swore he could hear her eyes roll. "Yes, *now*. I'm hungry. I'm tired. I'm not negotiating with you under cover of darkness, Pete."

He stepped into her and lifted the duffel from her shoulder. This close, the scent of her filled his nose. Something sweet, fruity maybe—but underneath that was the musk of a woman. She smelled good enough to eat. "What are you in the mood for?"

The air between them began to hum with tension. Chloe looked up at him, her face hidden in shadows and for one crazy second, he wanted her to say his name.

Hell.

"There's not much left open," she said and he might have been hearing things, but her words sounded breathless. "The bars…"

"Will have too many drunk cowboys and buckle bunnies." The thought of some young buck hitting on Chloe was enough to get his hackles up.

"I'm not eating fast food."

"I don't suppose there's a nice restaurant open this late, where I can buy you a good steak and a better bottle of wine?" A fancy candle-lit dinner with roses on the table and soft music in the background would…

Well, it'd be the wrong thing. She certainly didn't deserve to be wined and dined.

"First off, not this late. And second off, I'm not putting that dress back on." She pulled away from him. "As long as we're not at the same bar Flash is at, it'll be fine. And he likes Jeremy's better. So we'll go to Mike's and get a corner booth and I'm getting a bacon cheeseburger. Deal?" She started walking toward her truck, a sleek black Ram pickup with custom pink swirls along the side.

"I'll buy you a beer. To celebrate our new partnership."

She stopped so suddenly she almost stumbled and looked back over her shoulder. Even though he couldn't make out the details of her face, he could feel the distrust radiating off her. "Don't start celebrating just yet, Wellington."

Yeah, he'd definitely underestimated her.

It was going to be a hell of a ride.

Five

"I'll get us a table," Pete said, his breath caressing Chloe's ear as his hand rested briefly on the small of her back. Then he was gone, cutting through the drunken crowds with a grace she wasn't sure she'd appreciated before this exact moment in time.

She shook her head, trying to get her thoughts in order. Dinner at eleven thirty at night with Pete was a truly bad idea, capping off a day full of spectacularly bad ideas. Chloe was starving and exhausted and the last thing she should be doing was standing in a bar filled with All-Stars riders dancing to a bad band, waiting for Pete Wellington to…take *care* of her, for pity's sake.

She'd lost her mind. That was the only reasonable explanation. She was not operating on all cylinders and Pete was the kind of opponent who'd take full advantage of her at her weakest.

No way in hell was she drinking a beer around the man.

At least Flash wasn't here. She couldn't deal with the headaches a Flash-Pete brawl would bring. She just wanted her dinner and maybe a dance and...

No, wait—no dancing. Absolutely not. Not even if Pete asked. Because if he pulled her into his arms and two-stepped her around the dance floor, his arms around her waist...well, she might do something that would make all previous terrible decisions look positively well planned.

Damn that man.

He was not sweeping her off her feet and she was not being swept. This was all part of the same dance they always did around each other. He was just mounting a different sort of assault and she was doing her best to fend him off.

Wasn't she?

The noise was deafening and the bar was hot with the press of bodies. The rodeo was a huge deal in this small town, one of the biggest weekends in the entire year and it felt like half of Missouri was packed into this one bar. It wouldn't be any better at the other one, she knew.

Ugh, what a mistake. There was no way she could negotiate with Pete in here at any volume other than bellowing. It only got worse when he made his way back to her and shouted in her ear, "No place to sit."

She sagged into him a bit but then he yelled, "I found a waitress. If you don't mind, we can order to go and eat on the tailgate..."

Mind? Hell no, she didn't mind. What she minded was that Pete had not only come to the same conclusions she had, but had already found a workable solution that bordered on thoughtfulness.

She nodded.

"Bacon cheeseburger, right?"

Oh, Lord, she couldn't handle thoughtfulness, not from Pete Wellington. Not without some more sleep and distance between their bodies. "Double bacon cheeseburger and onion rings," she yelled back.

"Beer?"

"No."

He winked at her—a disturbing trend—and then disappeared into the crowd.

Chloe slipped out the door and instantly the volume ringing in her ears dropped to a manageable level. A breeze blew through, carrying away the smell of sweaty bodies and spilled beer.

Where had this day gone wrong? Oh, right—a bunch of sexist old men who might have been working with Pete. She had to remember that part.

So what was Pete trying to accomplish with all this thoughtfulness?

The same thing he was always trying to accomplish—getting his rodeo back. She didn't have any question about that. But she had to admire that he was going about it in a new way.

So he was trying to steal the All-Stars. Again. Reasoning with him had never worked before. How many times had she pointed out that it'd never really been his rodeo in the first place—it'd been his father's? He was not a fan of that logic.

So why was he turning on the charm now? Because he was and, heaven help her, she was in danger of being charmed.

Unless she missed her mark, he had one of two plans. Either he was going to push her out from the inside or...

A shiver ran down her back. Or he'd decided he could win her and get the rodeo all at once.

Sneaky. Very sneaky. The only problem with that second plan was that she wasn't anyone's prize to be won. Especially not his.

The door to Mike's swung open, bringing a blast of noise and heat. "Hey—" she started to say.

And pulled up short because it wasn't Pete.

Two men she'd never seen before all but fell out of the bar, giggling like schoolgirls. By the looks of their hats and T-shirts with the sleeves carefully torn off, she'd guess they were local boys out having a wild night.

They stumbled to a stop, holding each other up as they looked Chloe over with leering gazes. "Well, hellooo, nurse!" said the taller one, which made the shorter, beefier one giggle again.

She notched an eyebrow at the men and dropped back into a fighting stance. Bless her brothers for teaching her how to throw a punch. During her childhood in New York City, her mother and her nanny had shuttled Chloe to dance and gymnastics and music—all the standard classes for a girl of her social circle. Most of the time, Trixie Lawrence had also arranged shuttling for Renee Preston to the same classes. The two girls had been inseparable.

But when Chloe had started riding as the Princess of the Rodeo, her brothers had decided she should know how to throw a punch. And since it'd been one of those rare times when Oliver and Flash had agreed on something and since her father hadn't been in a big rush to get her back into dance classes, Chloe had gone along with it.

Thank God for that.

"Not interested," she said casually even as she slid

to the side, putting more space between her and the men while also making sure she had room to run if she needed. A good punch was a great thing, but if two guys got her pinned against the wall, the odds weren't in her favor.

"Ooh, lookie here," the shorter one said, leering drunkenly at her. "And I thought all the pretty girls were inside."

Hell, the odds already weren't in her favor. Outnumbered and outweighed—and these guys were drunk. Should she kick off her flip-flops? She knew she should have packed her sneakers, dammit. *"Not. Interested."*

"Waiting for us, honey?" the taller one added, stepping toward her. The shorter one almost tipped over without his support.

Why didn't men ever listen? Because they never did. How were these guys any different from Dustin Yardley refusing to try something just because a girl had suggested it? Or from Pete refusing to acknowledge that the damned All-Stars wasn't his?

"No means no," she said, shifting her weight and letting her fist fly as the tall guy made a clumsy grab at her. She couldn't deck Pete or Dustin or any of the other men who treated her as nothing but a pretty face, but by God she wasn't going to let this jerk assault her.

Her fist connected with a sickening-yet-satisfying crunch. Pain blossomed along her knuckles, making her gasp. But it was a good, solid punch. She hit him hard enough that he spun around, knocking back into his friend. The pair of them staggered until they landed in a heap next to the door.

"Why you little—" the one not bleeding said as the taller one made a muffled screaming noise.

"Leave me alone," she snarled, shifting her position again. Damn, her hand hurt. If she'd broken something, it'd be impossible to ride and carry the flag tomorrow night.

This was exactly why she never went out to the bars anymore. But the nice thing about anger was the adrenaline that came with it. Her hand stopped throbbing as the shorter guy threw off his buddy—still moaning—and scrambled awkwardly to his feet.

She couldn't throw another punch with the same hand, so she shifted again. She'd either get this one on an uppercut or she could try a well-placed kick, if she had the room to—

The door to the bar swung open and Pete came out. "They were out of onion...*hell*."

"Little help here?" Chloe said, trying to keep her voice calm. She didn't dare take her eyes off the guy on his feet.

"She bwoke my node!" howled the tall one. He'd made it to his knees, but blood was gushing down his face.

"Good." Pete cut past the one still on his feet. The shorter guy swayed, his fists up. "What the hell are *you* doing?" he demanded.

"Getting their asses kicked," Chloe muttered.

"Shut it," Pete snapped, thrusting the food back at her. Then he turned his attention to the men. "You've got five seconds to get the hell away from her."

The shorter one blinked before his hands fell to his side. "Sorry, dude—didn't know she was yours."

Oh, that just absolutely did it. "What the hell did you just say?" she shouted and suddenly Pete had her around the waist and was holding her back.

"Five," Pete growled. "Four. Then I'm letting her kick your ass while I laugh at you."

"Not worth the trouble," the shorter one muttered as he hefted his friend up.

Oh, she was going to show them trouble. "I'm gonna…"

"Chloe, stop," Pete hissed in her ear. Then he said, louder, "Three…"

"We're going, we're going. Come on, Jack."

"My *node*!" Jack howled.

"Two," Pete all but yelled, but the guys were already shuffling off into the dark, bouncing off parked cars and trucks and occasionally yelling insults over their shoulders.

Chloe twisted out of his grasp. "Do you have any idea how infuriating that is?" she yelled.

Pete backed up, his hands raised in the universal sign of surrender. "Easy, honey."

"I am *so* not your honey and you know it. I told them I wasn't interested. I told them to leave me alone and what do they do? Make a grab at me. All you had to do was show up and be a man and suddenly, there they go," she shouted, waving in the direction they had stumbled.

"…Be a man?" he asked, his confusion obvious.

She wanted to throw something. She'd already punched something and in all honesty, it hadn't helped. "Yes! Do you have any idea what that's like?"

"Being a man?"

"Of course you don't! Because you're a man!"

Pete stared at her as if a small alien had landed on her forehead. She groaned. Of course he didn't understand. He was probably enjoying the hell out of her emotional reaction—another thing he could throw back in her face to prove she wasn't capable of running the All-Stars.

Suddenly, she was tired. She looked down, trying to get her thoughts in order as the adrenaline burned away.

Oh. She'd dropped their dinner on the ground. Her eyes began to burn. "I... I'm sorry."

Pete stepped in front of her. "Chloe," he said softly, his hands resting on her shoulders. He gave her a little squeeze and she almost sank into him. "What on God's green earth are you apologizing for?"

"I dropped our food." She managed not to sniff, but it was a close thing. "And I lost my temper."

"And here I thought Flash had the short fuse in your family." His thumbs stroked over her shoulders and he made a low humming noise in the back of his throat. "Are you okay?"

No, not really. Her hand ached so much she could almost hear a high whine in her ears, and nothing had gone right today and she was so pitiful that she was on the verge of asking Pete Wellington, of all people, for a stinking hug.

Worst. Day. *Ever.*

"I'm fine," she said, trying to pull herself together because she couldn't give this man one more bullet to use as ammunition against her. She forced her head up, forced herself to meet Pete's gaze. "Why?"

"Why?" His lips quirked into a smile. "Oh, no reason." As he spoke, his hands drifted down her shoulders and then her arms until he lifted her hands and tilted them toward the street lamp. "Just that you broke the nose of an idiot who had a solid seven inches and sixty pounds on you."

"Seventy," she corrected. This time, she did sniff.

And then froze. Pete's gaze locked with hers as he lifted her bruised knuckles to his mouth and pressed his lips to her skin.

Heat flashed down her back and her knees weakened so fast that she staggered a little. Pete's arm was around her waist in a heartbeat even as he held on to her swollen hand. "Seventy, easy," he agreed as he supported her weight.

Which, of course, brought her chest flush with his. She wasn't strong enough, dammit. She just wasn't. Not after the day from hell, not after this man had come to her defense twice in one day. Yeah, it was a trap and a trick and a long con, but he was also thoughtful and charming and it was so damned nice not to have to fight another battle.

She didn't want to fight with him.

"Here's what we're going to do," he murmured, staring down into her eyes.

"What?" She couldn't even care that she sounded breathless as her nipples went hard.

He let go of her waist and her hand at the same time and she almost cried at the loss until, unexpectedly, he bent down and swept her off her feet.

Who knew Pete Wellington could be so bloody charming?

"I'm going to get you set up on the tailgate of my truck because my truck is farther from the front door, which means fewer idiots will be by to harass you." As he spoke, he carried her as if she was as light as a feather. "Then I'm going to get you dinner and a bag of ice for your hand."

"Ice would be great," she admitted, draping her arms around his neck and leaning her head against his shoulder. She shouldn't, but what the hell.

He wasn't lying, his truck was a heck of a lot farther away from the bar than hers. "Can I tell you something, if you promise you won't overreact?"

"Really?"

He looked down at her without breaking stride, that

quirky smile still in place. "Just don't punch me, Lawrence. I've seen the damage you can do."

Was that a compliment? "Fine. No punching. What?"

They finally reached his truck and he set her down so he could lower the tailgate. It was a really nice truck, top-of-the-line Ford Super Duty. "What happened to that old piece of crap truck you used to drive?" she asked. "The one that was half-rusted away?" She went to hop up, but she couldn't put her weight on her punching hand and hissed in pain.

He *tsked* and stepped in front of her. Before she could brace herself, Pete put his hands on her waist. Again, that delicious heat flashed over her skin. "The rust bucket? That's been gone a long time, hon. I've come up in the world."

She looked up at Pete as his grip around her waist tightened. This was where they'd been earlier today, before Flash had started banging on the door.

Flash wasn't here this time. "Clearly," she teased. "That's why you want to work for the All-Stars. Because you need the money."

But instead of coming back firing, he just stared down at her. "That's not why."

"Then why, Pete?" Her voice had gotten softer but then again, he'd gotten closer.

He didn't answer for a long time. Then, his mouth cocked into that half grin, he said, "You are, hands down, one of the most impressive women I've ever known," and the hell of it was he seemed completely sincere.

Before Chloe could react, he lifted her up and set her on the tailgate. Her eyes—and her mouth—were almost level with his now.

Not kissing Pete. No matter how good the compliments were.

"I bet you say that to all the girls who could break your nose with one punch," she managed to get out, but she couldn't bring herself to pull away.

"Nope. Just you."

Then he leaned forward and, despite all her resolve, her eyes fluttered closed in anticipation and one word floated through her mind—*finally*.

But instead of feeling his lips against hers, he kissed her on the forehead. Which was good. Great, even. It was sweet and it didn't presume anything and she was absolutely *not* disappointed.

Pete pulled away and headed back to the bar. "Stay here and try not to get into any more fights."

"They started it!" she called after him.

He stopped and looked at her over his shoulder. "But you finished it like a *boss*."

There was no mistaking the approval in his voice, warm and sweet.

Oh, heavens.

Was she starting to like Pete Wellington?

What else could go wrong today?

Six

As soon as Pete was sure Chloe couldn't see him, he took off at a dead run. If those assholes decided to double back, he had to get to them before they got to Chloe.

She might throw a hell of a punch against one drunk, but two would overwhelm her and if something happened…

He ran as fast as he could, weaving in and out of cars and trucks parked haphazardly around the bar. Finally, he found the idiots in question by a rusted-out Ford truck. The one with the busted nose was on his hands and knees, heaving up his guts, while the one who'd called Chloe rude names was sitting behind the wheel with his legs hanging out the door.

Man, Pete was tempted to go over there and finish what Chloe had started. They'd scared the hell out of her. No, she hadn't exactly admitted that, but Pete wasn't some clueless greenhorn. She'd been terrified. But her fear had been buried under anger.

For once, he was thankful for the Lawrence temper. Never thought he'd live to see the day.

It wouldn't take him long to dispose of these two—a couple of quick punches to make sure these guys stayed down for the rest of the night. But then...there might be witnesses and, knowing Chloe, she'd notice if he got blood on his shirt and then she'd tear into him again about how he was a *man*, as if that were a crime or something.

He needed to get back to her. So, after one final look to make sure the guys weren't going anywhere, he made his way to the bar.

What had she meant by that, anyway? Of course he was a man. He'd never had any question about who he was.

Their dinner was exactly where Chloe had dropped it. Pete checked the bags. The containers were dinged up and some fries had escaped, but it all still looked edible. He gathered everything up and then, rather than fighting his way through the crowd, he cut around to the back door and stuck his head into the kitchen. "Hey, can I get some ice? Please?"

The staff was none too pleased to be taking orders through the back door and they had no problem letting him know it, but every moment he stood here begging for ice was another moment Chloe was alone in his truck. He needed to get back to her.

He'd almost kissed her.

Hell, he had kissed her, but not where he'd wanted to. And as he'd touched her skin with his lips, he'd inhaled her scent. That close up, he'd been able to figure out what the fruity smell was—green apples. She'd smelled good enough to eat and he'd be lying if he said he wasn't tempted.

But he was stronger than temptation.

Kissing Chloe might be a nice fringe benefit in the moment, but it was not a part of his larger plans. Knowing how she thought, kissing her would most likely take his careful planning and throw it right out the window. Then where would he be?

Still on the outside, watching city slickers exploit his rodeo.

Finally, he got a grocery bag full of ice, although it was more thrown at his head than handed to him. He thanked the staff and hurried back to Chloe.

He slowed down once he had her in his sights. She'd scooted to one side and had one elbow resting on the edge of the truck bed, her chin resting on her forearm as she stared up at the night sky. Sweet merciful heavens, she looked like every girl in every country song and he had a wild impulse to drive off into the night until they found a quiet field and could curl up in the bed of his truck, watching the stars.

He shook his head to clear that vision away.

"It's me," he announced. Sneaking up on her tonight was a bad idea. "Any trouble?"

"No. It was as quiet as it gets this close to a bar." She sat up and took the ice from him. "Oh, that feels so good," she all but moaned as she covered her sore knuckles.

His body tightened at her words. And that was just for ice. How would she sound if he put his hands on her body? If he buried himself inside of her?

Focus, Pete.

"Here, wait." He opened the truck door and dug into his glove box, finally finding a clean bandanna. "Let me wrap that so you don't freeze your skin." She held her hand steady as he looped the bandanna over her knuckles. "Did you break anything, do you think?"

She shook her head as he got the ice situated. "It's sore, but everything moves like it's supposed to. Going to be hard to carry that flag tomorrow, though."

"If anyone could do it, it'd be you." He handed her the container with her burger and then hopped up next to her, putting the rest of the food between them. It seemed safer that way. "If you lost any fries, they're still in the bag. They look okay, just a little squashed." This felt wrong. She deserved so much more than greasy bar food.

"Thanks."

"Tell me about your plans for the All-Stars," he said after a few minutes had passed. "You really want to open up the events to women competitors?"

"Oh, yeah," she replied around a mouthful of fries. "I've analyzed the stats and the revenue streams from the Total Bull Challenge since June Spotted Elk made the circuit and, between the marketing aimed at new, mostly female viewers and the network distribution deals, she's responsible for a solid 15 percent bump in profits. Some people argue with that—but you can't tell me that the numbers are a coincidence."

"Huh," he said, mostly because he'd never figured Chloe would analyze revenue streams, much less stats.

"I'd love to find a breakout star like that," she went on. "Tex McGraw has a natural grasp of branding— have you seen his Instagram page?"

"I'm not real big on social media," he admitted. Which was to say, he wasn't on it at all. His mom had tried to get him to join Facebook but his sister, Marie, had shown him what sorts of things Mom put out there and, well, ignorance was bliss.

"Shocking," she teased. "Take my word for it—with a solid marketing push from the All-Stars at a corporate level, we could get Tex some major sponsorships deals and get the All-Stars name out there."

Pete had to swallow his surprise with his burger. "You'd rather promote Tex than your own *brother*?"

"Hell, yeah," she scoffed. "This is the All-Stars, not the Lawrence Family Hour. Besides, it doesn't have to be Tex—although he's laid down a great platform. I'd love to get June to ride in a few events—she grew up on a ranch and can rope calves with the best of them. Even if it's just for an exhibition, it'd bring in viewers and we could cross promote with her fans, let them know the All-Stars exists—that sort of thing. But someone like Tex, where we can control the narrative and build a storyline over a season—yeah," she finished with a wistful sigh. "That'd be amazing. And then there's the title of Princess…"

Pete snorted before he could help it. "What, going to promote yourself to Queen of the Rodeo now?"

She gave him a dull look that made him smile. "Seriously? I'm not a teenager anymore and it's a little ridiculous that I'm still doing it after a decade, don't you think?"

Pete felt like she'd punched him right in the gut. Was he supposed to agree with her? Because he did, but saying so felt like a trap.

Luckily, she kept talking. "What I'd like to do is open up the title to other girls—which, again, would only grow our audience. Maybe a national scholarship competition with a year's reign or… I don't know, exactly. But it's time to shake things up. Besides," she added, jabbing a fry in his direction, "I'm tired of men barging in on me while I change. I'd rather just run the show."

Now what the hell was he supposed to say to that?

He'd been operating under the assumption that Chloe *lived* to be the princess. He'd thought she was clinging to her moment of glory like barnacles to the hull of a ship. And...

And that she didn't care about the All-Stars beyond her moment in the spotlight.

Had he misread the situation? Had he misunderstood *her*? Because suddenly, he wasn't entirely sure who he was sitting next to. It certainly wasn't the same clueless city slicker he'd first laid eyes on ten years ago, barely able to stay in the saddle without dropping the flag.

He didn't like not knowing because he had a plan that was built on a set of undisputed facts, the most important of which was that Chloe Lawrence was an airheaded attention hog who was ruining his rodeo.

He felt dizzy, almost.

"Big ideas" was all he managed to say. Huge changes, really. But if they worked—and it sounded like she'd done the research—then it could be good for the rodeo.

"Yeah. But the old timers are going to fight me every step of the way, no doubt. Like they're afraid of girl cooties instead of seeing long-term growth as a positive. They'd rather stagnate and die of obsolescence, I guess."

He snorted. They fell silent as they finished eating, but his mind was spinning the whole time.

Chloe Lawrence was hell-bent on remaking the All-Stars into something different. No wonder Dustin Yardley and the others had been so mad this morning. The rodeo was about tradition and honor and legacy and, okay, maybe it was a bastion of male pride. What Chloe was talking about flew in the face of a lot of that.

But...she also had a point about stagnation. He didn't want the All-Stars to shrivel and die. He loved the rodeo and had ever since his dad had started the circuit back in the eighties. Pete's childhood had revolved around the All-Stars. It'd been the one time when his dad was around and interested and focused on Pete. Because Davey Wellington had never been focused on anything, including his family. Mom liked to say that if they'd known what attention deficit disorder was back when Dad was a kid, he'd have been the poster child for it.

Mom made the ranch profitable, all while getting dinner on the table. Dad had a nasty habit of getting distracted with bright, shiny ideas. Which could be good, like when he'd decided to start the All-Stars. But it could also be bad, like when he bet the rodeo in a poker game and lost. And now it was too late. Dad was gone.

But Pete could still honor the man's life and keep those special memories alive by taking control of his rodeo. But if the All-Stars lost riders to bull riding or other outfits and went into decline, where would that leave his legacy?

He was going to need a drink to deal with that answer. Several drinks.

He decided it was safer to change the subject. Chloe was flat out inhaling her food—which was all the more impressive, considering she was doing so one-handed. "You were hungry, weren't you?"

"I never eat before a show. It used to be because I got so nervous but now I'm just too busy. I try to eat a big breakfast but by this time of night…" She shrugged. "Man, that's a good burger."

"It'd be better with a beer."

"True." She sounded wistful about it. "But there's no way in hell I'm going to drink around you, Pete."

"Why not?" He was real proud that he managed to keep any hurt he might or might not have felt at that sideswipe out of his voice. "I'd never go after you like those idiots tried to. You know that."

She turned and gave him a long look—such a long look, in fact, he began to squirm. He hid it behind scrounging for fries in the bag.

"That begs the question, doesn't it?"

She was setting him up for something but damned if he could see where this was going. Was she about to remind him he was a man again? "What question?"

"How *would* you go after me?"

He almost choked on a fry. So much for changing the subject to something safer. "Pardon?"

There was no way she meant that question in a sexual sense and it definitely wasn't a come-on. Even if he'd like it to be.

She set her empty container aside and swung around, crossing one leg over the other and leaning back against the side of the truck. With the ice and her wounded hand in her lap, she stared at him. "How *are* you going after me? Like, right now? Because we've danced around each other for a decade, Pete. Ten years of push and pull and not once—not *once*—have you ever been nice to me, much less defended me twice in one day."

He was thankful it was dark because his cheeks got hot with something that felt like shame and he'd rather take a punch than let Chloe Lawrence see him blush.

"And don't you dare try to pass it off as if you haven't been *that* bad or *that* mean because I'm not in the mood for bull tonight, Pete."

"How about tomorrow? We could have this talk tomorrow."

Light from the street lamp across the way shone off her smile. "I've recently discovered that my tolerance for BS has lowered significantly. Why are you here,

Pete? Why are you defending me? Why, after all this time, are you treating me like a person? Like—" she swallowed but didn't look away "—like a friend?"

Man, it was tempting to protest his innocence. The phrase *you never could take a joke* danced right up to the tip of his tongue before he bit it back.

She was right. Trying to blow off all the ways he'd attacked and undermined the Lawrence family and their management of the All-Stars over the years would be complete BS. Because he'd thrown everything he had at them—including but not limited to lawsuits—and nothing had worked.

But what was he supposed to say now? She knew why he was here and he knew why he was here. But he couldn't come right out with the truth, not before he and Chloe had the terms of his new position in writing.

"Maybe things changed. Maybe…" He said something that was supposed to be a bald-faced lie. "Maybe I changed."

Funny how that felt a lot like the truth.

But it wasn't, not really. The Lawrence family still owned the All-Stars and Pete wouldn't stop until he got it back. Chloe was just an obstacle Pete had to work around.

He looked at his obstacle. She was watching him from under her lashes and Pete had the sinking feeling she could tell what color his cheeks were.

"It won't work, you know."

"What won't?"

"Don't play dumb, Wellington," she scoffed. "It's beneath you and it's beneath me. This scheme you're working on—it won't work. You're only here for one reason. You want your rodeo back."

What he wanted was to lean forward and kiss her.

Not just because he wanted to get her to stop talking—although he did. He wanted to know if things really had changed between them or if it was all just smoke and noise, like the fireworks they set off at the start of every rodeo.

He looked out at the night sky. The bar wasn't too far away from the highway but, aside from people coming and going from the bar, the rest of the street was quiet, with only the occasional semi rumbling over the overpass.

"Did it ever occur to you that you've won?" he heard himself say. "That you're right?"

"There, was that so hard?" She spoke softly, but he could hear the amusement in her voice.

He shot a hard look at her. "You've got a hell of a mouth on you, Chloe Lawrence."

It wasn't right, how much he liked that grin on her. "Don't change the subject. You were telling me I was right?"

"Yeah." He swallowed and had to look away. These words, they weren't the reason he was here but...did that make them any less honest? "It's been ten years and nothing's changed. I'm never going to pry the All-Stars away from your family. God knows I've tried everything, but you people are worse than deer ticks during a wet spring."

"There's the Pete Wellington I know," she muttered, but at least she didn't sound like she was going to punch him when she said it.

"I can either keep beating my head against the same brick wall that is Chloe Lawrence and her irritating brothers or..."

"Or you can get hired on to run the rodeo?" Yeah, she wasn't buying this.

But was he lying, really?

The darkness of midnight in Missouri blurred the hard edges around them, making buildings indistinct lumps on the landscape and he wasn't sure where one parked car ended and the next began. "The All-Stars is *everything* to me and I'm never going to get it back. I've lost more than one lawsuit and you won't sell. I'm running out of options."

That was the unvarnished truth and it hurt to admit it.

"So I can either cut my losses and walk away from the one thing I love in this life or I can suck up my pride and ask you to hire me on as a show manager. I won't try to undermine your authority, and I can keep doing the only thing I love—running the rodeo my father started."

He looked back at her. Had she bought that last bit? Because, yeah, some of that was the truth. But the part about not working against her was the mother of all whoppers.

She sat forward, her head tilted to one side as she studied him. Could she see where the truth ended and the lies began? Or had the darkness obscured the difference?

Chloe shook her head and swung her legs off the back of the truck. "And I'm supposed to believe that a man whose middle name might as well be Grudge is just going to turn over a new leaf and work under me?" She hopped down, cradling her hand, and began to walk away. "That you've decided my family hasn't ruined your life after all?"

He scrambled after her and caught her by the arm, spinning her around to face him. "Chloe, stop."

"I don't buy it, Pete," she said, her brows furrowed as she stared up at him. But she didn't pull away from him, so that was something. "It's a great story, a real heartbreaker. It'd make a hell of a country song but you're asking me to believe that you're going to back me up when I want to do things differently in your beloved rodeo? Because you've *changed*?"

"Yeah," he said, his tone gruff as he lowered his head to hers. "Yeah, I am."

Kissing Chloe Lawrence was not part of the plan but was that stopping him as he brushed his lips over hers? No, it wasn't.

Because he was kissing her anyway, dammit. Not the rodeo, not the princess—her, Chloe with the smart mouth and the right hook and it felt so *right*.

She sighed into him, one arm going around his neck as the ice bag landed on his boot with a *thud*. He didn't care because Chloe opened her mouth for him and Pete got a little taste of heaven when her tongue tested the crease of his lips.

Holy hell, this woman. Why hadn't he kissed her before this? He could have been doing this for years!

He groaned, pulling her into his arms as he took what she gave and came back to ask for more. Greedily, he drank her in, shifting until he had her backed against the side of the truck. "Chloe," he whispered against her skin as he trailed his mouth down her neck. "God, Chloe."

She knocked his hat off his head and dug the fingers of her good hand into his hair. "Don't talk," she said, sounding almost angry about it. But then she lifted his hand to her breast and even the touch of her chilled skin wasn't enough to cool him off. "Just don't talk, Pete."

"Yes, ma'am." But that was the last bit of thinking he was capable of as his fingers closed around her breast. The warm weight filled his palm and he moaned at the feeling of her nipple going tight between his fingers. He went rock hard in an instant and suddenly, he needed more.

He needed everything. From her.

"Yeah," she breathed, which was all the encouragement Pete needed. He shoved his knee between her legs and ground his thigh against her sex. She gasped and bore down on him.

Her heat surrounded him and he grunted, shifting back and forth while she rode his leg. She threw her head back, which seemed like the perfect time to explore her breasts. He had to keep one hand braced on the truck so he didn't lose his balance, but he slipped the other one under her loose tee and cupped her breast again, teasing her nipple through the thin fabric.

"Lace," he murmured as he tugged the bra cup down and finally, *finally* got a handful of nothing but Chloe. "I wondered."

"Shut up and kiss me," she growled, pulling his mouth down to hers and kissing him with such raw desire that he almost lost control right then.

He couldn't let her unman him—at least, not without returning the favor. So he kissed her back as he stroked her breast and tormented her nipple and swallowed the noises she made because he couldn't bear for a single one of her gasps and moans to escape.

She broke the kiss to thrash her head from side to side, her weight heavy on his leg. She was close, he realized.

He jerked her loose tee to the side and lifted her breast to his mouth, sucking hard on her tight nipple. Once he had her firmly in his mouth, he used his free hand to reach down between her legs and rub until he found the spot that made her back arch into him.

"Come for me," he growled against her, pressing hard against that spot as he scraped his teeth over her skin.

For once, Chloe Lawrence—the woman who'd *never* listened to him—did as she was told. With a shudder that was so hard she almost knocked him off his feet, she came apart in his arms. Pete looked up just in time to see her face as the climax hit its peak.

Jesus, she took his breath away. Had he ever seen a woman as beautiful, as vulnerable as she was right now?

He held her as the aftershocks swept over her and then she slumped in his arms, her forehead against his shoulder as she panted against his neck. His body was screaming for release, but he couldn't have moved if he'd wanted to—and he didn't want to.

She felt so good in his arms that, for an exquisite moment, he wondered if maybe his old plan sucked and he should come up with a new one—one that involved a whole lot more Chloe and much less clothing. One where they spent the rest of the weekend in bed, learning every story their bodies had to tell.

What if…what if he'd told the truth earlier?

What if it hadn't been a lie, any of it?

"Chloe," he began, but then stopped because what the hell was he even thinking? He wasn't.

Sweet Jesus, he'd just brought Chloe Lawrence, of all people, to orgasm, which was bad enough. But he'd done it in the parking lot of a bar, out in the open where anyone could walk by and see them tangled together.

Before he'd gotten a job contract in writing.

What the *hell* was he thinking?

It only got worse when she pushed him away. He had no choice but to take that step back, no choice but to look away as she fixed her bra. "Well. That was…" She cleared her throat. "Well."

That was *bad*, that's what that was. And he had no idea what he could say that wouldn't make things worse. All of his blood had abandoned his brain for his groin, clearly. Best laid plans and all that crap.

He adjusted his pants and winced. "Yeah."

"Right." Then, without another word, she turned and walked off into the darkness.

Hell. He couldn't have screwed this up worse if he'd tried.

He better start hoping for a miracle.

Seven

By the time Chloe arrived at the rodeo the next afternoon, she was on the verge of throwing up the half cup of yogurt she'd managed to choke down that morning.

She hadn't slept. Every time she closed her eyes, Pete appeared before her, his body pressing hers against the truck, his hands everywhere.

She'd let him do that.

Let? Hell. She'd practically *ordered* him to do that.

Him. Pete Wellington. In public.

Christ.

She'd played right into his hand—literally. Short of doing a striptease for him on the bar, she'd given him everything he needed to either blackmail her for her silence or oh-so-publicly cut her to shreds and honestly, Chloe had no idea which one was worse.

Because they both led to the same place—her losing control of the All-Stars.

The only question was, how would he play his hand? Because he held all the cards. And Chloe could barely move her fingers on her right hand.

She walked around the arena, forcing herself to say hello to the people she passed. Years of smiling big while galloping around the arena paid off. But it wasn't easy because no one met her gaze or returned her greetings. What the hell? So she smiled harder, made sure to say good morning a little louder, but people's gazes still cut away from hers.

Great. Wonderful. Pete had fed her a sob story about how he'd seen the light and become a better man and then he'd gotten her into a compromising position and there would be no grace period. He'd already run his mouth and told everyone about last night. As plans went to turn *her* crew and riders against her, it was brutally efficient.

She made it to her closet and got the door shut before her face crumpled. She needed a counterattack here. So he'd gotten her off? So what? She enjoyed orgasms as much as the next girl and heavens knew it'd been too long since her last assisted one. And who could blame her for taking advantage of what Pete had offered? He was ruggedly handsome and so damn *good* with his hands.

But she would not be ashamed of her sexuality, by God. And anyone who tried to make her feel that way would live to regret it.

Yes, she could do this. Pete had used her? Two could play at this game. She'd used *him*. She'd been in the mood and he'd been convenient. Simple as that. It was his problem if he couldn't tell the difference.

Yeah, that was a good attitude going forward but this was still going to be the most awkward day ever. To say nothing of what Flash would do when he found out. God, she hoped the police wouldn't have to get involved.

A knock on the door made her start, but not as much as Pete's voice saying, "Chloe? Are you dressed?"

She shuddered. Okay, so they were doing this now. Taking a deep breath, she spun and threw the door open, glaring at him. "Does this meet your high standards?" she snapped, waving her hand over her favorite pair of leggings, the ones where the pattern looked like a cozy fall sweater in purples.

"Whoa," he said, throwing his hands up in surrender. Again. He did that a lot around her. "Easy."

"I am not your freaking horse, Pete, and there is nothing *easy* about this."

He rubbed at the back of his neck. "Okay, that answers one question. But," he hurried on before she could dissect that statement, "we have bigger problems."

"Bigger than you telling everyone you got me off in a parking lot?"

"For God's sake," he hissed, pushing her back into the dressing room and kicking the door closed behind her, "keep your voice down! What is wrong with you?"

"I'm trapped in a closet with a serial liar and con man?" She retreated back against the dressing room table, which was as far as she could go. Crossing her arms over her chest, she glared at him. "Why the hell did you tell everyone about what happened last night?"

He goggled at her. "What? No—that's—where did you get the idea that I'd ever do something like that?"

"Oh, I don't know. Maybe by the way no one would even look at me this morning? I don't enjoy being treated like damaged goods, thank you very much."

The words shouldn't hurt, but they cut their way out of her throat and she had to look away before she did something stupid, like get all teary. She wasn't going to cry over this man. Not in this lifetime or the next.

Pete's features hardened. "I know you don't need me to defend you, but I swear to God, I will destroy the first person who treats you like that. For the record," he went on, almost shouting over Chloe's protests, "I didn't tell anyone anything about you and me because that was private and perfect. Jesus, Chloe—what kind of asshole do you take me for?"

Wait, what? Had he just said...*perfect*?

"Because," he continued, glaring at her, "whatever you think of me, I'm not that kind of jerk. I would never kiss and tell and I would never use sex to hurt a woman. For God's sake, Lawrence, give me a little credit."

She got the feeling that, if he had the room, he'd be pacing. How much of that was true? But he did look truly offended that she'd even suggest he'd do such a thing. "Did someone see us or something?"

"No," he ground out. "No one saw us. No one is talking about us at all."

"Okay...so, if that's not the problem, what is?" Because something had to have happened.

He stopped and gave her a look and she realized it wasn't a *something*, but a *someone* right as he said, "Flash got into it at the bar last night."

Her shoulders slumped. Of course. Because that was what Flash did. "With a local or with another rider?"

"Another rider."

Today was just full of surprises. Was it too late to go back in time? She'd like to restart this weekend completely.

She didn't have to ask what the fight had been about. It was always the same fight. Someone would suggest the only reason Flash did well in the rankings was his daddy owned the circuit or his sister ran the show. That was all it ever took for him to come up swinging and go down kicking. "Police?"

"And an ambulance."

Damn. "I don't suppose we'd be lucky enough that Flash was the one hospitalized?"

Pete shook his head.

"Who?"

"Tex McGraw."

Double damn. Not only was Tex one of the few people who could outride Flash, but he had several hundred thousand followers that could easily be mobilized to put Flash's head on a pike. He was popular, dammit.

And Flash wasn't. Of all the people her irritating baby brother could have gone after… She ground the heels of her palms against her eyes. "And that's why no one was feeling friendly toward me this morning."

"Could be." He cleared his throat. "But at least it wasn't personal. They aren't feeling too kindly toward any Lawrence right now."

If this were a nightmare, she'd love to wake up right now.

Alas, this was no nightmare. "How bad is Tex?"

Pete swallowed. "Broken jaw, broken knee."

"Knee?"

"Lawrences fight hard," Pete said with an attempt at a smile. But all he managed to do was look as sick as she felt. "He'll be out for the season. He's, uh, already contacted his lawyer."

"Usually Flash calls me." Because, in addition to running the rodeo, her other job was keeping Flash out of trouble. As if anyone could. "Why didn't he call me?"

Her phone rang. But it wasn't Flash, nor was it the Greater Sikeston Police Department. She glanced at the name, even more dread building. How much more dread could one person feel? "Oliver."

She needed to answer this. But...

"That'd be why, I figure." Pete took a step toward her. "Hon, I'm sorry."

"You didn't land Flash in the pokey," she replied.

He lifted her bruised hand and pressed another surprisingly tender kiss to her knuckles. "I'm sorry about how we parted last night. I'm sorry I gave you cause to worry this morning." A little of the tension drained from her shoulders. "I know we still haven't discussed the parameters of my job but..."

"Crisis management has to come first." Her phone buzzed again. "Look, Pete—"

But he beat her to the punch, so to speak. "Right. We have to protect the rodeo, first and foremost. And..." He swallowed. "And we probably shouldn't be involved while we're working together. More involved."

"Yeah." Sure, she'd been about to say that exact thing, but her pride still smarted a little. She covered it with a weak grin. "One of these days, we'll come to terms. But until then...help?"

"Always, babe. You deal with your family and the press. I'll deal with the rodeo. Okay?"

A small part of her wanted to argue against that because if Pete were really working to push her out, this was a gift-wrapped opportunity for him.

But what was she supposed to do here? Because, if the morning had been any indication, no one was going to talk to her for the rest of the weekend, much less follow her directions. Someone had to keep the rodeo on track and Pete had the skills and the connections. She needed Pete right now in a way that had nothing to do with how he filled out those Wranglers or how he'd made her feel last night.

So she swallowed her misgivings and gave her smile her level best. "Got it. Go, team?"

He leaned forward to brush a quick kiss against her lips and then he was gone, the ghost of his kiss still lingering there.

Well. At least things couldn't get any worse.

"Dare I ask what the hell you were thinking?" Chloe said, barely keeping her anger reined in. She was exhausted, worried, furious and still nauseous. But she didn't get the luxury of hiding under the covers until the world went away.

Flash might not have been carted off to the hospital, but he hadn't gotten away scot-free. Stripped of his Stetson and his boots, her little brother looked surprisingly young in jail-issue orange. He had two black eyes and the left side of his face was so swollen that he was almost unrecognizable. His knuckles were scraped raw and she could tell by the way he was sitting that he hurt.

Didn't matter. She wasn't going to feel bad for him. He had brought this on himself, just like he always did.

He looked up, his left eye completely bloodshot. Tex had gotten in a few good licks before he'd gone down. "You wouldn't understand," he said, his voice flat.

How had Chloe come to this place in her life, where the only man who treated her with anything that resembled respect was Pete Wellington? "No, I'm sure I wouldn't. I'm only your older sister and in charge of the rodeo, which, I'd like to point out, you've done more to destroy in a single night than Pete Wellington has done in ten years."

Flash tried to glare at her, but he winced in pain. "Now is not the time, sis."

"I beg to disagree," she said, feeling her temper slip through her fingers. "Because you do have time. Oliver and I agreed. You got yourself into this mess—you can get yourself right back out. You may have permanently ended the career of one of the best riders on the All-Stars circuit."

"And the biggest asshole," Flash muttered.

Chloe ignored that. She was not allowing a strong contender for that title to interrupt her tirade. "You may have torpedoed your own career in the process. And you undermined my position as a manager who can successfully run the rodeo. You don't have any friends left, Flash. No one wants to put up with this crap. Especially not me."

He crossed his arms and stared at the top of the table.

If she could reach through the mesh wire separating them, she would strangle him. "You wanted to prove that you got where you are without cashing in on the family name? Now's your chance, buddy. Because family is not going to bail you out. Not the rodeo family, and not me. You're going to sit in this jail cell. You got there all by yourself."

"You weren't there," Flash yelled, slamming his hands down on the table. "You didn't hear the things he said. I'm not going to let any man talk about a woman the way he talked about *her*!"

Chloe had grown up with Flash. Hotheaded, short fuse, quick on the trigger—he'd always been like this. Calm and sullen one moment, raging the next. She wasn't even a little surprised about his outburst. "Her who? And what was he saying?" she asked, trying to stay calm.

If Tex had gotten sloshed and was talking about women as disrespectfully as the way those two drunks outside of Mike's had treated her, then she could at least understand why her brother had flipped out. Flash *loved* women. Sometimes too much.

If what Tex said had been abusive or even just misogynistic, Chloe needed to know before she attempted to make amends with him. She wasn't going to make someone who denigrated women the focus of any future All-Stars marketing campaigns.

Flash fell silent again. Chloe rolled her eyes. "Fine. Oliver is sending a lawyer, but you're on your own for bail and damages. You are hereby suspended from the All-Stars until further notice."

"What?" Flash exploded again, but Chloe was already standing. "You can't do this to me!"

She shook her head as she walked away. "Flash, you did this to yourself."

She was done. As she waited for the officer to open the door, she tried hard to find a silver lining in this situation. The only one she could come up with was that at least no one had caught her and Pete together.

"Does Oliver know about the deal you made with Wellington?" Flash called out behind her.

Chloe froze. Point of fact, Oliver did not. Mostly because it wasn't relevant to the current situation she was dealing with. But also because she'd put good money on the fact that Flash had already threatened Pete and she'd be willing to bet Oliver would do the same thing. Except Flash's threats tended to involve fights and Oliver's threats tended to involve expensive lawsuits.

She couldn't bring herself to lie, because lies were easy to prove wrong. But this was Flash, after all. She had no problem hedging the truth a little. "Like he cares," she said, doing her best to sneer dismissively. "The only thing Oliver cares about is that the All-Stars runs smoothly and profitably without him having to get his hands dirty. So if you think you can redirect Oliver's anger away from you and onto Wellington, I'd think twice before waving that red flag in front of that bull. Wellington isn't the reason Oliver called me this morning."

Behind her, the door clicked open and, without waiting for a reply, she turned and walked away.

She didn't even wince as the door slammed shut behind her and locked with the dull, metallic *clunk*.

Of course things got worse. Because the rodeo was family and some family squabbles could be kept quiet but this? This was not one of them. Not with the front-page headline of the *Sikeston Standard-Democrat* blaring about the fight in huge type and the editorial asking if it was safe for the town to continue hosting the rodeo.

What Chloe pieced together made it clear that the *her* in question had been Brooke Bonner, country singer and Flash's current infatuation.

As best Chloe could tell, Tex had been remarking that he didn't like Bonner because…well, the *because* was fuzzy. Tex wouldn't say much beyond Flash was a crazy bastard who was going to pay and Flash refused to say anything else in his defense. She got seven conflicting stories from eyewitnesses that ranged from Tex saying Brooke was getting fat to stating she was a no-talent hack to observing he'd "tap that," as one rider put it.

In other words, Chloe was on the losing end of the world's worst game of telephone and it was a hell of a mess. She'd say things couldn't get worse, but she wasn't about to tempt fate right now.

The All-Stars had lost Tex McGraw, most likely permanently. At the very least, he was out for the rest of the season and no force on this earth could stop him from taking swipes at Flash on social media. At least half of which Flash deserved, as far as Chloe was concerned. But worse, Tex was making plenty of noise about how he'd never ride for the All-Stars again as long as a Lawrence was in charge and maybe he'd take his skills where they'd be appreciated in the Total Bull Challenge.

Flash was booked for assault and sued accordingly and Chloe refused to overturn his indefinite suspension, which meant two of the All-Stars' top ten riders were out. No one wanted Flash back, that much was clear. His hot temper had caught fire too many times and all his bridges had burned to ash.

Chloe looked weak as a leader because she couldn't manage her brother or the bad press. Even announcing that Flash had been suspended, pending trial dates, didn't help much. Somehow, she was responsible for Flash's behavior, which infuriated her all over again. Flash was a twenty-four-year-old adult. He was responsible for his own screw-ups. Not her. She wasn't her brother's keeper, dammit.

And what had she been doing when this whole thing had gone down? Getting to third base with Pete.

Chloe was comfortable with her decision to leave Flash locked up, but that didn't mean she still didn't have to clean up after his messes. Everywhere the rodeo landed, it felt like she gave the exact same interview. Yes, the All-Stars were hopeful that Tex McGraw would make a full and complete recovery. Yes, the All-Stars were doing everything they could to assist Tex in achieving that goal. Yes, Flash was suspended pending his trial for assault. No, Chloe had not personally been there when the fight broke out. No, she didn't know what had started it all. No, she hadn't heard any rumors swirling that somehow linked the brawl back to Brooke Bonner.

She'd love to talk about the changes coming to the All-Stars—but no one wanted to ask about those. They all wanted to prop up the click-bait headlines that seemed to follow the Lawrence family no matter where they went. Unfortunately, Flash's trouble with the law was the perfect opportunity to resurface all those terrible facts about the Preston Pyramid scheme and how the former Renee Preston, current Renee Lawrence, was related to the very criminals who'd ruined everyone's life.

There might not be such a thing as bad PR, but Chloe could do with a lot less of it.

The good news—because she was still clinging to whatever silver lining she could—was that not only did Pete Wellington do a damned fine job running the All-Stars while Chloe handled the media and the lawyers and, worst of all, her family, but he announced the changes she'd told him about when they had been sitting in the back of a pickup truck what felt like years ago.

Next season, women would be allowed to compete in both the team events and the individual events. Yes, it was infuriating that, for the most part, everyone nodded and smiled and said something along the lines of, *well, maybe it was about time.* Chloe knew damned well that if she'd announced the changes, she would've gotten nothing but heartbreak and heartburn. But those same ideas coming out of Wellington's mouth? Everyone signed on with remarkably little dissent.

Which was good for the rodeo. Not so much for her ego.

She rarely got the chance to talk to Pete, and when she did, they kept the conversations short and focused on the tasks at hand. He kept her up-to-date on what the riders were talking about and she apprised him of the media chatter. He didn't barge in to her dressing room anymore and she didn't ask him to get something to eat. They were both too busy keeping the All-Stars from collapsing under its own weight. And besides, they'd agreed—they couldn't be anything more than coworkers. It was better this way.

Except...except when she mounted up and waited to make her entrance into the arena, she looked for him. And she usually found him, on top of one of the chutes, watching her with what felt like far more than friendly interest. Every single time their gazes met, heat flashed down her back and she wished he'd barge into her dressing room, just one more time.

For those few moments, separated by fences and horses and cowboys, she wasn't the Lawrence in charge and he wasn't the de facto rodeo manager. When her gaze met his and he gave her that wink, she could still feel his hands on her body, still taste him on her tongue. And given the way he stared at her, she couldn't help but wonder if he felt the same.

But she wasn't going to ask. Yeah, for that brief moment in time against the side of his truck, she'd just been Chloe and he'd been Pete and there hadn't been any past betrayals or family dramas. They'd only been a man and a woman outside a honky-tonk bar on a Friday night and it'd been *good*.

Too bad she might never get another moment like that.

Eight

The woman's voice cut through the hotel lobby. "What do you mean, I don't have a reservation?"

Chloe?

Pete's head whipped up so fast that he almost tripped over his own boots. Desire slammed into his gut. It *was* Chloe. There was no mistaking that backside in those stretch pants. She normally got to the rodeo a day before he did, but the way the flights to Pendleton, Oregon, had worked out, he was here early.

Good thing, too. As he got closer, he could see she was physically shaking.

The clerk behind the desk looked mortified as he apologized profusely, saying, "I'm so sorry but there's no record of a reservation under that name and we're booked solid—there's a convention in town and then the rodeo. There isn't a room in town." He cleared his throat, looking as hopeful as possible. "Did someone else make the reservation?"

"No, I did. I thought…" Her voice broke as she dropped her head onto her forearms.

The clerk shot Pete a pleading look, one that begged for patience.

This should have been Pete's moment of victory and he hadn't even done anything to earn it. Chloe was about to crack under the pressure of running the rodeo, just like he'd known she would. She was going to fall apart and Pete would be right here to pick up the pieces and show the world that Chloe Lawrence didn't have what it took—while he did.

Except… Her back rose and fell with a shuddering breath.

This wasn't right. He wanted her out of the All-Stars, but did he really want her broken?

Dammit all, he didn't.

"Problem?" he asked.

Chloe spun around. She looked terrible—pale, with dark circles under her eyes and so obviously upset. What the hell? His Chloe wouldn't buckle just because of a wayward reservation.

He moved without thinking, dropping his bag and pulling her into his arms. "What's wrong, hon?"

She took a ragged breath as her arms wrapped around his waist and she all but crumpled into him. Chloe Lawrence *clung* to him as if he were a rock in the middle of the stormy sea. "I don't have a room and there are no rooms and it's been a terrible week and…" She took another shuddering breath and Pete knew she was trying not to cry.

He hugged her harder, his heart pounding. He had seen Chloe angry, defensive, seductive, flirty and happy. She always looked so danged happy sitting at the head of the procession in her princess finery, ready to ride and wearing the hell out of her chaps.

He'd wanted her back in his arms, wanted her vulnerable and open like she'd been against the side of his truck. But this? He didn't want her destroyed. The urge to fix this mess was almost overwhelming.

He wanted to help her.

The realization left him feeling dazed. The burr under his saddle that was Chloe Lawrence? The thorn in his backside that he'd give anything to be rid of? He was being gifted with a golden opportunity to finish the job he'd started.

Her body was pressed against his and he realized he was stroking her hair. He couldn't do it, dammit. Fool that he was, he was going to protect her. Didn't matter from what. What mattered was that she needed someone on her side right now and by God, Pete was going to be that man.

She stiffened in his arms and pulled away, blinking hard. "Sorry, sorry," she said, trying to smile—or maybe look confident and in control? Either way, she failed miserably. "Just a little tired."

He leaned down, his mouth close to her ear. "You're a terrible liar." Her cheeks shot red as he added in a regular voice, "I have a room and you're taking it. I'll find another hotel."

"You can't do that," she said, like she had a choice in the matter. "There aren't any rooms!"

He stepped around her. "Wellington, Peter. I should have a reservation?" Looking relieved, the clerk nodded and started tapping on the keys.

Pete could hear Chloe huffing behind him. He grinned. Giving his room to Chloe was the right thing to do. Besides, it would go a long way toward earning her trust. He'd kept his nose clean for the last month, doing nothing that would make her suspicious of his ulterior motives.

Of course, he hadn't exactly had the time to work on any of those ulterior motives. Flash Lawrence had screwed up his plans but good. Just keeping the wheels from falling off the All-Stars took everything he had and that was with Chloe managing the marketing and PR and high-level decisions. He should be grateful for the chance to start pushing her out.

Why wasn't he?

He cut a glance to her. She was somewhere between confused and…angry, maybe? "Pete, what are you doing?" she asked. At least she didn't sound shattered anymore.

"If it's not obvious, then I'm doing it wrong," he replied with a wink. That got him a full-on glare which, oddly, made Pete felt better. If he were going to best Chloe Lawrence, he wanted her to go down fighting. There was no pride in kicking her when she was already down.

"Sir?" the clerk said. "We have you down for a king suite, no smoking. How many keys?"

Pete looked back at Chloe. She'd gotten close enough to touch and oh, how he wanted to touch her. What would it be like if this wasn't an accident? What if they'd planned to get in a night early and spend the evening wrapped up in each other? He had to shift his legs to relieve the pressure. "One," he said, nodding in her direction. "Give it to her."

"No, wait." She touched him on the upper arm, her lower lip tucked under her teeth. "You can't drive off tonight. It isn't right."

He snorted. "I'm not the kind of man who would kick a woman to the curb when there's a perfectly fine room available."

Her hand flattened on his arm, sending heat through the fabric of his shirt. Last time she'd touched him, there'd been too many clothes and not enough bare skin. "Pete…" she said, his name soft on her lips. "Maybe we could share?" She said it like she knew it was a bad idea.

And it was. It was a freaking terrible idea because he didn't want to be a gentleman about Chloe and a king-size bed. He turned into her to warn her off but the movement brought their bodies close together and that night against his pickup truck, where he'd made her come apart under his touch—it all came roaring back to him.

He could do a lot more than make her shatter in a hurried series of blunt touches dulled through layers of fabric. He could strip her down slowly, properly worshipping each inch of skin he revealed like the goddess she was.

He shook his head, trying to get a grip, but it wasn't easy. She was only inches away, staring up at him with her big brown eyes. What would a gentleman do? Hell if he could remember because he did not want to be a gentleman right now. He wanted to give and take and give some more until Chloe was breathless beneath him, his name a cry of pleasure on her lips.

He shifted again. It didn't do a damned thing for the roaring erection barely being held in check by his belt buckle. "Are you sure that's a good idea?"

Her eyes darkened and he saw her throat work to swallow. No, it wasn't a good idea. But she said, "It'll be fine, I'm sure."

Oh, he was sure, too. Sure he could bare her body and

be inside of her in minutes, if not sooner. He wanted her naked this time, her body spread open for him to feast on.

The gentlemanly thing to do would be pick up his bag, do an about-face and march his butt right back out to his car. If he drove long enough, he'd find a small town with a room available. The smart thing to do would be to put as much distance between him and this woman as possible.

Pete had never claimed to be *that* smart.

The clerk cleared his throat. "How many keys?"

Pete cupped her cheek in his hand, watching her eyelashes flutter at the touch. She was so warm, so soft. "You can have the room."

It wasn't his last grasp at decency, but it was damned close.

Chloe took a long breath and said, "Two, please. But I'm paying you back for the room, Wellington."

He chuckled. Yeah, this was how he wanted her—a battle of the equals. God, he liked her like this. "Like hell you are, Lawrence." He turned to the clerk. "Two keys. One bill."

The clerk nodded, his relief obvious. He made promises about giving Chloe extra rewards points and maybe Pete got some, too—he wasn't paying attention. He was busy trying to game plan the rest of his night.

The mess Flash had made had been both a blessing and a curse. It had kept Pete busy trying to reassure everyone associated with each All-Stars rodeo—riders and contractors, not to mention the local rodeo boards— that the All-Stars was safe and solid and going strong. The other parts of his plan had languished under the sheer amount of work he had to do, but he was happy to do it because he wanted his rodeo back in one piece, not in tattered remains.

But it was a blessing, too, because even though he hadn't moved forward with his plans to push Chloe out, it'd happened almost by accident anyway. She dealt with the press, smoothing over the losses of both Tex and Flash. She handled the marketing and distribution and her clothing line. She hadn't dealt with a single stock contractor in almost a month. How much would it take to turn the contractors away from her?

The clerk handed her both keys and she turned to him. "Shall we?"

"Let's."

That one blisteringly hot moment against his truck notwithstanding, Chloe was making it almost too easy to wall her off from the day-to-day operations. As long as Pete could keep his hands and other body parts to himself, he could just keep on letting things play out. The further Chloe got from the running of the actual rodeo, the harder it would be for her to step back in and the more people would resist Pete leaving.

On the other hand, he had one night alone in a hotel room with her. This was the sort of opportunity that didn't come around every day. But was it worth it, wrapping himself up further in her?

They walked down the hall to the elevator silently. Chloe clutched both key cards in her hand. All Pete needed to do was to keep walking out the other exit door at the end of this hall and back out to the parking lot. That was it.

But then she turned to him as the elevator door dinged open and said, "Coming?"

To hell with his long-term plans. Chloe was a once-in-a-lifetime opportunity and he'd be a fool to pass her up. "Yeah."

They maneuvered their bags into the elevator and

stood silently as the door closed. Pete gave her to the count of three to lay down her rules, but all she did was fiddle with the key cards. So he took the reins. "Thinking about how you want this to go?"

She startled and stared at him with her huge eyes. "What?"

"Tonight. How you want this to go." She blinked a few times at him, her mouth opened slightly. Was he imagining things or was she breathing harder? "The way I see it, we have three options."

No, he wasn't imagining it. Her body canted toward his ever so slightly. "And those are?"

He was more than tempted to press her against the back of the elevator and skip the first two options. But this was his very last attempt at decency. "The first option is that I spend the night on the sofa while you sleep on the far side of the king bed and neither of us moves for fear of disturbing the other, leaving us tired and cranky tomorrow."

Her brow wrinkled. "That's an option?"

"Not my favorite. Or," he went on, "option two is that we decide we're rational, mature adults who can share a bed while keeping our hands to ourselves and then, in a bold display of that maturity, we line up pillows down the center of the bed so we each stay on our own side. We'll lay awake all night, staring at the ceiling, wondering if the other person is thinking the same thing we are, leaving us tired, cranky *and* frustrated tomorrow."

The elevator began to slow as they reached their floor. "So, that leaves option three as…"

He reached out, stroking his fingertips over the curve of her cheek. "We take a small break from our previous agreement that, as coworkers, we shouldn't spend the night together and then whatever happens, happens."

A furrow appeared between her eyebrows but even so, she leaned into his touch. Not a lot, but enough. "*Whatever*, huh?"

He grinned. Because that had not been a *no*.

"Let me love on you a little, Chloe. I'll take care of you tonight. Tomorrow, we can go back to the way we were."

"What if we can't?"

It was a fair question and one he didn't have an answer to. He stroked her skin as the elevator doors opened. With a nod of his head toward the hallway before them, he replied, "Then we go forward as best we can."

She gasped as he grabbed her bag and headed toward the room. After a moment, he heard her behind him.

He had to stop at the door and wait for her because she held all the cards here—key and otherwise. She didn't look at him as she unlocked the door, but she held it open for him, so that counted for something. He set her bag down on the bed but left his on the floor. Then he crossed to the small desk and flipped on the light.

When he turned around, Chloe was half in shadows. Every fiber of his being was screaming to go to her, to pull her into his arms and kiss her hard, to make that decision for her. Or at least, make it easier. But he didn't want to overwhelm her better angels because he knew if he did, tomorrow would be that much harder. Worse, because tomorrow they wouldn't have Flash's messes to clean up. It would, God willing, be a normal day at a normal rodeo.

Speaking of... "What about the rodeo?" she asked, taking a small step toward the light.

"What about it?"

She gave him a dull look. "Look, option three is a

bad idea twice over. Either you'll hold *whatever* over my head in this plot you're working on to steal the rodeo away or we'll still be coworkers who shouldn't even attempt the maturity of pillow barriers."

Yeah, that stung. He hadn't said a damned thing about what'd happened in Missouri, except to tell her he wouldn't use sex against her. But then again, he couldn't blame her for being cautious. "Either you trust me or you don't."

She looked away first, running her hands through her hair. "I'm going to take a shower. I had a bad meeting and a terrible flight and—" she swallowed. "And I'm grateful that you're sharing the room with me."

Hell. He crossed the room in a few long strides and pulled her into his arms. "I'm sorry you had a crappy day," he said into her hair.

She stiffened, as if she expected him to press his case, but all he did was hold her and after a long moment, she melted into him. "It did suck," she admitted. "What are you doing here early?"

He chuckled. "Do you know how hard it is to get from East Texas to this part of Oregon? It would've been less painful if I'd driven. What was your meeting?"

"Oh, that." She sighed heavily, causing her chest to rub against his. "Family stuff."

That couldn't be good. If Milt or Oliver Lawrence decided to take a more active role in the All-Stars, Pete would be in danger of losing everything he'd worked for because he wasn't exactly on friendly terms with either man.

But then again, this was the Lawrence family, so he made an educated guess. "Flash causing trouble again?"

She didn't quite pull off a grin, but the eye roll was classic Chloe. "You have no idea."

"No," he murmured, lowering his head to hers, "but I'm starting to get one."

Unlike the kiss a month ago, this was not hard or hurried. It was a soft meeting of the lips, a promise of something more. Chloe's arms tightened around his waist, making her breasts press against his chest and his groin hit her hipbone. Fire licked through his veins and he started praying that she'd decided on option three because *frustrated* was not going to be strong enough to describe his state if he had to bunk down on the sofa.

Her tongue traced the seam of his lips and he almost groaned at the touch because it sure seemed like option three was going to be the big winner. But instead he pulled away and forced himself to say, "You—shower."

Which was not the most verbose thing he'd ever said, but it was all he was capable of. Another moment in her arms, and he wouldn't be able to walk away. Hell, he wouldn't be able to walk, not with the erection he was working on.

She nodded and took that all-important step away, touching her fingertips to her lips as if she couldn't believe he had just kissed her.

When she got to the bathroom door, she looked back. The full force of her desire hit him hard and threatened to send him to his knees. But before he could take another step toward her, she closed the door and shot the lock.

Oh, yeah. It was stupid to risk everything for a night with Chloe, but one thing was clear—that woman was worth it.

Nine

What the hell was she doing?

That was the question Chloe asked herself repeatedly as hot water sluiced over her shoulders and down her back. The fact that she was even considering spending the night with Pete was insane. What happened before in Missouri had been…just one of those things. Her adrenaline had been pumping from the fight and she'd needed to let off a little steam. She hadn't been there for Pete—he'd just been the safest, most convenient option. They'd gotten swept up in the moment and that was that. No big deal.

And this was Pete Wellington, for heaven's sake. The man had done his level best to make her life a living hell for the last ten and a half years. At every turn, he had criticized, undermined and generally made a huge pain of himself. She could still hear her father's ranting in her ear from this morning, demanding to know how she could dare trust him, how she could dare risk the All-Stars? Or, worse, when Dad had stopped yelling long enough to take a breath, Oliver's sullen glares and his quiet accusation, "I thought you said you could handle the rodeo yourself."

Yeah, well—that had been before Flash had committed assault *and* before Flash made good on his promise to tell Dad and Oliver about Pete unless Chloe ended his suspension early so he could ride again.

It'd also been before Pete had turned out not to be the villain she had pegged him for.

The next time she saw Flash, she was going to wring his neck. The nerve of that idiot. Seriously, all he did was get pissed whenever someone suggested he'd only gotten ranked in the All-Stars because he traded on the family name. But the moment things got messy, what did Flash do? Tried to blackmail his own sister so he could get around the rules that applied to everyone else.

By God, if he had the nerve to show up at the rodeo in two days' time and do anything that even looked like *smirk*, she was going to finish him, and he'd deserve it.

She heard a thump from the room. Flash was *a* problem but he wasn't *the* problem she had to deal with right now. That honor went to Pete freaking Wellington and his thoughtful gift of a hotel room and his tempting offers to take care of her.

She shouldn't even be considering option three. She should offer to take the sofa or sleep on the floor or anything, really, that kept at least a modicum of distance between her and Pete.

But she was considering it. Oh, she was.

If it were just because he'd brought her to a shattering orgasm in less than five minutes with nothing more than his fingers, that'd be enough of a reason to give him a second chance. He'd been hot stuff back when she'd first laid eyes on him almost ten years ago, and since then? Pete was the finest of wines, getting better with age until he was perfect. And last time, she hadn't gotten to see the rest of him. She'd barely gotten to touch him.

She wanted him. Not just for a quick climax—although she was never one to pass on those. A night with him loving on her? God, she'd never heard anything so tempting as that.

And then he had to go and offer up his room—multiple times—before he'd even mentioned option three. She had no doubt he could take care of her sexual needs but the man had made her health and well-being his priority and *that* was a dangerous thing. She knew how to protect herself from the Pete Wellington who hated her guts, detested her brothers and lived to exact his revenge on her father.

She didn't know how to protect herself from the Pete who cared for her.

Ever since he'd barged into her dressing room a month ago, he'd done nothing but defend her, promote her ideas and who could forget about the orgasm? For the last month, he'd worked his butt off for the All-Stars and there hadn't been so much as a single whisper of betrayal.

She wasn't so stupid that she hadn't been checking up on him. Of course she had. He was doing his job well. Sadly, better than she could because no one wanted to take the All-Stars in a new direction simply because the Princess of the Rodeo said so.

But all of her ideas, coming from Pete? People got on board. Fast.

Truly, it had been an awful day. And there was no

guarantee that her father or Oliver or, worst of all, Flash wouldn't show up at this weekend's rodeo and cause all sorts of trouble. No, the worst would be if all three of them came together.

She shuddered and pushed the thought from her mind. The important thing was that they weren't here now—Pete was, with his thoughtful gestures and full-on charm, his good hugs and better kisses, his beautiful damned eyes and hot body.

And his bed. His big, soft bed.

She ran her hands over her breasts. They were heavy and tight and she knew what'd make them feel better. Some things had changed in a month and one of those things—the only relevant one at the moment, it seemed—was the fact that she wanted him again. *Still*. A month of pretending she had no interest in Pete was just that—pretending.

Better, he still wanted her. A man didn't casually mention sex if he weren't ready, willing and able to deliver the goods.

A knock on the bathroom door startled her so hard that she almost slipped. "Yes?"

"Got to get something. I'll be back in a bit."

"Oh. Okay." She heard the room door open and then realized—he might be leaving. "Pete?" she yelled in a panic because if he decided to be all noble, she'd kill him for leaving her aching for his touch.

"Yeah?" his voice came right back to the bathroom door.

"You're coming back, right?"

There was a pause that was long. Too long. Damn that man, he was torturing her, wasn't he? He'd brought up the possibility of sex and thrown in that gentle kiss and now he was going to leave her high and dry and—

"Do you want me to?" Even through the door and over the sound of the shower running, his voice resonated through her body.

Everything about her tightened and she came pitifully close to climbing out of the shower and dragging him onto the bed. "Yes." She swallowed, her hand gripping the shower curtain. "Please."

"Then I'll see you in a few."

As lines went, it wasn't the most romantic thing she'd ever heard. But there was no denying the relief that coursed through her as the door shut. Hopefully, he'd remembered to grab a key.

He was coming back. For her.

She wanted him. It was that simple. She wanted him, and she could have him. Was that a problem? After all, they'd been able to do this before—engage in certain liberties and then go on as if nothing had happened. What's to say they couldn't do that again?

Just for one night. They'd overlook the sound business practice of keeping business and personal separate and whatever happened…happened.

If she were really lucky, *whatever* would happen several times. But only this once and then things would go back to the way they'd been before.

She dropped her head into her hands. This wasn't the sort of thing that people could pretend had never happened. This would change everything between her and Pete. And yet, she was going to let that man love on her and hold her all night long because…

No. She didn't need him. Absolutely not. But she needed *something* and he was here.

Oh, she was in trouble, wasn't she?

Her mind made up, she took her time shaving her legs and moisturizing. Because it made her feel better, not because she was primping for a man. Or even one specific man.

She was in the middle of brushing her teeth when the door clicked open and Pete said, "It's me."

A thrill shot through her. He'd kept his word. "I'm almost done."

"Honey," he said through the door, his voice warm and rich, "I'd wait all night for you."

Her breasts tightened almost to the point of pain and heat flooded her center. "Would you really?"

"Yup. But, Chloe?"

She forced herself to breath. The woman looking back at her in the steamy mirror was nude and aroused and cupping her own breasts. But it wasn't enough. She needed more. "Yes?" It came out needy.

He could tell—she heard it in his voice when he said, "Don't make me wait forever."

She was absolutely not going to open this door and throw herself at him. Nope. She might desperately want everything he was offering, but she wasn't about to come off as desperate. A girl still had her pride.

He could just keep waiting, even if only for another five minutes. She forced herself to go slow as she slid her nightgown over her head. It wasn't a peek-a-boo lace teddy or anything. She liked to sleep in a dove gray silk slip that came to almost her knees. But when she looked in the mirror, she could see the hard points of her nipples and, really, what more did a girl need when it came to seduction?

She twisted her damp hair into a messy high bun so it would dry with curls in it and then, taking a deep breath, she walked out into the room.

And stumbled to a stop at the sight of Pete in a white T-shirt, his buckle undone and the top two buttons on his fly hanging open. He wasn't naked, not even close. But dear God, he was a wonder to behold. Had she ever properly appreciated his biceps? Or his forearms? The muscles bulged as he worked a cork loose from a bottle of wine. Her gaze dropped to those open buttons and the faint outline of a bulge still hidden that promised amazing things.

He popped the cork and looked up. His jaw fell open and he almost dropped the bottle. The cork was a lost cause. "My God, Chloe," he murmured with what sounded like awe. "Look at you."

She wouldn't have thought it possible, but her nipples got even harder. She positively ached for his touch. But again, she didn't fling herself at him. Instead, she skimmed her hands over the cool silk of her nightie. His eyes almost bulged out of his head.

This was good. She'd had a hot shower and time to calm down and she wasn't some delicate flower. She was his equal, by God, and she was going to make him sweat. Was he even breathing? When he lifted his gaze to her face, he seemed dazed. She nodded toward the bottle—*not* his bulge, which looked like it was actively growing. "Is that for me?"

He seemed startled to realize he was holding an open bottle. "Oh. The wine. Yes, and some chocolate," he added. "And ice cream. Vanilla's okay?"

Sweet merciful heavens, this man. She couldn't remember the last time a man had brought her chocolate, much less wine and ice cream. How was she supposed to be all cool and seductive when she was so stupidly grateful he was here?

Chloe had put a hand over her chest to try to keep her heart from beating so hard he'd be able to see it.

"Where did you get all of this?"

He stood, grinning. She felt a little dazed, too. "I have my ways." He grabbed another glass from next to another ice bucket—which was full of ice—and poured her some white wine.

"I can't remember the last time I had someone do something this nice for me." She wasn't including Renee in that, though. Girlfriends operated at a different level than men she was sleeping with. And right now, Pete was blowing every other man she'd ever known out of the water.

He handed her the glass of wine. When Chloe took it, she let her fingers skim over his. His breath caught in his throat, but he held her gaze and said, "That's a damned shame. You deserve nice things, Chloe."

She looked up at him. "What if…" She swallowed. They'd already had almost-sex. He'd already offered even more sex. Why did she suddenly feel so shy? "What if I want more than *nice*?"

He was suddenly in front of her, the heat radiating off his chest, warming her through her silk slip. She tensed when he lifted a hand but instead of pulling her into his arms, he wrapped one curl around his finger. He whispered, "You deserve every good thing, babe," then he kissed that little curl, his chest coming flush with hers. "And I want to give it to you. Anything you want, it's yours."

This time, she did melt into him, as best she could while holding a glass of wine. Her arm went around his waist, bringing her chest flush with his and, as her nipples slid against the warming silk, they went rock-hard.

Pete released her wayward curl and brushed his lips over her ear. "Did you decide?" His breath caressed her skin and then his teeth tugged on her earlobe.

"Did you really get me wine and chocolate?" It was a

stupid question because of course he had. Those things hadn't materialized out of thin air. But he'd gone out of his way and done something wonderfully sweet. For her.

He was the most dangerous man she'd ever known.

"Darlin'," he said, his voice pure Texas drawl as his lips skimmed over her jaw, "I'm starting to think that there's not much I wouldn't do for you."

Oh. *Oh, my.* "Option three," she breathed. "Please."

She didn't know if she kissed him or if he kissed her or if it even mattered. Pete was here, for her.

"Just for the night," she murmured as he took the glass of wine from her hands and pivoted to set it on the table, turning her at the same time. Her back hit the wall and then he was pressing against her.

"Well," he chuckled, running one hand down her thigh and lifting her leg so it wrapped around his waist, "maybe the morning, too."

She gasped as his erection bumped against her sex. "God, yes," she managed to get out, but then Pete was kissing her, devouring her and she gave herself over to him.

What she needed was this man, hot and hard against her. He nipped at her lower lip as his hips rocked into her and she couldn't fight back the moan.

"Could I make you come, just like this?" he growled against the skin of her neck, thrusting against her. He had one hand holding up her leg, the other braced against the wall by her head. Her arms around his neck, she hung on for the ride.

Chloe whimpered. It wasn't dignified or logical, but this man had the ability to reduce her to panting desperation in a matter of seconds. Standing up, even! And not for the first time. How good would he be in an actual bed?

He rocked against her and she bit down on his neck, which made him groan. "I think you're going to come for me," he said, but his voice was rough and she knew he felt it, too—this connection between them, however tenuous it was. "Then I'm going to lay you out on that bed and make love to you until you come again."

She shuddered at the words, the tension coiling inside her becoming sharper, almost painful. How did he do this to her?

But he did. Easily. The hand under her leg pushed the hem of the slip up. Not that the silk was a great barrier between their bodies but when he lifted it out of the way, she gasped as she came into contact with the stiff denim of his jeans.

"So beautiful," he got out in a strained whisper, his forehead resting on hers. Her eyes flew open and what she saw reflected in his gaze made her gasp again.

Please let this be real. She didn't think that on purpose, but there it was. She wanted *whatever* this was with Pete to be real.

That feeling only got stronger when he repeated, "God, Chloe. So damned beautiful." But this time, he pulled his other hand away from the wall and covered her breast with it, pulling the silk tight over her nipple. Then he kissed her as he squeezed.

And Chloe came for him, moaning loudly as the tension in her body snapped back. He sucked down the noise and didn't stop thrusting against her, not even when her legs began to shake. Everything began to shake, and she knew she was in danger of falling. She pulled away from his mouth and said, "I can't stand."

And that man had the damned nerve to wink at her. And pivot his hips so his erection ground against her.

"That," he said, sounding way too pleased with himself, "was the plan."

She liked a confident partner, she really did. But this was beyond confident. This was Pete like she knew him—cocky. Convinced he knew best. And okay, maybe he did. But he wasn't in charge here.

She was. And it was high time he remembered that.

She pushed at his chest, but that barely moved him, so she used the wall for leverage. "You forgot something," she said, managing to keep her balance as he stumbled back and dropped her leg.

"What?" But he didn't look worried or even mildly concerned. Instead, he had that teasing smile tucked into the corners of his lips.

She took a deep breath, making sure her knees were going to hold before she stepped toward him. "You work *underneath* me."

The man licked his lips and then Chloe was pulling his shirt over his head and shoving his jeans and shorts down. Then she pushed him, and he fell back onto the bed with a muffled *whump*. And he grinned at her the whole time, like he'd just found the golden ticket.

She stared at his body, hoping her mouth was shut. Good lord, the man was built. His chest was broad and muscled without being fastidiously ripped. A working man's muscles, ones he'd earned the hard way. But that wasn't the part that caught her attention. Oh, no. She couldn't look away from his erection, hard and long and curved ever-so-slightly to the right. He was big without being huge and he hadn't manscaped. She liked that hair on him, liked the calluses on his hands. She liked him rough around the edges but most of all, she liked him underneath her.

As she looked her fill, he twisted until he was able

to reach his back pocket, where he grabbed a small box of condoms. "Yes?" he asked, tossing them on the bed.

She shot him a look. "You were counting on option three, weren't you?"

He didn't even have the decency to blush. "Been waiting for this moment for a month, hon." He kicked the rest of the way out of his jeans and propped himself up on his elbows, his legs draped over the edge of the bed. "Ever since Missouri, I haven't been able to get you off my mind, so you're damned right I'd want to be prepared. I want to see you this time."

She mounted up and straddled him, smacking his hands away when he tried to lift her slip over her head. "Hey," he protested but then she settled on him, his thick erection rubbing against her sex.

"I'm the boss," she told him when he reached for the slip again. This time, she grabbed his hands and held them tight, using his arms to help her stay balanced. Instead of fighting her, he laced his fingers with hers and another part of her melted. She was still shaky, her pulse still pounding through her sex as the last of the climax worked through her. Without layers of fabric between them, she could feel the heat of his body against hers, the pulse of his erection as she slid back and forth. "Pete," she started but then stopped because she wasn't sure what she was going to say next.

As she moved over him, his head fell back and he began to pant. "You're killing me, Lawrence," he moaned, his body quaking under hers.

"Just returning the favor." But even as she said it, that tension began to coil within her body again. For a month, they'd both been dreaming of this moment. Every time she caught him watching her from the top of the chutes, this was the heat that flashed down her body. All roads led here. It'd been pointless to fight it, she realized. This time was theirs.

This time, she wanted him inside her.

So she scooted back and reached for the condoms. Now it was Pete who batted her hands away and got the packet open. "I could have done that," she scolded as he quickly rolled the condom on.

"And let you keep torturing me?" He tried to give her another cocky grin, but that was when Chloe peeled the slip off.

And held her breath. Pete sucked in air as he stared. She arched her back to put her perfectly average breasts in the best light. After her second boyfriend had taken one look at her bare breasts and said in a pitying tone, "they're not *that* bad," she'd made a concerted effort to master all the tricks to make them look their best. Arch the back, suck in the stomach, try not to lie flat on her back lest her poor breasts all but disappear.

So she braced herself because she was naked in bed with Pete Wellington and he could be the man of her dreams and he could still also cut her to shreds if he wanted to.

Did he want to?

He sat up and stroked his fingers over the tops of her breasts, over her nipples. Then he leaned forward and pressed his lips to the tip of her left breast. "Perfect," he murmured against her skin and then he sucked her whole nipple into his mouth.

"Oh, God," she whispered, clutching his head as his teeth skimmed over her delicate skin. The pull of his mouth drew an answering pull from deep inside her. His sheathed erection continued to rub against her from below and it was just that damned easy for him to take her breath away.

There was no negotiation about how it was his turn, how he needed to let go, how he couldn't wait another second. He didn't push or rush or demand. Instead, he just sucked at her sensitive skin and let her body bear down on his as he took his sweet time.

This was what it meant to let a man love on her. To let a man take care of her. She'd had plenty of boyfriends and lovers but she'd never had a man who put her first like this. For heaven's sake, she was already naked and he had on the condom!

But instead of lifting her bottom and thrusting into her, he just kissed his way to her other breast and began to torment that nipple, too.

She stared down at him as he lavished her with attention, her fingers twined in his thick hair. It almost didn't feel real, this moment with him. But if it was a dream, she didn't want to wake up.

Finally, she couldn't take it anymore. She needed him inside of her. "Lie back." She didn't have to tell him twice.

Chloe scooted forward, raising her bottom in the air as she kissed him. His erection sprang up against her and, because she was absolutely not done torturing him, she let herself sink back onto him—slowly. Years of gripping a saddle with her thighs while she rode around arenas gave her the strength to move so slowly that Pete began to cuss.

"Dammit, Chloe," he growled, trying to sit up and thrust into her.

She shoved him by his shoulders until he was flat on his back and shifted until she had his thighs pinned to the bed with her feet. "My turn, Pete. You like to see how fast you can make me come? Fine. I'm going to see how slow I can go without making you come."

He groaned in pure agony, but she slid down another centimeter onto his erection. She sat up and let her legs fall to the side again, sinking down on him completely. "Pete," she moaned as her body stretched to accommodate his.

"Babe, I need to feel you come around me." He started to thrust again and for a moment, Chloe forgot that she was in charge here because if Pete had been amazing before, he was simply breathtaking now.

Because he was filling her and she wasn't sure she'd ever felt anything so good, so *right*.

Pete Wellington had always been the wrong man. How had he become the right one?

His hands went to her breasts again, tweaking her nipples and making her moan. "Come with me, Chloe." It wasn't a request—it was an order.

She laced her fingers with his and then kissed his knuckles. "Slow, Pete," she told him when he tried to go faster. "I want this to last."

If it were possible for him to look insulted and aroused at the same time, he did. "This isn't a one-time thing, Chloe." His voice was rough with need and that, combined with the way he was moving inside of her, made her shudder. "It can't be."

She shook her head. "Tonight." She used his arms to balance herself, unable to keep her slow pace as he drove her mad. Again. "Just tomorrow morning."

Suddenly, he pulled her down, chest to chest, and kissed her fiercely. Light exploded behind Chloe's eyes as she went stiff and then completely limp, a climax unlike anything she'd ever experienced before. She collapsed on top of him and in seconds, he had her on her back and was pounding into her, saying, "God, Chloe—yes!" Then, with a grunt that was almost a shout, he buried himself inside her and it was all she could do to hold on to him, to hold on to herself. When he fell onto her, she wrapped her arms and legs around him and held on. Breathing hard, they lay there in silence.

Had she thought the orgasm against the side of his truck was good? Or the one a few minutes ago against the wall? She'd had no idea, had she?

Now what was she supposed to do with him? There was no going back to the way they'd been before. She'd known that going in, but she hadn't counted on how much sex with Pete would change her.

He propped himself up on one elbow and stared down at her. "My God, Chloe," he said, his voice a reverent whisper as he touched her cheek with the tips of his fingers. There was no deception in his eyes, no hidden joke at her expense. Nothing but a swell of emotions that made her breath catch in her throat because being with Pete had changed everything.

Because she wasn't the same. She would *never* be the same.

Oh, no. What had she done?

Ten

While Chloe used the bathroom, Pete took care of the condom and chugged the now-warm wine so he could pour her a fresh glass. He moved the ice bucket to the nightstand, then put the chocolate next to it. There. Everything was in easy reach. Including the condoms.

It was easier to do these small things than to think about what had just happened. What, God willing, would happen again. Soon.

He'd made love to Chloe Lawrence. He was a little fuzzy on the details, but he was pretty sure they'd even managed to have an argument in the middle of sex.

Had he really told her he didn't want this night—and tomorrow morning—to be a one-time thing? And had she really told him this was all that could be?

Idiot. He scrubbed his hand over his face, which was a mistake because he could smell her scent on his skin. He'd promised her one night. He was pushing his luck with one night and one morning. Asking—*demanding*—anything more was tantamount to failure.

Because how was he supposed to push Chloe out of the rodeo while he was having sex with her? And not just any old sex. The kind of sex that overrode every single one of his plans and intentions. The kind of sex that made him forget the last ten damned years.

Shit.

This was the problem with being scrupulously unscrupulous. Because he knew he could very well be at Chloe's beck and call in the bedroom and still push her out of the All-Stars. It'd make everything easier because she might assume their physical closeness would mean he couldn't pull the trigger. It'd be easy.

But it wouldn't be right. If he were going to steal his rodeo back, he didn't want to muddy the issue with emotions, dammit. Sex was fine. Everyone enjoyed a good time and that was that.

Or that was *supposed* to be that.

But just then, the bathroom door opened. Chloe came back out and even though she'd put the gray nightie back on, his heart skipped a beat and he was already pulling her into his arms and burying his nose in her hair and sighing in relief when she hugged him back.

Stupid emotions. They were going to ruin everything.

Somehow, he managed to break away. He couldn't think and touch her at the same time. "Wine," he said gruffly as he handed her the glass. "Chocolate is here, ice cream is in the fridge. I'm going to take a quick shower."

She blinked up at him and he was more than relieved that she looked dazed. Thank God he wasn't the only one left reeling by the best sex he'd ever had.

He was to the bathroom door—moving quickly, *not* running away from her—when she said, "Pete?"

He just needed another few minutes to figure out how to put all these damned feelings on lockdown and then he'd be happy to work under her again. But if she asked him to hold her right now, he knew he'd be at her beck and call. Happily.

As it was, he managed to stop and look back at her without rushing to her side. "Yeah, hon?"

She had the wine almost against her lips and she shot a look at him over the glass that made his pulse began to pound again. "Don't make me wait."

He didn't even bother to fight the groan that ripped itself out of his chest. He all but tripped over his own damned tongue into the bathroom and proceeded to take the world's fastest shower.

He needed to get a grip on something other than Chloe's amazing body. Making love to her wasn't a detour, it was…just a speed bump. He could do exactly what he'd told her he could—keep whatever happened in this room separate from whatever happened at the rodeo. He didn't need to revise his plans. All he needed to do was make sure that neither of them got tangled up in emotions. Simple.

But *simple* wasn't why he barely toweled off and hurriedly rushed through brushing his teeth. *Simple* wasn't why he didn't even bother putting on a pair of shorts, instead wrapping a towel around his waist. And *simple* had nothing to do with the way he all but jogged out of the bathroom.

It was Chloe. Dammit.

She was sitting cross-legged on the bed, her perfect little toes just visible under her calves. He had an irrational need to suck on each toe, just to see if she'd giggle or threaten him with bodily harm or what. She had the pint of ice cream in one hand and a square of chocolate in the other, all while she grinned at the TV.

For just that moment, she looked young, like a girl full of wonder and mischief.

A memory came crashing out of the past, of Chloe full of a brazen kind of hope as she'd come up to him at a rodeo and said, "I know our dads have their issues, but I wanted to tell you that my brother Flash says you're the best rider here," and then she'd stuck out her hand like they could shake on that compliment and let bygones be bygones.

And he'd been young and stupid and so, *so* angry at her just waltzing into his rodeo like she owned it, which she had and he'd...

But that was bullshit, wasn't it? He hadn't been young. He'd been a twenty-three-year-old man and he'd had three whole years to adjust to the fact that the All-Stars wasn't his anymore. But he hadn't. He'd been furious that she'd had the nerve to even try to make nice. Instead of shaking her hand, he'd sneered, "You tell your daddy that next time he wants to talk to me he shouldn't send a *girl* to do his dirty work," before he'd stomped off, cussing out the entire Lawrence family at top volume.

That was when he'd seen pain etched on her young face. That was the first time he'd watched her lift her chin and refuse to be put in her place. By him.

He could not have been a bigger asshole.

She giggled again and Pete put away that old memory. "What are you watching?"

She looked at him and her whole face softened. "I found *I Love Lucy* reruns."

That look killed him. "A classic." Was there a point

in apologizing for how he'd treated her a decade ago if he was still hoping to wrestle control of the All-Stars away from her?

"This is a really good wine," she said, taking another sip. "Where on earth did you get it? Pendleton isn't known for its high-dollar wine selection."

He snorted. "Ah, the guy at the front desk was happy to point me in the correct direction." Point of fact, it had not been cheap, since the cute little wine store downtown had already closed for the night. But Pete was not going to let a little thing like regular business hours stop him from getting the very best for Chloe.

And, given how pleased she was with his choice— a nice Riesling—he was glad he'd basically bribed the store's owner to reopen for him. "I'm glad you like it."

Her gaze dropped to his towel. "Want some?"

He nodded and, losing his towel, climbed into bed next to her. She passed him her glass and he took a sip. Maybe it was that the wine was chilled. Or maybe it was the taste of Chloe on the rim of the glass. Either way, the wine was better for it.

She leaned into him, her shoulder bumping his. "Did I thank you for all this?" She waved her spoon around in what he took to be a gesture encompassing the wine, the sweets and the bed.

"Yes."

"Well, I meant it."

He grinned at her, at the matter-of-factness in her tone. "Duly noted." And then, maybe because he'd had a little wine or because his brain hadn't started fully functioning again after the mind-blowing sex, he heard himself say, "I'm sorry."

She shot him a surprisingly hard look. "For what?"

Crap. "Uh, for…you know. For being an asshole for, uh, the last ten years."

Brilliant, Pete. Way to go.

He had no idea what he was expecting her to do with that lousy attempt at an apology, but it certainly wasn't the way her shoulders slumped forward and she said, "Oh, Pete, don't start that."

Dimly, he was aware that the smooth thing to do would have been to say anything *but* an apology. Tell her how amazing she looked. Compliment her skills in bed. Hell, even asking what he'd missed in the *Lucy* episode would have been better than leading off with an apology after great sex. He knew that.

But the sheer dismay radiating off her put him on the defensive, dammit. "Start what? I've been a jerk in the past and I want to apologize for it."

She shot him the kind of look that normally he only saw on her face when Flash was doing something idiotic. "Well, don't. It's enough that we've both matured to the point where we can work well together and the sex is…" She cleared her throat, her cheeks bright pink. "The sex is very good."

He didn't like where this was going. "But…"

"But that doesn't make us friends." She looked away. "Or more than friends."

He knew he was staring at her, but he was powerless to stop. "That horse is out of the barn, Chloe, and there's no point in shutting the barn door behind it. We're way past more than friends."

She groaned and it wasn't a sensual sound. It was a sound of aggravation. "You don't get it, do you?"

That was a trap of a question if he'd ever heard one and, even in his muddled state, he knew better than to reply, *get what?* Instead, he crossed his arms and waited for her to answer her own question.

"Don't make me like you, Pete. It's enough that I respect you and you respect me. I couldn't handle it if we were anything else." She shifted, leaning back against the pillows and pulling her knees up, as if she could block him with her legs.

It took him a beat or two to make sense of those words. Respect? Hell, yeah, he respected her. He'd seen her in a new light in the last few weeks. She wasn't a ditzy, self-absorbed teenager whose only concern was how many people liked her. She was a business-focused horsewoman with big plans and the numbers to back up those plans. She put the All-Stars ahead of her family, for God's sake. He never would have believed it if he hadn't seen her handle the Flash debacle with his own eyes.

But this *whatever* between them? This wasn't respect. This was white-hot attraction that went beyond professional courtesy and far beyond their messy history.

What did she mean, she couldn't handle it?

He was going to find out, by God. He reached over her to grab the remote and shut the TV off. "Hey," she said, her voice muffled as he practically sprawled on top of her. "I was watching that!"

"Lucy gets a crazy idea, Ricky gets mad and yells in rapid Spanish, Fred and Ethel save their bacon and everyone lives happily ever after," he said, taking her wine and ice cream and half setting, half throwing them onto the nightstand.

"Pete?"

Good. Better. She was a little nervous now. She should be, after saying they couldn't be friends right after she'd ridden him better than any bucking bronco, by God.

He *knew* all the reasons they couldn't be friends. He was going to screw her over in a nonsexual sense and she was going to hate him and her brothers might try to kill him. They could *not* be friends. Not in this lifetime, not in the next.

"Pete?" she said again and he went hard at the sound of his name on her lips. "What are you doing?"

He grabbed her legs and pulled her down. "This," he said, skimming his hands up her legs, "is how I respect you."

He buried his face against the soft hair that covered her sex. She gasped, in pleasure or surprise, he didn't know. He didn't care. He licked her, the taste of her arousal flooding his mouth, pushing everything else away.

They weren't friends.

He found her already tight and swollen with need, and swept his tongue over her. "This is how I honor you," he murmured against her delicate flesh.

They weren't friends with benefits, either.

Her hands found his hair and she gripped him tightly, holding him against her, asking for more. Begging for more.

They weren't enemies. Not anymore.

He slipped a finger inside her and had to hold her legs down when her back came off the bed. God, she was so responsive, so beautiful. He loved that he could make her come in moments, when he put his mind to it. "This is how I love on you."

This was how he loved her.

He almost snorted to himself. This was not love. This was lust. This was emotions running high. This was them straddling the fine line between love and hate in a purely physical way.

Hell. He didn't know what they were.

He added a second finger and focused on timing the thrust of his hand with the movement of his tongue, finding the right rhythm to push her higher and higher. His erection bounced against the sheet beneath him, each contact making him even harder for her.

"Pete, *oh*…" she breathed, her whole body twisting underneath his touch. He pinned her thighs open and pushed her body to the breaking point.

They were *not* friends, dammit.

"I love making you come," he all but hummed as he tasted her again and again. He couldn't get enough of her. "Come for me, babe."

She broke, her shoulders coming off the bed as she damned near ripped his hair from his scalp. Her sweet body pulsed around his fingers, against his tongue as wave after wave crashed over her. Every twitch of her body pushed his own need higher until he was in danger of coming just from the act of satisfying her.

Three, he thought as the tension began to drain away from her body and she collapsed back against the bed, breathing hard and making little mewing sounds of satisfaction. He'd made her come three times tonight.

Three was a good number. *Four* was better.

He kissed her inner thigh and then sat up, pausing only long enough to grab a condom and then roll it on. "Yeah?"

She looked up at him, her eyes glazed and her mouth open. "You're going to be the death of me," she murmured as he wrapped her legs around his waist and fit his tip against her sex.

He sank into her with one thrust; she was still quivering from the last orgasm. His body jerked in response and he wanted desperately to let go. But she wasn't at four yet and by God, by the time they collapsed into sleep tonight, he was going to make damned sure that she'd forgotten every other man in the world. That every time she looked at him, thought of him, she'd remember how he'd taken care of her.

This was not a race to see how fast he could make her come but there was no way in hell he was going to go slow, like she'd done when she was in control. She wasn't in charge of this *whatever* anymore.

He set a steady rhythm, determined to keep the upper hand. But then her nails dug into his ass as she pulled him into her, demanding more from him and he lost himself in her.

Not friends. Not enemies. Just him and her and *whatever* this was.

She bit him on the shoulder and he knew he couldn't hold out much longer, not with the way she was overwhelming his senses, his everything. He shifted so he could reach between their bodies and press her right… there.

She bit him again, harder, muffling her screams of pleasure against his skin, and he gave up the fight. He surrendered to the way her body pulled him in, to the way she felt surrounding him, to the indescribable pleasure of his climax deep inside of her.

He was hers.

Dammit.

Eleven

Despite the large, comfortable bed and despite the sheer exhaustion that obliterated the need to come up with appropriate post-sex pillow talk, Pete slept badly.

Every time Chloe turned in her sleep, he woke up wanting to make sure she was still there. To make sure she wasn't leaving and, most important, that he hadn't dreamed her.

At five, he gave up trying to keep his eyes closed. He lay on his back, with Chloe curled against his side, and tried to picture how either of them were going to move forward from this. Going back to the way things had been was out of the question.

At six, enough light seeped around the curtains that he could watch her while she slept. He'd been so lost in lust last night that he hadn't properly appreciated Chloe Lawrence without her fake eyelashes or over-the-top makeup. She was simply gorgeous.

At seven, he had to get up. Moving as carefully as he could, he shifted her off his arm and went to the bathroom.

Was it possible they could pretend nothing had happened? Could he look at her ready to ride out into the arena without seeing the way she'd ridden him? If he caught some local yokel hitting on her—which happened far more than he'd thought possible—would he let Chloe deal with it without punching someone?

Could he work under her? No, that still wasn't the right question.

Could he take the All-Stars away?

He could. It wasn't a matter of possibility. The plan would still work. Easily.

But if he pushed her and the Lawrences out of the rodeo business, would he ever have another chance to count the number of times he brought her to orgasm? Another chance to save the day? Hell, would he ever get to lounge around laughing at the wackiness of classic TV sitcoms with her?

He knew the answer to those questions. *No.*

If he locked Chloe out of the All-Stars, he'd never get another shot at her. It was either Chloe or the All-Stars. There was no possible *and*.

Was that an answer he was willing to live with?

And why the hell was he trying to have this conversation with himself before he'd had his coffee? *Dumbass.*

He opened the bathroom door and immediately noticed the room was brighter. Although Chloe was curled up in bed, she'd clearly gotten up to open the blinds. "Morning, hon," he said, filling the single-serve pod coffeemaker.

"Hmm," she murmured. "Come back to bed." Then, after a brief pause, "Please."

He really needed that coffee but…yeah, Chloe was his priority. He slid back between the sheets and pulled her into his arms and something in his chest loosened as she curled into him.

"So polite." He kissed her forehead. "Morning," he said again.

"Are you coming back here tonight?" she asked around a yawn.

That was not the deal. Yeah, this room was technically his but when they went their separate ways this morning, that was the end of whatever. It had to be.

Didn't it?

"The room is yours. I can find another place to crash. One night, that's what we agreed on."

She yawned again. He began to think that Chloe Lawrence was not a morning person. "One night and one morning," she corrected.

That was what she'd said last night when he'd stupidly asked for more. He wasn't going to be stupid again.

She flung her leg over his. He could feel the warmth of her sex against his hip, closer now. "Come back to me tonight," she whispered, her hand stroking over his chest.

Aw hell. "Riders will be coming in," he said, grasping for something reasonable even as his body started to respond to her touch, her voice. "We might be seen."

That got her attention. Her leg slid off his and she stopped petting him, instead rolling over onto her back. He tried not to shiver at the loss of her heat and, when she flung her hand over her head, he contented himself to admire this particular view of her breasts. And to trace their outline with his fingers. And maybe his tongue.

"I need to tell you something," she sighed. But at least she went back to stroking him—his hair this time.

"That doesn't sound good," he murmured against her skin before shifting so he could pay attention to her other very lovely breast. He loved how easily the tips hardened to little points at the slightest touch.

She sighed dramatically. "It's not. But...there's a slight chance that one or more Lawrence men might show up at the rodeo this weekend."

That got Pete's attention. He sat back. "Is there a particular reason for that?"

He could see her trying to put on a brave face and he didn't like it. He didn't want her to have to hide. Not from him. "The meeting yesterday did not go as planned."

"The one that upset you?"

She nodded. Pete took comfort in the fact that she hadn't turned on her vapid charm. Right now, Chloe was still very much the woman who held his feet to the fire. "It was with my family. I mean, I had a not-great meeting about the Princess clothing line, which was bad enough—distribution problems—but then Oliver called me into his office. He was waiting with Dad and Flash."

Hell. Had they found out about him and Chloe? But how? No one had so much as breathed a whisper about what had happened in Missouri last month and the whole part about them being naked in bed together hadn't happened until afterward.

She took his hand. It was both comforting and alarming, frankly, and he didn't enjoy that feeling one damned bit. "I hadn't exactly informed Oliver or my father that I had hired you to help me run the rodeo."

It didn't take a genius to figure this one out. "Flash told them." He'd had it up to here with that twerp. It was one thing for him to threaten Pete, another to beat up a fellow rider. But a man should protect his loved ones, not throw them to the wolves.

She gave him a look that was full of regret. "I might have failed to mention that Flash was attempting to use the small detail of your employment to *persuade* me to let him back onto the circuit early."

That did it. He wasn't doing another single thing without coffee. He gave her hand a squeeze and then went to get the first cup.

Which, of course, he immediately handed over to her. They were silent while he got the second cup going. While it perked, he sat down on the edge of the bed and fought the urge to bury his head in his hands. "I take it that revelation didn't go over real well."

"No," she said quietly. "Not particularly."

He gave up and let his head drop. "Just so I understand what you're saying, your jackass brother—the younger jackass—was attempting to use me to blackmail you?"

"It sounds bad when you put it like that." He spun and stared at her. Hard. "Yes," she admitted, taking a long drink of the coffee. "I didn't give in, though."

"How mad were they? Oliver and Milt?" Because Pete had been on the receiving end of their anger on more than one occasion and if the Lawrence men were well and truly pissed, they could make Chloe's life a living hell. Just like they'd done to Pete.

"Well," she said weakly, "my father managed not to give himself a heart attack, so that counts for a lot, right?"

"Jesus." In other words, he'd probably been throwing things. "And?"

She shrugged, staring at her coffee. "And…that was all."

"Chloe," he said, the warning in his voice. Because they both knew there was no way in hell that was all.

"Dad made it clear he thought I was stupid to let you use me like this. Oliver wanted to know why I'd told him I could manage the rodeo if I so obviously couldn't and Flash gloated."

"Of course he did." Man, he wished Flash had just punched him. Pete would take a black eye over the almost detached way Chloe was relating this story of family "bonding." He could just see it, her being called on the carpet while Milt raged, Oliver glowered and Flash made everything worse. Three against one was never fair.

"Then they informed me they wanted you gone before you destroyed the All-Stars for good."

He processed that statement. In his personal experience, telling Chloe she had to do anything was never a good idea. "And?"

If she was going to fire him, that seemed like the sort of thing she might have mentioned before he went down on her.

She looked at him and the raw vulnerability he saw in her eyes almost knocked him right off the bed. "And I told them they were wrong about you. Because they are." She swallowed hard, her eyes taking on a suspicious shimmer. "Aren't they?"

She wasn't going to kick him out of the All-Stars. She'd defied her family for him. For the man who'd treated her like total crap for years. For the one person who hated anything and anyone associated with the Lawrence name.

And that was before he'd slept with her. Before everything had changed.

There was no possible *and*. It was either the All-Stars *or* Chloe. He could destroy her faith in him and take back his rodeo or he could stay wrapped around her and wait for her family to destroy him. Because they would.

No *and*.

No happy endings. Not for them.

He cupped her cheek, stroking his thumb over her soft skin and a few creases from where she'd slept on the pillowcase funny. "Chloe Lawrence—were you protecting me?"

It felt so right to touch her, to pull her into his arms and marvel at how perfect she fit there. It sure as hell made it easier to ignore things like long-simmering family feuds. "Don't let it go to your head." She sniffed and the sound of her trying not to cry—because of him!—almost destroyed him. "I was protecting myself, too."

"Did they say they're coming to check on you?" Because if there was a chance that one or more Lawrence men were about to barge in at any moment, he at least wanted to have on a pair of pants before the brawl broke out.

She shook her head. "But I wouldn't put it past them. Dad's pissed because I'll never be anything more the Princess of the Rodeo to him. And Oliver's pissed at me because even though he hates the damned rodeo, he took a chance on me, and because I brought you in, I've proven that I can't do the job—which makes him look bad. Funny," she said, leaning away from his touch and taking another drink of her coffee, "that no one seems pissed at Flash."

"Except you." And him. Because he was *livid* at that hotheaded jerk.

"Oh, yeah," she agreed and he was unreasonably relieved to see that fighting spirit light up her eyes. "He doesn't see it. He picks all these fights with anyone who dares even think that he's only ranked because his daddy owns the rodeo, but the moment I treat him like just another rider, he goes crying to Dad that the rules shouldn't apply to him."

"How old is he?"

"Twenty-four."

"That explains everything." Pete smiled and then he began to chuckle when she looked at him like he'd lost his mind. "God, I was *such* a jerk to you at that age."

"Don't start," she said, but he didn't miss the way her cheeks colored.

Did she remember the way he'd refused to shake her hand? Oh, hell, who was he kidding? This was Chloe Lawrence. Of course she remembered. "The odds of Flash apologizing to you are a thousand to one—"

"If that," she snorted.

"So you're going to let me apologize to you on behalf of dipshit young rodeo riders everywhere, okay?" He didn't know why he was pushing this, only that he had to get this out. "You deserve better, Chloe. You shouldn't have to take this much crap from anyone, much less your family or—" he paused, remembering how the stock contractors had talked down to her in Missouri "—or any of the riders or contractors or anyone, dammit. Not even me." She didn't exactly roll her eyes at this, but he could tell she wasn't buying it. "We don't have to be friends for me to regret how I treated you in the past. We don't have to be *anything* for me to do better by you in the future. So I'm sorry. I never should've used you as an emotional punching bag when we were younger. You weren't the problem. I was. And I'm trying to do better. I *will* do better by you."

It felt good, saying those words. It felt better meaning them. But underneath all those warm, possibly even fuzzy, feelings was a slithering sense of guilt because it was all 100 percent true. Except for the part where he was going to do better in the future.

Because, assuming her family didn't descend upon the All-Stars in the next forty-eight hours and destroy everything, he wasn't going to do better by her.

Even so, a small voice, one that sounded a little like Chloe, whispered inside his head—why couldn't there be an *and*? Why couldn't he have *both*? Did he have to sacrifice *whatever* this was with her for the rodeo?

Or did he just have to make sure she was on his side when he made his move? Her against her family? Could he do that?

"Pete," she said, her voice soft. Because she was still nude and so was he and this bed was plenty big enough for both of them and she was staring at him like she'd never seen him before. "You really mean that?"

"Yeah, hon," he said gruffly, cupping her chin and lifting her mouth to his. He could make this work. He could keep Chloe and the rodeo. He just had to be on her side. Them against the world. Because he needed her in his bed, in his life.

He needed her.

Go, team.

He tasted the coffee on her lips and that woke him up but quick. They tangled together, legs and arms and mouths all touching and moving and it was even better by the light of day than it was in the deep shadows of the night.

Chloe was even better and, heaven help him, Pete

thought he might be a better man, too. Because what if he could keep the rodeo and hold Chloe tight? What if loving on her like this wasn't a one-time thing?

What if he could love her forever?

"Come back to me tonight," Chloe moaned in his ear as he thrust into her again and again.

"Yeah," he agreed, because this—she—was what he wanted.

It could work. He'd make it work.

Failure was not an option.

Twelve

How much longer until she and Pete could slip back into the hotel, like they had the last few nights? Not that Chloe was counting the hours—or minutes. Not at all.

Okay, she was. And the answer was a long time because the show at the Pendleton Round-Up didn't even start for an hour and a half. The rodeo would take a few hours, then there was the concert with Johnny Jones, a new up-and-comer that Chloe would have to put in an appearance for and…

Seven hours, give or take. Surely she could make it seven measly hours. Then maybe she and Pete could order a pizza and more wine and kick back. Because she wanted to jump his bones again but she also just wanted to hang out with him.

She liked him, dammit. Maybe too much.

She smiled and posed and told people that their Princess of the Rodeo shirts looked great on them and tried not to watch the clock. She was in the middle of posing with a group of little girls with pink cowboy hats when an icy chill ran down Chloe's back at the same moment the hairs on the back of her neck stood straight up. Everything about her body went into fight-or-flight mode, which could only mean one thing.

The Lawrence men were here. Of course they were.

She didn't let her big smile falter as she signed autographs and told everyone that, next year, there was going to be a brand-new competition to crown the next Princess of the Rodeo which, in general, was getting her one of two responses—excitement and sadness that it wouldn't be her. Sometimes in the same sentence.

"I'll still be here," she promised another young mother who said she'd been watching Chloe since she was a kid. As she talked and posed, she kept scanning the crowd.

Where were they? Or had she gotten lucky and only one relative had showed up? Please, let it be Oliver. He was disappointed in her for bringing in Pete, yes. But Oliver was far and away the most rational of her relatives. If she could make her case that Pete was helping the bottom line and also ensuring that Chloe didn't need to bother Oliver about the rodeo at all, she might be able to make him see reason.

That was a pretty freaking huge *might*, though.

A lull in the crowd showed her how far-fetched the idea of making anyone see reason was because that was when she heard it—shouting. And not just the normal yelling that went on before a rodeo. No, it was clear this was the kind of shouting that went with a fight.

Nope. Not just Oliver, then.

She did not want to deal with this, dammit, but what choice did she have? "If you all will excuse me for a moment," she said, making sure her smile stayed so bright that her face began to hurt. Then she took off toward the commotion at a fast walk. Not a run. Running would draw attention.

A huge crash reverberated throughout the rodeo grounds, followed by more shouting. Lots of it. The kind of noise that practically guaranteed all three Lawrence men were in attendance and potentially brawling in the dirt with Pete.

People turned toward the noise and she heard them asking what was going on as she hurried past. So much for not drawing more attention.

This was going to be a mess. The kind of mess that made Flash getting arrested and pleading no contest to assault look like a cake walk. The kind of mess that couldn't be easily smoothed over with some pretty words and a well-placed distraction.

The temptation to walk away was huge. She could turn her boots around and hide until the dust had settled. Ignore the fact that her family was ruining everything she'd worked for. Because why else were they here? Why didn't they have just a little faith in her and give her a season to make it work or fail on her own? Why did they seem hell-bent on destroying the rodeo and blaming her for it?

Why couldn't they see that Pete had changed? That he cared about the rodeo and the riders and…

And her.

Because he did. She knew he did. What else could explain sharing his room and the best sex she'd ever had?

No, she couldn't walk away. This was her rodeo and her family, regrettably. But she could give them a piece of her mind because dammit, she was freaking *furious*.

It was Friday night. How dare they pitch this fit right before showtime?

Another loud crash. It sounded like some of the metal fence panels used to pen up the animals were toppling. *Goddammit.* She started running, which wasn't easy in these chaps.

Her only consolation was that the fight was happening behind the grandstand, where the general public wasn't allowed. The crowd in attendance would know something had gone wrong, especially if they had to delay the start of the show to reset the pens, but Chloe needed a little time before the details of the brawl got out.

She had to push her way through a knot of riders and local staff before she found them.

What she saw made her heart sink because there they were. "You limp-dick rat bastard!" Flash yelled, struggling against two cowboys who were barely able to hold him back. His lip was split and blood poured out of his nose. It was a lot of blood.

And right next to him, practically foaming at the mouth, with his face an unnatural shade of purple, was her father. "You lying, cheating thief!" he screamed, spittle flying everywhere. Milt Lawrence was so mad that he also had two men holding him back. At least he wasn't bleeding.

"That's the best you can do, old man?" Pete taunted. One of his eyes was swollen shut and, oddly, Oliver was physically lifting Pete off the ground. Chloe had no idea if he was about to body slam Pete or what. "You can't even throw a punch, you fake cowboy!"

"Shut up!" Oliver hollered. Pete kicked him in the shins with his boot and Oliver cursed with much more creativity than Dad.

Fencing was on the ground and a couple of cowboys were trying to herd calves that had escaped and were panicking in the crowd. But as bad as all that was, that wasn't the thing that made Chloe want to howl with frustration.

No one else seemed interested in breaking things up. Instead, people were recording the fight on their phones. So much for that cushion and any hope she had of spinning this to her advantage. She had, at best, thirty seconds before the whole world knew that the feud between the Lawrences and the Wellingtons was back on in a big way.

Thirty seconds before people began to speculate if the All-Stars could survive the Lawrence family.

Her eyes burned and her throat closed up, but Chloe did not have time to mourn the All-Stars rodeo. It wasn't dead yet, despite the attempted murder happening before her eyes.

That was the moment when, with a scream of rage, Flash broke free and headed straight for Pete.

Chloe moved without thinking. She launched herself across the space and hip-checked Flash from the side. The impact jarred her hard enough her teeth clacked together but she kept her feet underneath her, which counted for a lot.

Flash didn't fall, damn him, but he lost his balance and staggered to the side where—thank God—a local stock contractor grabbed him several feet from Pete and Oliver.

"That's enough!" Chloe yelled. And for once, men listened. Her family stopped screaming. Pete stopped yelling. A hush fell over the crowd.

Every eye was on her.

"Cameras off, please," she said in what she hoped

was a polite voice, but she didn't think everyone would listen and, sure enough, only a few people lowered their phones. Great. Might as well play to the cameras.

"Now," she went on in a loud but hopefully not furious voice. "Anyone care to explain?"

"He started it!" Flash yelled, gesturing with his chin to Pete.

"What are you, four?" Pete snarled back, but at least his feet were on the ground and Oliver only had a hand on him.

"Gentlemen," she tried again, although there weren't any of those currently in attendance. Pete shot her a look that walked the fine line between *sorry* and *not sorry*.

Well, he could stuff his sorry ass. This was exactly why she hadn't wanted him to apologize earlier—because it wasn't enough. It'd never be enough.

She was so tired of this.

"At least be man enough to admit you've screwed this up," Pete went on.

Which of course was when Milt Lawrence decided to reenter the fray. "This isn't your rodeo, Wellington. Hasn't been for years! What are you even doing here?"

"Shut up!" Chloe spun to face her father. "I don't want to hear another word out of you—out of any of you," she added, spinning in a slow circle. "This rodeo is due to start in an hour and fifteen minutes and the calf pen has been destroyed. The show *will* go on, by God. So you," she said, pointing at her brothers and her father and Pete—and all the various people holding them back, "Come with me. Everyone else, get this pen reassembled, the calves contained and get ready to ride."

No one moved.

"You heard her," Pete bellowed. "Move!"

Everyone jumped to attention because of course they

did. Pete was a man and he could give orders. Who was she? Just the Princess of the Rodeo. Just another pretty face and an empty head and it'd be an affront to the men here and God above if she dared to ask people to do something.

She was so damned tired.

"Do you need a keeper?" she fired at Flash as she stalked past him. "Or can you at least pretend to be a grown man for fifteen damned minutes?"

"Hey, I'm not the problem here," he protested, but he shrugged out of the hold of the contractor.

"The hell you aren't." But she wasn't getting into this with him, not in public. "Follow me or else."

The Pendleton Round-Up was held every year at an outdoor arena, with rooms tucked underneath the stands. She marched toward her dressing room—which was thankfully larger than a closet. Would these dumbasses destroy it and possibly each other? Yeah, the odds were good. But she couldn't let any more of this out onto social media.

To their credit, Dad, Oliver, Flash and Pete all followed her back without punching each other. Dad grumbled about who owned the rodeo. Flash mumbled about how none of this was his fault. Pete and Oliver were thankfully silent.

When she had the door shut behind her, she turned to look at these men. Her men. Not that Pete was really hers but after the last few nights…maybe he was, just a little.

"Now," she said in as calm a voice as she could because even if they weren't punching each other, she could see that these four were like gas-soaked rags, just waiting to catch a spark and go up in flames. "What happened?"

They all started to talk at once—except for Oliver, who was leaning against her dressing room table, arms crossed and watching the whole thing.

"Boys," Dad roared. Under different circumstances, Chloe would've enjoyed the way both Flash and Pete clammed up like chastised schoolboys, except that was when Dad turned to her, finger jabbing in her direction. "I told you to fire this whelp."

There was a part of Chloe that was just as chastised. This was her father, who'd been a loving dad and had done his best to raise his kids after the death of his wife.

But she wasn't thirteen anymore. She was a grown woman, doing her best to run a successful rodeo. "Yeah, and?"

"What do you mean *and*, young lady?" he asked indignantly.

Pete smirked but Chloe ignored him. "You provided input on how this business should be run. I took that input into consideration and made a decision that was in the best interests of the business. Which was not to fire Pete." She took a step toward her father. "And?"

Dad's mouth opened and closed and his eyes all but bugged out of his head. "Do you know who he is?" he finally spluttered. "What he's done to our family? What he's doing to our livelihood right now?"

"Trying to keep Flash from destroying the All-Stars?" she replied in her most innocent voice.

"Hey, this is not—"

"Pete hasn't done anything to our family that we haven't done to his," she went on, ignoring Flash. "Did any of you consider that maybe things had changed? That we didn't have to keep doing *this*?"

Her gaze locked with Pete's and for the barest second she was encouraged by what she saw there. Support.

Understanding. He was listening to her and he agreed with her and that was a good thing.

It didn't last.

"I'll tell you what's changed," Flash spit into that second of silence. "Oliver went behind Dad's back and put you in charge of the All-Stars and it's all gone to hell since then."

She spun on her baby brother. If his nose wasn't already broken, she'd break it for him. "Oh? Is that so? Well tell me this, Frasier—who attacked Tex McGraw in Missouri, huh?" She used his real name because if ever he needed to be reminded that life was not all buckles and bunnies, it was now. "Who turned the most popular rider and all his fans against him and the All-Stars, single-handedly dropping take-home revenue by almost 7 percent? Whose actions, I wonder, created such a freakin' PR *disaster* that I had no choice but to hire a manager to keep the rodeo going while I worked overtime trying to contain the damage?" Flash opened his mouth in protest, but Chloe cut him off. "And for what? Because Tex insulted a *woman*?"

"That's not what happened!"

"Like hell it's not," Pete growled. Chloe glared at him.

"You," she went on, walking up to her baby brother and jabbing him in the chest, "need to grow up. You will not be allowed back on the All-Stars until you've completed your sentence for assault and demonstrated that you can control your behavior."

"That's not fair!" he yelled. "Tex started it and he didn't get suspended!"

That did it. She snapped. "Tex quit rather than be around you!" she screamed. "At least he has that option! You want to talk fair? How is it fair that you got into a fight and I'm the one being punished for it? How is it fair that I had to hire Pete because no one listens to me when I tell them to do something, but the moment he says jump, everyone asks how high?"

"People don't—" Oliver tried to say.

No one listened. Not a one of them. Chloe knew she was past the point of no return now, knew it was a good thing Pete was holding her back because she was done. *Done.*

"Did you not see the same thing I did not five minutes ago? Where I told everyone the show must go on and not a single person moved an inch until Pete told them to? You didn't even listen to my explanation about why I need Pete's help, Oliver. Instead, I got scolded like a little kid because of Flash. Why is it my job to manage his behavior, not his?" She spun back to Flash. "So you just tell me how it's fair that Dad lets Oliver run the company but I have to go behind his back to even get a chance to prove myself and, when I do get that chance, *you screw it up*? How is any of this fair, huh?" Her voice cracked.

Oh, no. She couldn't cry. Not now. For the rest of her life, anytime Flash wanted to get under her skin, he'd just casually bring up the time she cracked under the pressure and started sobbing. She took a step back and tried to breathe. She'd rather break her hand on Flash's jaw than do anything as unforgivable as *cry.*

"Me? You treat me like a child!" Flash shot back.

"I'm not—"

But Pete cut her off. "You act like a child," he replied, sounding exactly like a disappointed big brother. "You want to be treated like a man? Act like one."

"Hear, hear," Oliver added, as if it were necessary.

"And you!" Pete turned to him. "You act all high

and mighty? You play God with people's lives and you don't care what happens to them. Your wife's family stole money from half the country and your father stole my rodeo and do you care? Of course not."

"Pete, that's not fair," she tried to say.

But Oliver talked right over her. "You keep my wife out of this," he said, pushing off the table, his voice deadly.

"Or what? Do any of you realize that this all could have been avoided if you'd just treated Chloe like an adult? You," he said, staring at her father, "you act like the only thing she's good for is carrying a flag. If you paid attention, you'd realize that she's got some brilliant ideas to take the All-Stars to the next level. You," he said, spinning to Oliver, "back her up next time when it's clear these two won't listen to reason. And you," he said, turning to Flash, "if you want to prove yourself, then stop expecting her to bail your ass out when you screw up."

Yes, because talking about her as if she weren't here was treating her like an adult. It was nice of Pete to defend her, but she could defend herself, dammit.

"You're one to talk," Flash said, getting right up into Pete's face.

"Wait—" But no one listened to her.

"I am," Pete ground out. "You think I don't know what it's like to be young and angry and lash out at every single person because of something you have no control over? Jesus Christ, *kid*," he said, hitting *kid* extra hard, "open your damned eyes and man the hell up. Stop running to your father every time something goes wrong and stop hiding behind *her* skirts."

"Guys," she tried again because this was already spiraling out of control. *"Listen."*

No one did. Not even Pete. For all his big words, he was just as bad as they were.

"All you want," Flash said in an unnaturally calm voice, "is to get *into* her skirts and then, when you're done with her, push her out of this rodeo. You're using her—if you haven't already. She's nothing more than a pawn in your plans, and it's not my fault if she's not smart enough to see you for what you really are."

She gasped, pain slicing through her chest. Oh, God—was that how Flash saw her? Too dumb to even realize that Pete's betrayal was a possibility? She wrapped her arms around her waist, trying to hold herself together.

Dad swung around to stare at her, his face taking on that purple tinge again. Even Oliver looked concerned by this announcement.

"Chloe?" Oliver asked. "Is he using you?"

She was a grown woman. She was in charge. This was fine. She was fine.

"Did he touch you?" Dad roared, because the only thing that could apparently get her family to pay attention to her was a discussion of her sex life.

"It was his plan from the beginning," Flash crowed, shooting her a mean smile. "I tried to warn Chloe but no. She said *she* knew best."

"You watch your mouth," Pete said in a deadly whisper.

What happened next was utterly predictable. Flash took a swing at Pete's face. Pete managed to block the blow and got off a shot to Flash's ribs. Dad yelled. Oliver tried to break it up. Someone punched him and he punched back and within seconds, it was an all-out brawl.

Chloe just stood there, trying not to despair. Trying

not to lose all hope that this *whatever* could work. It couldn't. She'd been a fool to think it might.

Something crashed to the ground and shattered, probably off her dressing table. Oliver yelled and Chloe…

She walked. She grabbed her purse off the hook by the door and walked right out of that room, softly closing the door behind her. The sounds of the fight didn't quiet down, which meant they hadn't even noticed her leaving. Because, when it got down to brass tacks, she wasn't relevant to the feud. She was merely another sore spot to fight over, just like the All-Stars.

Did she even matter? To any of them?

She *so* wanted the answer to be yes. She wanted to believe, with her heart and soul, that she mattered to Pete. She had the last few nights, after all.

But Flash's words echoed in her ears as she wove her way through the arena grounds, ignoring the people who called her name. It didn't matter if she responded to them or not. They wouldn't listen until her orders came out of Pete's mouth.

When had she lost track of the fact that Pete was a Wellington, first and foremost? She'd known from the beginning that he was plotting to get his rodeo back. But then Flash had acted like a dick and they'd gone into crisis mode and Pete had been so damned good at his job.

So damned good at listening to her. To her big ideas and her grand plans. To translating those plans into concrete progress on the ground. To running the All-Stars rodeo.

At making her feel like she mattered.

What if it were all a trick?

What if none of it was real?

But then again, what if it were? He wasn't in there tearing her down. He was defending her to her own family. He had her back, even if no one else did. That counted for something. It'd come so close to counting for everything.

What did it matter? Yeah, the sex was amazing. And for a few days, it'd been...almost too good to be true.

Dammit, Pete had made her like him. Even now, he was standing up for her—in spectacularly wrong fashion, but still, he was trying. And she'd begun to think...

That there could be more. That they could go forward together.

She didn't care what the hell Flash said. What happened in private between her and Pete was just that—private. She would not be shamed for her sexuality, dammit.

But it was *so* much more than that, wasn't it? She couldn't run the rodeo as long as those four kept playing tug-of-war and using her as the rope.

Her eyes burned. To hell with this. She didn't need them or their "help." If any of them thought they could run the rodeo without her, they were free to do so. She had options. She was a successful clothing designer and businesswoman. She could...

Well. She'd keep moving forward. But she was going to do it alone.

But even thinking that made her look back over her shoulder. Please let Pete come after her. If he really wanted her and not just the damned rodeo, let him come with her. Because it was one thing to say that he was going to do better by her. It was another thing for him to put action behind those words.

Please, she thought. *Come back to me tonight. Every night.* Please.

The crowds parted and she held her breath, but Pete didn't appear. Even above the din of the animals and people getting ready for the show, she thought she heard a howl of pain and a huge crash.

Right. Pete wasn't coming for her. He'd rather brawl over the All-Stars.

Fine. She didn't need this. She didn't need them. Not even Pete.

She kept walking. Right out of the arena grounds, all the way to where she'd parked. She just kept going.

Would they notice she was gone? Would they even care?

The question made her cringe and here, in the safety of her car, she felt the first tears begin to fall. Because as bad as that question was, it wasn't *the* question.

No, that was this—would Pete care?

Or would he be glad because she'd ceded the field to him? She'd admitted that she couldn't handle the All-Stars or her family. She was done.

After all this time, he'd finally gotten what he wanted.

He'd gotten rid of the Princess of the Rodeo.

Thirteen

Pete sat on the floor, his legs sprawled out in front of him as he tried to take stock.

He couldn't see out of his left eye, it was that swollen. His nose was broken for sure. Two of his teeth were loose but his jaw still moved like it was supposed to. Unlike his right hand—probably a broken bone or three there. And his ribs—damn, breathing hurt. Whoever'd caught him in the ribs had a hell of a punch. Or had he been kicked? Lord. Pete had been stepped on by bulls that hadn't hurt him this much.

A stillness settled over the dressing room, quiet except for the sounds of wet breathing. Pete coughed, tasted blood. He rolled his head to the side, trying to get his good eye to focus. Flash had come to rest against the door. His face looked like it'd been through a meat grinder. Oliver was next to the tipped clothing rack that held Chloe's dress for the evening, holding his wrist and moaning softly, a black eye blooming on his face. Milt was in the only chair still standing, leaning his head against his hands. Blood trickled out of the corner of his mouth, but he didn't look as bad as his sons. As much as Pete hated the old man, he hoped he hadn't hurt him too much.

And Chloe...

Wait. "Where's Chloe?"

"What?" Milt said, lifting his head.

"Chloe. Your daughter." Panic began to flare in his chest. Pete pushed himself up but had to sit back down when his head spun dangerously. "Where is she?"

"Gone," Flash said. He sounded funny and he wasn't moving his mouth—yeah, Pete had broken his jaw.

That he didn't feel bad about. But Chloe wasn't in here and as the adrenaline from the fight began to fade, worry replaced it. "Gone where?"

Flash shrugged and winced.

Pete rested his head on the wall, trying to think. It wasn't easy—his whole face felt like he'd run into a brick wall with it. Repeatedly.

She'd brought them back here so they could sort through their differences in private. And Flash had run his mouth and Milt had acted affronted and Pete had attacked Oliver's wife and then Oliver had attacked Pete and...

Chloe had left.

Had she tried to break up the fight? Of course she had—this was Chloe. But they hadn't listened to her.

Jesus, he hadn't listened to her. No wonder she'd walked.

"I need to get her," he said, struggling to his feet.

"You're not going anywhere until this is done, Wellington," Oliver said. "And it isn't done. Not yet."

Pete tried to give him a dirty look, but it hurt too much. "Get out of my way, Lawrence."

"Sit your ass down, Pete," Milt said, like Pete was a teenager instead of a grown man who'd...

Who'd possibly ruined everything.

Chloe was gone and there was no way in hell her family could be reasoned with, not after that fight. "I'm going after her."

Milt waved a dismissive hand. "Chloe can take care of herself and Oliver's right—we're not done yet."

"I'm done with you. With all of you." Pete tried to get to his feet again, but his boots slipped on something wet and he landed back on his ass with a dull groan. "But not with her."

Dear God, he hoped she wasn't done with him.

He hadn't meant to let things get this far. He'd wanted Chloe to be on his side when he confronted Milt, Oliver and Flash. He'd wanted to even the odds. But Flash had a way of making a man lose all sense of reason and besides, Pete hadn't thrown the first punch. He never did.

But he always threw the last one.

"I'm too old for this," Milt said, leaning back in his chair. A nasty bruise was forming along his jaw. "This is exactly why I kicked you off the circuit."

Pete gaped at the older man. "What?"

Because he'd been a hothead back then, but he hadn't brawled like this. The room was trashed—clothing scattered, furniture tipped, the mirror over the dressing table broken. Someone was going to have a lot of bad luck. Pete hoped it wasn't him. "I didn't fight like this and you know it."

"Not that," Milt scoffed and then grimaced. "Didn't like how you and Chloe looked at each other. Even back then, I could see it."

"See *what*?" This didn't make any sense. Pete hadn't been anything but a jerk to her. "How did we look at each other?"

"There's a thin line between love and hate, young man," Milt explained, sounding reasonable—for once. "Young, good-looking buck like you? I'm not blind. She had a crush on you something fierce and it was only a matter of time before you took advantage of that." He tried to look mean. "When you tried to buy the circuit off me and said she could keep riding as the Princess— that's when I knew I couldn't risk my daughter with you." Given all the bruising, Milt still managed to put a lot of heat into his glare. "And what do you know, I was right about that, wasn't I?"

"I'm going to be sick," Flash moaned, although who could tell if that was because Pete had landed a few punches to the gut or because the idea of Pete and Chloe together was too much for him.

Oliver explained, "So Flash and I taught her how to fight, in case…"

In case Pete ever cornered her. So that was why she could throw a punch. Because of him. Anger burned through him all over again. These men saw nothing but the worst in him. "I never took advantage of her." At least, not in a sexual sense. Not then, not now.

How could he have missed that Chloe had had a crush on him? And he'd treated her like crap. He owed her a better apology. But right alongside that thought was another. "That's why you kicked me out?"

He was having trouble putting all the pieces together right now. He managed to get one hand lifted to the back of his head. It came away wet. That explained the headache.

"Well, that and you were trying to turn the local

rodeo boards against me," Milt went on. "Then you sued me and I sued you back and—"

"*That* I remember," Pete said quietly.

But… Chloe?

Where was she? He needed her.

"And it was a huge mess," Oliver finished. "The feud was doing real damage to both Lawrence Energies' bottom line and the All-Stars. So I mounted a semi-hostile takeover."

"Can't say it was a bad thing," Milt agreed, sounding not even a little put out. "Retirement suits me just fine."

"Wait, wait." Pete had actually succeeded in getting the All-Stars away from Milt? Four damned years ago? And he was just now finding out? "So who owns the All-Stars? Or is it just a part of the energy company?"

"Not me," Flash mumbled.

"Flash sold his stake to Chloe when he started riding. I insisted," Oliver translated. "And I bought Dad out."

"Impudent whelp," Milt said to Oliver, sounding both angry and proud at the same time. "Outmaneuvered by my own son."

"I see," Pete said, even though he didn't.

His pounding head wasn't helping anything, but how did this make sense? If Chloe and Oliver were the only two Lawrences who owned the circuit, then Pete hadn't been trying to steal it from Milt. He'd been trying to steal it out from under Chloe.

"How the hell did we get here?" he asked, mostly to himself.

Flash groaned again, but Oliver was the one who answered. "Davey Wellington, may he rest in peace, was a lousy poker player and Dad had a massive midlife crisis."

"For a good reason," Milt said quietly, his hands clasped in what looked like prayer.

"I'm sorry for your loss," Pete said weakly. He knew that Milt had lost his wife, but he hadn't realized how much it still affected the old man.

"Appreciate that," Milt went on in that same quiet voice.

Oliver righted a second chair and dropped into it. "What are you doing here, Wellington? Honestly. I don't want to have to beat you up again."

"You can try," Pete replied, but he hurt too much to put any menace into it. He tested out his loose teeth. They still felt attached, just wobbly. "I'm helping Chloe run the rodeo."

This pronouncement was met with a palpable distrust, even though no one said anything.

"Well, I am," Pete went on defensively. "Rodeo is a family but ever since my dad lost that poker game, you guys have run this as a vanity project."

"Screw you," Flash mumbled from the side, but he didn't say anything else. Pete considered breaking his jaw more often.

"You," Pete went on, pointing to Milt, "you made friends here, but you didn't know a damned thing about running a rodeo. You," he pointed at Oliver, "can't be bothered with anything other than the bottom line, leaving all the work to Chloe. And for some reason, that includes managing *him*," he said, pointing at Flash. "And you treat the All-Stars like it's your personal playground, where you make up the rules. None of you *care* about the rodeo, not like Chloe does."

"You mean, not like *you* do, you whelp," Milt said, but he was rubbing his temples as he said it.

Pete refused to rise to that piece of bait. "Not like

Chloe does. When was the last time any of you noticed everything she does? Maybe thanked her for all her hard work?"

"Man, I hate you," Flash replied, but he sounded tired.

Pete could ignore the small barbs. He was a bigger man than that. Also, he was pretty sure his hand was broken. "I mean, yeah she's aware that I want the All-Stars back."

"Bastard," Milt growled. Given that they'd all beaten the hell out of each other, the older man still managed to make it sound menacing.

"You can call me all the names you want, but you're going to listen to me—the way you should have listened to your own daughter."

All three men looked at him. They weren't happy about it, but they were paying attention. Why couldn't they give Chloe this chance?

"She knew damned well my showing up wasn't an accident, but she couldn't get the stock contractors to listen to her ideas. Then Flash beat the hell out of Tex McGraw. You don't seem to realize how close he came to destroying the rodeo." Shame hit him low and he swallowed. "How close we've *all* come to destroying the rodeo. I wouldn't be surprised if she washed her hands of all of us after this."

The thought left him with a growing sense of dread. She'd walked away and the hell of it was, he didn't blame her a single bit. He'd been fighting for her, for her ideas and her right to run this rodeo as she saw fit.

Hadn't he?

God, he hoped so.

"Because of all of that, she had no choice but to trust me because she knows how much I care about the

All-Stars." He swallowed, which tasted only faintly of blood, so that was progress. "Which I do."

"And?" Oliver asked, pinning Pete with a look from his good eye.

"And she's an amazing woman," Pete admitted. "I always thought she was vain and shallow and the only thing she cared about was being the Princess of the Rodeo—but I was wrong. She cares about this rodeo and the rodeo family. She has so many amazing ideas— which you'd think you bunch of ingrates would appreciate, since it'll directly benefit your bottom line. But instead, all she gets is pushback."

The amazing thing was, they were still listening. Even Flash. Unless he'd blacked out? Pete wasn't sure.

"You saw how it was. No one takes her seriously, but when I tell them the exact same thing, they snap to it. Because I'm one of them."

Because he was a man. Was that any different?

With a growing sense of shame, he realized it wasn't. She'd brought them here to try to get them to listen and instead, the four of them had pounded the crap out of each other.

"God," he moaned, closing his eye. A vision of Chloe's face, stunned and hurting, assembled itself to torture him. "We're doing it right now. You all didn't listen to her when you ambushed her three days ago. You didn't listen to her here. But you're listening to me, aren't you?" When a Lawrence took a Wellington more seriously than they did Chloe, something was definitely wrong with the world. "She's your equal, dammit. Treat her like it."

"Like you do?" Flash sneered.

"Yes, like I do," Pete shot back, trying to get to his feet. He didn't land on his ass this time, but he wobbled. "Which she tried to tell you."

Oliver was at his side, steadying him with his good hand. "Did you seduce my sister as part of a plan to push her out of the rodeo?"

"If you think I'm going to answer that question, then Flash isn't the biggest jackass in this room," Pete shot back. "I thought you were supposed to be the smart one."

Oliver didn't exactly glare at Pete, but it was obvious he wasn't buying that. A quick glance around told him that none of them were and Pete was still outnumbered.

"I want it all," he said. This was it, all his cards on the table. "I want her—because she's got a wicked right hook and she knows how to ride and she's a part of this rodeo family. And I want the rodeo. This is where I belong. It's…" he sighed. "I rode this circuit with my dad when I was a kid and that was our time together. That was when I mattered to him and then he treated it like he treated his wife and children—disposable." It hurt to admit that. "The truth is, he bet the All-Stars that night because it didn't mean much to him. Because I didn't mean much to him."

An uneasy silence settled over the room. Then Milt spoke. "Now, son…"

Pete shook his head, cutting the old man off—and making his head spin. "It's the truth. The All-Stars has always been there for me, even when my own father wasn't. Rodeo is family and I couldn't let it go. It's my father's legacy, the best part of him. Of me. And if you'd just open your damned eyes, you'd see it's a pretty amazing part of Chloe, too. She's the heart and soul of this rodeo. She's…"

Things had changed. *Pete* had changed and that was in no small part thanks to Chloe. She'd shown him that they didn't have to stay locked in the same roles, fighting the same battles. If they worked together, they could be something more. Something good.

"I need this rodeo *and* I need Chloe. Together, we can make it something more than my dad ever could have, something better than you ever dreamed, Milt. It's…it's home. Chloe makes it home."

He hadn't realized the truth until the words hung in the air around them. But once they were out, Pete felt them deep in his soul.

Chloe *was* home.

"We don't have to like each other," he said, struggling to keep his voice level. The longer he stood here trying to talk sense into these stubborn mules, the farther away Chloe got and the harder it'd be to apologize to her. "But can't we at least agree that Chloe is more important to all of us than this?" he asked, waving one hand over the destruction of the dressing room. He had to use the other hand to hold on to the wall so he didn't tip over.

"You really care for my girl?" Milt asked after a long moment.

"I think I love her."

The room spun at that statement. He didn't know if it was love or a concussion. He braced for impact, but no one rushed him and no one threw a punch. Instead, the three Lawrence men shared a look.

Then Oliver cleared his throat. "Does she feel the same?"

After the last few days with her, Pete wanted to say yes. But there was one problem with that. "After this? I can't be too sure she'll ever want to talk to me again. And she'll probably bar me from the All-Stars for life. But if you all give her the respect she's due, it'll have been worth it."

The weird thing was how much he meant it. This was

him waving the white flag and leaving the field. If he'd lost Chloe, he'd lost, period. She might well wash her hands of him, but as long as her family started taking her seriously...

This was the end of the feud, another failed attempt at misplaced revenge. He was going to lose his legacy. He was out of options when it came to the All-Stars and the Lawrence family.

He'd lost. Funny how that wasn't what he was worried about.

Where the hell was Chloe? And how was he going to get to her if he couldn't even walk without collapsing in a heap?

The final blow to his pride was that he couldn't go after Chloe without help. Or some really good painkillers.

Another look went around the room. "Well?" Pete finally demanded. "Are we going to go after her or what?"

"I have an idea," Oliver finally said.

"I can't believe either of you are considering this," Flash added. At least, that's what Pete thought he said.

"However—if she says no..." Milt jabbed a finger in Pete's direction. "Then you're gone. This is a one-time-only deal."

Wait, what? What was she saying no to? How was whatever they were talking about different from her leaving them to figure things out on their own?

Yeah, Pete had missed something. And it might be the head trauma, but it sure as hell sounded like her family was maybe going to help him? He had a sinking feeling that he was going to need all the help he could get.

"Fine. What's the deal?"

"I don't know about anyone else," Oliver said, awkwardly pulling out his phone with one hand while he cradled the other hand against his chest, "but I need to go to the hospital. We can discuss it on the way there. But don't screw up this *whatever* there is between you two, Wellington."

Pete just managed not to smile at that *whatever*. Probably because his lip was busted in three, maybe four places. "I won't."

He hoped.

Man, he hoped.

Fourteen

"Do you mind if I drink?" Chloe said to Renee Lawrence as she carried the tray out to the porch, where Renee had somewhat uncomfortably wedged her enormous pregnant belly into one of Chloe's rocking chairs.

It was still hard to think of her oldest, dearest friend as a Lawrence. Renee and Oliver had only been married for a few months and Renee was now only a few weeks shy of her due date.

"Help yourself," Renee said with a soft smile, waving her hand toward the tray that held Chloe's longneck beer and a pitcher of iced tea for Renee. "Drink one for me while you're at it."

"Thanks."

Because Chloe needed a drink. It'd been three days since she'd walked away from the disaster at the rodeo and she hadn't heard a single thing from Pete. Or her family. But that was fine. She needed a break from overprotective, bullheaded male relatives.

Did she need a break from Pete?

Renee rubbed the side of her belly and winced. "I still can't believe Oliver flew all the way to Oregon to start a fight. I can barely get him to go to work. He's terrified that I'll go into labor without him."

Chloe nodded meaningfully. "Because he has so much experience delivering babies."

She and Renee looked at each other and burst out laughing because of course Oliver had never had a single thing to do with pregnancy before Renee had walked into his life. No, he was just a control freak. Which was exactly why he'd gone to Oregon. He must have thought he could control Chloe, too.

So typical.

Renee clutched her belly as she giggled. "Careful or you'll make me pee," she warned, which set Chloe off again.

She was happy for her brother and Renee. It'd always been her fondest wish growing up that Renee could be her sister and now she was. But there was something about the way Renee stroked her huge belly that made Chloe want to cry.

She'd never wanted a baby before, beyond a general *maybe someday* feeling. She'd never had a guy who'd inspired her to move past that feeling. But Pete...

But nothing.

Pete had gotten sucked back into his personal feud instead of putting the rodeo first.

Instead of putting her first.

And he hadn't even bothered to call or text since she'd walked away. Which made his feelings really clear. He liked her, sure. They were great in bed together. But she would never be the most important thing in his life and Chloe wasn't about to settle for anything less than everything.

"Do you want to talk about it?" Renee asked, snapping Chloe out of her thoughts.

"Not really."

"Hmm." Renee sipped at her tea.

That *not really* lasted all of thirty seconds. "It's just that I'm so damned mad at them. At all of them," Chloe went on, the truth bursting out of her. "I guess I'm not surprised at Dad and Oliver and Flash because this is how they've always treated me. But Pete…" Her voice caught and she had to take a long swig of beer. "I wanted things to be different. Between us. And they're not. He's the same, too."

"You didn't tell your family you'd fallen for him, did you?"

Leave it to Renee to get to the heart of the matter. "No, I didn't tell them that, but that doesn't make it not true. And because I couldn't see him for what he was, now I've screwed everything up. The rodeo, my family…everything. God, I'm such an idiot," she groaned.

Renee patted Chloe's hand. "You know, you don't actually have to take responsibility for their actions."

"What?"

Renee shrugged. "Take it from me—you can love your family and still want to lock them in prison and throw away the key." Her cheeks colored as she slid a glance at Chloe. "I happen to have some experience in this sort of situation."

"Who could forget?"

After all, Renee's father, brother and first husband had all worked together to pull off the largest pyramid investment scheme in history. Her husband had committed suicide and her father was going to die in prison.

Her brother had bargained his sentence down to seven years. "Did your mother get extradited to America yet?" Because it was easier to talk about Renee's messy life than Chloe's, apparently.

"The lawyers are still negotiating," Renee said with a dismissive shrug. "But don't change the subject. What are you going to do?"

Chloe shrugged. "The Princess clothing line is still mine, thank God. I can do a lot with it."

"Big plans?" Renee said with a knowing smile.

"Always," Chloe agreed, taking another long drink. It'd be heaven—her own business, run her way, without any interfering men. Pure *heaven*.

"And what about you and Pete?"

Chloe groaned. "There's nothing to do—not with him and not with my family, anyway," she said in frustration. "Until they listen to me, what's the point? I'll always be Daddy's little girl or the irritating sister or the woman who shouldn't do anything other than smile big. Besides—" she sniffed "—it's not like they noticed when I left. It's not like Pete tried to come after me. It's not like anyone bothered to apologize."

"Hmm," Renee murmured again. "Well, I'm sorry this sucks."

"Thanks," Chloe said, swiping at the tears that threatened to trickle down her face. If she wanted to get emotional with Renee, she could. Renee understood, thank God. "Even though you don't have a single thing to apologize for."

"I should have kept Oliver home," she said, a note of steel in her voice. "Faked Braxton Hicks contractions or something. But I thought he was going to keep a short leash on Flash…"

"No one can keep that boy on a leash."

"Yeah, there's something going on with him. But," she added quickly before Chloe could launch into the seemingly endless list of ways Flash had screwed things up, "that doesn't excuse his behavior. It doesn't excuse any of their behavior."

"Right, you know?" Chloe said, unable to keep the bitterness out of her voice. "I'm not their mother *or* their keeper. I just wanted to do my job and then the thing with Pete happened and..." She dropped her head back and stared at the horizon.

The afternoon sun was hot on Sunshine Ridge, the ranch she'd bought to give her a place to get away from well-meaning relatives. Wonder, her mare, was prancing in the paddock. After Renee left, Chloe would saddle her for a long ride and maybe Chloe could leave all her heartache and frustration in the dust.

That was a hell of a *maybe*.

"And it was *so* good, Renee," she went on. "He listened to my ideas and then translated them into man speak, I guess—but he got people to buy into the changes. He didn't call me a 'pretty little thing' or say," she added, dropping her voice down in an attempt to match Pete's baritone, "'that's not how we did things when my family was in charge' or any of that."

"*That's* what made it good?" Renee scoffed. "Don't get me wrong—a man who listens is worth his weight in gold but come on, Chloe. You do realize we're talking about the same man you used to send me messages about? How many times did you write about his butt in a pair of chaps?"

"Who could count that high?" Chloe sighed, because she had only ever allowed herself to admit that she thought of Pete in a non-enemy kind of way when she was talking to Renee.

"Uh-huh," Renee snorted in a highly unladylike way.

"He was amazing," she admitted, because this *was* Renee. "Better than I'd ever allowed myself to dream he'd be. But we'd only just gotten started. Barely one freaking week," she went on. "And only because Dad had yelled at me and the hotel screwed up my room and I was a mess. Pete was there and he offered me his bed and got me wine and chocolate."

Renee's eyes were huge. "He *didn't*."

"Oh, he totally did." The memory left a bittersweet taste in her mouth and her eyes stung again. "And I thought... I thought he was in my corner. I could depend on him because he'd finally let go of the past. I thought we could go forward together."

Maybe things changed, he'd told her in the bed of his truck a long time ago. *Maybe I changed.*

And maybe he hadn't. She was more the fool for having trusted him at all.

"Anyway," Chloe said, somehow getting the words out around the lump in her throat, "are you sure you should be this far outside of Dallas? Not to sound like Oliver—"

"God forbid." Renee laughed.

"But what are you doing here?"

Renee gave Chloe a sharp kind of smile, one that didn't seem natural on her face. "Besides supporting my best friend in her time of need?" As she spoke, a new sound reached Chloe's ears—the sound of tires on pavement. "Stalling."

Chloe pushed herself to her feet and leaned over the porch railing. It wasn't a truck—two trucks were barreling down her drive. She recognized her father's but... was that Pete's truck behind it?

She spun on her best friend, who was trying to get

out of the chair. Chloe extended her hand and helped Renee to her feet. "Renee, what did you do?"

Renee wrapped her arms around Chloe's shoulders in an awkward, A-frame hug. "I'll apologize for this later—but only if you want," she said.

"Renee…" she warned, but Renee pulled away and walked down the top two porch steps.

The trucks pulled up in front of the house, and Dad and Flash got out of his truck, and Pete and Oliver got out of Pete's truck and both Renee and Chloe gasped in horror at the mass of bruises and casts the four of them were sporting.

Her father's jaw was a sickly shade of purple that spread up the side of his face to ring his eye. But Dad had nothing on Flash, who looked like he'd been run through a wood chipper. He had a cast on one hand and she could barely see his eyes between the broken nose, the bruising and swelling. Oliver looked better than that, but the cast on his right arm went all the way up to his elbow and he had a hitch in his stride as he made his way to his wife.

"You're late," Renee scolded.

"But we're here now," he said, meeting Renee on the steps to give her an exceedingly gentle kiss with his hands on her belly.

Chloe had to look away. Which of course meant her gaze landed on Pete, who was hanging back. The left side of his face was so swollen and discolored that his eye was nothing but a tiny slit. He also had a cast on his hand and, as he stood there staring at her with his good eye, she noticed he held himself stiffly.

If his face was that bad, what did the rest of him look like?

She took in the group they made, matching bruises

and casts and contrite looks. At least they weren't yelling and punching, unlike the last time she'd seen them. "What are you all doing here?" Chloe demanded. Because she was sure she'd remember if she'd invited them to her ranch. Which she had no plans to do, ever again.

Oliver turned and looked at the others. "Well," he said, managing to look slightly embarrassed. "We thought we'd apologize."

"All of us," Dad added, giving Flash a little shove.

"Yeah," Flash said without moving his mouth. "Sorry."

"His jaw is wired shut," Oliver explained. "It's been the most peaceful three days of my life."

Flash flipped off his brother with the hand that wasn't in the cast and she saw that his knuckles were a painful shade of purple. But Chloe had to agree—it was very peaceful not to have to listen to Flash escalate a fight.

"That's...nice," she told them. She looked at Pete, standing a few feet behind Flash and Dad. He met her gaze without hesitation. But he kept quiet.

"I should've had your back," Oliver said. "I know you're more than capable of running the rodeo and it wasn't fair to jump to conclusions."

Chloe cut a look at Renee, who pushed Oliver on the shoulder. He winced and added, "And you were doing a great job with the All-Stars." Renee pushed him again, harder this time. "I mean, you've always done a great job with it. I appreciate everything you've done to keep it going for the last four years."

"Um," Chloe said. She was completely at a loss. Apologies weren't beyond Oliver, but had he ever complimented her business skills before? Not that she could remember. "Thank you?"

Dad stepped forward because they were going in

a predetermined order or something. "And I'm sorry, sweetie. I shouldn't have stood in the way of your taking on more responsibilities like I did. Your mother would've had my head on a platter for treating you differently, may she rest in peace."

"Okay?" Chloe had to blink a few times. She always got teary when Dad talked about Mom.

"You'll always be my princess," Dad went on, his eyes watery. "But you're a grown woman, too, and a sharp businesswoman and I want you to know that I'm mighty proud of you."

She couldn't reply to that because her throat wasn't working. So she managed to nod, which was enough for Dad. He gave her another shaky smile and then turned back to Flash.

Chloe braced herself as Flash stepped forward. The apology tour was making all the stops, it seemed, but she wasn't sure she was ready to hear anything from Flash.

He pulled a folded up sheet of paper out of his back pocket and handed it to her. "Read it," he got out, but then added, "please."

Chloe gave him a long look, but what the hell. They were family, after all. She unfolded the paper and read, "I have enrolled in anger management classes and I won't come to any rodeo until I have completed them and my community service sentence. I accept your decision to suspend me from the All-Stars because of my actions and won't ask to have the suspension lifted until the beginning of the next season. I'm going to work on growing up and being a better man. I am also going to quit drinking. I'm sorry I was a dick. Flash."

"Yes," she mumbled, "you were."

"Sorry," Flash gritted out again.

That only left one. Chloe looked to Pete again, but he still hung back.

Instead, it was Oliver who spoke. "Okay?"

Pete lifted an eyebrow at her, almost in challenge. Chloe tore her gaze away from him and looked at the contrite faces surrounding her. "We're family," she said. "So, yeah, okay. But that doesn't solve the problem we have with who runs the All-Stars." Or the problem with Pete. She looked back at him and the man had the nerve to wink at her! At least, she thought it was a wink. He might just be grimacing in pain. Hard to tell, what with all the swelling.

"Actually, it does. See, sis, here's the thing—I hate the rodeo," Oliver said.

"And neither Flash nor I own any part of it," Dad went on. "Not anymore."

"While I value the All-Stars in terms of marketing," Oliver said, "I can't be bothered with the day-to-day management of it. I'm running a company, I just got married, the baby is due any second and, well, I'm busy."

"I've recently come to realize that, while I love the rodeo," Dad said, "that I was never that great at running it."

"And I'd just screw it up," Flash said. At least, Chloe thought he said that. She couldn't be sure.

"But?" she said because she was positive she heard one in there. Oliver was grinning like he was about to get to the bad news.

"But running the rodeo isn't a one-person job," Pete said, making her jump. Even now, after everything that had happened between them and with her family standing around her, the sound of his voice still sent a shiver down her back.

Dammit, she'd missed him. She didn't want to, but she did anyway.

"Exactly," Oliver replied. "It'd be best if there was a team who could manage it together."

"A couple of people who love the rodeo and treat it like family," Dad added.

"Like home," Pete said, his voice warm.

Chloe was getting dizzy trying to keep up with the thread of the conversation. "What are you saying?"

"I'm out of the rodeo business," Oliver announced, his arm around Renee's waist. He kissed her forehead and looked down at her, the love in his gaze painfully obvious. "I no longer own my stake."

"You are? You don't?" Which meant she was the only Lawrence who still owned the All-Stars? Was she even hearing this right?

But even as she said it, she looked to Pete again. Even with his face kind of swollen, there was no mistaking the grin on his face. And this time, he *definitely* winked.

"It's time to end this feud," Dad announced. "The All-Stars will always belong to a Lawrence but now they'll always belong to a Wellington, too. It's right."

Chloe's legs wobbled and she had to grab on to the porch railing to hold herself up. "You sold your stake to Pete?"

"Actually," Pete said, finally stepping toward her, "he tried to give it to me."

Oh. Of course. Because she couldn't be trusted to run the rodeo on her own. Her family thought she needed a man to keep tabs on her, apparently. All this nice talk about how they were going to trust her instincts and treat her as an equal was just that—talk.

She spun on Oliver, ready to beat a few more knots into his head. "You *gave* your stake to Pete? Without asking *me*?" Her chest felt like someone had wrapped steel bars around it. She couldn't breathe.

Everyone took a step back—except for Pete, who moved closer. "Hon," he said quietly. "Wait."

"Wait for what?" Somehow, she managed to keep her fists at her sides. But her arms began to shake with the effort. "I notice that everyone else here has apologized, Pete—but not you."

The damned man had the nerve to look amused by this. Chloe was real proud she didn't take a swing at him—but she did plant her hands on his chest and shove as hard as she could.

That wiped the smile right off his face. "Easy, hon. I've got three cracked ribs."

"I don't care," she snapped. "You all will never change. You'll never give me a seat at the table. You make a major change in ownership to the All-Stars and can't even be bothered to run it by me? I'm done. I don't want your self-serving apologies or your condescending attitudes. I wanted you to have faith in me. I wanted you to trust me. But you don't. None of you do." Tears streaming down her face, she turned on Pete. "Not even you, Wellington. I hope you're happy. You got what you wanted. You can have the All-Stars."

Somehow, he'd gotten closer. The look in his good eye about broke her heart. "Chloe," he said and she heard regret and sadness in his voice.

She couldn't take this final humiliation. Bad enough that she'd surrendered. But did she have to do it in front of an audience?

"Just go," she whispered, squeezing her eyes tight. It didn't stem the tide of her tears, though.

She felt his warmth seconds before his arms went around her shoulders and she wanted to push him away, wanted to knee him in the groin—to make him pay for using her. For letting herself get used. But she couldn't because this was her last chance to hold him. Fool that she was, she clutched at his shirt, pulling him closer, and leaned her head against his shoulder.

"I didn't take it," he said, low in her ear.

It took a second for his words to sink in. "You didn't take what?" she sniffed.

"I didn't take Oliver's share." She stumbled back from him, but he caught her before she lost her balance. "I don't want it."

"But…you love the rodeo," she told him. "Getting the All-Stars back—that's all you've ever wanted." She looked around, but her brothers and her father didn't seem to be in any rush to explain what the hell was going on.

Pete tucked a strand of hair behind her ear and then trailed the tips of his fingers down her wet cheek. "I found someone I want more."

She gasped but it didn't get any air moving into her lungs.

"The rodeo is yours, Chloe. Your ideas, your energy—you're the one who keeps the wheels from falling off and keeps the rest of us in line. It belongs to you."

Then the man did something she never saw coming. He got down on bended knee. Slowly and awkwardly, but still.

Oh, God.

"I belong to you," he said, holding on to her hands. "You showed me there was more to life than this stupid feud. You showed me what I'd forgotten—that rodeo was family. My family," he went on. "When I'm with you, I'm home. So let me be your home, too. Let me love on you for a little while longer. For the rest of our lives."

Pete Wellington was proposing. Just to make sure she hadn't passed out and was dreaming this whole thing, she glanced over at Renee, who gave her a look that clearly said, *Go for it*.

"Pete—are you sure?"

Yes, she was crying. No, she didn't care.

"I've never been more sure of anything in my life. I will always be in your corner, fighting for you—even if you say no. I promise I'll listen to you and, when I forget because I'm a man and I probably will, you have my permission to punch me. *After* I heal," he added with a wink.

"That's... I...but what about Oregon?" Because Pete Wellington was proposing to her and she was terribly afraid she was about to say *yes*, but he hadn't apologized for flying off the handle last weekend and she wasn't about to let him off the hook for that. "It's been days, Pete, and I haven't heard from you and when I do, you show up with an *audience*?" The words settled around the silence and she realized that probably hadn't come out right. She glanced up at her family. "No offense."

"We're leaving," Renee announced. "Right after I pee." She hurried inside as fast as a woman in her condition could.

Chloe snuck a glance at Pete, who had blushed. She thought. Stupid bruises.

"We wanted to apologize, sweetie," Dad said as Oliver helped Pete to his feet. Dad wrapped his arm around her shoulder and gave her a gentle squeeze. "And we wanted to show you that we've all agreed to let bygones be bygones."

"Plus, we wanted to make sure there was no misunderstanding," Oliver told her. "I did offer my stake to Pete—after we all got done beating the crap out of each other. But he was right." Oliver pulled a folded manila envelope out of his back pocket and handed it over to her. "You'll need to come into the office to sign all the paperwork, but the All-Stars is yours."

"Damned impressed, really," Dad drawled, giving Pete a long look. "I reckon he might just be good enough for you, after all."

"Daddy!"

Dad kissed her on the cheek. "But the decision is yours, sweetie. Yes, no, maybe—it doesn't matter. We'll back you up because we love you. Always." He kissed her on the cheek again. "We want you to be happy. It's all your mother and I ever wanted for you and if a Wellington is the one who does it, then we'll welcome him to the family."

"With minimal fistfights," Flash said. Or at least it sounded like he said that. Oh, she was going to enjoy the weeks of near silence.

She hugged her father and then Oliver and settled for carefully patting Flash on the least-injured-looking shoulder. Then Renee came back out and hugged Chloe again and whispered, "Do what you want but remember— *chaps*."

Chloe giggled. "Call me when you go into labor," she told Renee, then Oliver was helping Renee into her car and Flash and Dad were climbing into Dad's truck and suddenly, she and Pete were alone.

Finally.

When the last sounds of the vehicles had faded, Chloe took a deep breath and turned to Pete. She was startled to realize he was holding her hand, their fingers laced together as if they'd always been that way.

"Well," she started but that was as far as she got before

he pulled her into his chest and kissed her with so much passion and need that her knees got all wobbly again.

"Babe," he murmured against her lips as his arms went around her. His hard cast dug into her back but she didn't care. "Marry me. *Please.*"

"No more fighting with my family," she replied, pulling him toward the house, her hands already at the buttons on his shirt.

"No more fighting," he agreed. "I think we got it all out of our systems."

He pulled her shirt over her head just inside the front door. "And you'll ride the circuit with me?"

"I'll manage the show, but it's your rodeo." She got his shirt over his cast and then he spun her around to get her bra undone. "What you say, goes."

"And..." She swallowed, suddenly shy as he stared at her breasts. "And you'll love me?"

He stepped into her, staring down at her with a look she recognized. It was the same look that'd been on Oliver's face when he'd looked at Renee.

It was love.

"Always," he said, gingerly touching his forehead to hers. "I plan to show you every single day for the rest of our lives how much I love you." He swallowed. "If you'll let me. Will you let me?"

She touched his face, carefully stroking his bruises and then leaning up on her tiptoes to kiss the less damaged side. "Come back to me tonight," she whispered. "Come back to me every night, Pete. For the rest of our lives."

Rodeos and hotels and ranches—and Pete by her side.

"I'm yours," he said, a solemn promise.

She knew he'd keep it.

Epilogue

Flash Lawrence smiled at the buckle bunny who'd sent him a drink. Blonde and buxom, she was everything he normally looked for in a one-night stand, especially when she batted her eyelashes and thrust out those amazing breasts. Her offer couldn't be clearer.

So why didn't he take her up on it?

Instead of asking her for a dance, which would've turned into another dance, then a trip to her place or his hotel or, hell, even his pickup truck parked outside this bar in Topeka, he tipped his hat and turned away.

"Send her a beer," he told the bartender who'd given him the woman's drink. Then he paid his tab—Sprite was cheap—and headed out.

What the hell was wrong with him? This was his life—riding in the All-Around All-Stars, racking up the points to make a run at a world ranking and then, when the dust had settled, hitting the bars and enjoying the ladies to the fullest extent allowed by law.

At least, it had been his life last season, before he'd screwed everything up. But not this year. Not anymore.

Instead, he climbed into the cab of his truck, dropped his hat on the seat next to him and pulled out his phone.

She hadn't texted. Of course she hadn't. Why would she?

Logically, he knew why. Yes, he and Brooke Bonner had shared one of the most electric thirty-six hours of his life. It wasn't an exaggeration to say that she'd left him a changed man.

But that was a year ago. Brooke probably didn't remember their wild night together at the All-Stars rodeo in Fort Worth last year, right before Flash had spun completely out of control.

Brooke had gone on to tour five other countries after that show. Her album had hit in a major way. She'd won Grammys and CMA awards and broken sales records. Hell, she'd even made the covers of several high-fashion magazines. All Flash had done in that time was almost destroy his rodeo riding career, trash his relationships with his family and accrue way too many legal bills.

So yeah, he could see how one night with a cowboy might have slipped her mind. Or she'd looked him up online and found nothing but the headlines. One glance at his conviction for assault and she'd probably decided to pass. He couldn't blame her for that. The best possible option was that she thought of him the way he thought of all the ladies he'd danced around—with a fond smile and nothing else.

Brooke Bonner should be that to him. A fond memory of a wild night.

Why wasn't she?

As hard as he'd tried, Flash hadn't been able to forget her, not when her voice filled the arenas in between rides, when her face smiled knowingly at him from a magazine cover every time he was in line at a store. Not when she was waiting for him in his dreams, driving him the best kind of crazy.

It should've gotten better. After an all-out publicity blitz, Brooke had basically gone dark a few months ago, reportedly to work on her follow-up album. She wasn't everywhere anymore.

Except in his dreams. Night after night, she was waiting for him, his name on her lips, her body underneath his, surrounding him. He hadn't been with another woman since her. And, pitiful as it was, he was doing his best to keep a grip on his temper and stay on the straight and narrow because he was no idiot. No woman, much less one as wildly successful as Brooke, wanted to deal with an immature, unemployed jerk.

Flash had a brand-new season to make his run at the All-Stars world rankings. He had a new grip on sobriety and his temper under control. He was going to make this second chance count.

For her.

She'd gotten under his skin, that was all. And he knew the cure—a little hair of the dog. He checked Brooke's social media—and what he saw made his heart pound.

"Just announced—I'll be at the Bluebird Café with an exclusive sneak-peek at material off my upcoming album in three days! Can't wait!"

Flash couldn't believe what he was seeing. The Bluebird Café—that was just south of Nashville.

The All-Stars were rolling into Nashville next week. If he left now...

Hands shaking, Flash fired up the engine. Maybe it was fate. Maybe it was just dumb luck. Either way, one thing was clear—it was high time he looked up Brooke Bonner.

* * * * *

COMING SOON!

We really hope you enjoyed reading this book. If you're looking for more romance, be sure to head to the shops when new books are available on

Thursday
12th July

To see which titles are coming soon, please visit
millsandboon.co.uk

MILLS & BOON

LET'S TALK
Romance

For exclusive extracts, competitions
and special offers, find us online:

- **f** facebook.com/millsandboon
- **○** @millsandboonuk
- **𝕏** @millsandboon

Or get in touch on 0844 844 1351*

For all the latest titles coming soon, visit
millsandboon.co.uk/nextmonth

Want even more
ROMANCE?

Join our bookclub today!

'Mills & Boon books, the perfect way to escape for an hour or so.'

Miss W. Dyer

'Excellent service, promptly delivered and very good subscription choices.'

Miss A. Pearson

'You get fantastic special offers and the chance to get books before they hit the shops'

Mrs V. Hall

Visit millsandbook.co.uk/Bookclub
and save on brand new books.

MILLS & BOON